image comics presents

THE WALKING DEAD™

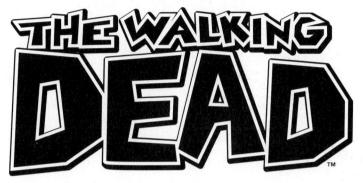

ROBERT KIRKMAN
CREATOR, WRITER

CHARLIE ADLARD
PENCILER, INKER

CLIFF RATHBURN
GRAY TONES

RUS WOOTON
LETTERER

CHARLIE ADLARD
&
CLIFF RATHBURN
COVER

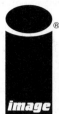

IMAGE COMICS, INC.

Robert Kirkman - chief operating officer
Erik Larsen - chief financial officer
Todd McFarlane - president
Marc Silvestri - chief executive officer
Jim Valentino - vice-president

Eric Stephenson - publisher
Todd Martinez - sales & licensing coordinator
Betsy Gomez - pr & marketing coordinator
Branwyn Bigglestone - accounts manager
Sarah deLaine - administrative assistant
Tyler Shainline - production manager
Drew Gill - art director
Jonathan Chan - production artist
Monica Howard - production artist
Vincent Kukua - production artist
Kevin Yuen - production artist

www.imagecomics.com

THE WALKING DEAD, VOL. 7: THE CALM BEFORE. Third Printing. Published by Image Comics, Inc. Office of publication: 2134 Allston, 2nd Floor, Berkeley, California 94704.

PRINTED IN USA

ISBN: 978-1-58240-828-6

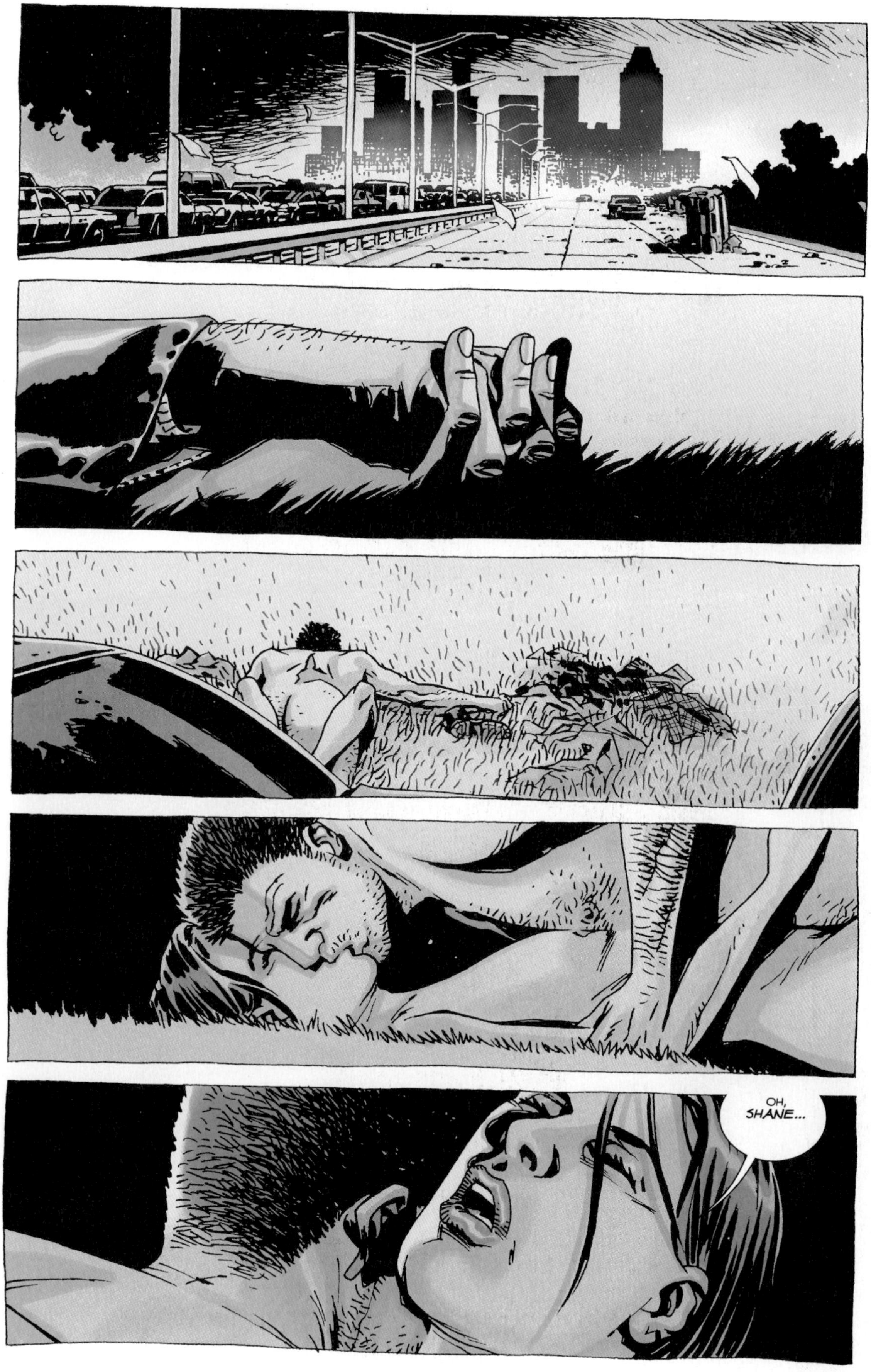
OH, SHANE...

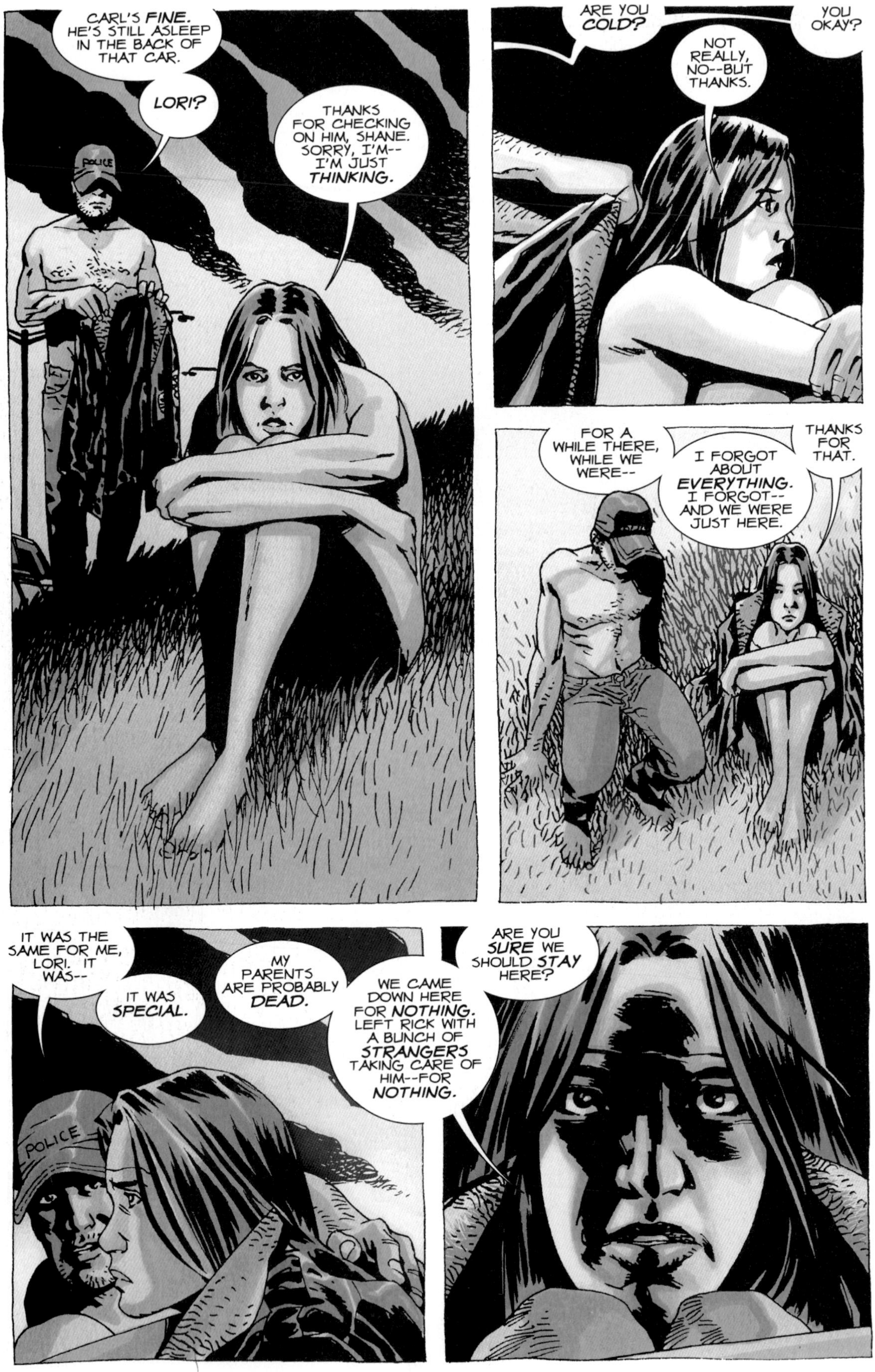
CARL'S FINE. HE'S STILL ASLEEP IN THE BACK OF THAT CAR.
LORI?
THANKS FOR CHECKING ON HIM, SHANE. SORRY, I'M-- I'M JUST THINKING.
ARE YOU COLD?
NOT REALLY, NO--BUT THANKS.
YOU OKAY?
FOR A WHILE THERE, WHILE WE WERE--
I FORGOT ABOUT EVERYTHING. I FORGOT-- AND WE WERE JUST HERE.
THANKS FOR THAT.
IT WAS THE SAME FOR ME, LORI. IT WAS--
IT WAS SPECIAL.
MY PARENTS ARE PROBABLY DEAD.
WE CAME DOWN HERE FOR NOTHING. LEFT RICK WITH A BUNCH OF STRANGERS TAKING CARE OF HIM--FOR NOTHING.
ARE YOU SURE WE SHOULD STAY HERE?

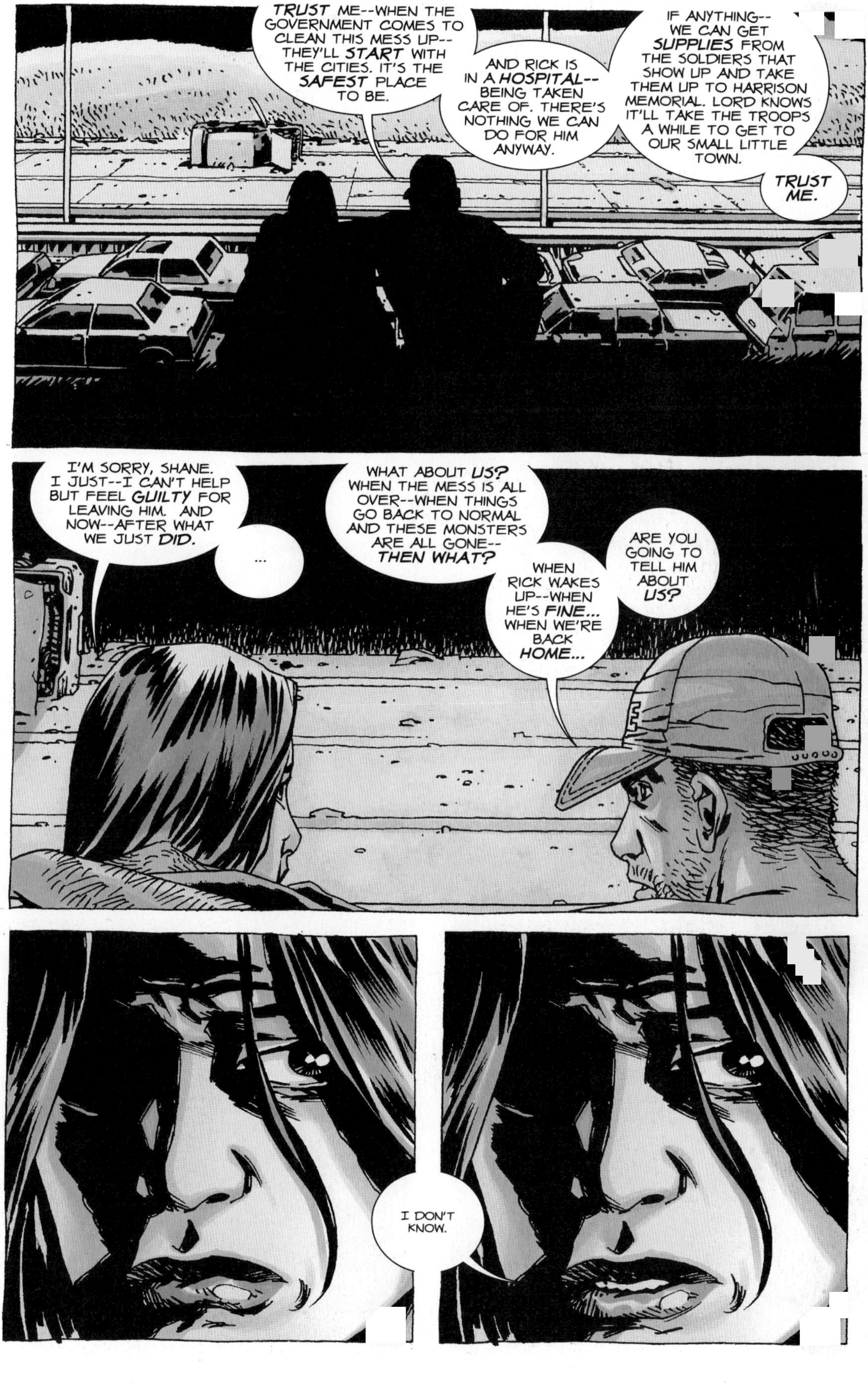
TRUST ME--WHEN THE GOVERNMENT COMES TO CLEAN THIS MESS UP--THEY'LL START WITH THE CITIES. IT'S THE SAFEST PLACE TO BE.
AND RICK IS IN A HOSPITAL--BEING TAKEN CARE OF. THERE'S NOTHING WE CAN DO FOR HIM ANYWAY.
IF ANYTHING--WE CAN GET SUPPLIES FROM THE SOLDIERS THAT SHOW UP AND TAKE THEM UP TO HARRISON MEMORIAL. LORD KNOWS IT'LL TAKE THE TROOPS A WHILE TO GET TO OUR SMALL LITTLE TOWN.
TRUST ME.
I'M SORRY, SHANE. I JUST--I CAN'T HELP BUT FEEL GUILTY FOR LEAVING HIM. AND NOW--AFTER WHAT WE JUST DID.
...
WHAT ABOUT US? WHEN THE MESS IS ALL OVER--WHEN THINGS GO BACK TO NORMAL AND THESE MONSTERS ARE ALL GONE--THEN WHAT?
WHEN RICK WAKES UP--WHEN HE'S FINE... WHEN WE'RE BACK HOME...
ARE YOU GOING TO TELL HIM ABOUT US?
I DON'T KNOW.

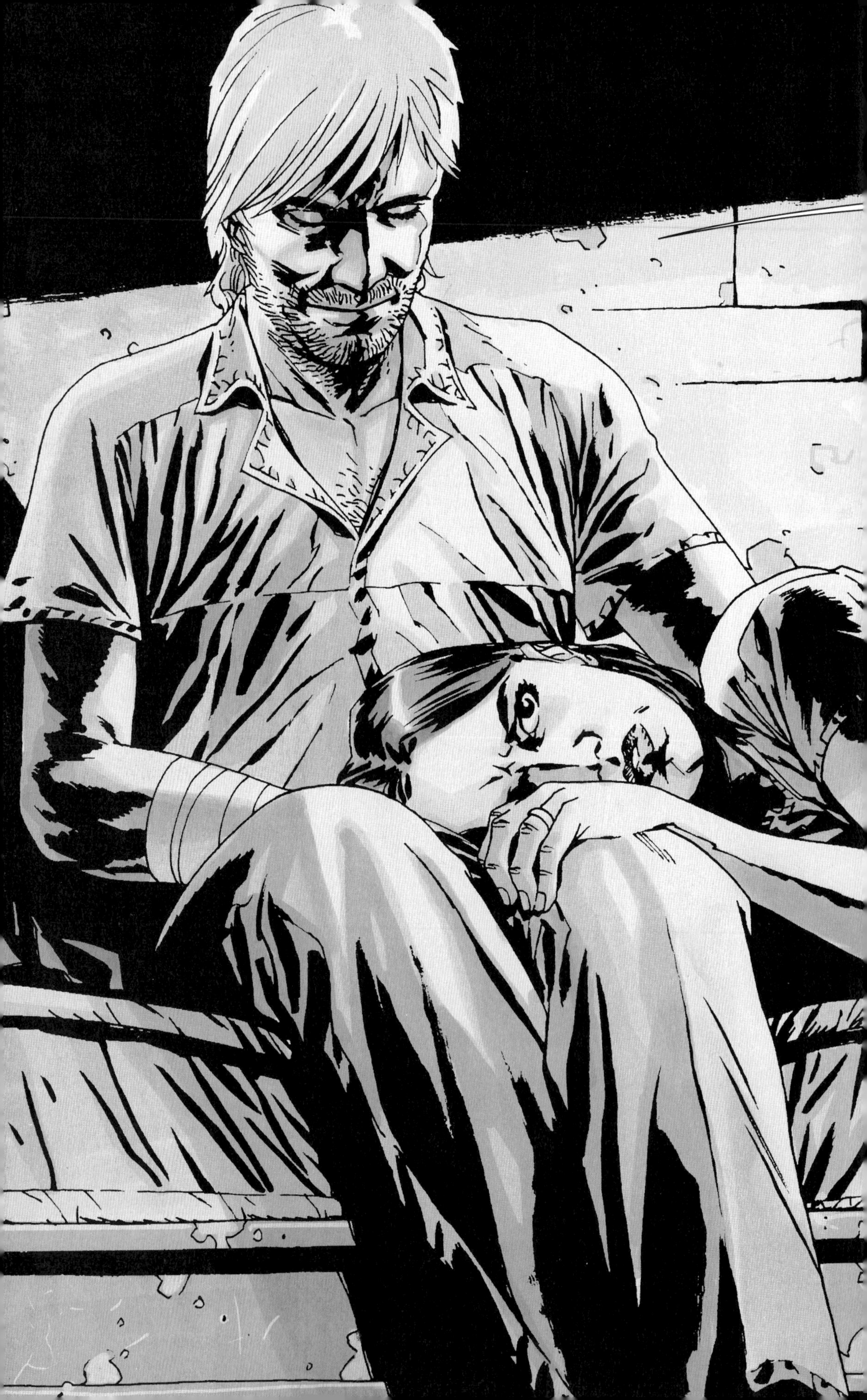

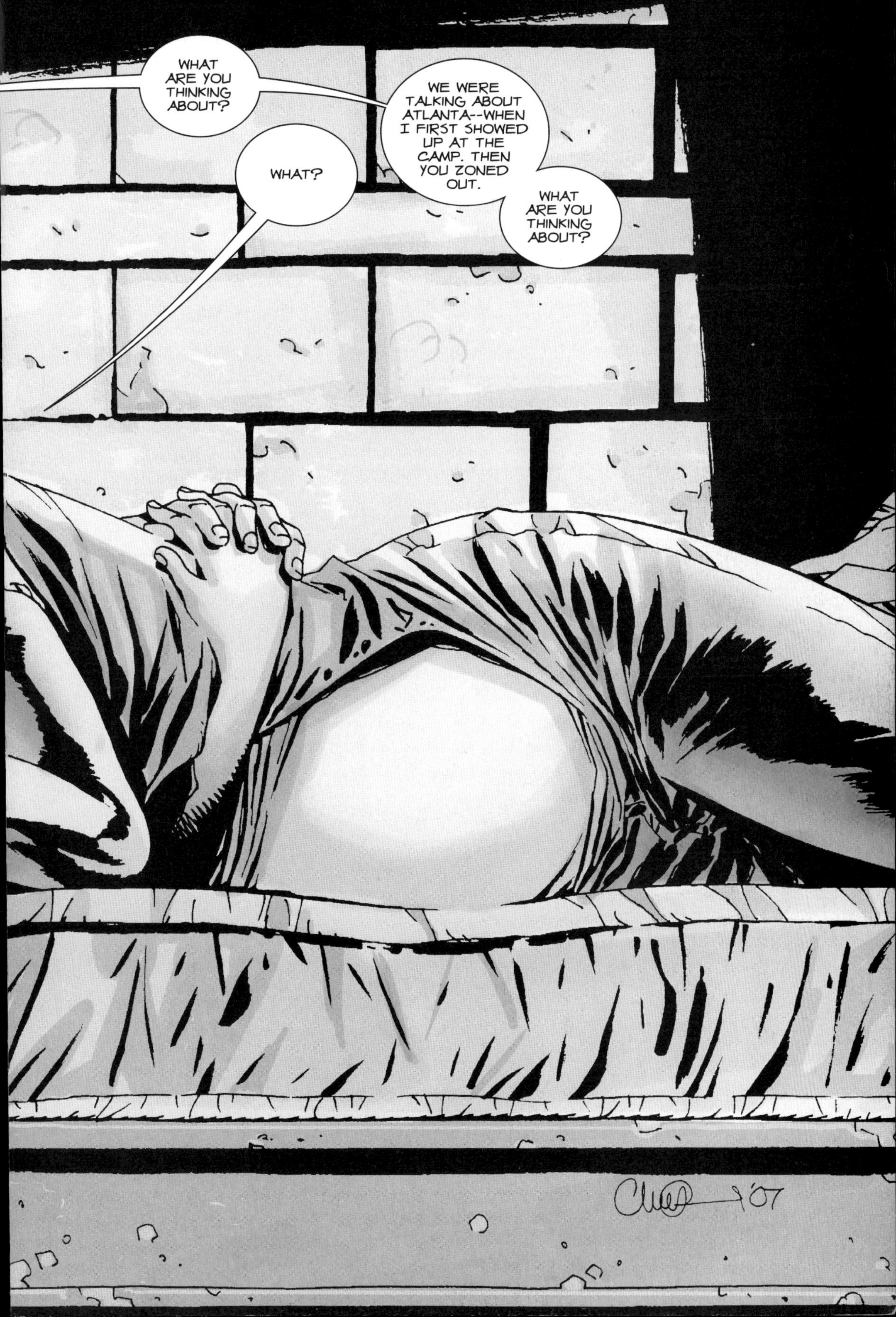
WHAT ARE YOU THINKING ABOUT?
WE WERE TALKING ABOUT ATLANTA--WHEN I FIRST SHOWED UP AT THE CAMP. THEN YOU ZONED OUT.
WHAT?
WHAT ARE YOU THINKING ABOUT?
'07

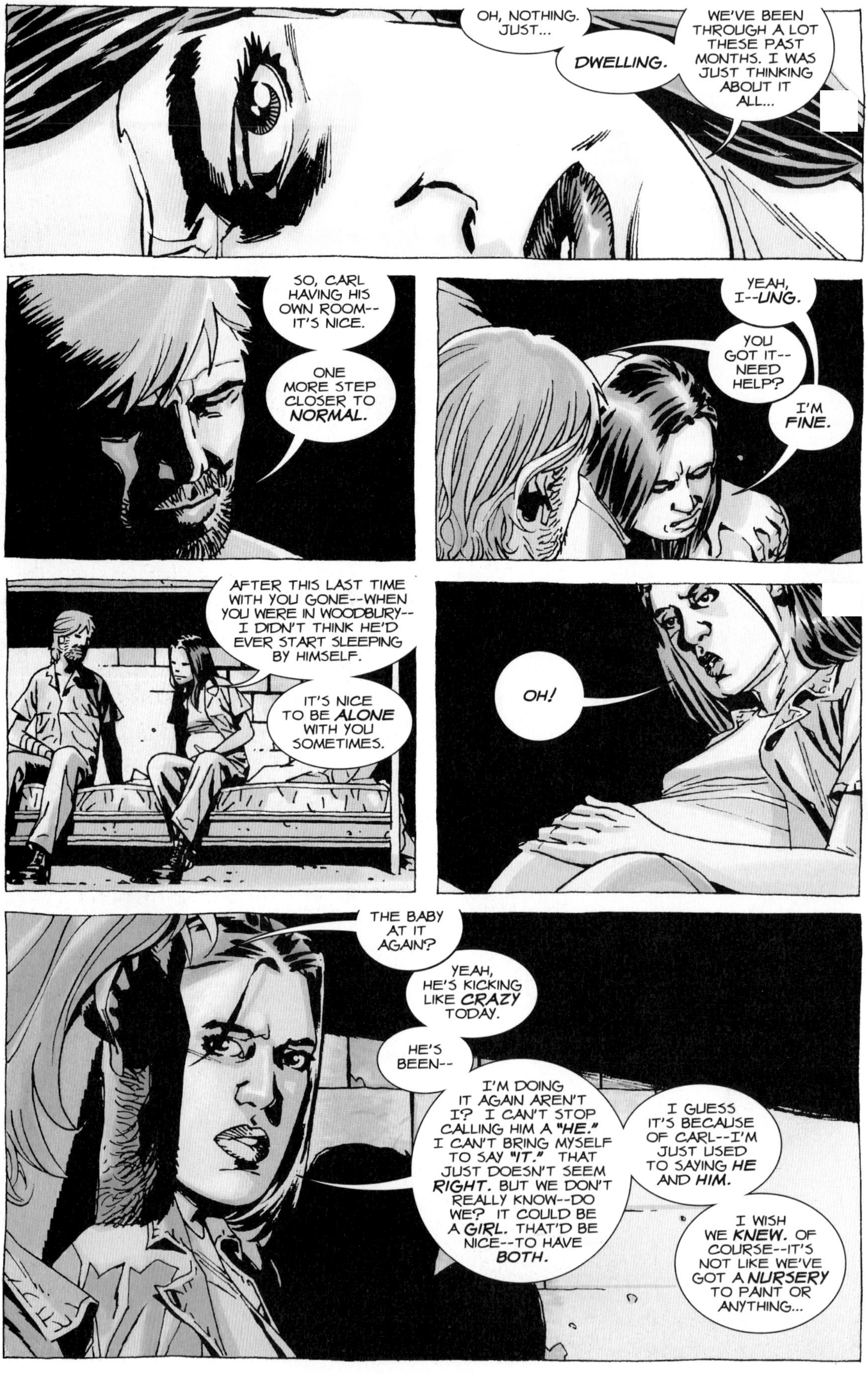
OH, NOTHING. JUST...
DWELLING.
WE'VE BEEN THROUGH A LOT THESE PAST MONTHS. I WAS JUST THINKING ABOUT IT ALL...
SO, CARL HAVING HIS OWN ROOM-- IT'S NICE.
ONE MORE STEP CLOSER TO NORMAL.
YEAH, I--UNG.
YOU GOT IT-- NEED HELP?
I'M FINE.
AFTER THIS LAST TIME WITH YOU GONE--WHEN YOU WERE IN WOODBURY-- I DIDN'T THINK HE'D EVER START SLEEPING BY HIMSELF.
IT'S NICE TO BE ALONE WITH YOU SOMETIMES.
OH!
THE BABY AT IT AGAIN?
YEAH, HE'S KICKING LIKE CRAZY TODAY.
HE'S BEEN--
I'M DOING IT AGAIN AREN'T I? I CAN'T STOP CALLING HIM A "HE." I CAN'T BRING MYSELF TO SAY "IT." THAT JUST DOESN'T SEEM RIGHT. BUT WE DON'T REALLY KNOW--DO WE? IT COULD BE A GIRL. THAT'D BE NICE--TO HAVE BOTH.
I GUESS IT'S BECAUSE OF CARL--I'M JUST USED TO SAYING HE AND HIM.
I WISH WE KNEW. OF COURSE--IT'S NOT LIKE WE'VE GOT A NURSERY TO PAINT OR ANYTHING...

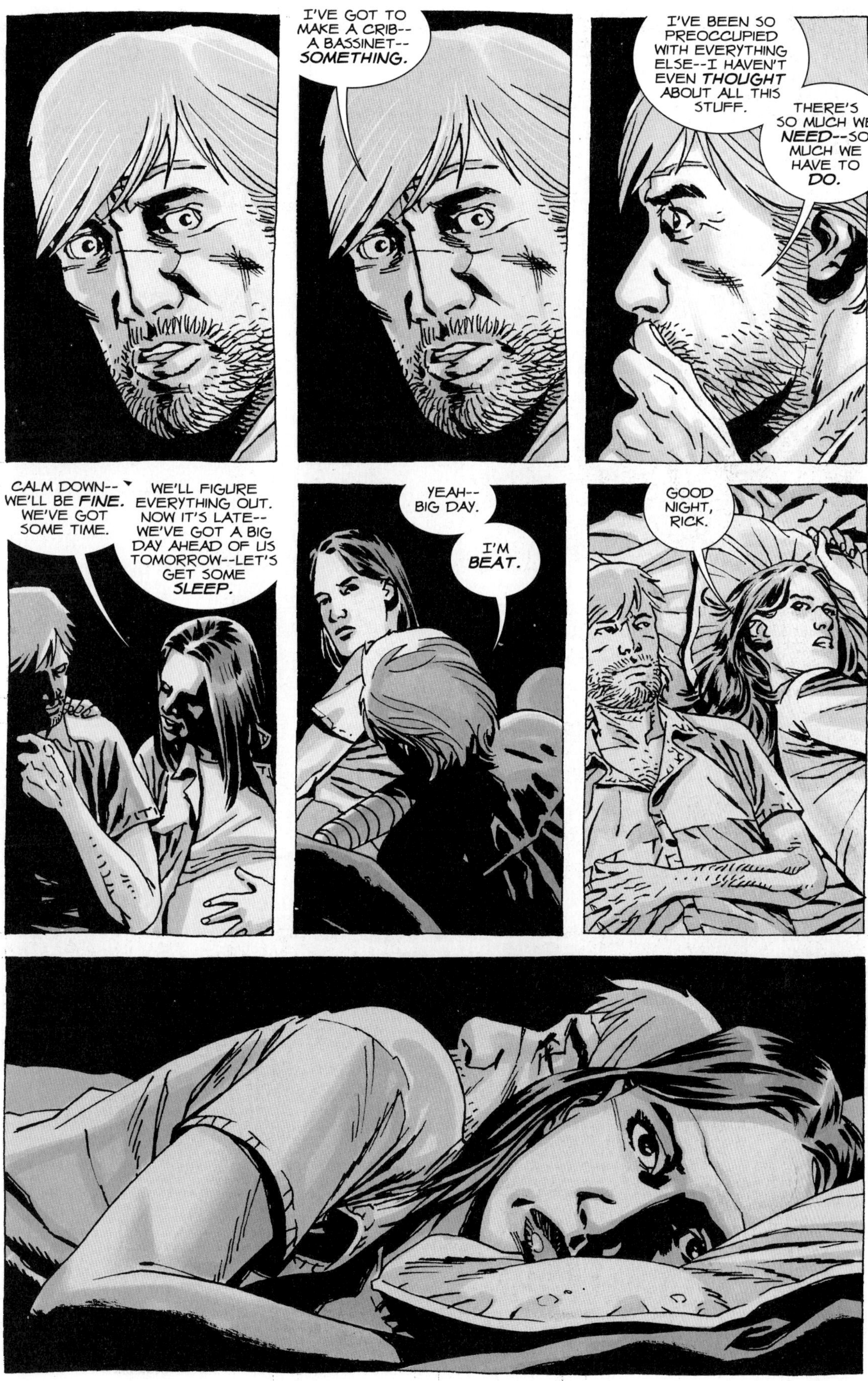
I'VE GOT TO MAKE A CRIB-- A BASSINET-- SOMETHING.
I'VE BEEN SO PREOCCUPIED WITH EVERYTHING ELSE--I HAVEN'T EVEN THOUGHT ABOUT ALL THIS STUFF.
THERE'S SO MUCH WE NEED--SO MUCH WE HAVE TO DO.
CALM DOWN-- WE'LL BE FINE. WE'VE GOT SOME TIME.
WE'LL FIGURE EVERYTHING OUT. NOW IT'S LATE-- WE'VE GOT A BIG DAY AHEAD OF US TOMORROW--LET'S GET SOME SLEEP.
YEAH-- BIG DAY.
I'M BEAT.
GOOD NIGHT, RICK.

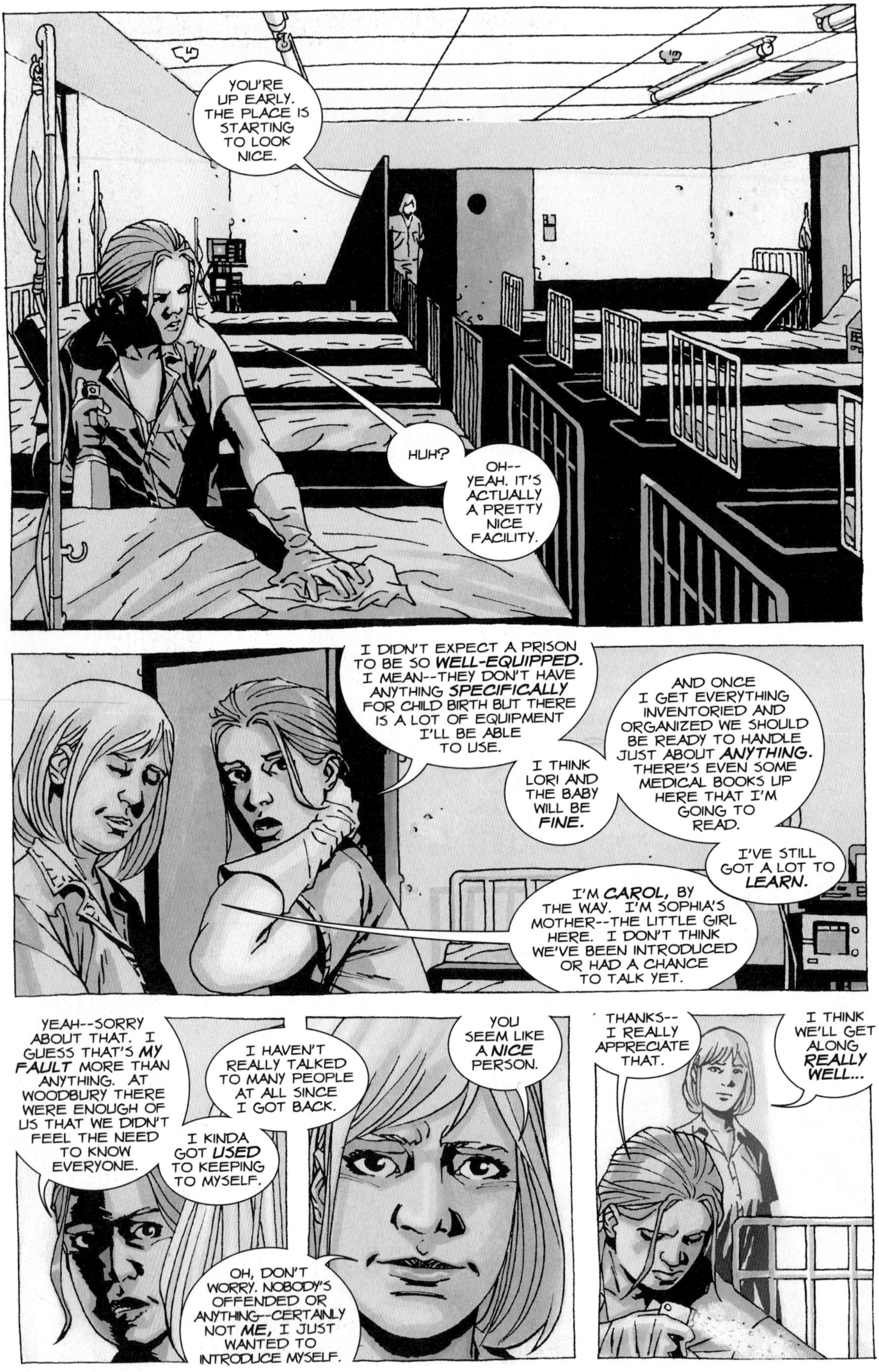
YOU'RE UP EARLY. THE PLACE IS STARTING TO LOOK NICE.
HUH?
OH-- YEAH. IT'S ACTUALLY A PRETTY NICE FACILITY.
I DIDN'T EXPECT A PRISON TO BE SO **WELL-EQUIPPED.** I MEAN--THEY DON'T HAVE ANYTHING **SPECIFICALLY** FOR CHILD BIRTH BUT THERE IS A LOT OF EQUIPMENT I'LL BE ABLE TO USE.
I THINK LORI AND THE BABY WILL BE **FINE.**
AND ONCE I GET EVERYTHING INVENTORIED AND ORGANIZED WE SHOULD BE READY TO HANDLE JUST ABOUT **ANYTHING.** THERE'S EVEN SOME MEDICAL BOOKS UP HERE THAT I'M GOING TO READ.
I'VE STILL GOT A LOT TO **LEARN.**
I'M **CAROL,** BY THE WAY. I'M SOPHIA'S MOTHER--THE LITTLE GIRL HERE. I DON'T THINK WE'VE BEEN INTRODUCED OR HAD A CHANCE TO TALK YET.
YEAH--SORRY ABOUT THAT. I GUESS THAT'S **MY FAULT** MORE THAN ANYTHING. AT WOODBURY THERE WERE ENOUGH OF US THAT WE DIDN'T FEEL THE NEED TO KNOW EVERYONE.
I HAVEN'T REALLY TALKED TO MANY PEOPLE AT ALL SINCE I GOT BACK.
I KINDA GOT **USED** TO KEEPING TO MYSELF.
YOU SEEM LIKE A **NICE** PERSON.
OH, DON'T WORRY. NOBODY'S OFFENDED OR ANYTHING--CERTAINLY NOT **ME,** I JUST WANTED TO INTRODUCE MYSELF.
THANKS-- I REALLY APPRECIATE THAT.
I THINK WE'LL GET ALONG **REALLY WELL...**

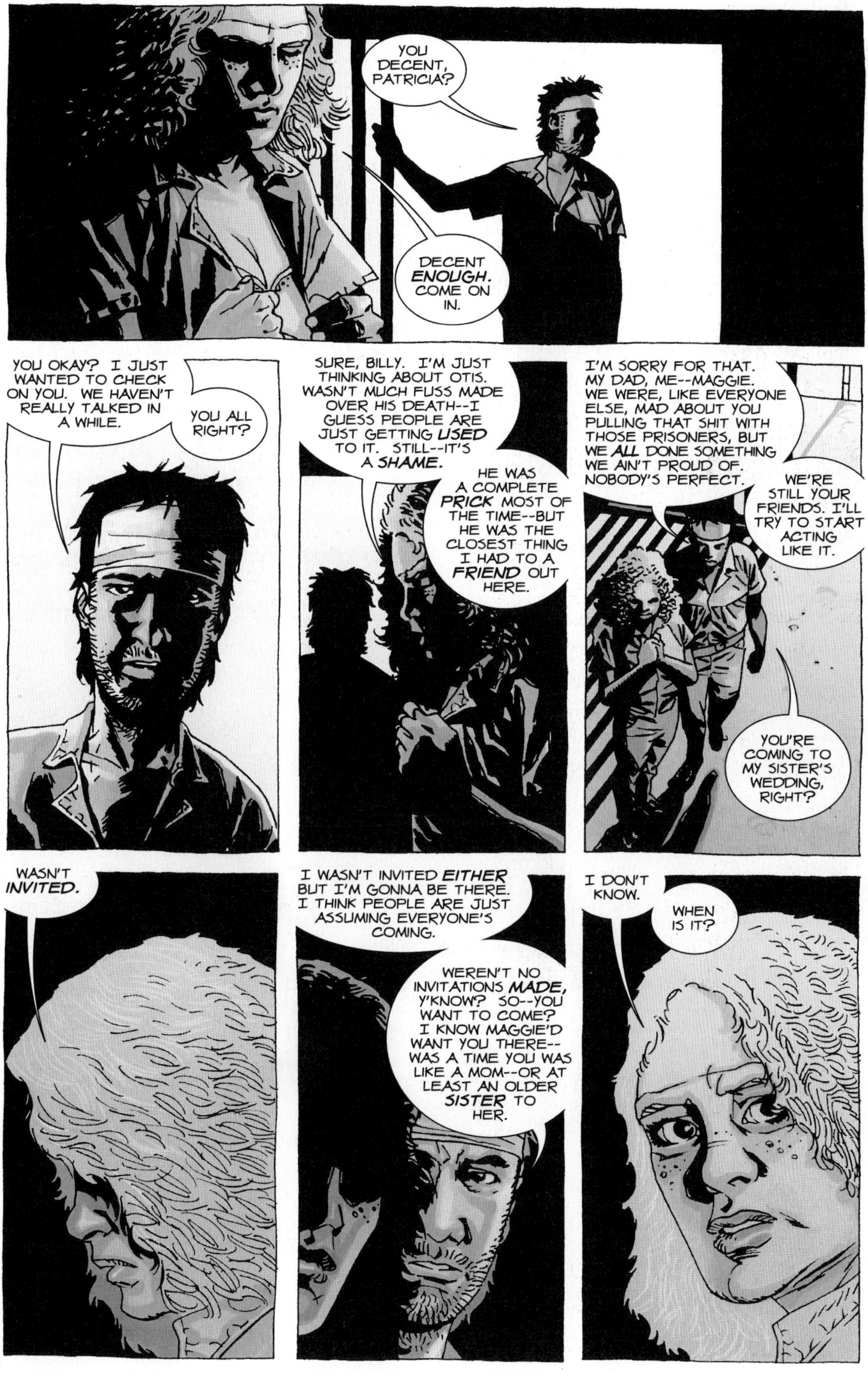

YOU DECENT, PATRICIA?
DECENT ENOUGH. COME ON IN.
YOU OKAY? I JUST WANTED TO CHECK ON YOU. WE HAVEN'T REALLY TALKED IN A WHILE.
YOU ALL RIGHT?
SURE, BILLY. I'M JUST THINKING ABOUT OTIS. WASN'T MUCH FUSS MADE OVER HIS DEATH--I GUESS PEOPLE ARE JUST GETTING USED TO IT. STILL--IT'S A SHAME.
HE WAS A COMPLETE PRICK MOST OF THE TIME--BUT HE WAS THE CLOSEST THING I HAD TO A FRIEND OUT HERE.
I'M SORRY FOR THAT. MY DAD, ME--MAGGIE. WE WERE, LIKE EVERYONE ELSE, MAD ABOUT YOU PULLING THAT SHIT WITH THOSE PRISONERS, BUT WE ALL DONE SOMETHING WE AIN'T PROUD OF. NOBODY'S PERFECT.
WE'RE STILL YOUR FRIENDS. I'LL TRY TO START ACTING LIKE IT.
YOU'RE COMING TO MY SISTER'S WEDDING, RIGHT?
WASN'T INVITED.
I WASN'T INVITED EITHER BUT I'M GONNA BE THERE. I THINK PEOPLE ARE JUST ASSUMING EVERYONE'S COMING.
WEREN'T NO INVITATIONS MADE, Y'KNOW? SO--YOU WANT TO COME? I KNOW MAGGIE'D WANT YOU THERE--WAS A TIME YOU WAS LIKE A MOM--OR AT LEAST AN OLDER SISTER TO HER.
I DON'T KNOW.
WHEN IS IT?

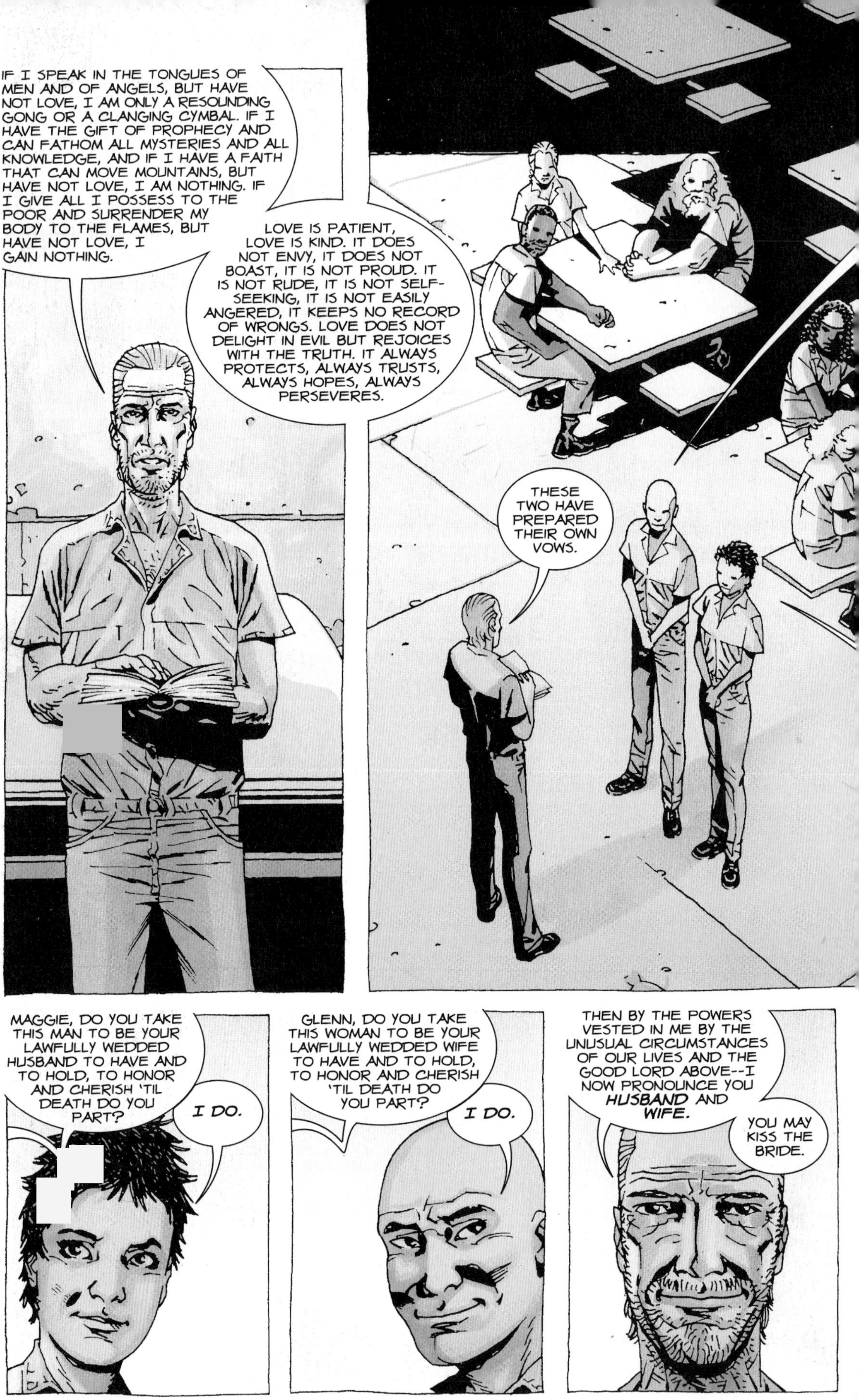
IF I SPEAK IN THE TONGUES OF MEN AND OF ANGELS, BUT HAVE NOT LOVE, I AM ONLY A RESOUNDING GONG OR A CLANGING CYMBAL. IF I HAVE THE GIFT OF PROPHECY AND CAN FATHOM ALL MYSTERIES AND ALL KNOWLEDGE, AND IF I HAVE A FAITH THAT CAN MOVE MOUNTAINS, BUT HAVE NOT LOVE, I AM NOTHING. IF I GIVE ALL I POSSESS TO THE POOR AND SURRENDER MY BODY TO THE FLAMES, BUT HAVE NOT LOVE, I GAIN NOTHING.
LOVE IS PATIENT, LOVE IS KIND. IT DOES NOT ENVY, IT DOES NOT BOAST, IT IS NOT PROUD. IT IS NOT RUDE, IT IS NOT SELF-SEEKING, IT IS NOT EASILY ANGERED, IT KEEPS NO RECORD OF WRONGS. LOVE DOES NOT DELIGHT IN EVIL BUT REJOICES WITH THE TRUTH. IT ALWAYS PROTECTS, ALWAYS TRUSTS, ALWAYS HOPES, ALWAYS PERSEVERES.
THESE TWO HAVE PREPARED THEIR OWN VOWS.
MAGGIE, DO YOU TAKE THIS MAN TO BE YOUR LAWFULLY WEDDED HUSBAND TO HAVE AND TO HOLD, TO HONOR AND CHERISH 'TIL DEATH DO YOU PART?
I DO.
GLENN, DO YOU TAKE THIS WOMAN TO BE YOUR LAWFULLY WEDDED WIFE TO HAVE AND TO HOLD, TO HONOR AND CHERISH 'TIL DEATH DO YOU PART?
I DO.
THEN BY THE POWERS VESTED IN ME BY THE UNUSUAL CIRCUMSTANCES OF OUR LIVES AND THE GOOD LORD ABOVE--I NOW PRONOUNCE YOU HUSBAND AND WIFE.
YOU MAY KISS THE BRIDE.

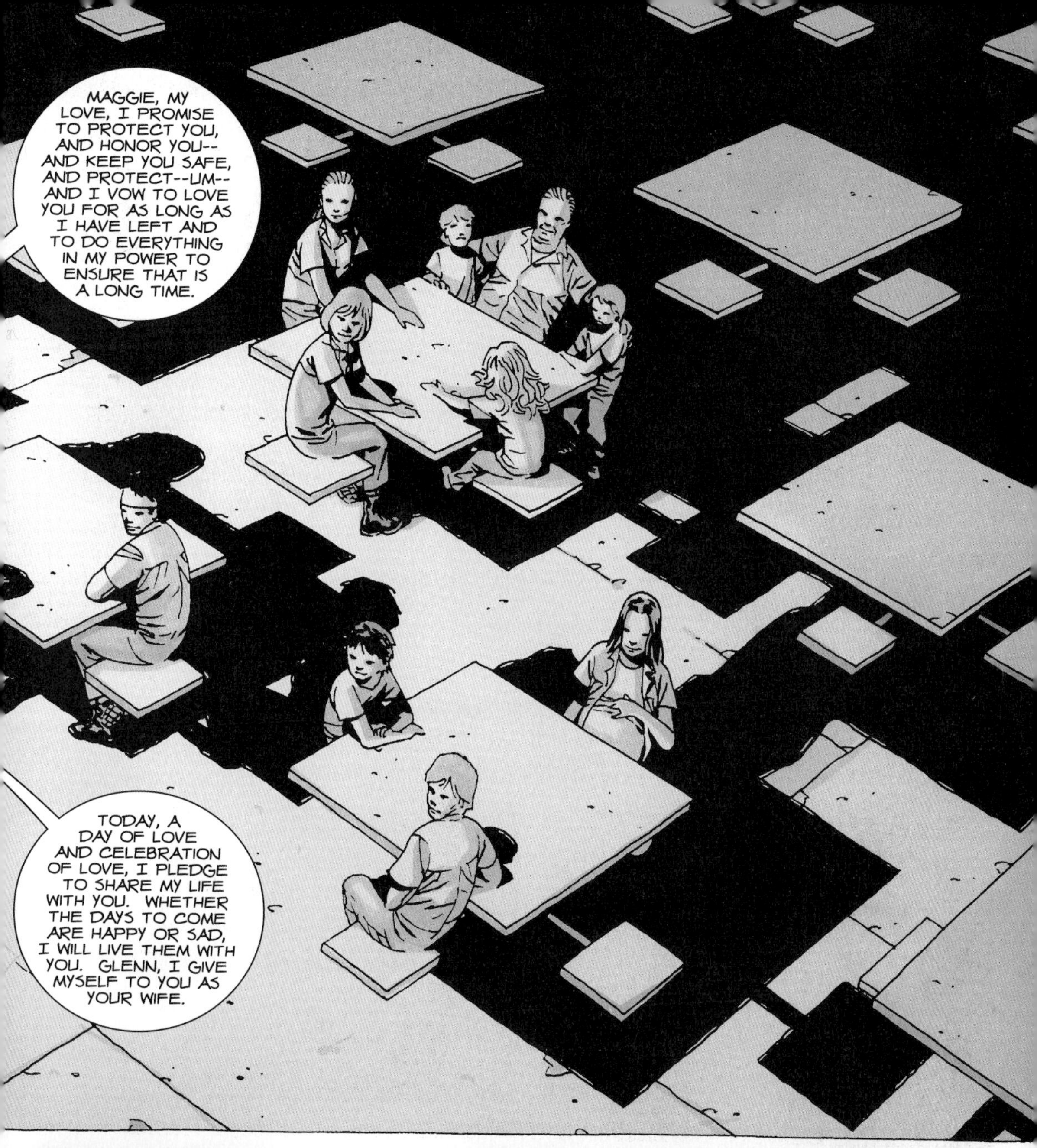
MAGGIE, MY LOVE, I PROMISE TO PROTECT YOU, AND HONOR YOU-- AND KEEP YOU SAFE, AND PROTECT--UM-- AND I VOW TO LOVE YOU FOR AS LONG AS I HAVE LEFT AND TO DO EVERYTHING IN MY POWER TO ENSURE THAT IS A LONG TIME.
TODAY, A DAY OF LOVE AND CELEBRATION OF LOVE, I PLEDGE TO SHARE MY LIFE WITH YOU. WHETHER THE DAYS TO COME ARE HAPPY OR SAD, I WILL LIVE THEM WITH YOU. GLENN, I GIVE MYSELF TO YOU AS YOUR WIFE.

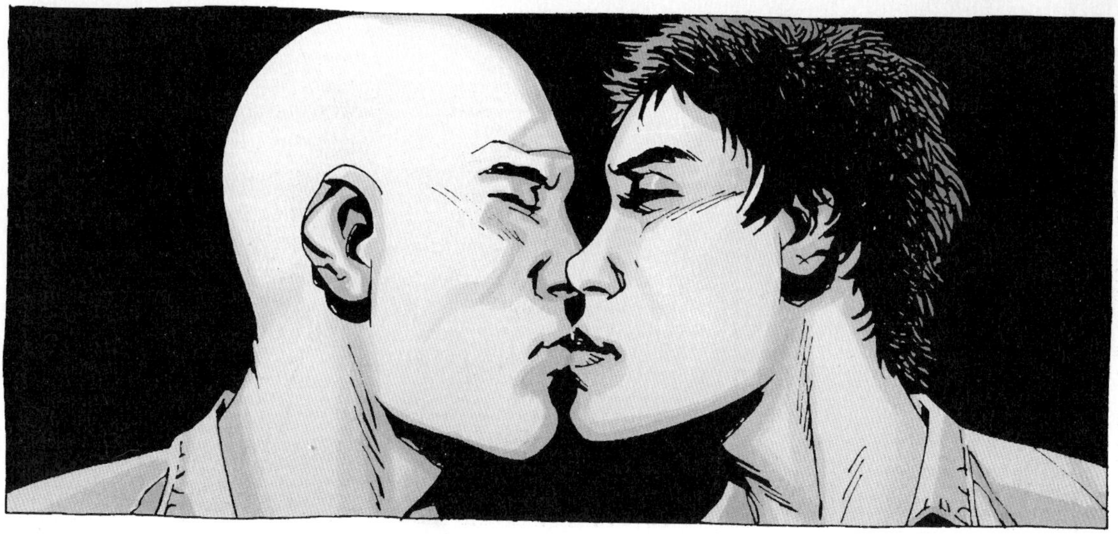

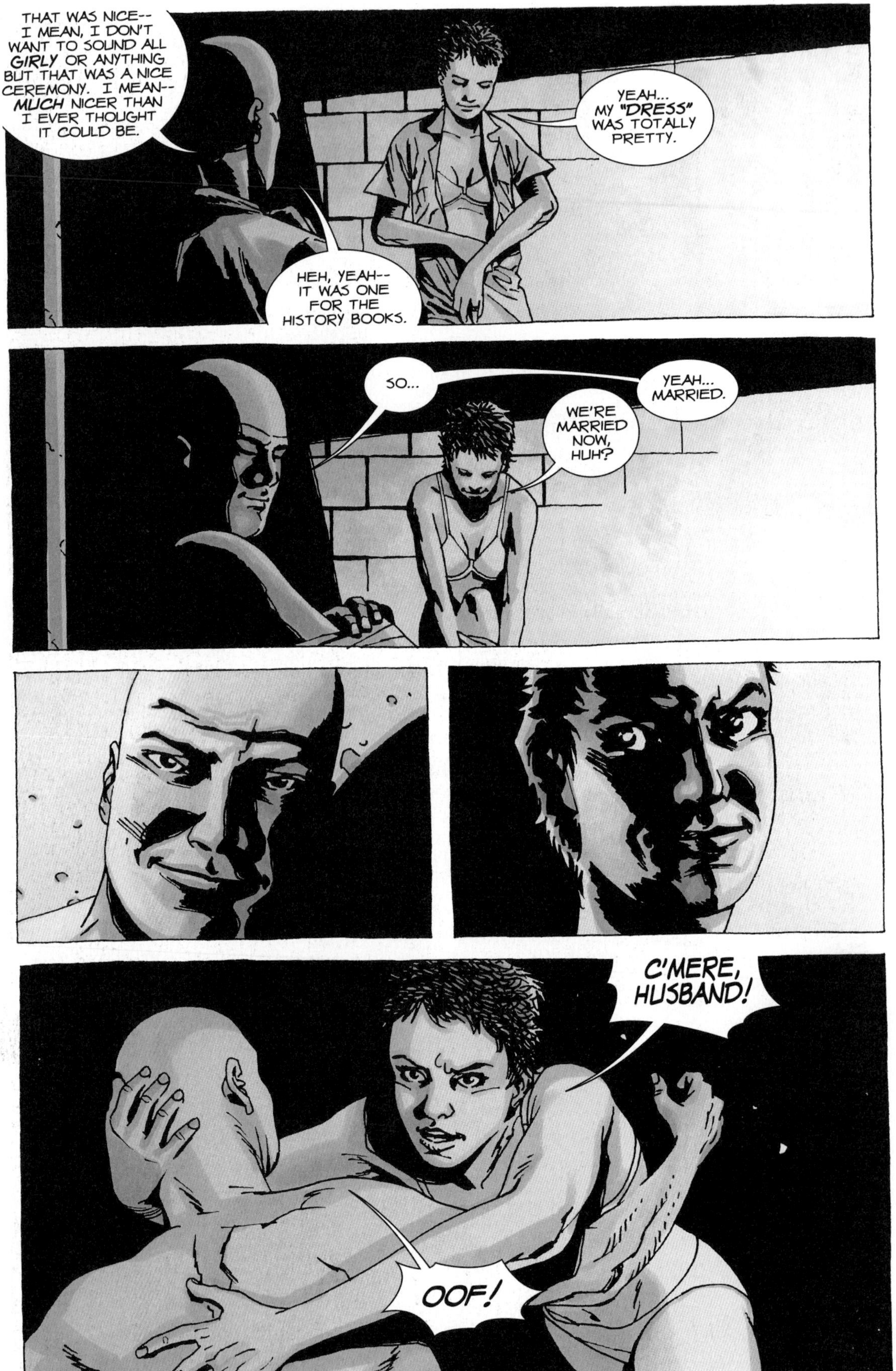
THAT WAS NICE-- I MEAN, I DON'T WANT TO SOUND ALL GIRLY OR ANYTHING BUT THAT WAS A NICE CEREMONY. I MEAN-- MUCH NICER THAN I EVER THOUGHT IT COULD BE.
YEAH... MY "DRESS" WAS TOTALLY PRETTY.
HEH, YEAH-- IT WAS ONE FOR THE HISTORY BOOKS.
SO...
WE'RE MARRIED NOW, HUH?
YEAH... MARRIED.
C'MERE, HUSBAND!
OOF!

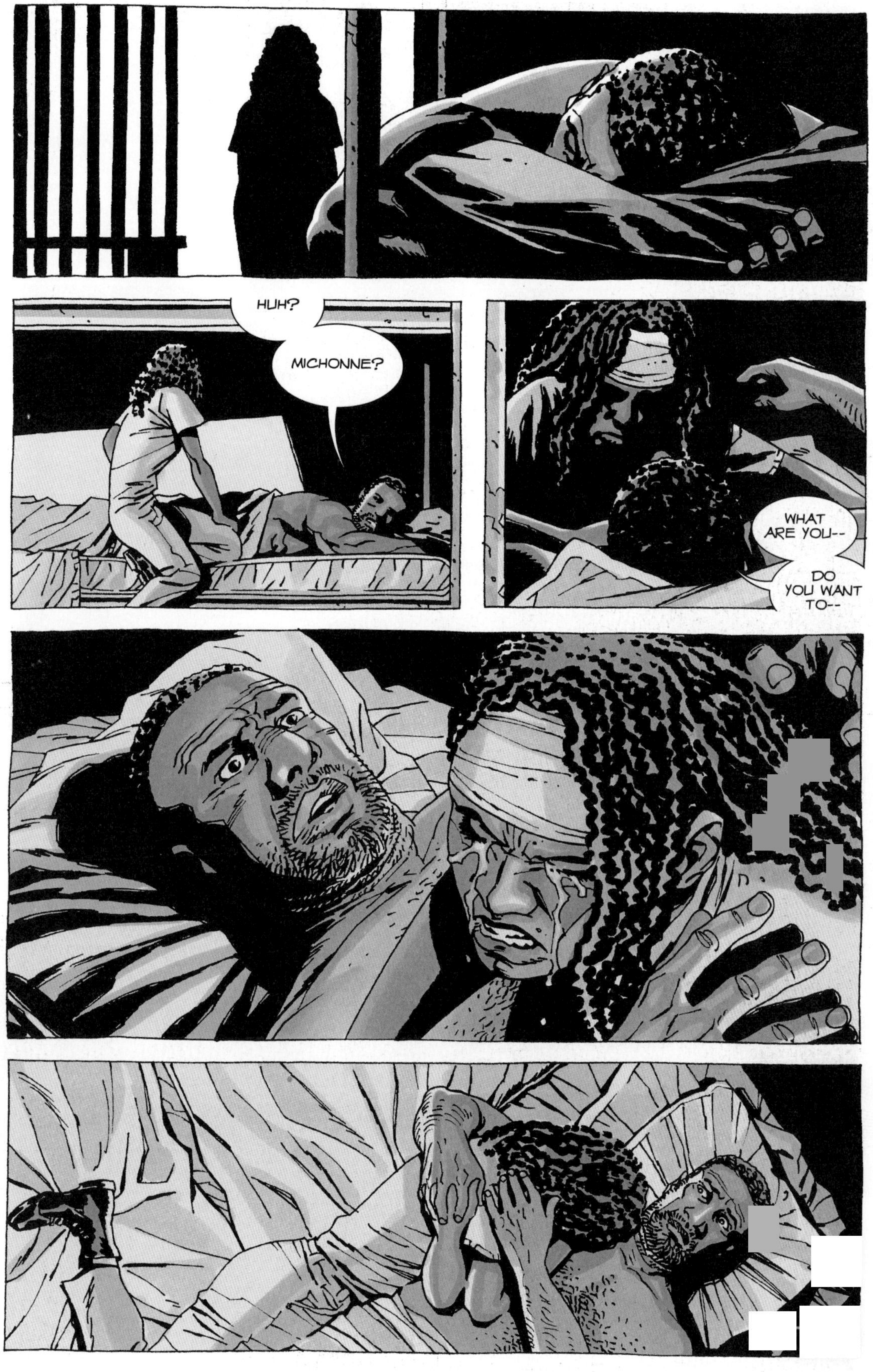
HUH?
MICHONNE?
WHAT ARE YOU--
DO YOU WANT TO--

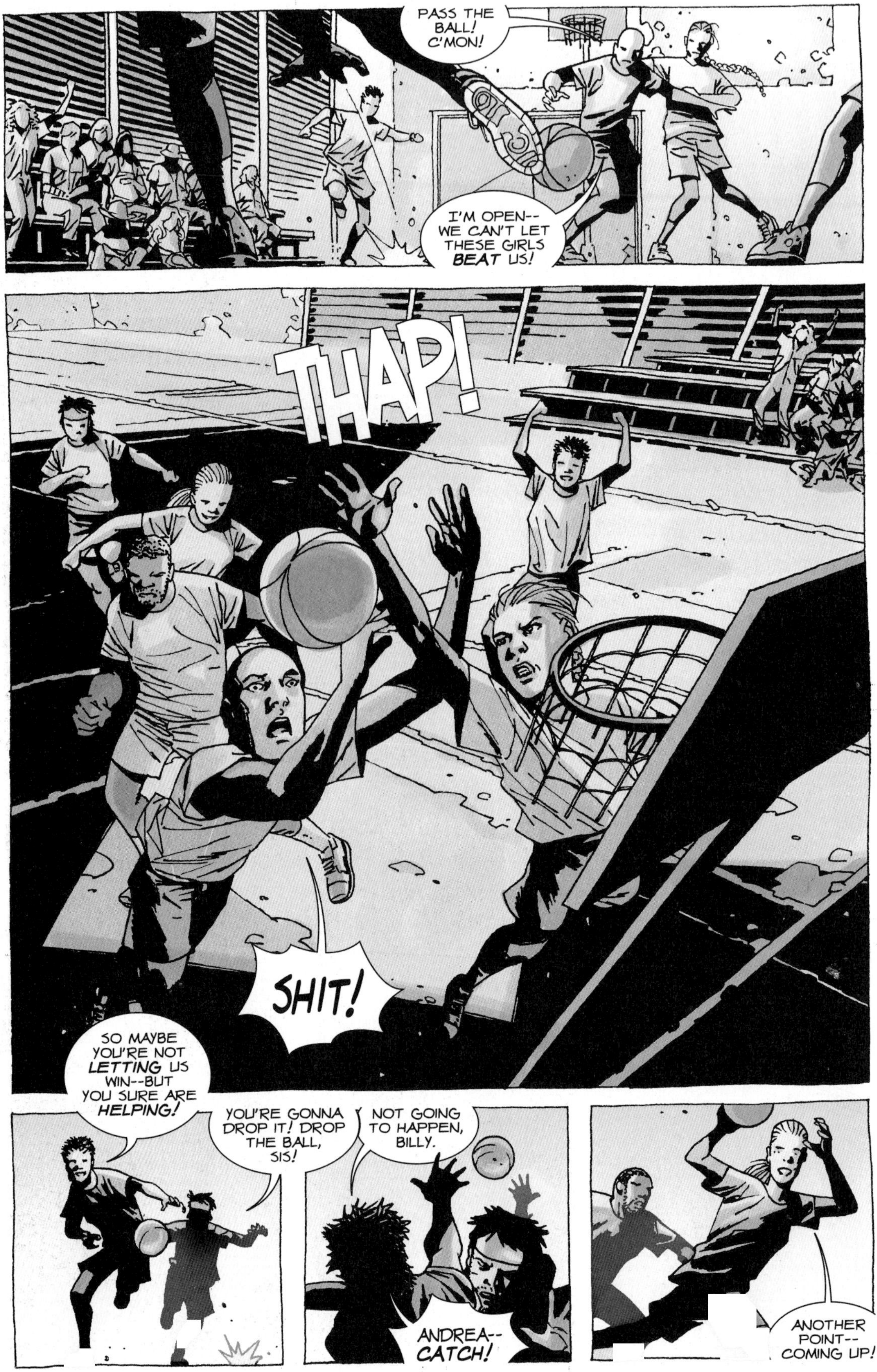
PASS THE BALL! C'MON!
I'M OPEN-- WE CAN'T LET THESE GIRLS BEAT US!
THAP!
SHIT!
SO MAYBE YOU'RE NOT LETTING US WIN--BUT YOU SURE ARE HELPING!
YOU'RE GONNA DROP IT! DROP THE BALL, SIS!
NOT GOING TO HAPPEN, BILLY.
ANDREA-- CATCH!
ANOTHER POINT-- COMING UP!

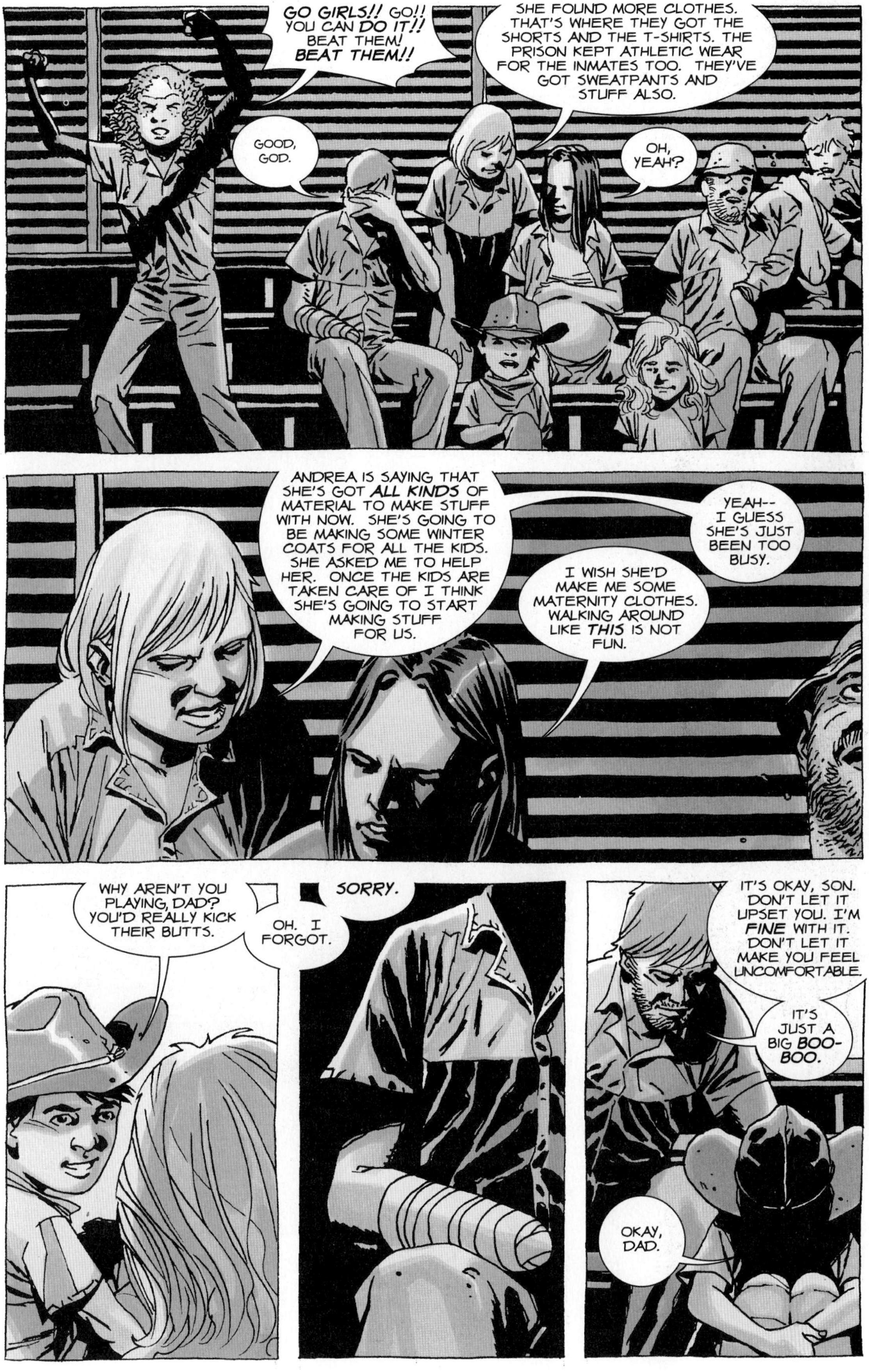
GO GIRLS!! GO!! YOU CAN DO IT!! BEAT THEM! BEAT THEM!!
GOOD, GOD.
SHE FOUND MORE CLOTHES. THAT'S WHERE THEY GOT THE SHORTS AND THE T-SHIRTS. THE PRISON KEPT ATHLETIC WEAR FOR THE INMATES TOO. THEY'VE GOT SWEATPANTS AND STUFF ALSO.
OH, YEAH?
ANDREA IS SAYING THAT SHE'S GOT ALL KINDS OF MATERIAL TO MAKE STUFF WITH NOW. SHE'S GOING TO BE MAKING SOME WINTER COATS FOR ALL THE KIDS. SHE ASKED ME TO HELP HER. ONCE THE KIDS ARE TAKEN CARE OF I THINK SHE'S GOING TO START MAKING STUFF FOR US.
YEAH-- I GUESS SHE'S JUST BEEN TOO BUSY.
I WISH SHE'D MAKE ME SOME MATERNITY CLOTHES. WALKING AROUND LIKE THIS IS NOT FUN.
WHY AREN'T YOU PLAYING, DAD? YOU'D REALLY KICK THEIR BUTTS.
OH. I FORGOT.
SORRY.
IT'S OKAY, SON. DON'T LET IT UPSET YOU. I'M FINE WITH IT. DON'T LET IT MAKE YOU FEEL UNCOMFORTABLE.
IT'S JUST A BIG BOO-BOO.
OKAY, DAD.

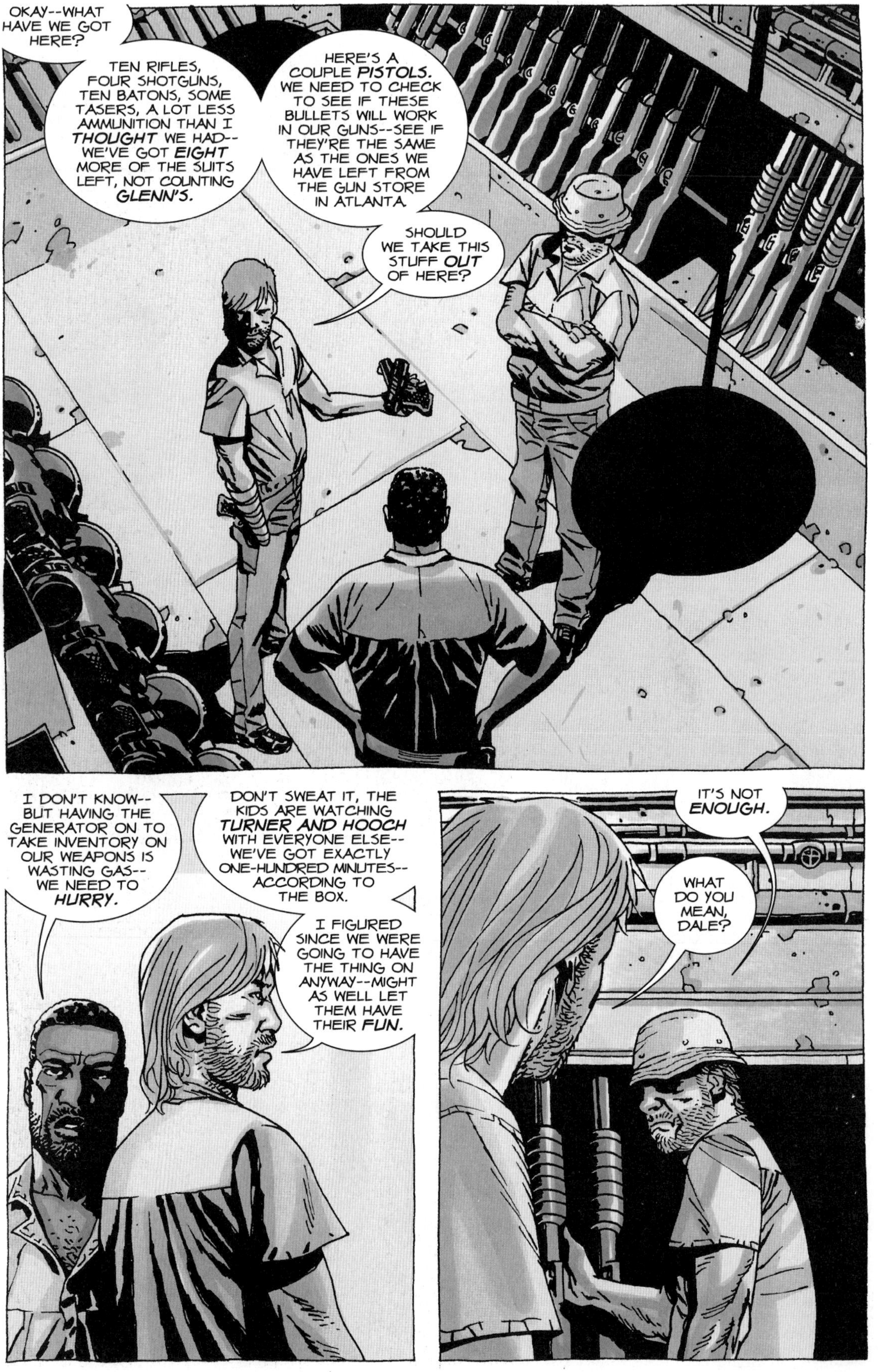
OKAY--WHAT HAVE WE GOT HERE?
TEN RIFLES, FOUR SHOTGUNS, TEN BATONS, SOME TASERS, A LOT LESS AMMUNITION THAN I THOUGHT WE HAD-- WE'VE GOT EIGHT MORE OF THE SUITS LEFT, NOT COUNTING GLENN'S.
HERE'S A COUPLE PISTOLS. WE NEED TO CHECK TO SEE IF THESE BULLETS WILL WORK IN OUR GUNS--SEE IF THEY'RE THE SAME AS THE ONES WE HAVE LEFT FROM THE GUN STORE IN ATLANTA.
SHOULD WE TAKE THIS STUFF OUT OF HERE?
I DON'T KNOW-- BUT HAVING THE GENERATOR ON TO TAKE INVENTORY ON OUR WEAPONS IS WASTING GAS-- WE NEED TO HURRY.
DON'T SWEAT IT, THE KIDS ARE WATCHING TURNER AND HOOCH WITH EVERYONE ELSE-- WE'VE GOT EXACTLY ONE-HUNDRED MINUTES-- ACCORDING TO THE BOX.
I FIGURED SINCE WE WERE GOING TO HAVE THE THING ON ANYWAY--MIGHT AS WELL LET THEM HAVE THEIR FUN.
IT'S NOT ENOUGH.
WHAT DO YOU MEAN, DALE?

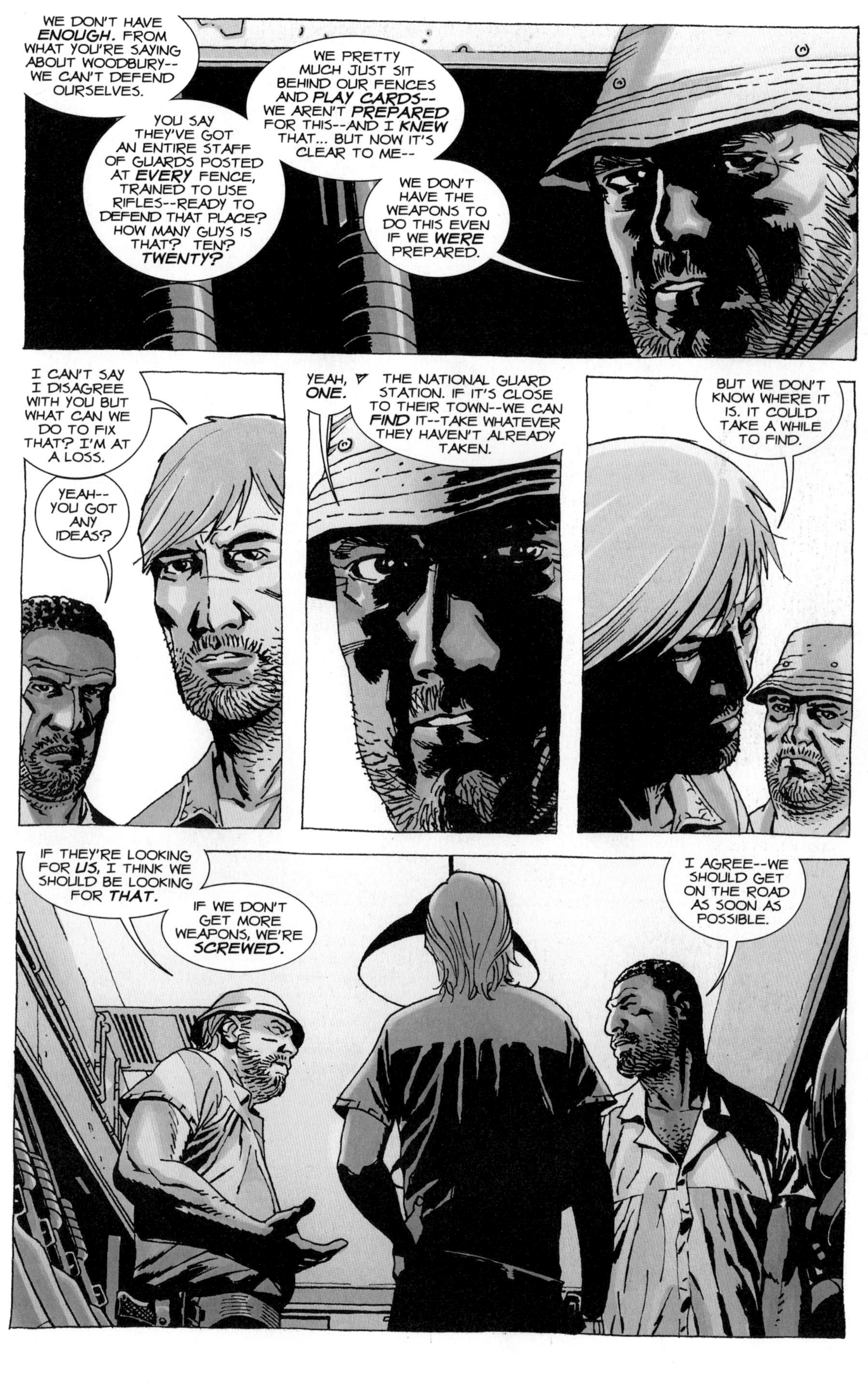

WE DON'T HAVE ENOUGH. FROM WHAT YOU'RE SAYING ABOUT WOODBURY-- WE CAN'T DEFEND OURSELVES.
YOU SAY THEY'VE GOT AN ENTIRE STAFF OF GUARDS POSTED AT EVERY FENCE, TRAINED TO USE RIFLES--READY TO DEFEND THAT PLACE? HOW MANY GUYS IS THAT? TEN? TWENTY?
WE PRETTY MUCH JUST SIT BEHIND OUR FENCES AND PLAY CARDS-- WE AREN'T PREPARED FOR THIS--AND I KNEW THAT... BUT NOW IT'S CLEAR TO ME--
WE DON'T HAVE THE WEAPONS TO DO THIS EVEN IF WE WERE PREPARED.
I CAN'T SAY I DISAGREE WITH YOU BUT WHAT CAN WE DO TO FIX THAT? I'M AT A LOSS.
YEAH-- YOU GOT ANY IDEAS?
YEAH, ONE.
THE NATIONAL GUARD STATION. IF IT'S CLOSE TO THEIR TOWN--WE CAN FIND IT--TAKE WHATEVER THEY HAVEN'T ALREADY TAKEN.
BUT WE DON'T KNOW WHERE IT IS. IT COULD TAKE A WHILE TO FIND.
IF THEY'RE LOOKING FOR US, I THINK WE SHOULD BE LOOKING FOR THAT.
IF WE DON'T GET MORE WEAPONS, WE'RE SCREWED.
I AGREE--WE SHOULD GET ON THE ROAD AS SOON AS POSSIBLE.

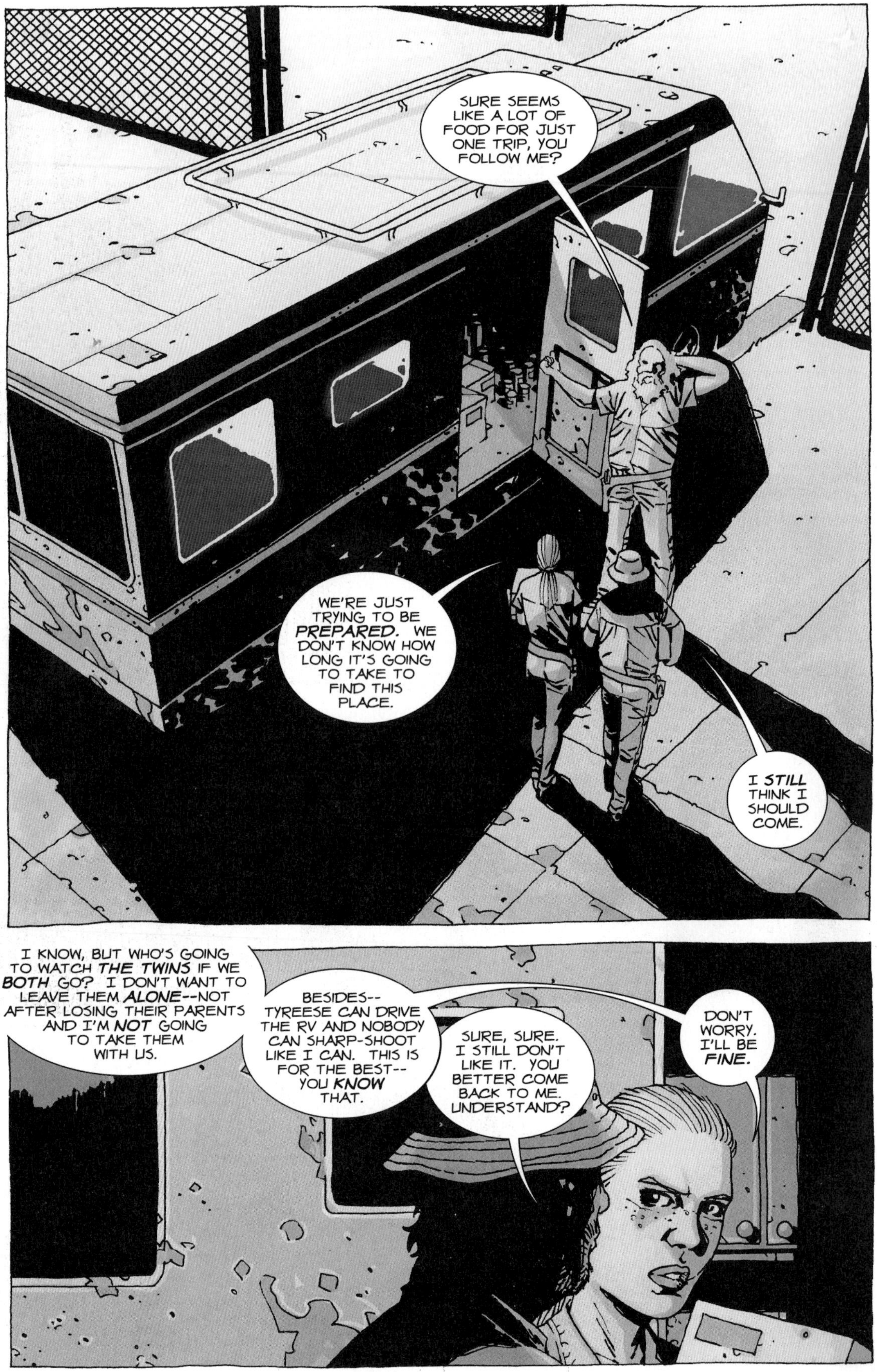
SURE SEEMS LIKE A LOT OF FOOD FOR JUST ONE TRIP, YOU FOLLOW ME?
WE'RE JUST TRYING TO BE PREPARED. WE DON'T KNOW HOW LONG IT'S GOING TO TAKE TO FIND THIS PLACE.
I STILL THINK I SHOULD COME.
I KNOW, BUT WHO'S GOING TO WATCH THE TWINS IF WE BOTH GO? I DON'T WANT TO LEAVE THEM ALONE--NOT AFTER LOSING THEIR PARENTS AND I'M NOT GOING TO TAKE THEM WITH US.
BESIDES-- TYREESE CAN DRIVE THE RV AND NOBODY CAN SHARP-SHOOT LIKE I CAN. THIS IS FOR THE BEST-- YOU KNOW THAT.
SURE, SURE. I STILL DON'T LIKE IT. YOU BETTER COME BACK TO ME. UNDERSTAND?
DON'T WORRY. I'LL BE FINE.

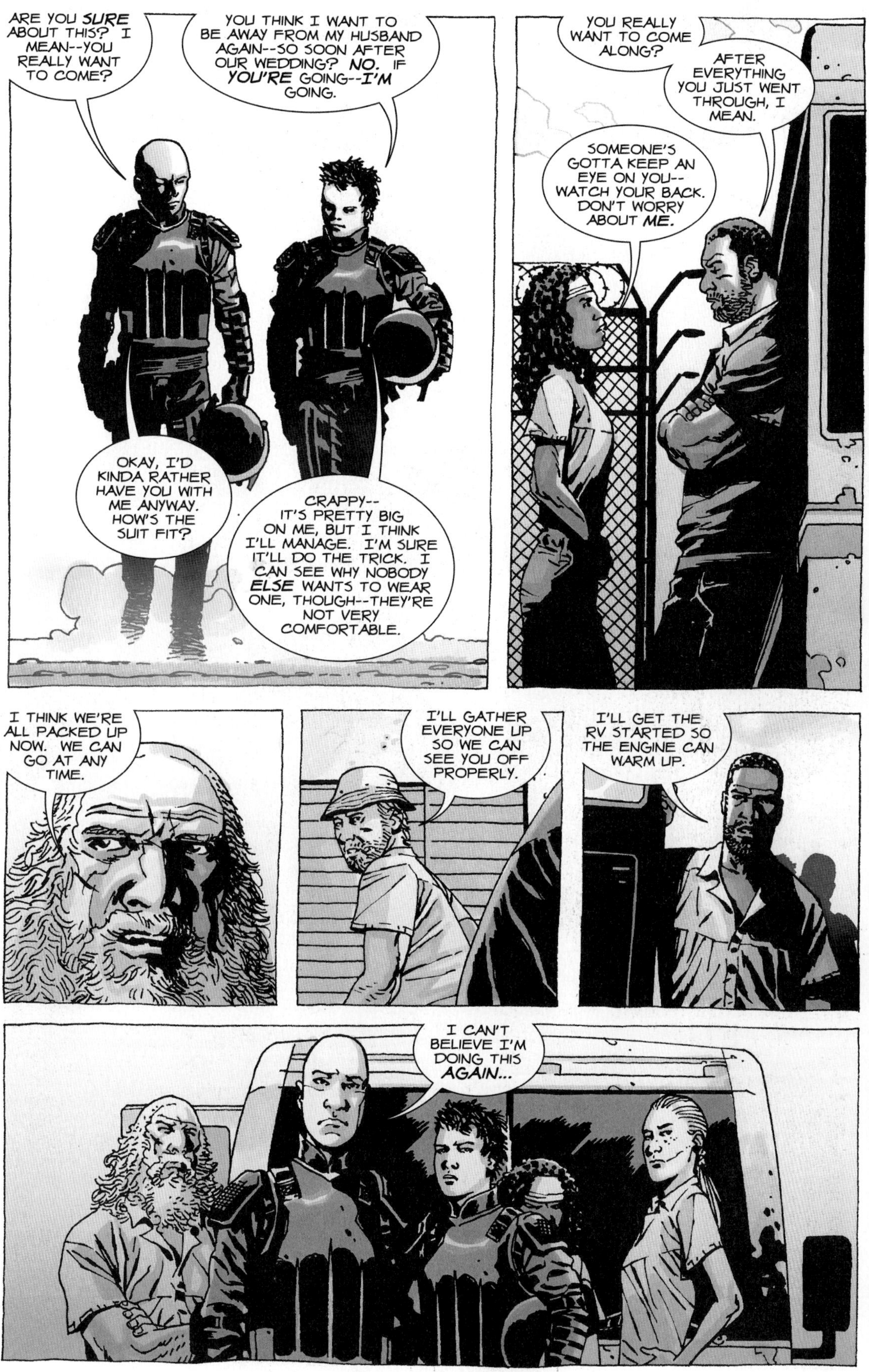
ARE YOU SURE ABOUT THIS? I MEAN--YOU REALLY WANT TO COME?
YOU THINK I WANT TO BE AWAY FROM MY HUSBAND AGAIN--SO SOON AFTER OUR WEDDING? NO. IF YOU'RE GOING--I'M GOING.
OKAY, I'D KINDA RATHER HAVE YOU WITH ME ANYWAY. HOW'S THE SUIT FIT?
CRAPPY-- IT'S PRETTY BIG ON ME, BUT I THINK I'LL MANAGE. I'M SURE IT'LL DO THE TRICK. I CAN SEE WHY NOBODY ELSE WANTS TO WEAR ONE, THOUGH--THEY'RE NOT VERY COMFORTABLE.
YOU REALLY WANT TO COME ALONG?
AFTER EVERYTHING YOU JUST WENT THROUGH, I MEAN.
SOMEONE'S GOTTA KEEP AN EYE ON YOU-- WATCH YOUR BACK. DON'T WORRY ABOUT ME.
I THINK WE'RE ALL PACKED UP NOW. WE CAN GO AT ANY TIME.
I'LL GATHER EVERYONE UP SO WE CAN SEE YOU OFF PROPERLY.
I'LL GET THE RV STARTED SO THE ENGINE CAN WARM UP.
I CAN'T BELIEVE I'M DOING THIS AGAIN...

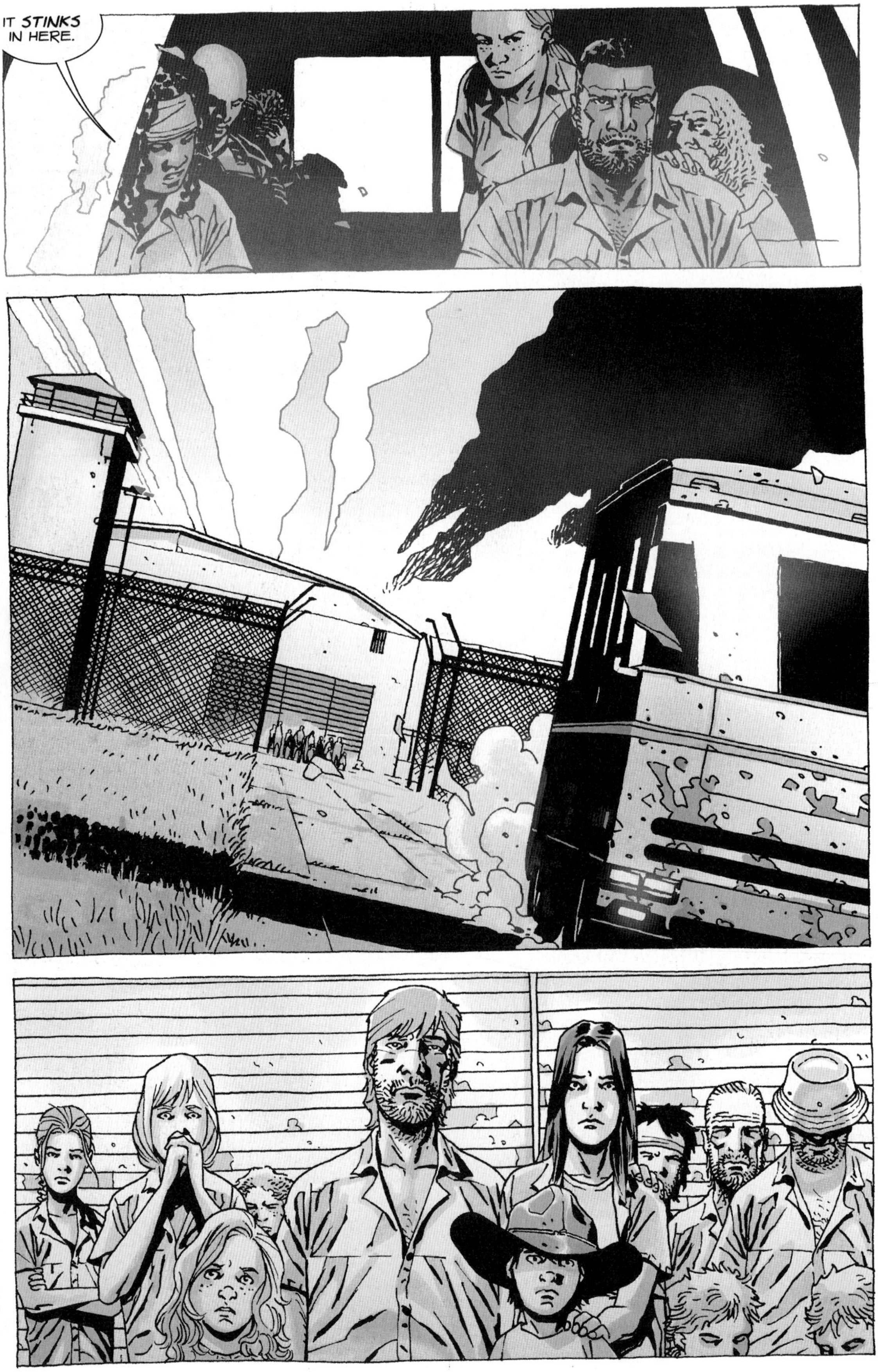
IT STINKS IN HERE.

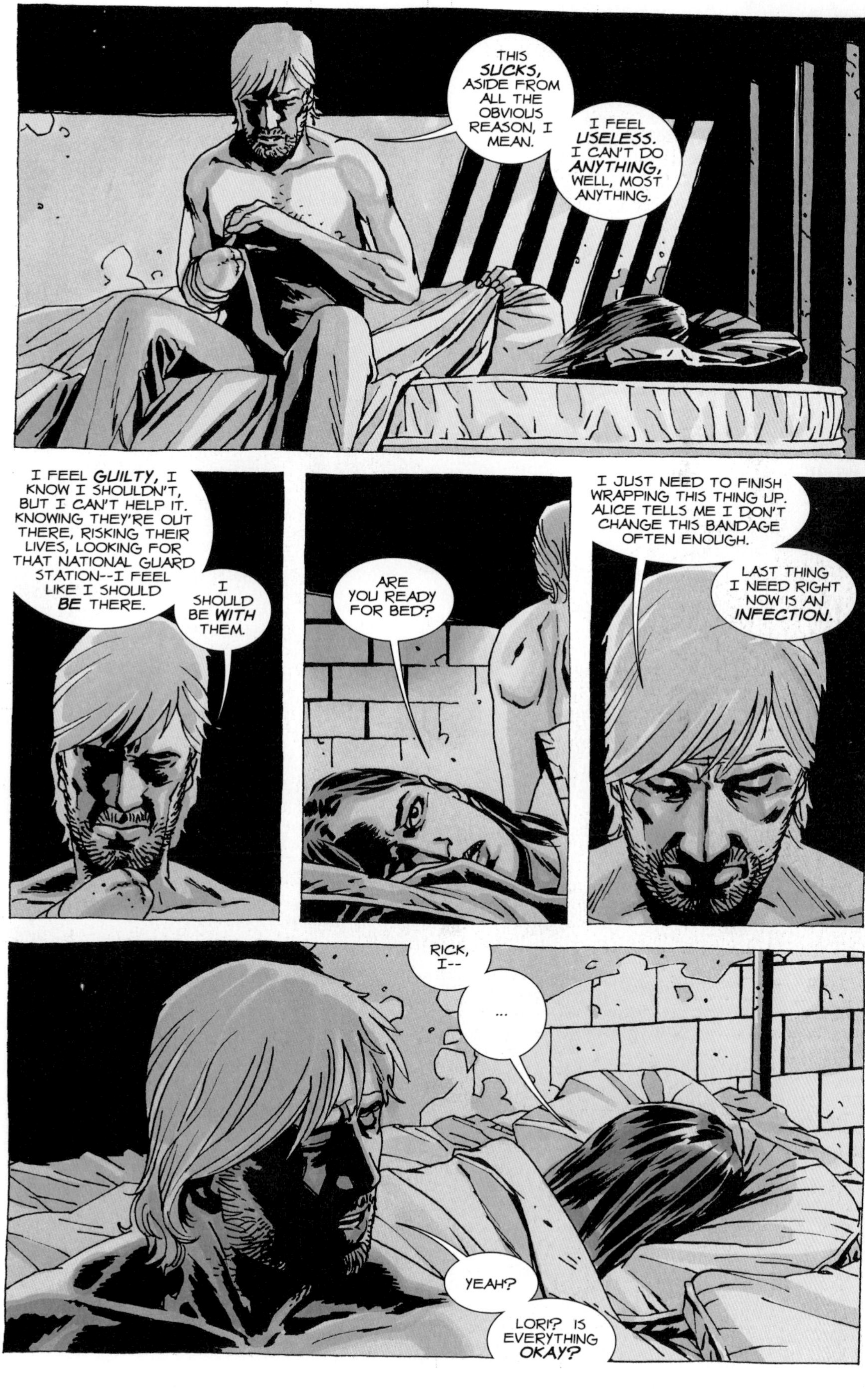
THIS SUCKS, ASIDE FROM ALL THE OBVIOUS REASON, I MEAN.
I FEEL USELESS. I CAN'T DO ANYTHING, WELL, MOST ANYTHING.
I FEEL GUILTY, I KNOW I SHOULDN'T, BUT I CAN'T HELP IT. KNOWING THEY'RE OUT THERE, RISKING THEIR LIVES, LOOKING FOR THAT NATIONAL GUARD STATION--I FEEL LIKE I SHOULD BE THERE.
I SHOULD BE WITH THEM.
ARE YOU READY FOR BED?
I JUST NEED TO FINISH WRAPPING THIS THING UP. ALICE TELLS ME I DON'T CHANGE THIS BANDAGE OFTEN ENOUGH.
LAST THING I NEED RIGHT NOW IS AN INFECTION.
RICK, I--
...
YEAH?
LORI? IS EVERYTHING OKAY?

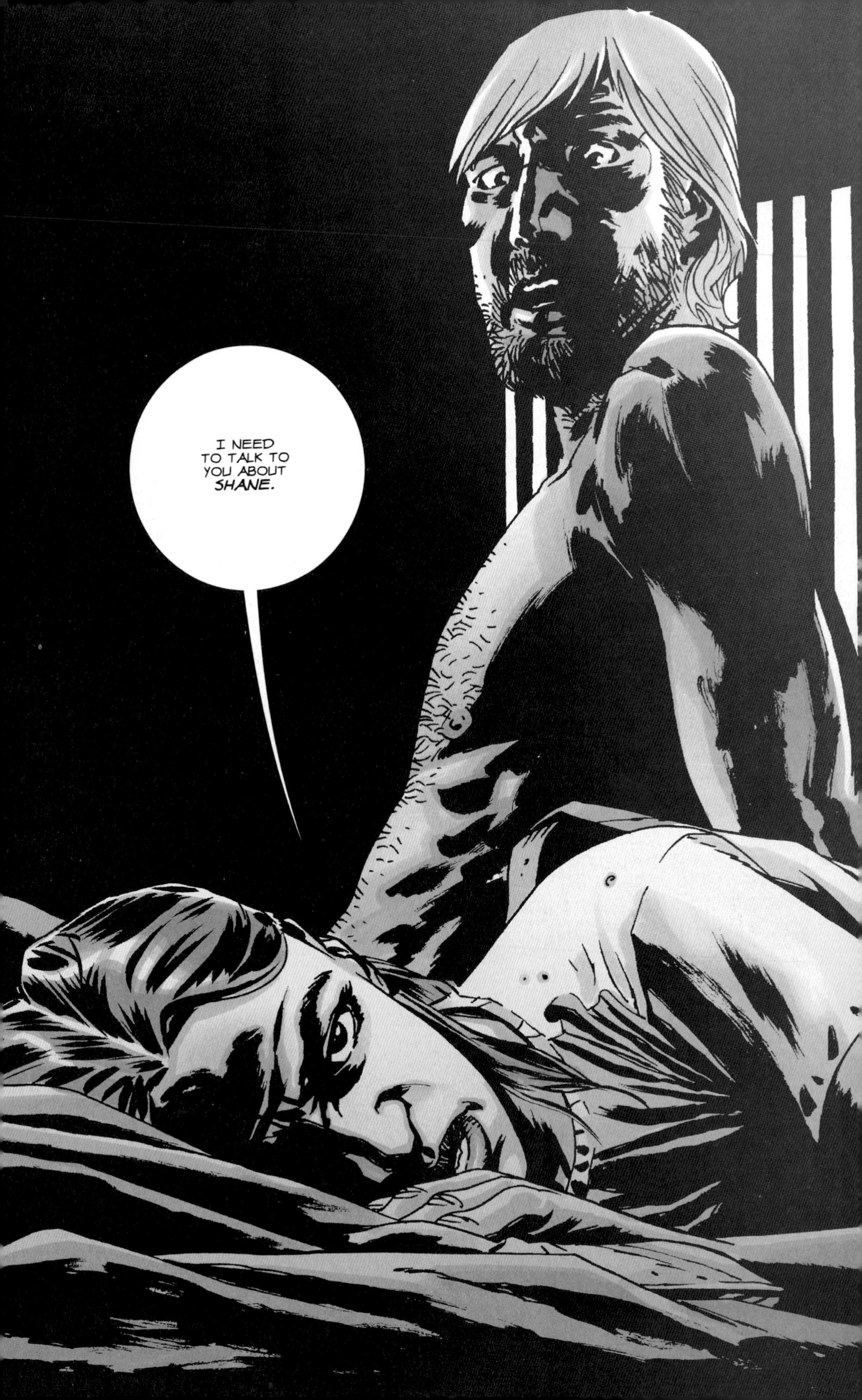
I NEED TO TALK TO YOU ABOUT SHANE.

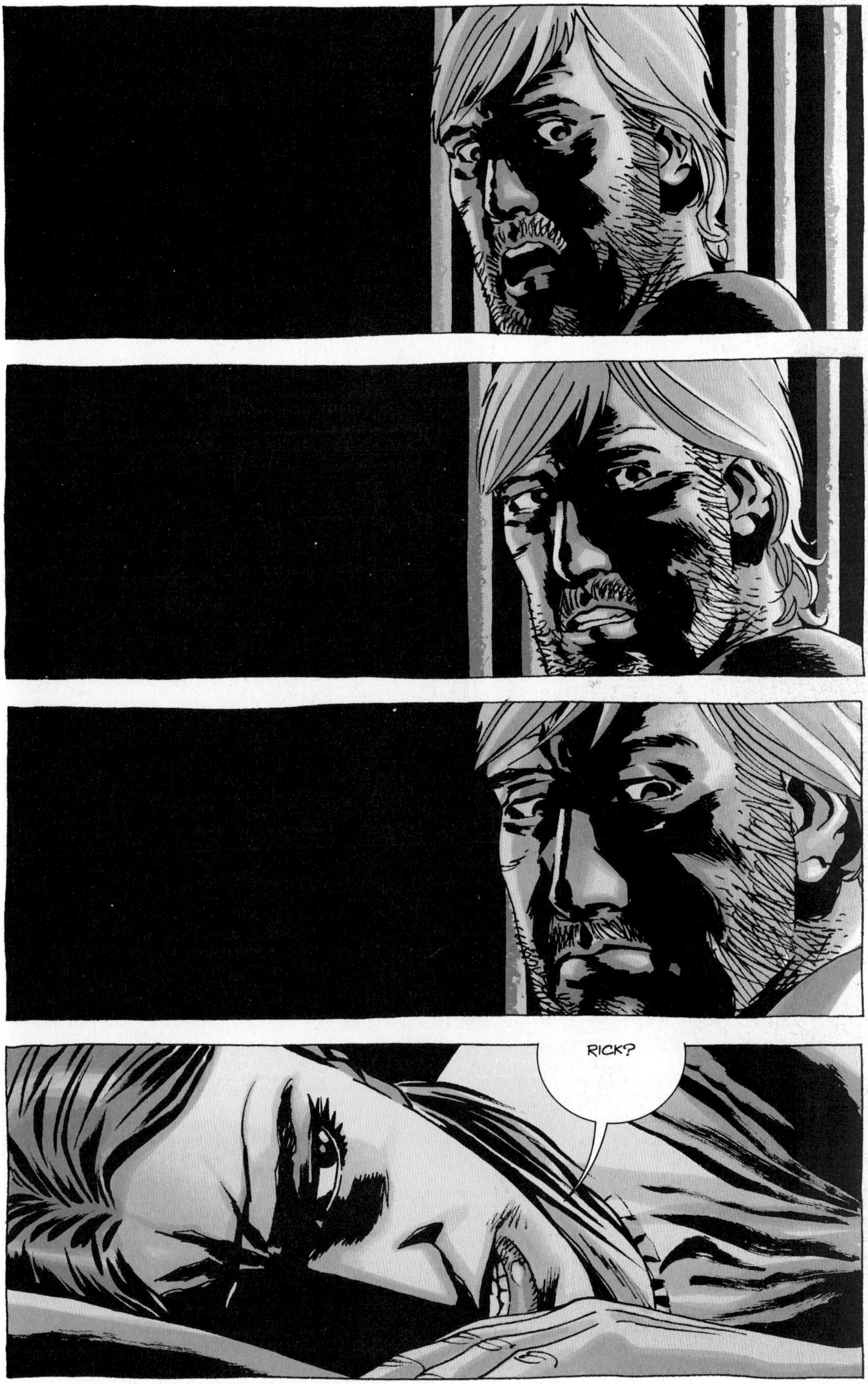
RICK?

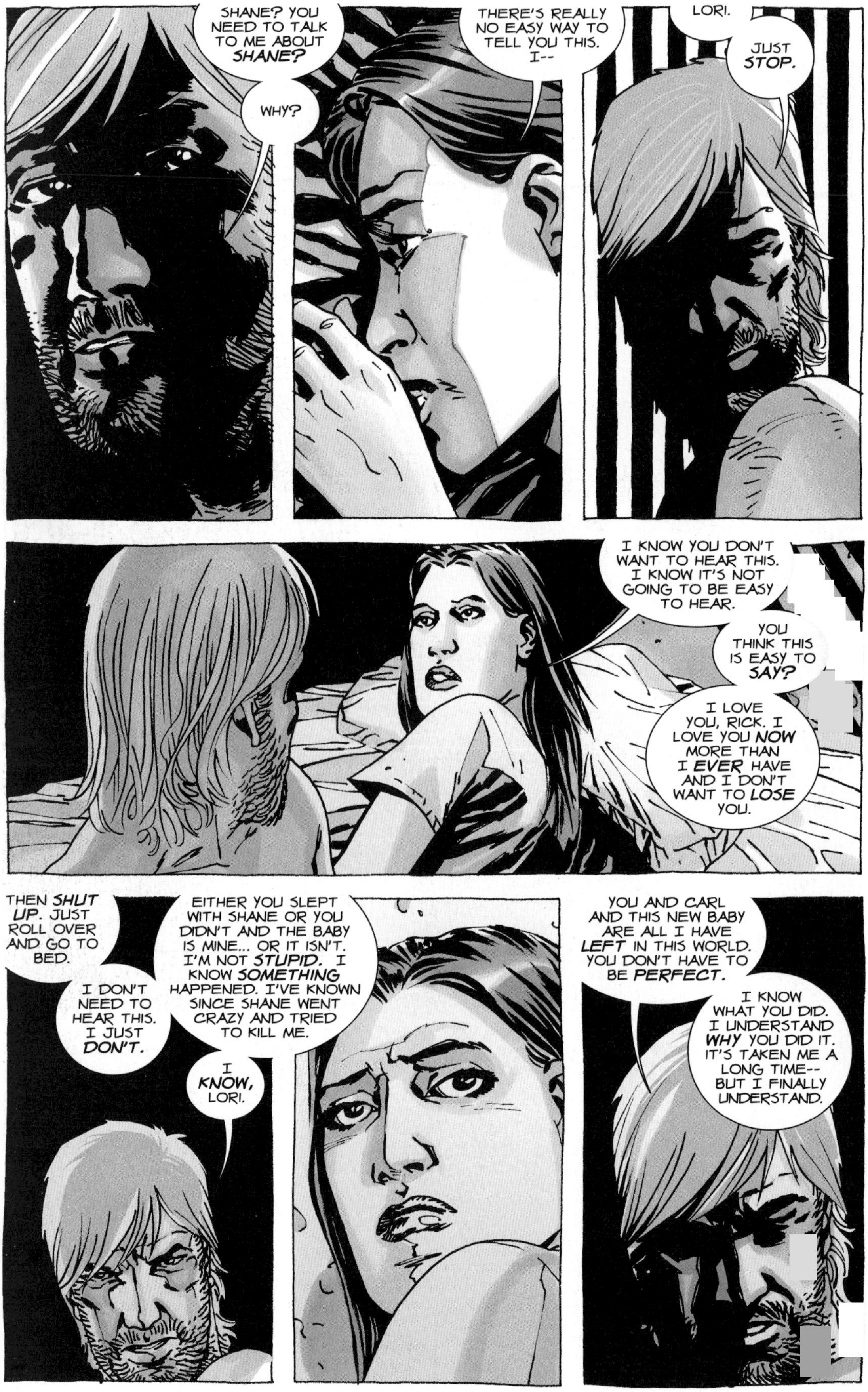
SHANE? YOU NEED TO TALK TO ME ABOUT SHANE?
WHY?
THERE'S REALLY NO EASY WAY TO TELL YOU THIS. I--
LORI.
JUST STOP.
I KNOW YOU DON'T WANT TO HEAR THIS. I KNOW IT'S NOT GOING TO BE EASY TO HEAR.
YOU THINK THIS IS EASY TO SAY?
I LOVE YOU, RICK. I LOVE YOU NOW MORE THAN I EVER HAVE AND I DON'T WANT TO LOSE YOU.
THEN SHUT UP. JUST ROLL OVER AND GO TO BED.
I DON'T NEED TO HEAR THIS. I JUST DON'T.
EITHER YOU SLEPT WITH SHANE OR YOU DIDN'T AND THE BABY IS MINE... OR IT ISN'T. I'M NOT STUPID. I KNOW SOMETHING HAPPENED. I'VE KNOWN SINCE SHANE WENT CRAZY AND TRIED TO KILL ME.
I KNOW, LORI.
YOU AND CARL AND THIS NEW BABY ARE ALL I HAVE LEFT IN THIS WORLD. YOU DON'T HAVE TO BE PERFECT.
I KNOW WHAT YOU DID. I UNDERSTAND WHY YOU DID IT. IT'S TAKEN ME A LONG TIME-- BUT I FINALLY UNDERSTAND.

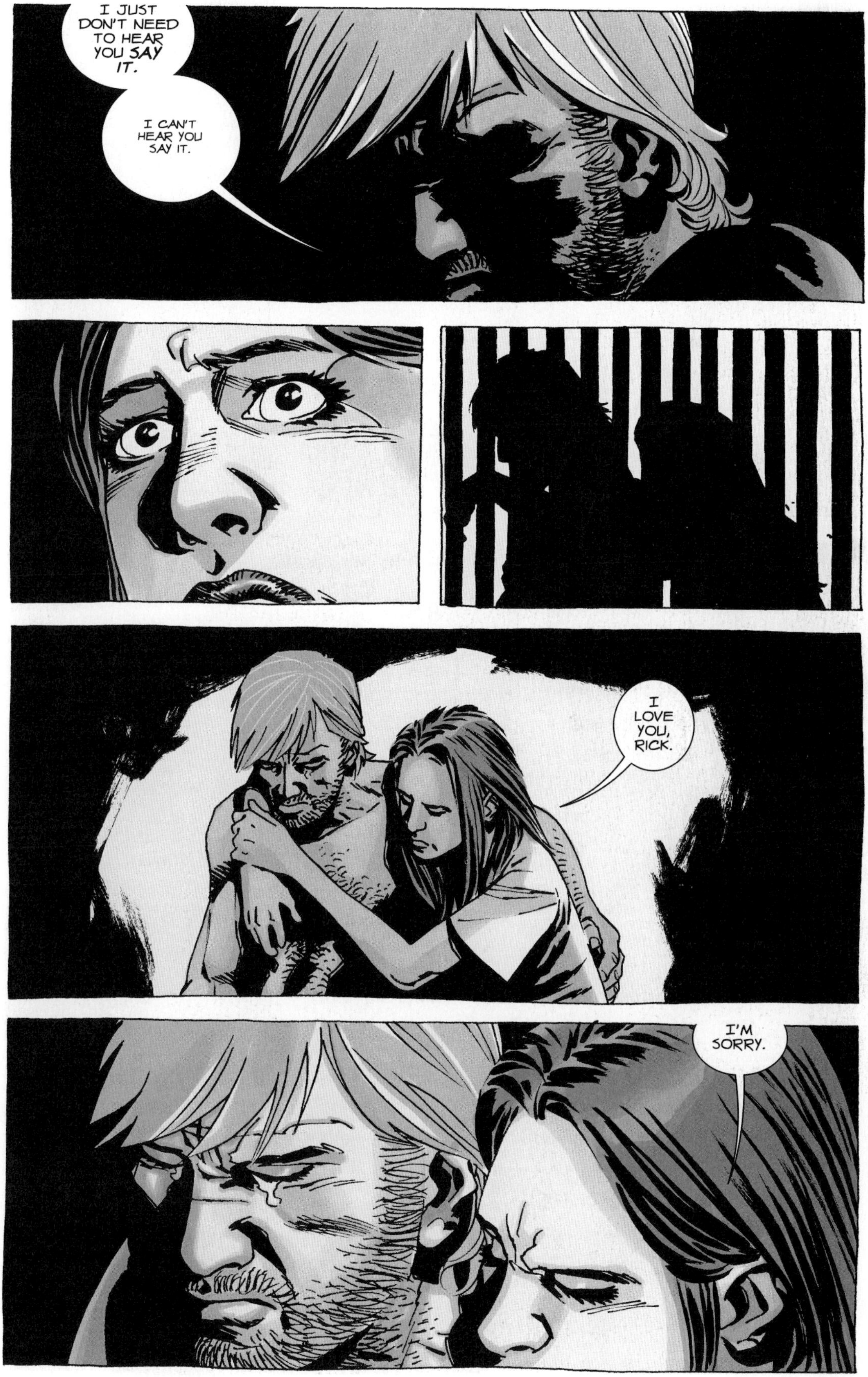
I JUST DON'T NEED TO HEAR YOU *SAY* IT.
I CAN'T HEAR YOU SAY IT.
I LOVE YOU, RICK.
I'M SORRY.

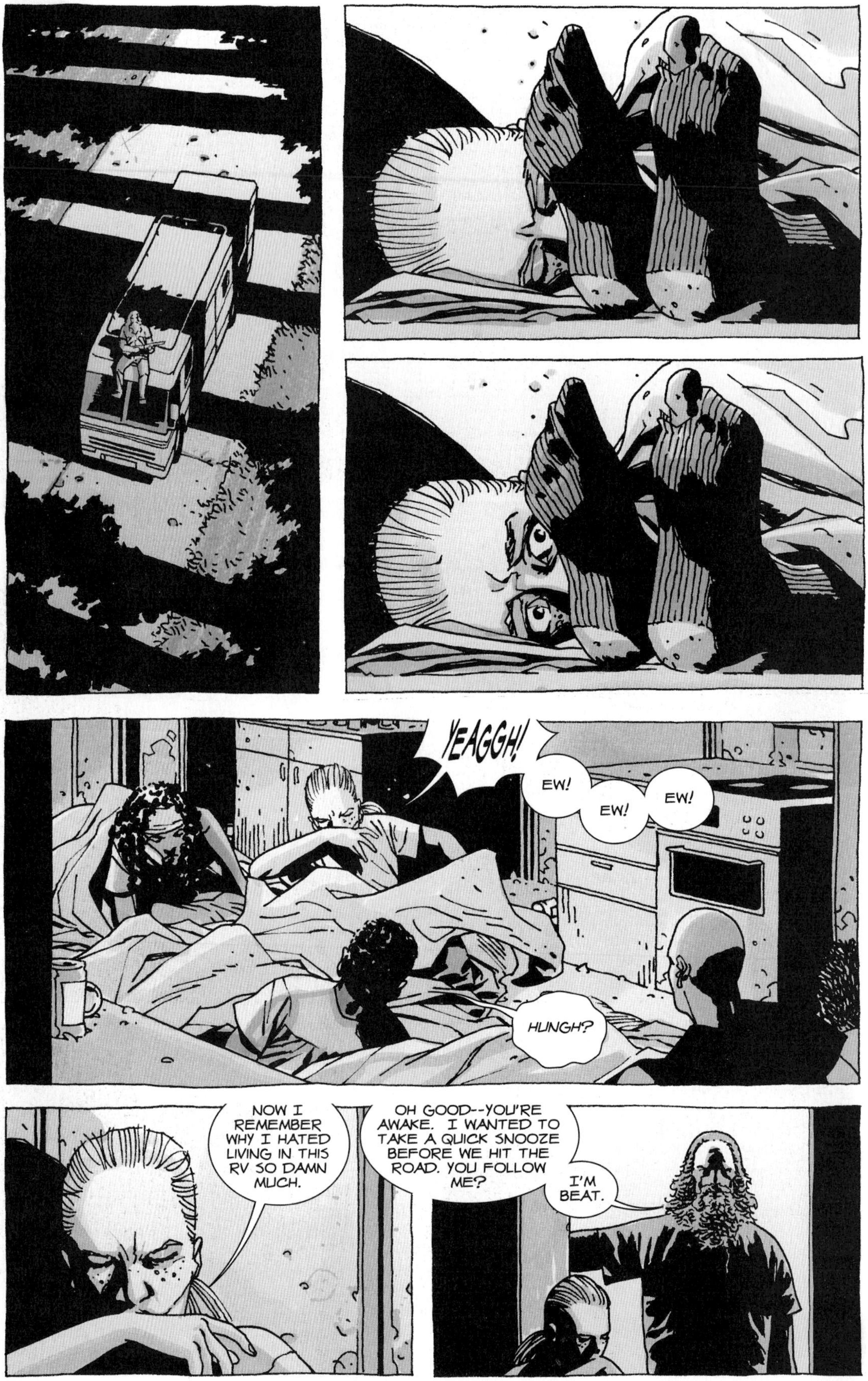
YEAGGH!
EW!
EW!
EW!
HUNGH?
NOW I REMEMBER WHY I HATED LIVING IN THIS RV SO DAMN MUCH.
OH GOOD--YOU'RE AWAKE. I WANTED TO TAKE A QUICK SNOOZE BEFORE WE HIT THE ROAD. YOU FOLLOW ME?
I'M BEAT.

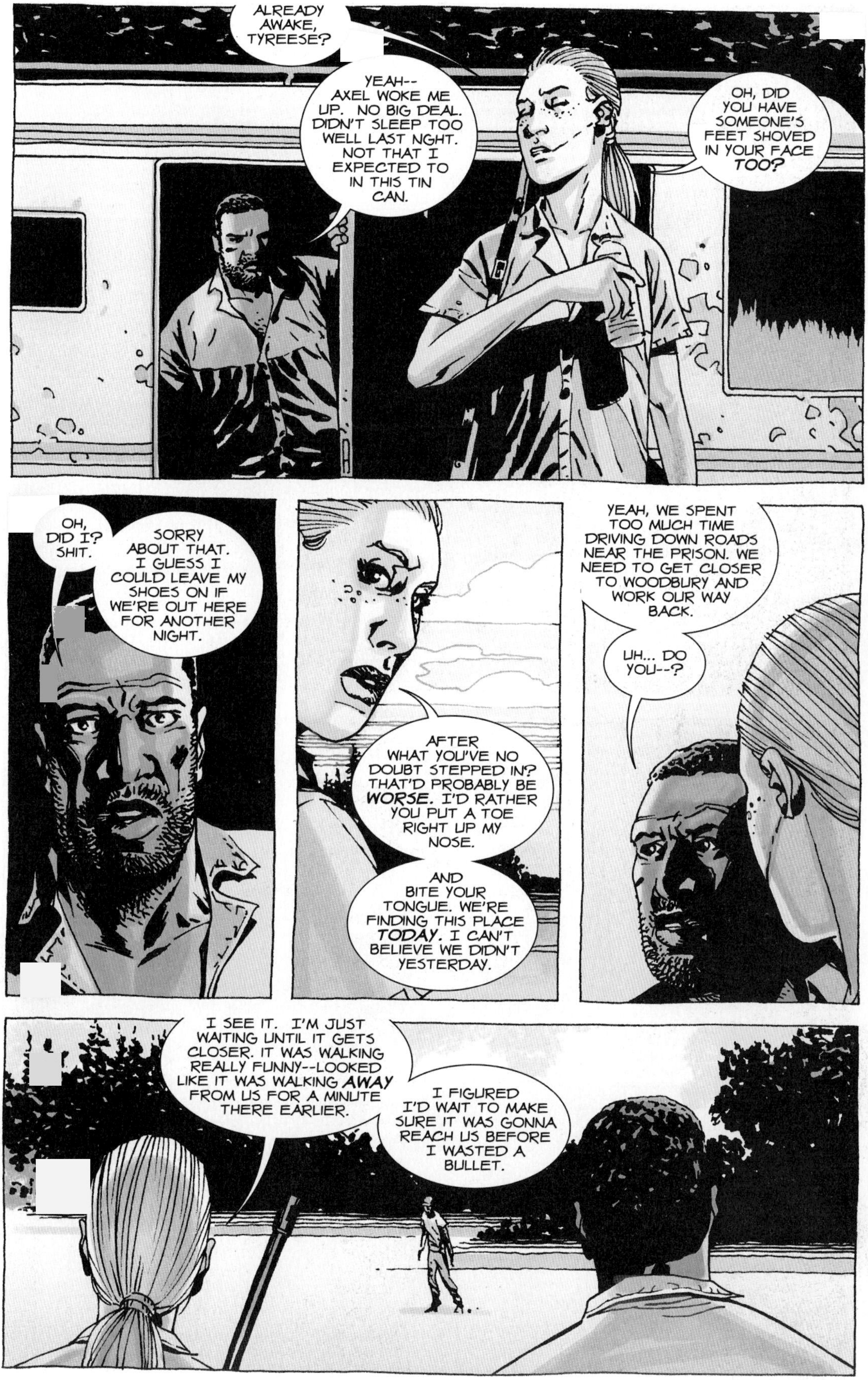
ALREADY AWAKE, TYREESE?
YEAH-- AXEL WOKE ME UP. NO BIG DEAL. DIDN'T SLEEP TOO WELL LAST NGHT. NOT THAT I EXPECTED TO IN THIS TIN CAN.
OH, DID YOU HAVE SOMEONE'S FEET SHOVED IN YOUR FACE *TOO?*
OH, DID I? SHIT.
SORRY ABOUT THAT. I GUESS I COULD LEAVE MY SHOES ON IF WE'RE OUT HERE FOR ANOTHER NIGHT.
AFTER WHAT YOU'VE NO DOUBT STEPPED IN? THAT'D PROBABLY BE **WORSE.** I'D RATHER YOU PUT A TOE RIGHT UP MY NOSE.
AND BITE YOUR TONGUE. WE'RE FINDING THIS PLACE ***TODAY.*** I CAN'T BELIEVE WE DIDN'T YESTERDAY.
YEAH, WE SPENT TOO MUCH TIME DRIVING DOWN ROADS NEAR THE PRISON. WE NEED TO GET CLOSER TO WOODBURY AND WORK OUR WAY BACK.
UH... DO YOU--?
I SEE IT. I'M JUST WAITING UNTIL IT GETS CLOSER. IT WAS WALKING REALLY FUNNY--LOOKED LIKE IT WAS WALKING ***AWAY*** FROM US FOR A MINUTE THERE EARLIER.
I FIGURED I'D WAIT TO MAKE SURE IT WAS GONNA REACH US BEFORE I WASTED A BULLET.

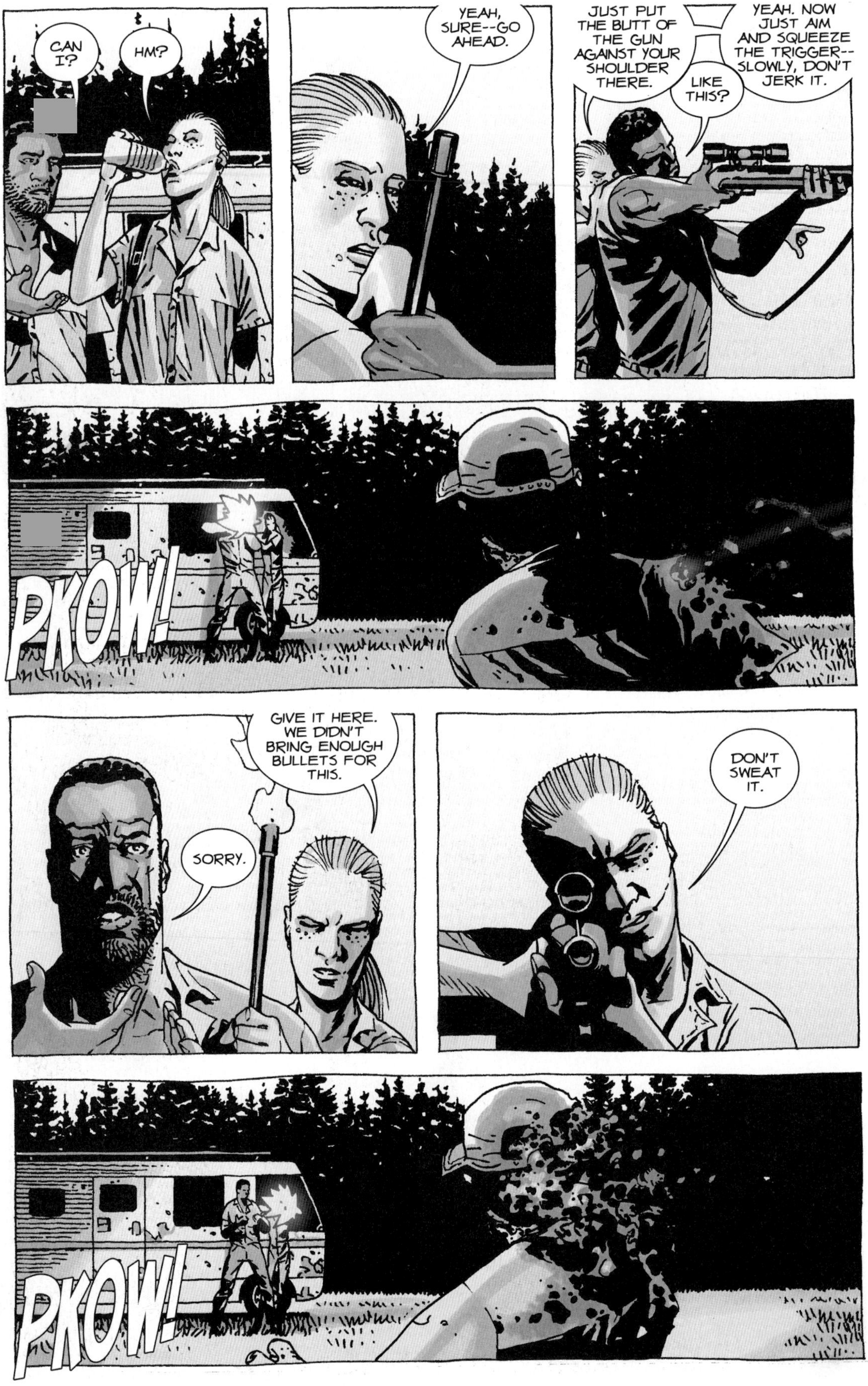
CAN I?
HM?
YEAH, SURE--GO AHEAD.
JUST PUT THE BUTT OF THE GUN AGAINST YOUR SHOULDER THERE.
LIKE THIS?
YEAH. NOW JUST AIM AND SQUEEZE THE TRIGGER-- SLOWLY, DON'T JERK IT.
PKOW!
GIVE IT HERE. WE DIDN'T BRING ENOUGH BULLETS FOR THIS.
SORRY.
DON'T SWEAT IT.
PKOW!

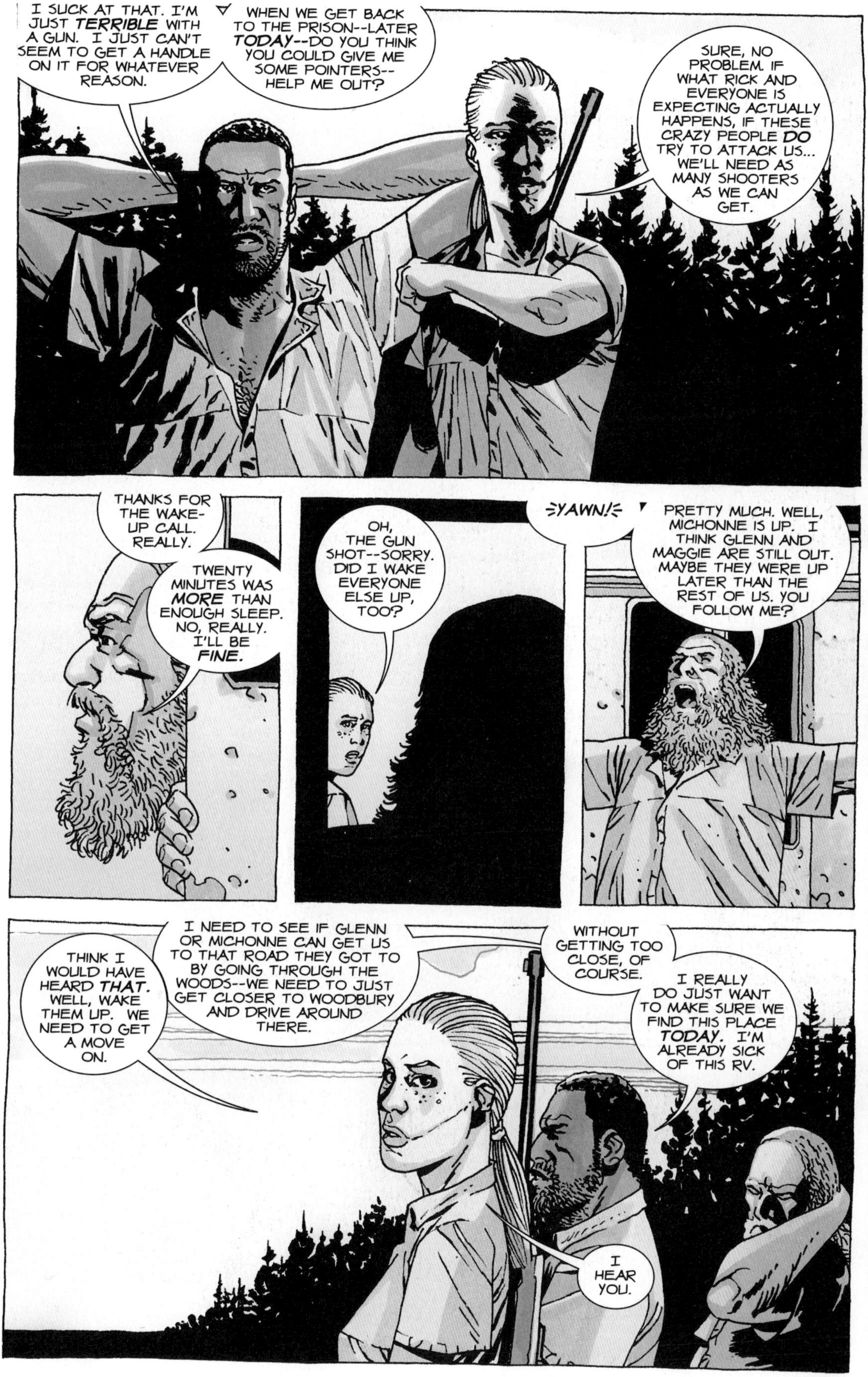
I SUCK AT THAT. I'M JUST TERRIBLE WITH A GUN. I JUST CAN'T SEEM TO GET A HANDLE ON IT FOR WHATEVER REASON.
WHEN WE GET BACK TO THE PRISON--LATER TODAY--DO YOU THINK YOU COULD GIVE ME SOME POINTERS-- HELP ME OUT?
SURE, NO PROBLEM. IF WHAT RICK AND EVERYONE IS EXPECTING ACTUALLY HAPPENS, IF THESE CRAZY PEOPLE DO TRY TO ATTACK US... WE'LL NEED AS MANY SHOOTERS AS WE CAN GET.
THANKS FOR THE WAKE-UP CALL. REALLY.
TWENTY MINUTES WAS MORE THAN ENOUGH SLEEP. NO, REALLY. I'LL BE FINE.
OH, THE GUN SHOT--SORRY. DID I WAKE EVERYONE ELSE UP, TOO?
YAWN!
PRETTY MUCH. WELL, MICHONNE IS UP. I THINK GLENN AND MAGGIE ARE STILL OUT. MAYBE THEY WERE UP LATER THAN THE REST OF US. YOU FOLLOW ME?
THINK I WOULD HAVE HEARD THAT. WELL, WAKE THEM UP. WE NEED TO GET A MOVE ON.
I NEED TO SEE IF GLENN OR MICHONNE CAN GET US TO THAT ROAD THEY GOT TO BY GOING THROUGH THE WOODS--WE NEED TO JUST GET CLOSER TO WOODBURY AND DRIVE AROUND THERE.
WITHOUT GETTING TOO CLOSE, OF COURSE.
I REALLY DO JUST WANT TO MAKE SURE WE FIND THIS PLACE TODAY. I'M ALREADY SICK OF THIS RV.
I HEAR YOU.

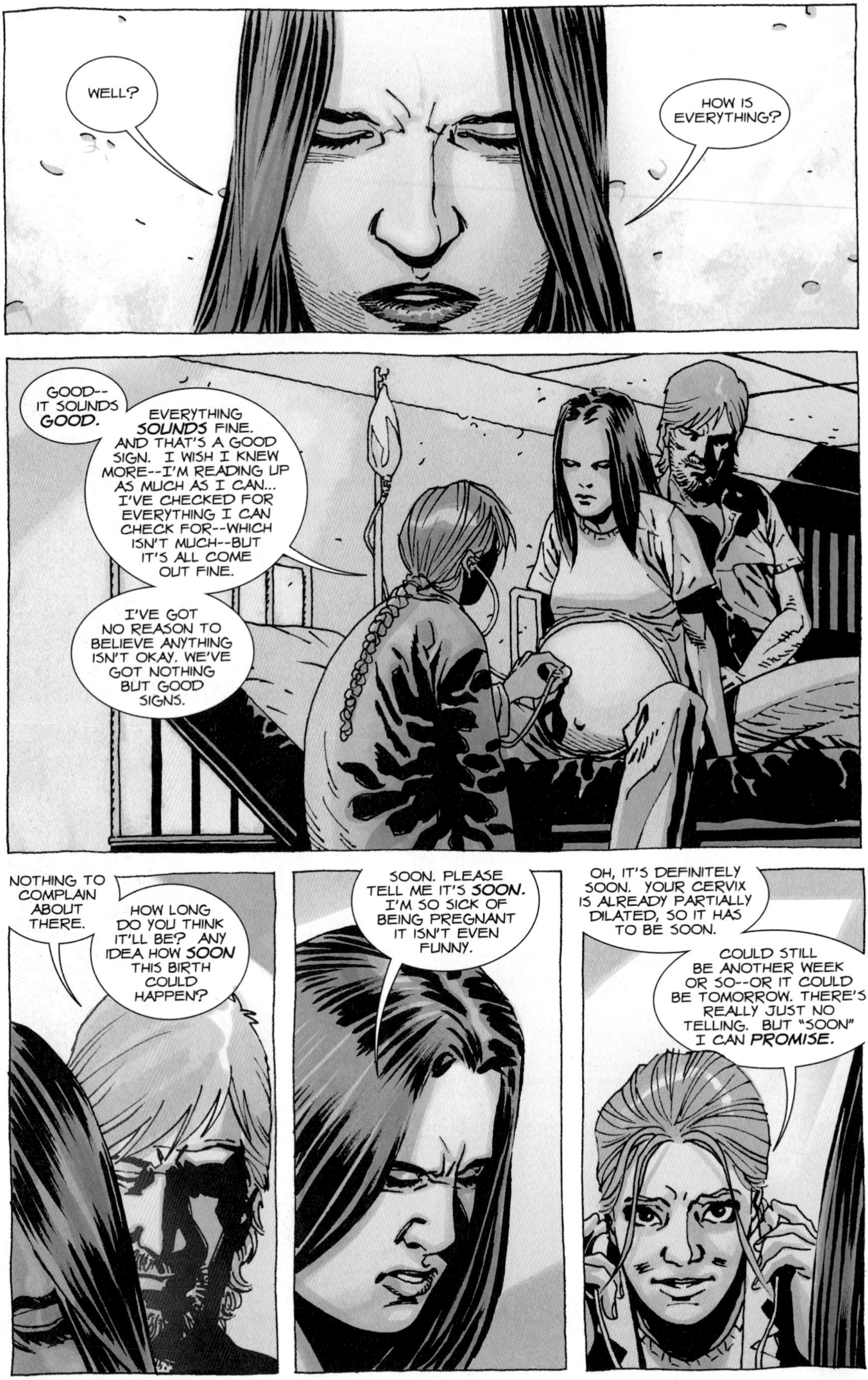

WELL?
HOW IS EVERYTHING?
GOOD-- IT SOUNDS GOOD.
EVERYTHING SOUNDS FINE. AND THAT'S A GOOD SIGN. I WISH I KNEW MORE--I'M READING UP AS MUCH AS I CAN... I'VE CHECKED FOR EVERYTHING I CAN CHECK FOR--WHICH ISN'T MUCH--BUT IT'S ALL COME OUT FINE.
I'VE GOT NO REASON TO BELIEVE ANYTHING ISN'T OKAY. WE'VE GOT NOTHING BUT GOOD SIGNS.
NOTHING TO COMPLAIN ABOUT THERE.
HOW LONG DO YOU THINK IT'LL BE? ANY IDEA HOW SOON THIS BIRTH COULD HAPPEN?
SOON. PLEASE TELL ME IT'S SOON. I'M SO SICK OF BEING PREGNANT IT ISN'T EVEN FUNNY.
OH, IT'S DEFINITELY SOON. YOUR CERVIX IS ALREADY PARTIALLY DILATED, SO IT HAS TO BE SOON.
COULD STILL BE ANOTHER WEEK OR SO--OR IT COULD BE TOMORROW. THERE'S REALLY JUST NO TELLING. BUT "SOON" I CAN PROMISE.

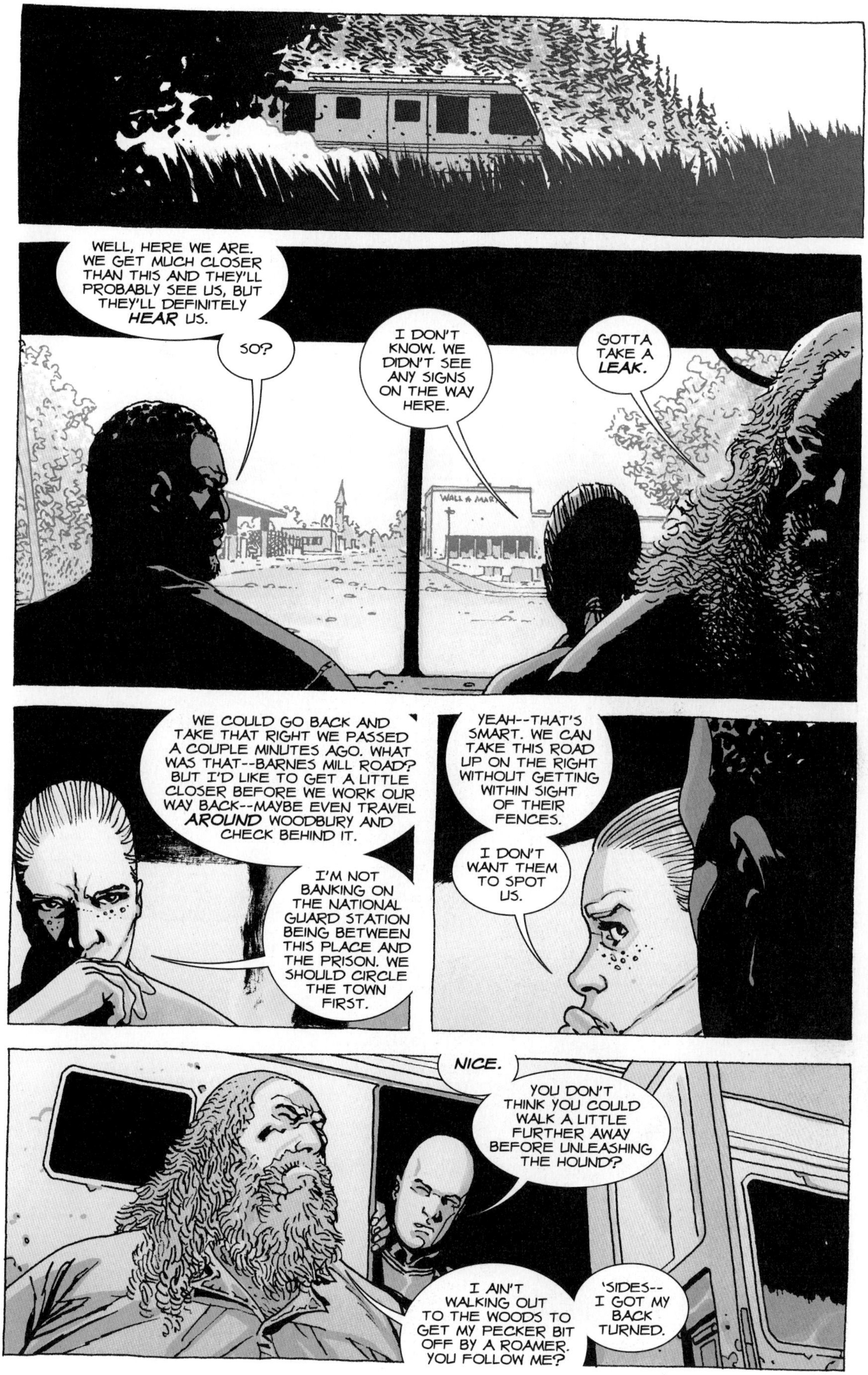

WELL, HERE WE ARE. WE GET MUCH CLOSER THAN THIS AND THEY'LL PROBABLY SEE US, BUT THEY'LL DEFINITELY *HEAR* US.
SO?
I DON'T KNOW. WE DIDN'T SEE ANY SIGNS ON THE WAY HERE.
GOTTA TAKE A *LEAK.*
WALL ★ MART
WE COULD GO BACK AND TAKE THAT RIGHT WE PASSED A COUPLE MINUTES AGO. WHAT WAS THAT--BARNES MILL ROAD? BUT I'D LIKE TO GET A LITTLE CLOSER BEFORE WE WORK OUR WAY BACK--MAYBE EVEN TRAVEL *AROUND* WOODBURY AND CHECK BEHIND IT.
I'M NOT BANKING ON THE NATIONAL GUARD STATION BEING BETWEEN THIS PLACE AND THE PRISON. WE SHOULD CIRCLE THE TOWN FIRST.
YEAH--THAT'S SMART. WE CAN TAKE THIS ROAD UP ON THE RIGHT WITHOUT GETTING WITHIN SIGHT OF THEIR FENCES.
I DON'T WANT THEM TO SPOT US.
NICE.
YOU DON'T THINK YOU COULD WALK A LITTLE FURTHER AWAY BEFORE UNLEASHING THE HOUND?
I AIN'T WALKING OUT TO THE WOODS TO GET MY PECKER BIT OFF BY A ROAMER. YOU FOLLOW ME?
'SIDES-- I GOT MY BACK TURNED.

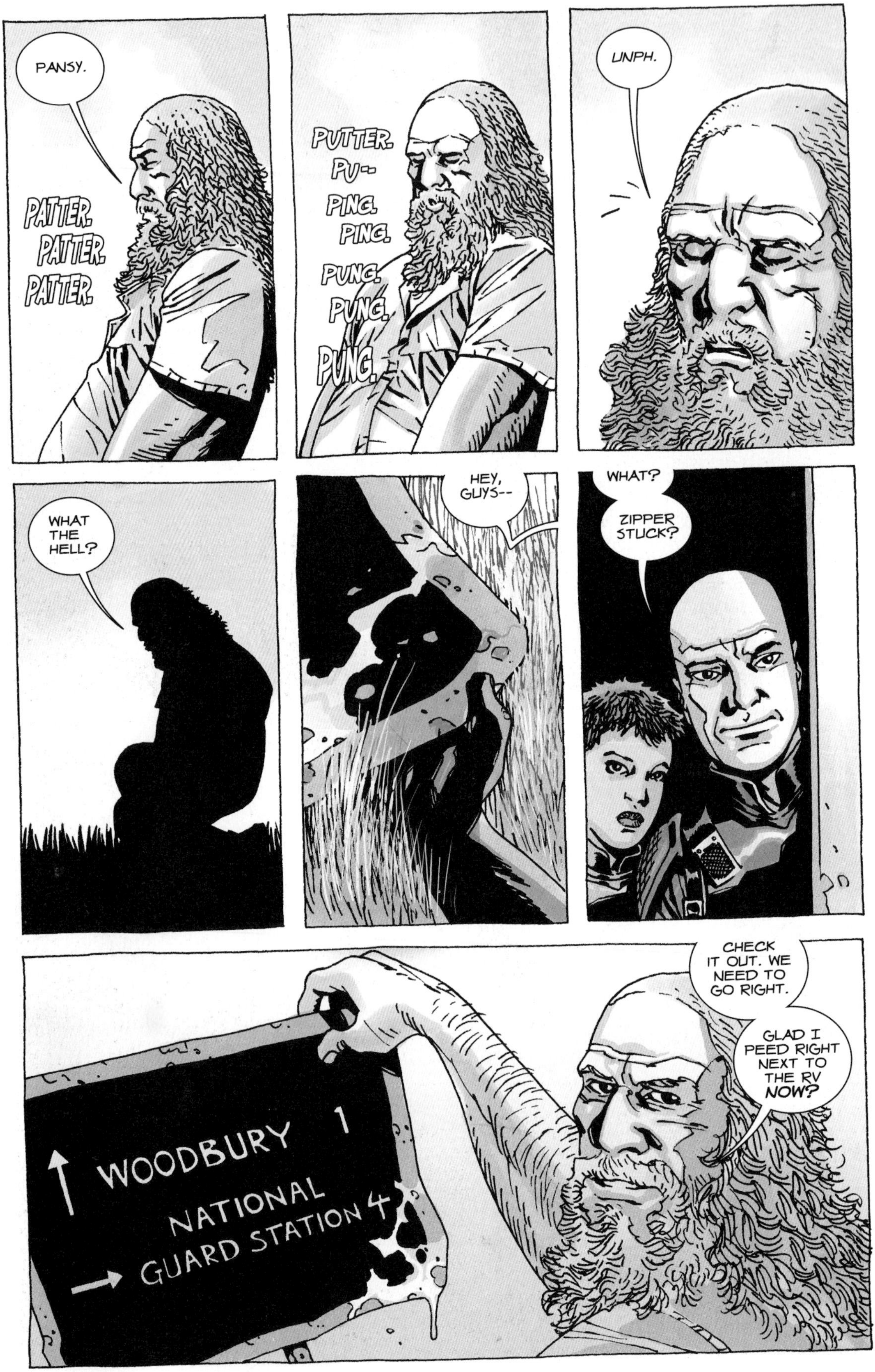
PANSY.
PATTER. PATTER. PATTER.
PUTTER. PU--
PING. PING.
PUNG. PUNG. PUNG.
UNPH.
WHAT THE HELL?
HEY, GUYS--
WHAT?
ZIPPER STUCK?
WOODBURY 1
NATIONAL GUARD STATION 4
CHECK IT OUT. WE NEED TO GO RIGHT.
GLAD I PEED RIGHT NEXT TO THE RV NOW?

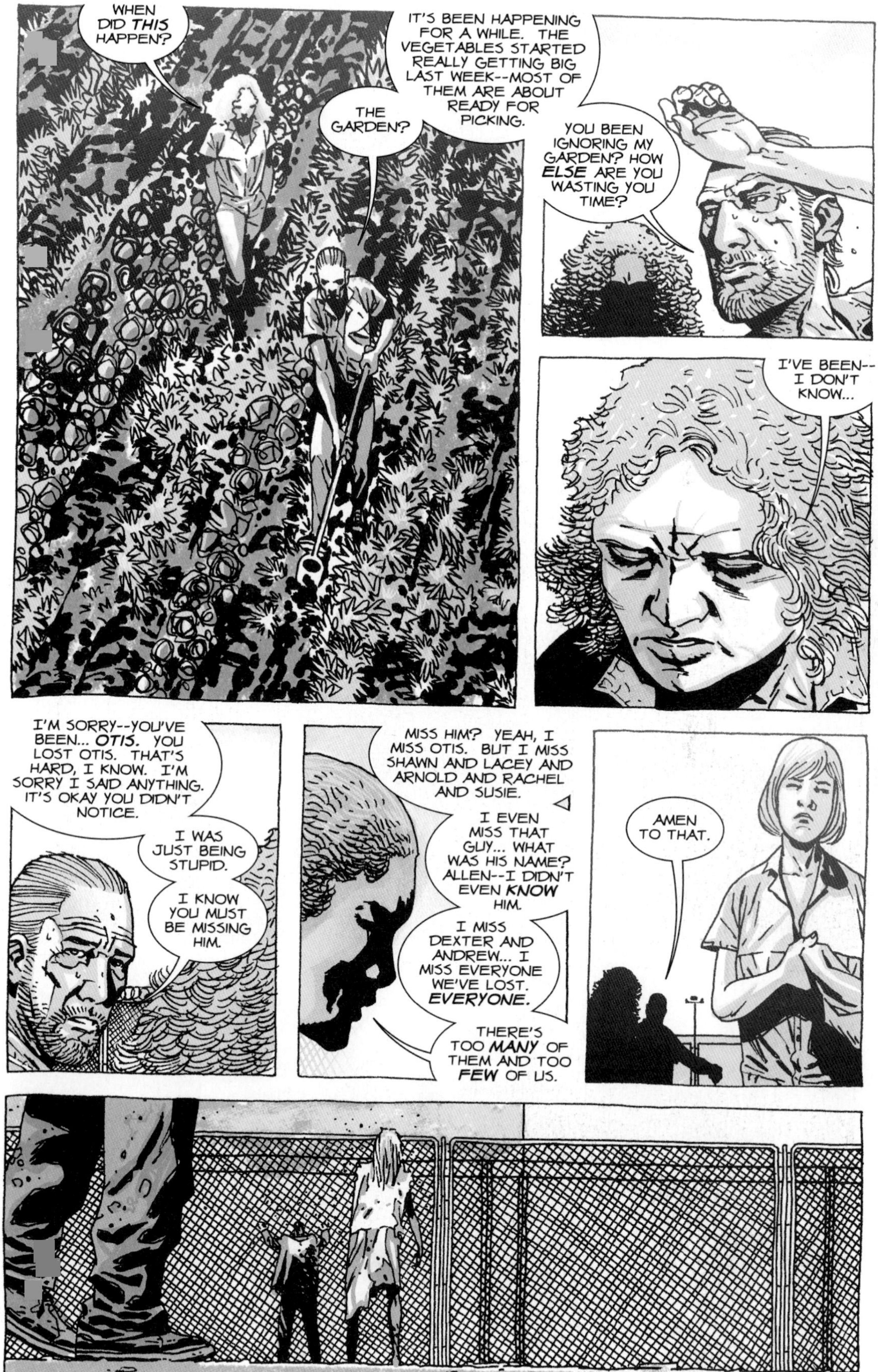
WHEN DID THIS HAPPEN?
THE GARDEN?
IT'S BEEN HAPPENING FOR A WHILE. THE VEGETABLES STARTED REALLY GETTING BIG LAST WEEK--MOST OF THEM ARE ABOUT READY FOR PICKING.
YOU BEEN IGNORING MY GARDEN? HOW ELSE ARE YOU WASTING YOU TIME?
I'VE BEEN-- I DON'T KNOW...
I'M SORRY--YOU'VE BEEN... OTIS. YOU LOST OTIS. THAT'S HARD, I KNOW. I'M SORRY I SAID ANYTHING. IT'S OKAY YOU DIDN'T NOTICE.
I WAS JUST BEING STUPID.
I KNOW YOU MUST BE MISSING HIM.
MISS HIM? YEAH, I MISS OTIS. BUT I MISS SHAWN AND LACEY AND ARNOLD AND RACHEL AND SUSIE.
I EVEN MISS THAT GUY... WHAT WAS HIS NAME? ALLEN--I DIDN'T EVEN KNOW HIM.
I MISS DEXTER AND ANDREW... I MISS EVERYONE WE'VE LOST. EVERYONE.
THERE'S TOO MANY OF THEM AND TOO FEW OF US.
AMEN TO THAT.

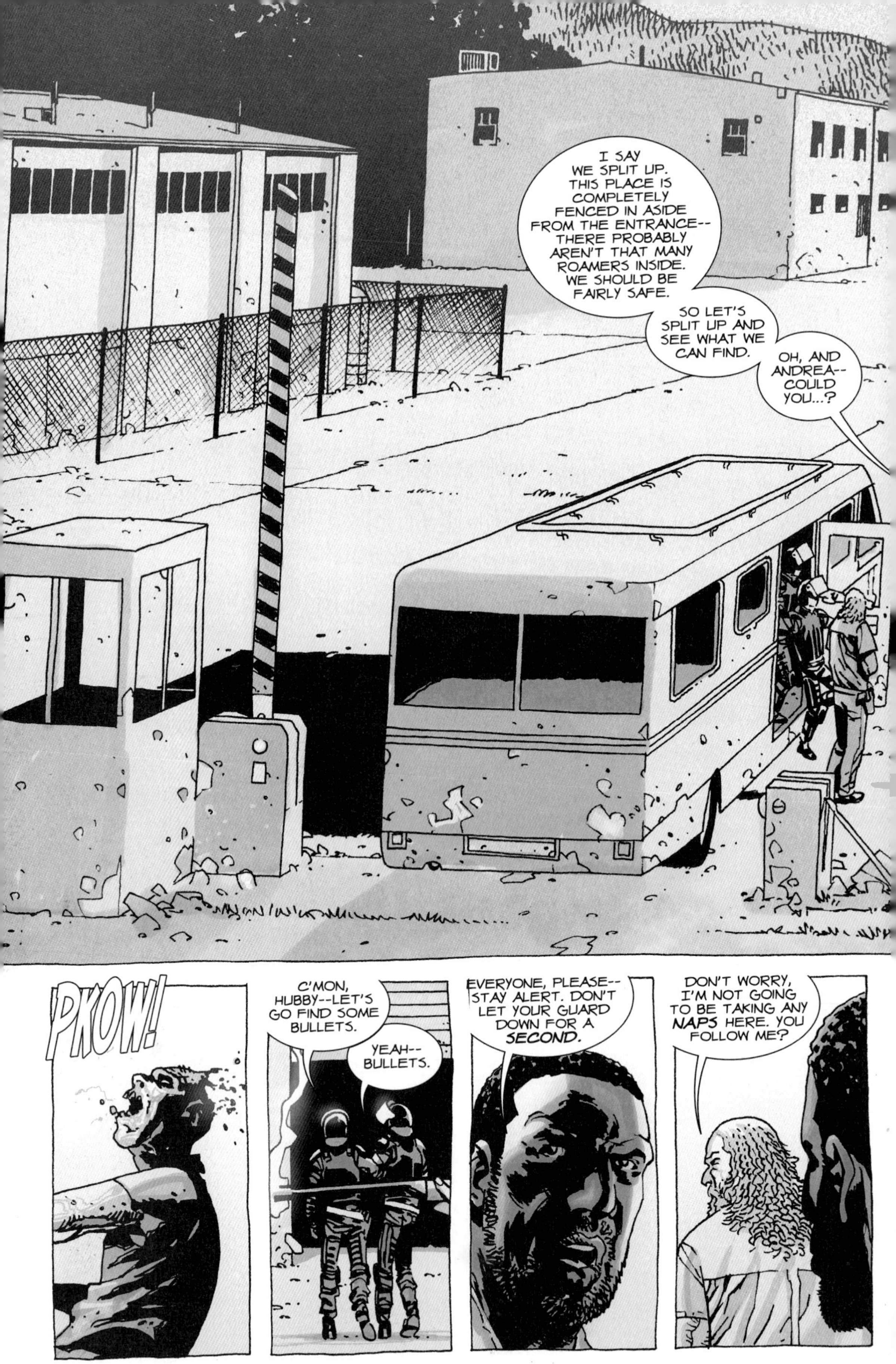
I SAY WE SPLIT UP. THIS PLACE IS COMPLETELY FENCED IN ASIDE FROM THE ENTRANCE-- THERE PROBABLY AREN'T THAT MANY ROAMERS INSIDE. WE SHOULD BE FAIRLY SAFE.
SO LET'S SPLIT UP AND SEE WHAT WE CAN FIND.
OH, AND ANDREA-- COULD YOU...?
PKOW!
C'MON, HUBBY--LET'S GO FIND SOME BULLETS.
YEAH-- BULLETS.
EVERYONE, PLEASE-- STAY ALERT. DON'T LET YOUR GUARD DOWN FOR A SECOND.
DON'T WORRY, I'M NOT GOING TO BE TAKING ANY NAPS HERE. YOU FOLLOW ME?

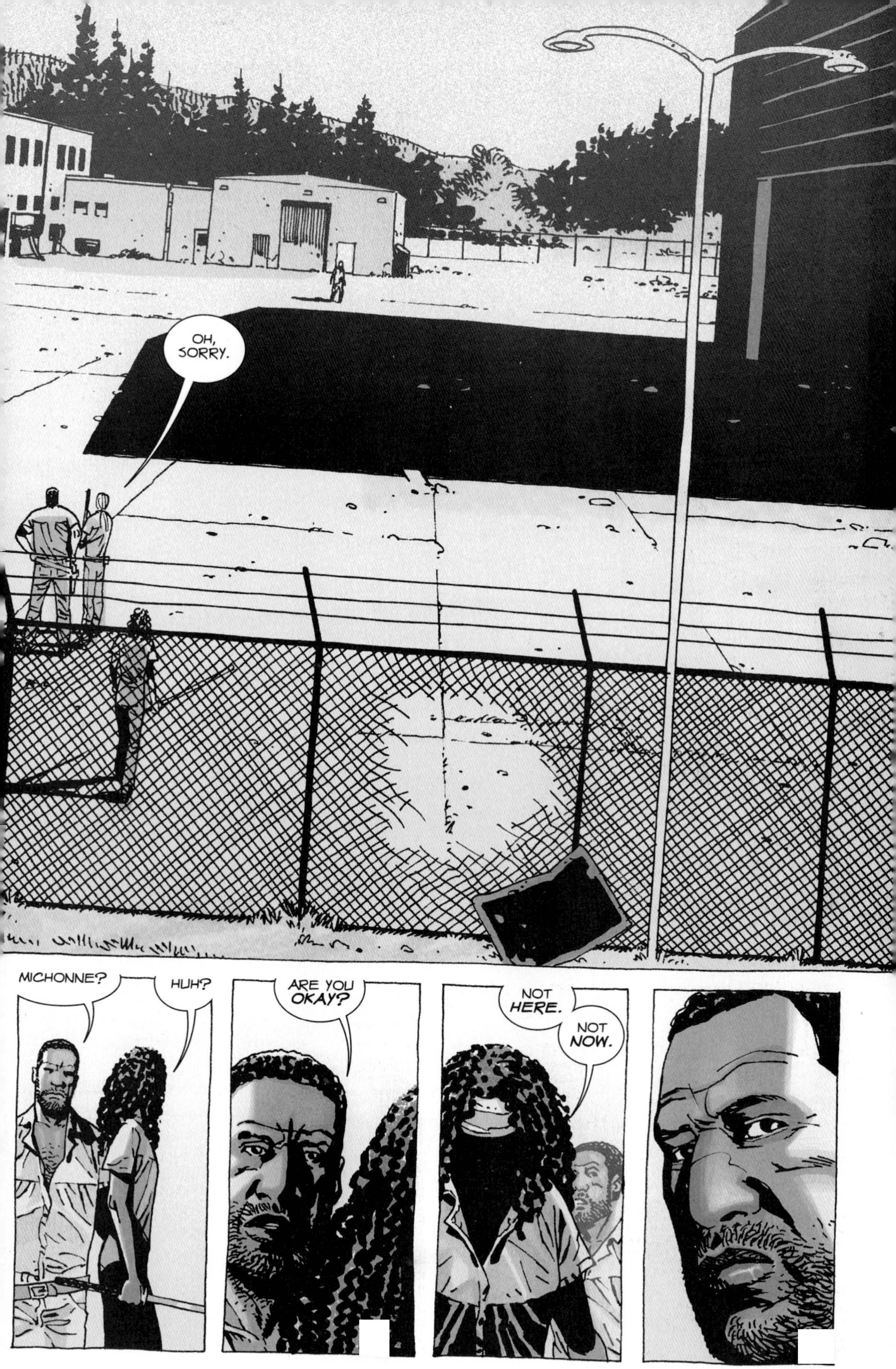
OH, SORRY.
MICHONNE?
HUH?
ARE YOU OKAY?
NOT HERE.
NOT NOW.

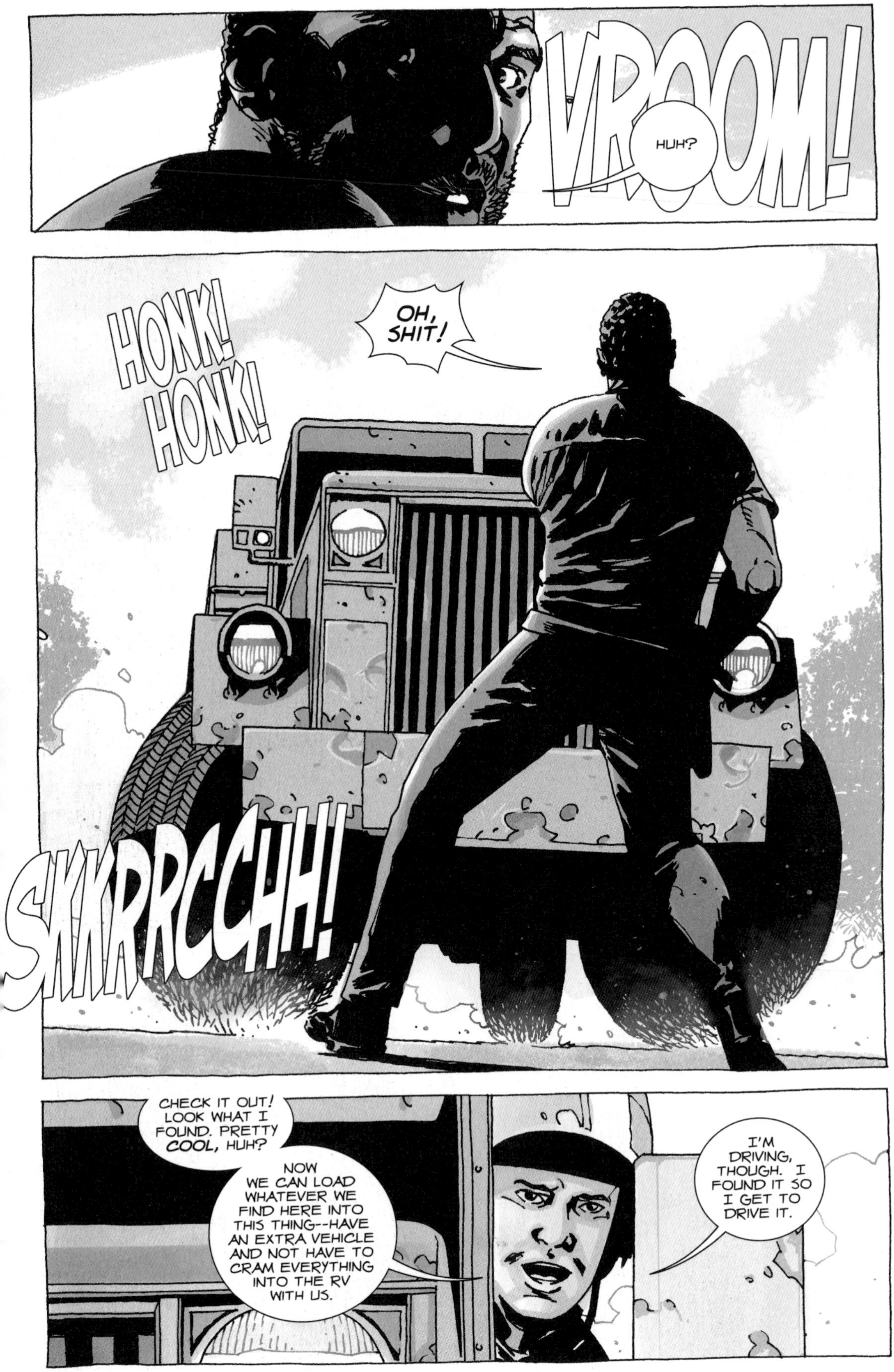
VROOM!
HUH?
HONK! HONK!
OH, SHIT!
SKKRRCCHH!
CHECK IT OUT! LOOK WHAT I FOUND. PRETTY COOL, HUH?
NOW WE CAN LOAD WHATEVER WE FIND HERE INTO THIS THING--HAVE AN EXTRA VEHICLE AND NOT HAVE TO CRAM EVERYTHING INTO THE RV WITH US.
I'M DRIVING, THOUGH. I FOUND IT SO I GET TO DRIVE IT.

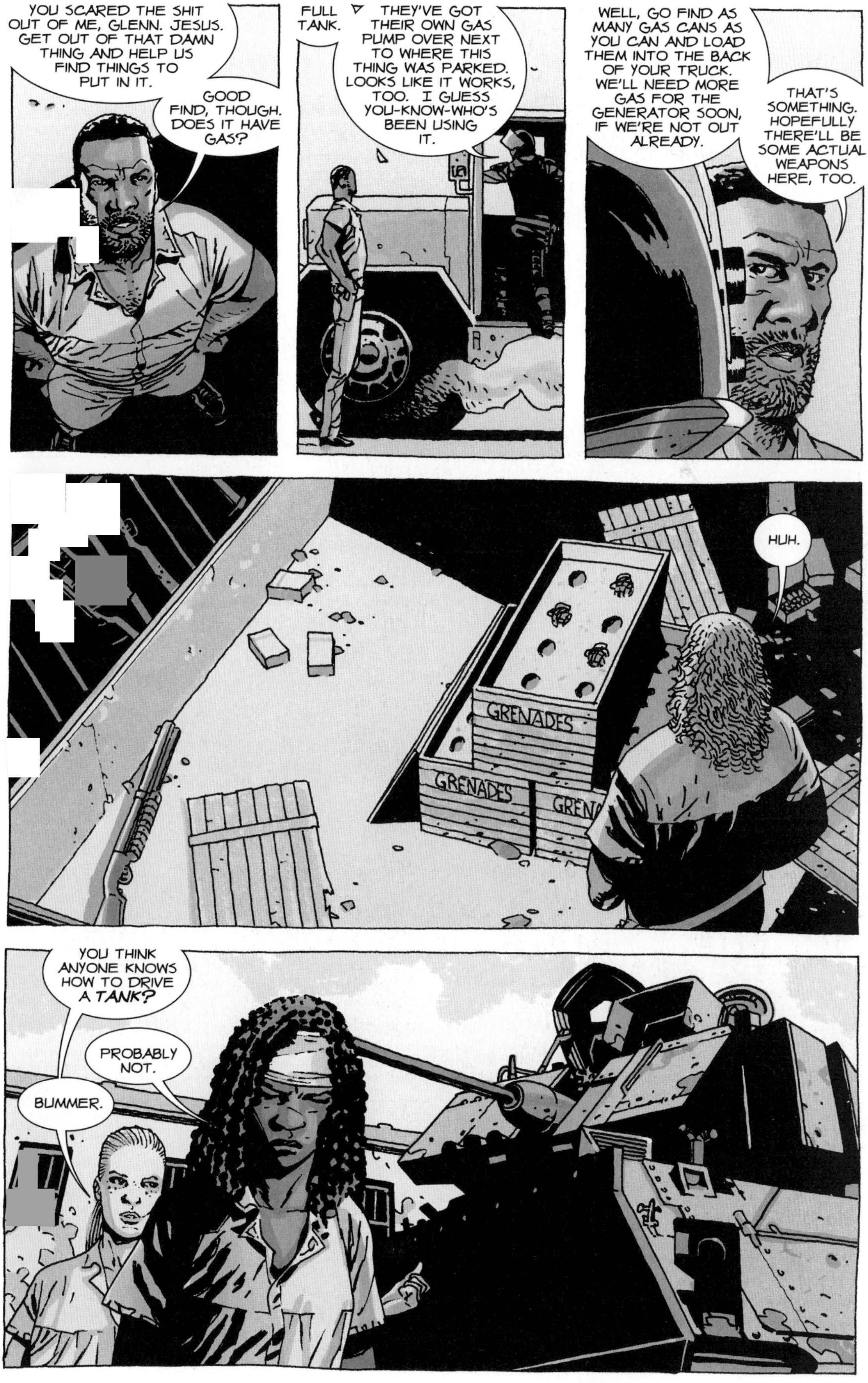
YOU SCARED THE SHIT OUT OF ME, GLENN. JESUS. GET OUT OF THAT DAMN THING AND HELP US FIND THINGS TO PUT IN IT.
GOOD FIND, THOUGH. DOES IT HAVE GAS?
FULL TANK.
THEY'VE GOT THEIR OWN GAS PUMP OVER NEXT TO WHERE THIS THING WAS PARKED. LOOKS LIKE IT WORKS, TOO. I GUESS YOU-KNOW-WHO'S BEEN USING IT.
WELL, GO FIND AS MANY GAS CANS AS YOU CAN AND LOAD THEM INTO THE BACK OF YOUR TRUCK. WE'LL NEED MORE GAS FOR THE GENERATOR SOON, IF WE'RE NOT OUT ALREADY.
THAT'S SOMETHING. HOPEFULLY THERE'LL BE SOME ACTUAL WEAPONS HERE, TOO.
HUH.
GRENADES
GRENADES
YOU THINK ANYONE KNOWS HOW TO DRIVE A *TANK?*
PROBABLY NOT.
BUMMER.

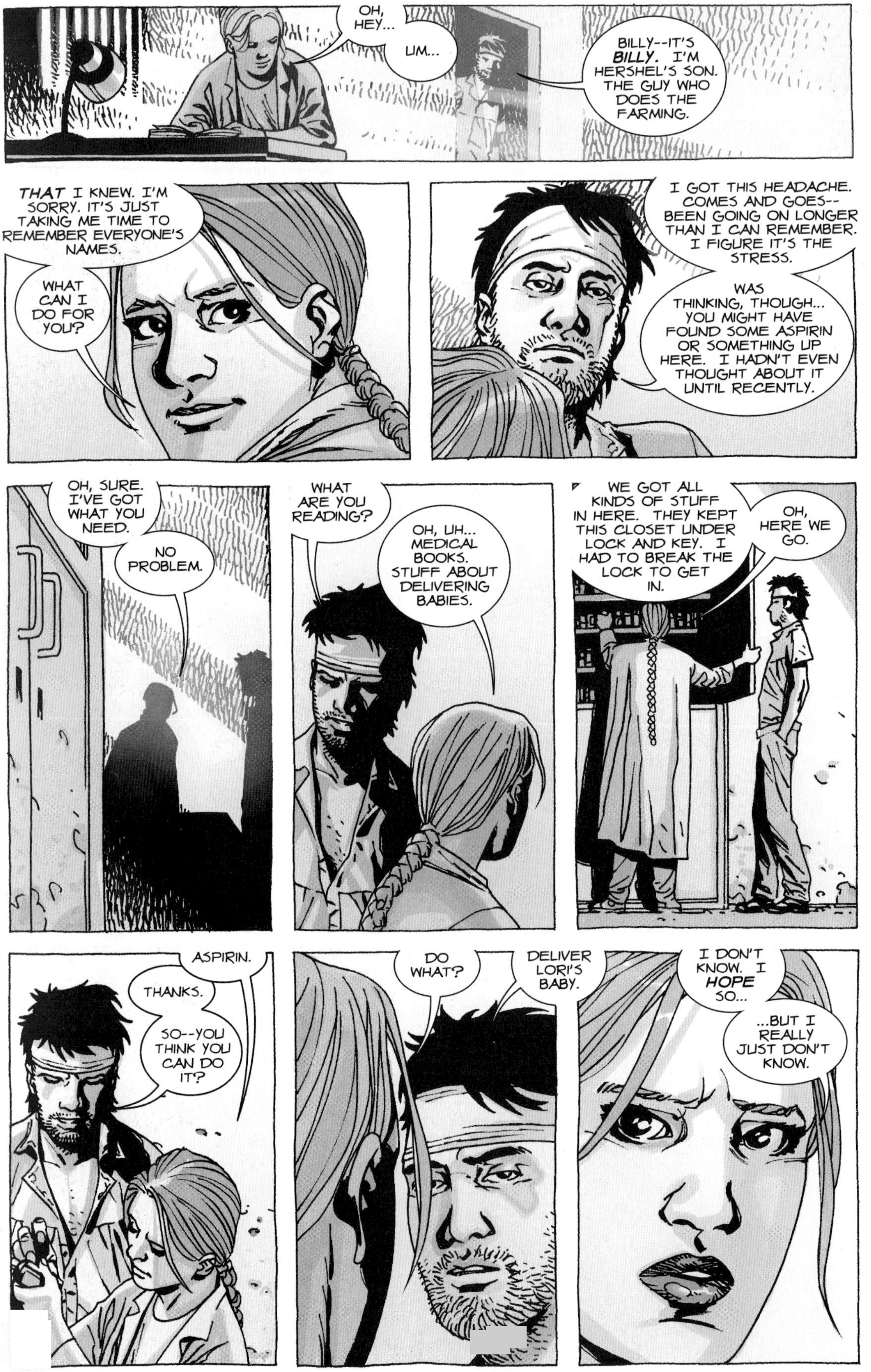
OH, HEY...
UM...
BILLY--IT'S BILLY. I'M HERSHEL'S SON. THE GUY WHO DOES THE FARMING.
THAT I KNEW. I'M SORRY. IT'S JUST TAKING ME TIME TO REMEMBER EVERYONE'S NAMES.
WHAT CAN I DO FOR YOU?
I GOT THIS HEADACHE. COMES AND GOES-- BEEN GOING ON LONGER THAN I CAN REMEMBER. I FIGURE IT'S THE STRESS.
WAS THINKING, THOUGH... YOU MIGHT HAVE FOUND SOME ASPIRIN OR SOMETHING UP HERE. I HADN'T EVEN THOUGHT ABOUT IT UNTIL RECENTLY.
OH, SURE. I'VE GOT WHAT YOU NEED.
NO PROBLEM.
WHAT ARE YOU READING?
OH, UH... MEDICAL BOOKS. STUFF ABOUT DELIVERING BABIES.
WE GOT ALL KINDS OF STUFF IN HERE. THEY KEPT THIS CLOSET UNDER LOCK AND KEY. I HAD TO BREAK THE LOCK TO GET IN.
OH, HERE WE GO.
ASPIRIN.
THANKS.
SO--YOU THINK YOU CAN DO IT?
DO WHAT?
DELIVER LORI'S BABY.
I DON'T KNOW. I HOPE SO...
...BUT I REALLY JUST DON'T KNOW.

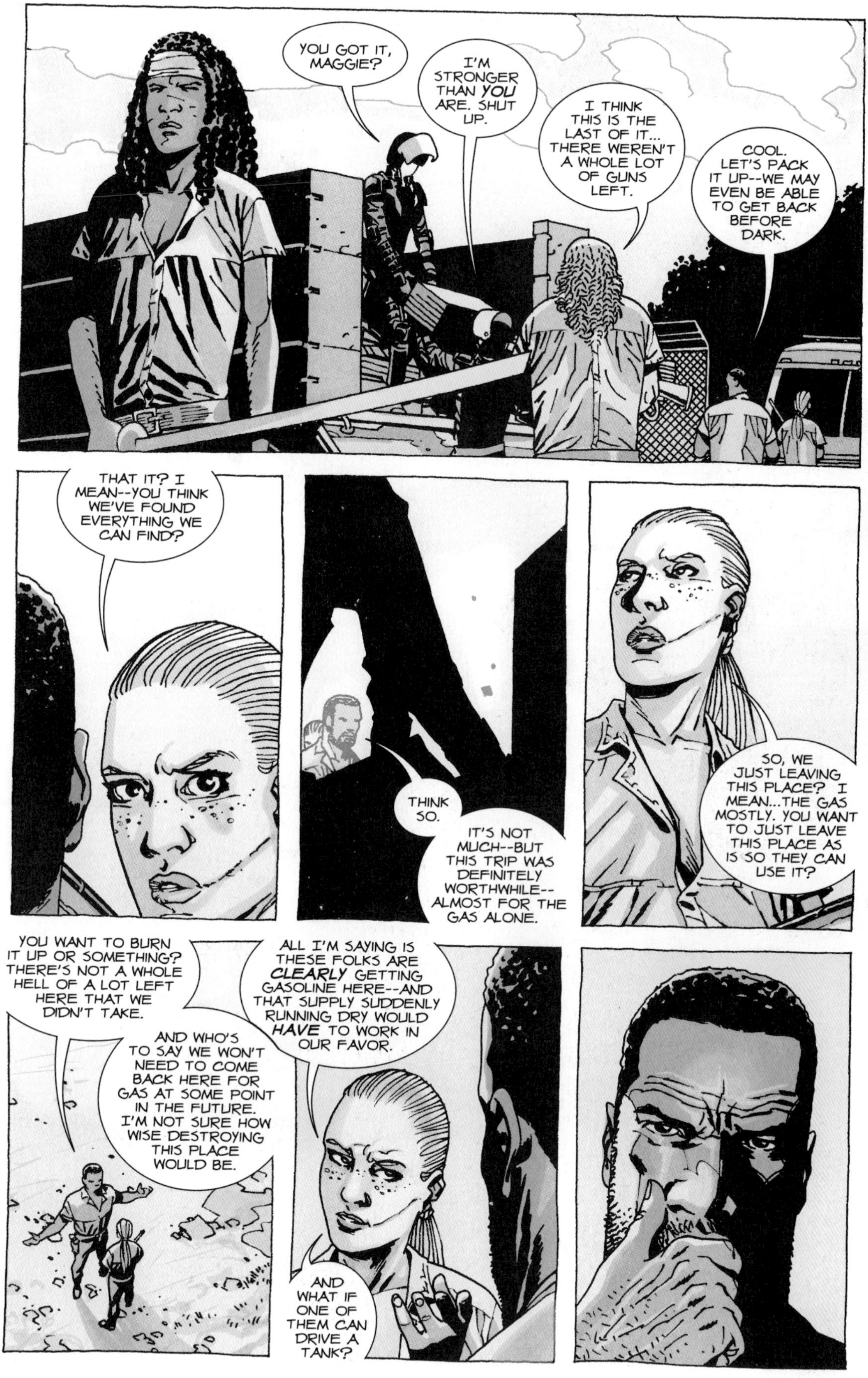
YOU GOT IT, MAGGIE?
I'M STRONGER THAN YOU ARE. SHUT UP.
I THINK THIS IS THE LAST OF IT... THERE WEREN'T A WHOLE LOT OF GUNS LEFT.
COOL. LET'S PACK IT UP--WE MAY EVEN BE ABLE TO GET BACK BEFORE DARK.
THAT IT? I MEAN--YOU THINK WE'VE FOUND EVERYTHING WE CAN FIND?
THINK SO.
IT'S NOT MUCH--BUT THIS TRIP WAS DEFINITELY WORTHWHILE-- ALMOST FOR THE GAS ALONE.
SO, WE JUST LEAVING THIS PLACE? I MEAN...THE GAS MOSTLY. YOU WANT TO JUST LEAVE THIS PLACE AS IS SO THEY CAN USE IT?
YOU WANT TO BURN IT UP OR SOMETHING? THERE'S NOT A WHOLE HELL OF A LOT LEFT HERE THAT WE DIDN'T TAKE.
AND WHO'S TO SAY WE WON'T NEED TO COME BACK HERE FOR GAS AT SOME POINT IN THE FUTURE. I'M NOT SURE HOW WISE DESTROYING THIS PLACE WOULD BE.
ALL I'M SAYING IS THESE FOLKS ARE CLEARLY GETTING GASOLINE HERE--AND THAT SUPPLY SUDDENLY RUNNING DRY WOULD HAVE TO WORK IN OUR FAVOR.
AND WHAT IF ONE OF THEM CAN DRIVE A TANK?

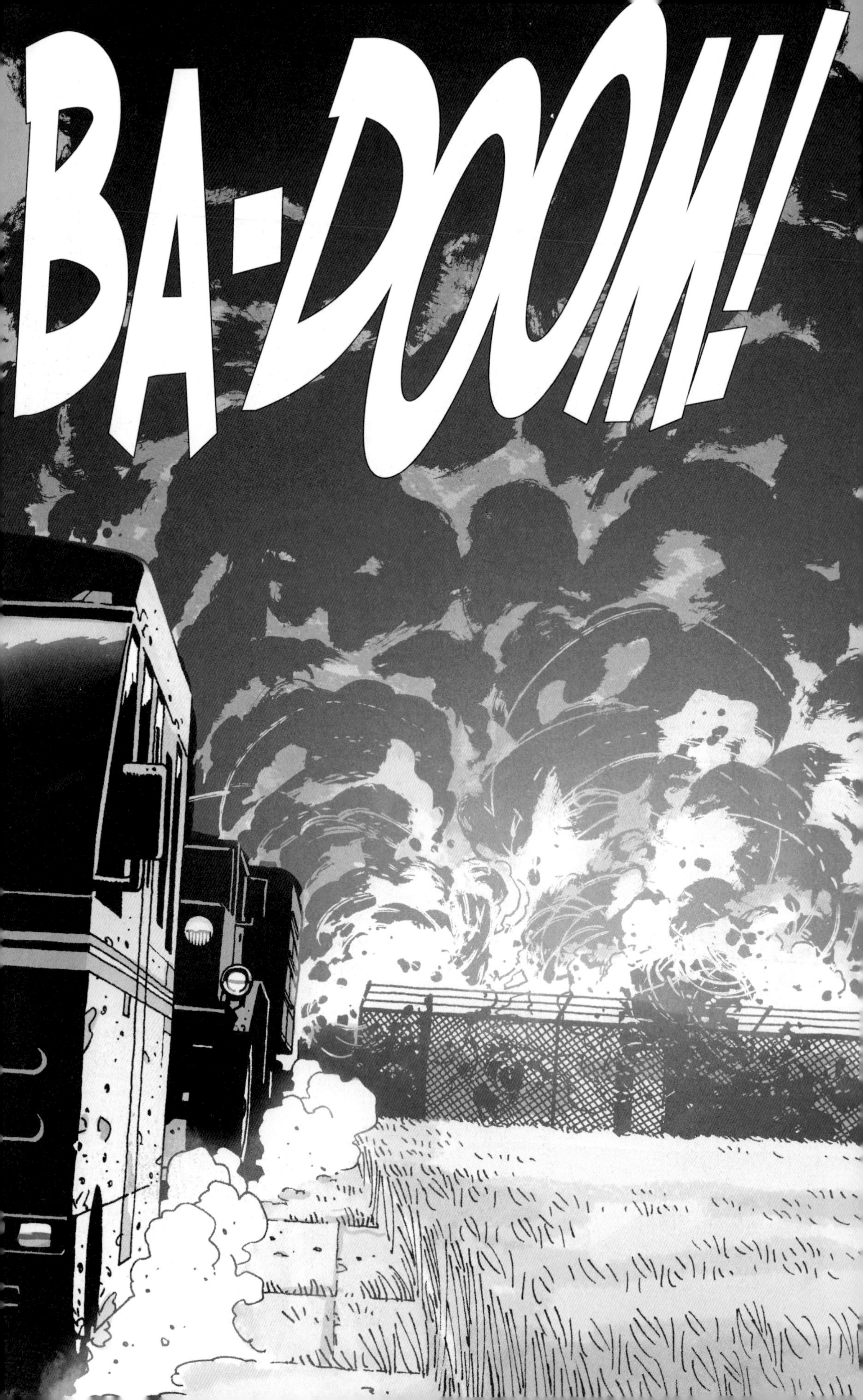
BA-DOOM!

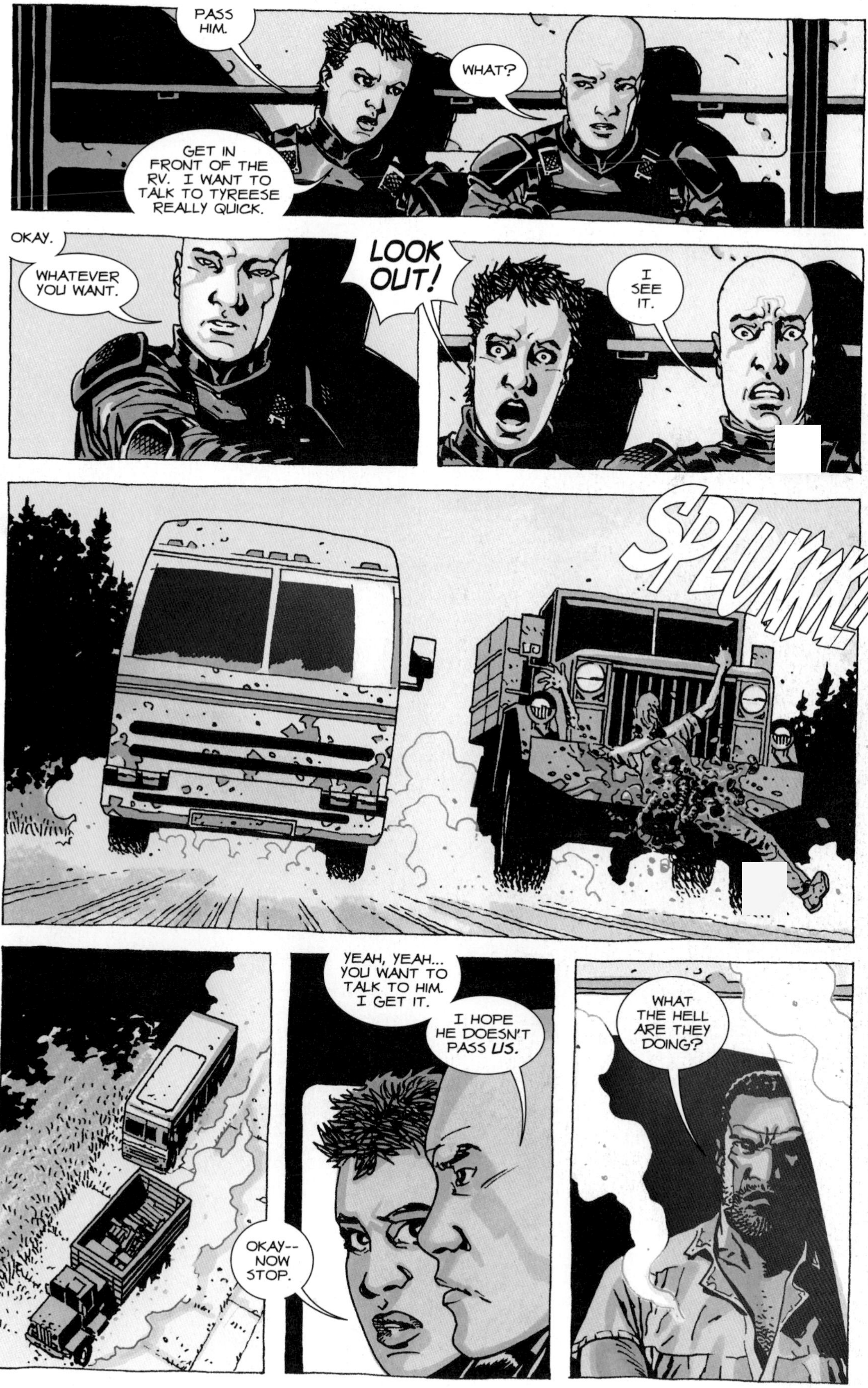
PASS HIM.
WHAT?
GET IN FRONT OF THE RV. I WANT TO TALK TO TYREESE REALLY QUICK.
OKAY.
WHATEVER YOU WANT.
LOOK OUT!
I SEE IT.
SPLUNKK!!
YEAH, YEAH... YOU WANT TO TALK TO HIM. I GET IT.
I HOPE HE DOESN'T PASS US.
OKAY-- NOW STOP.
WHAT THE HELL ARE THEY DOING?

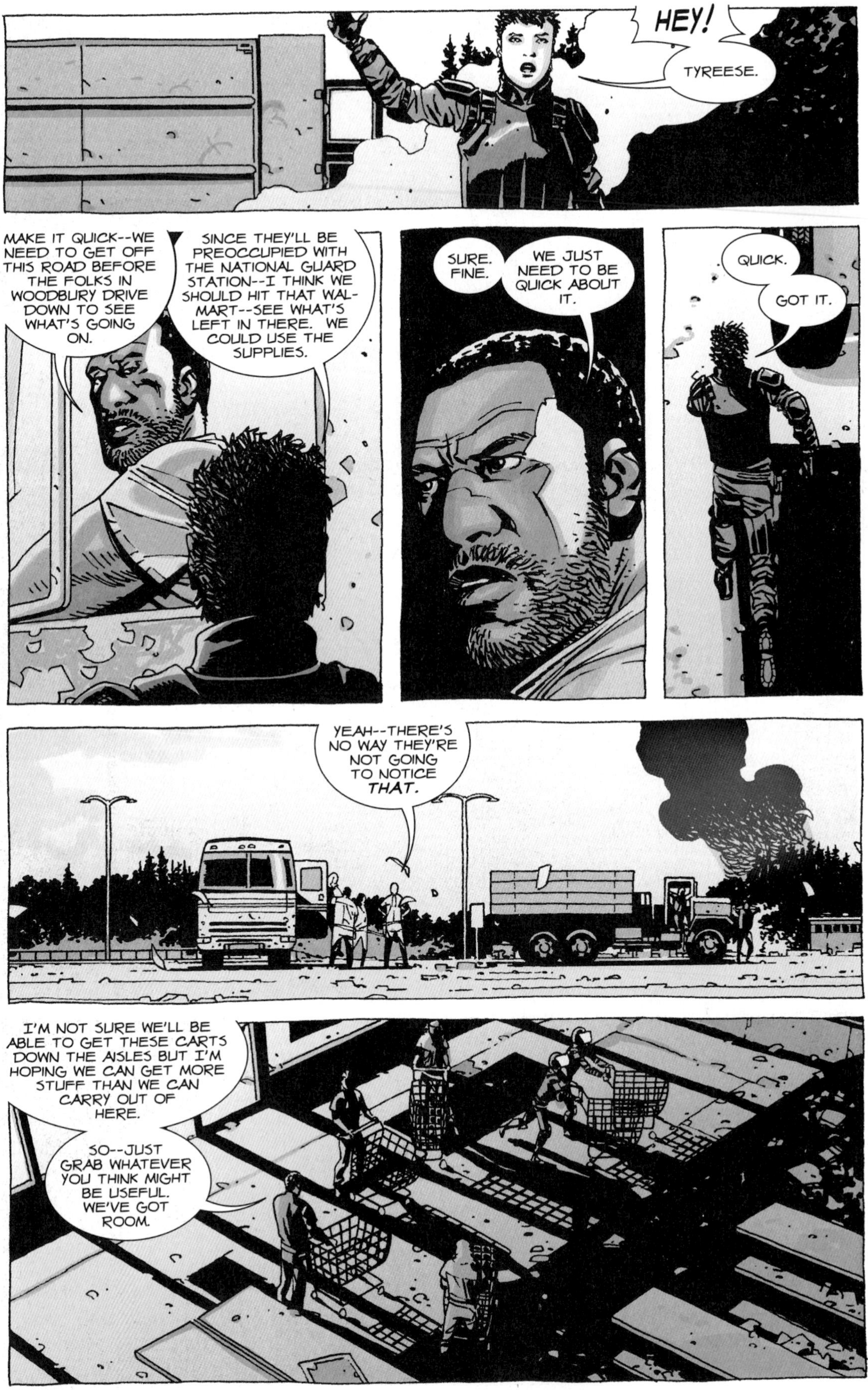
HEY!
TYREESE.
MAKE IT QUICK--WE NEED TO GET OFF THIS ROAD BEFORE THE FOLKS IN WOODBURY DRIVE DOWN TO SEE WHAT'S GOING ON.
SINCE THEY'LL BE PREOCCUPIED WITH THE NATIONAL GUARD STATION--I THINK WE SHOULD HIT THAT WAL-MART--SEE WHAT'S LEFT IN THERE. WE COULD USE THE SUPPLIES.
SURE. FINE.
WE JUST NEED TO BE QUICK ABOUT IT.
QUICK.
GOT IT.
YEAH--THERE'S NO WAY THEY'RE NOT GOING TO NOTICE *THAT.*
I'M NOT SURE WE'LL BE ABLE TO GET THESE CARTS DOWN THE AISLES BUT I'M HOPING WE CAN GET MORE STUFF THAN WE CAN CARRY OUT OF HERE.
SO--JUST GRAB WHATEVER YOU THINK MIGHT BE USEFUL. WE'VE GOT ROOM.

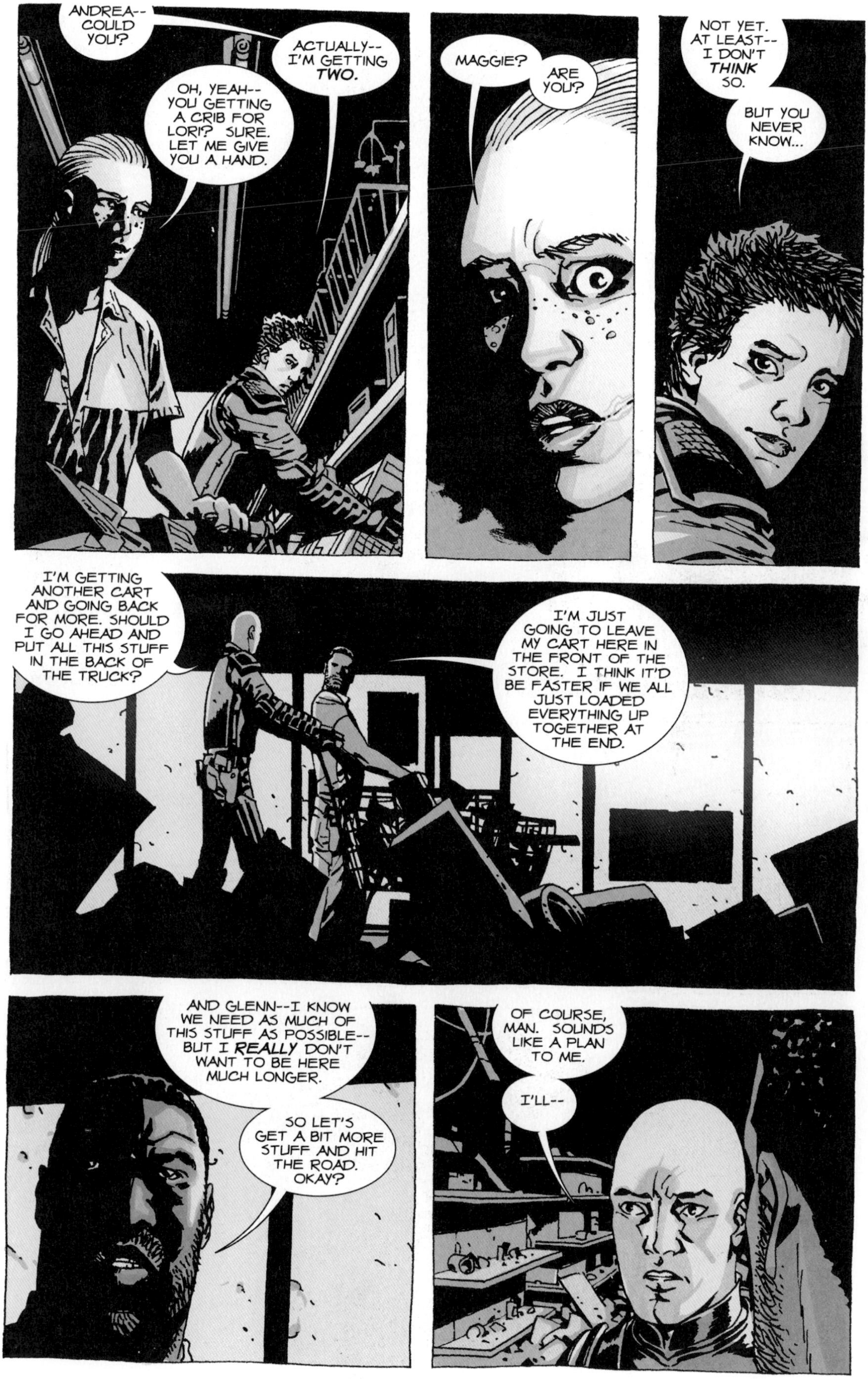
ANDREA--
COULD
YOU?
OH, YEAH--
YOU GETTING
A CRIB FOR
LORI? SURE.
LET ME GIVE
YOU A HAND.
ACTUALLY--
I'M GETTING
TWO.
MAGGIE?
ARE
YOU?
NOT YET.
AT LEAST--
I DON'T
THINK
SO.
BUT YOU
NEVER
KNOW...
I'M GETTING
ANOTHER CART
AND GOING BACK
FOR MORE. SHOULD
I GO AHEAD AND
PUT ALL THIS STUFF
IN THE BACK OF
THE TRUCK?
I'M JUST
GOING TO LEAVE
MY CART HERE IN
THE FRONT OF THE
STORE. I THINK IT'D
BE FASTER IF WE ALL
JUST LOADED
EVERYTHING UP
TOGETHER AT
THE END.
AND GLENN--I KNOW
WE NEED AS MUCH OF
THIS STUFF AS POSSIBLE--
BUT I *REALLY* DON'T
WANT TO BE HERE
MUCH LONGER.
SO LET'S
GET A BIT MORE
STUFF AND HIT
THE ROAD.
OKAY?
OF COURSE,
MAN. SOUNDS
LIKE A PLAN
TO ME.
I'LL--

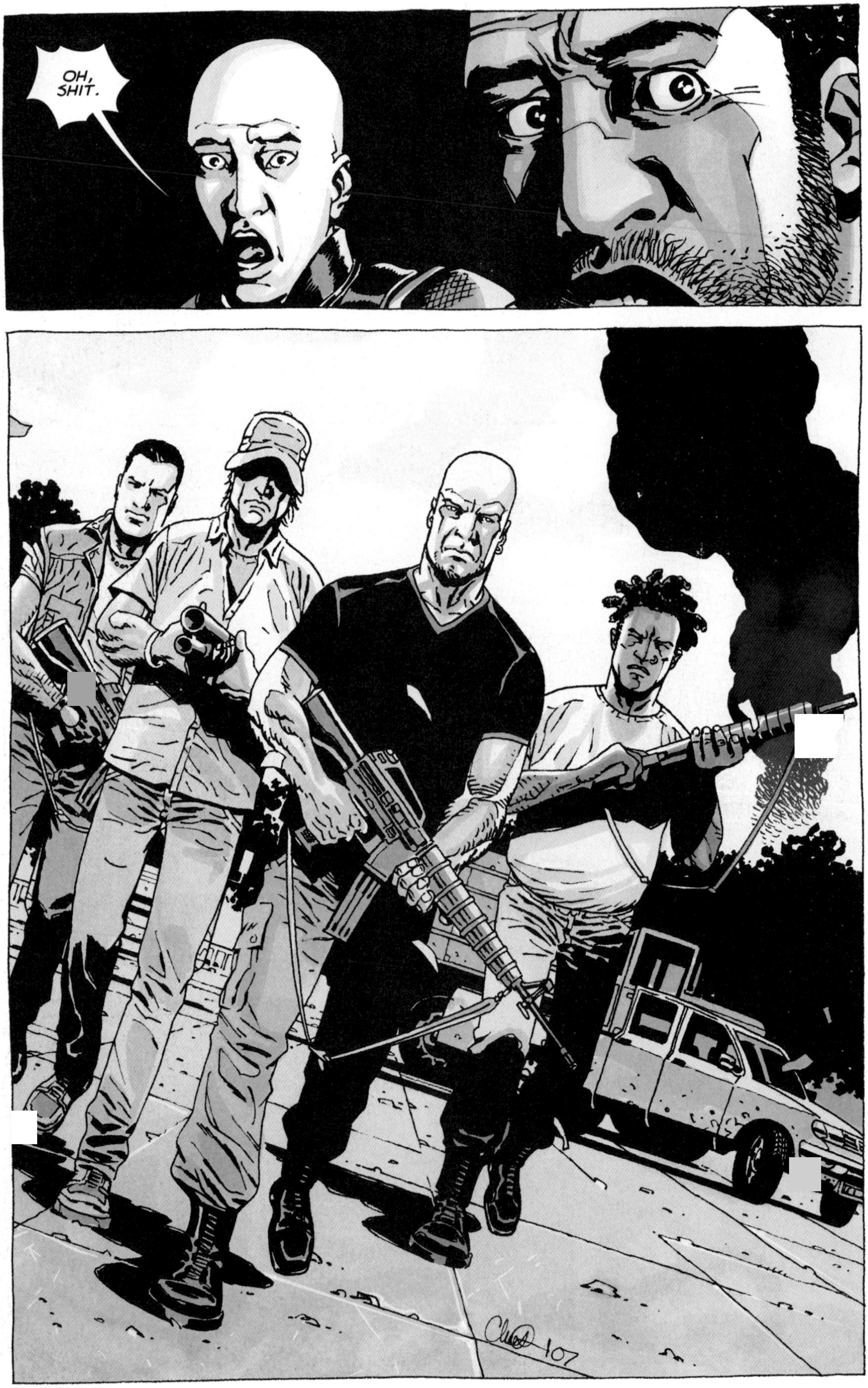
OH, SHIT.

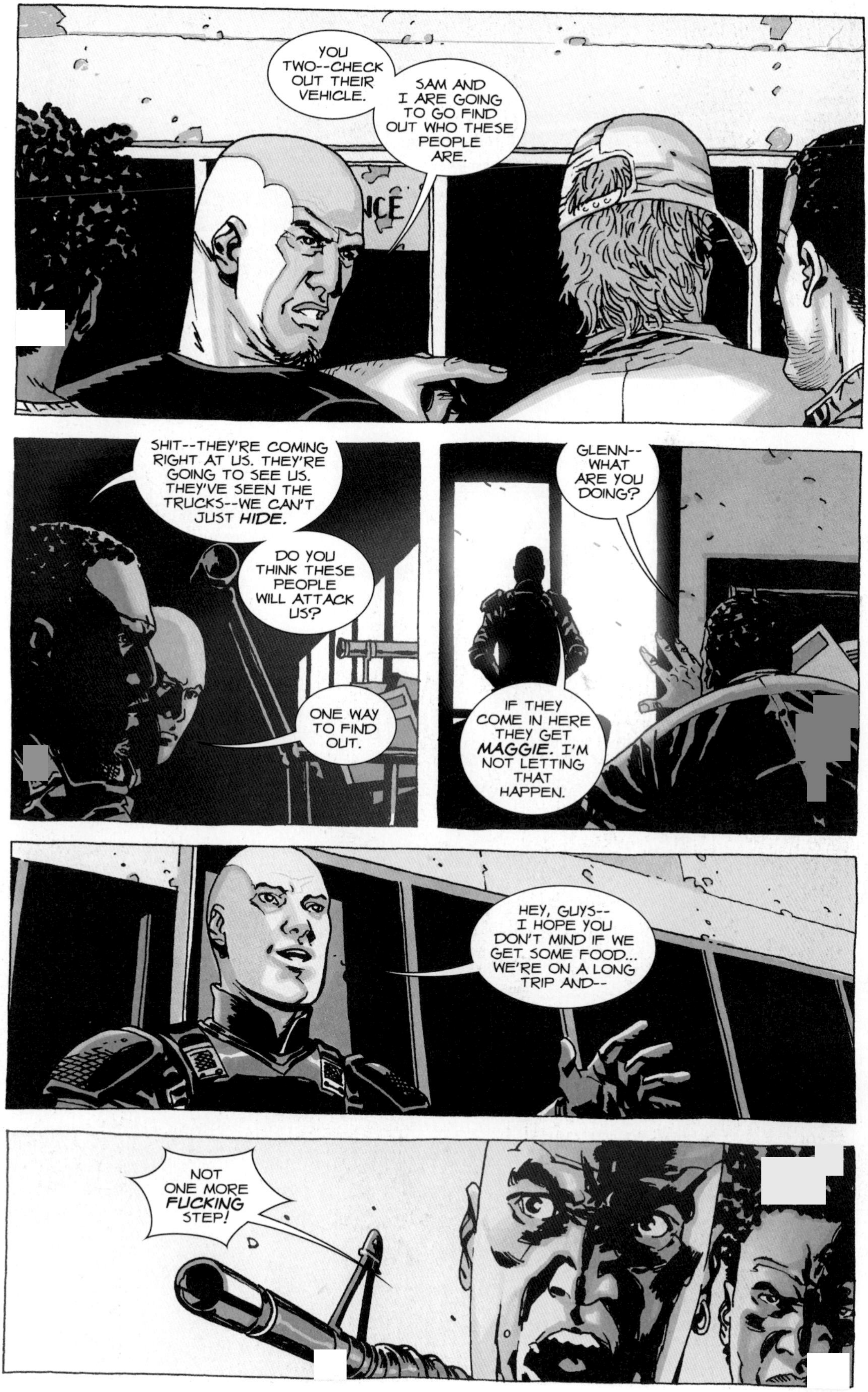
YOU TWO--CHECK OUT THEIR VEHICLE.
SAM AND I ARE GOING TO GO FIND OUT WHO THESE PEOPLE ARE.
SHIT--THEY'RE COMING RIGHT AT US. THEY'RE GOING TO SEE US. THEY'VE SEEN THE TRUCKS--WE CAN'T JUST HIDE.
DO YOU THINK THESE PEOPLE WILL ATTACK US?
ONE WAY TO FIND OUT.
GLENN-- WHAT ARE YOU DOING?
IF THEY COME IN HERE THEY GET MAGGIE. I'M NOT LETTING THAT HAPPEN.
HEY, GUYS-- I HOPE YOU DON'T MIND IF WE GET SOME FOOD... WE'RE ON A LONG TRIP AND--
NOT ONE MORE FUCKING STEP!

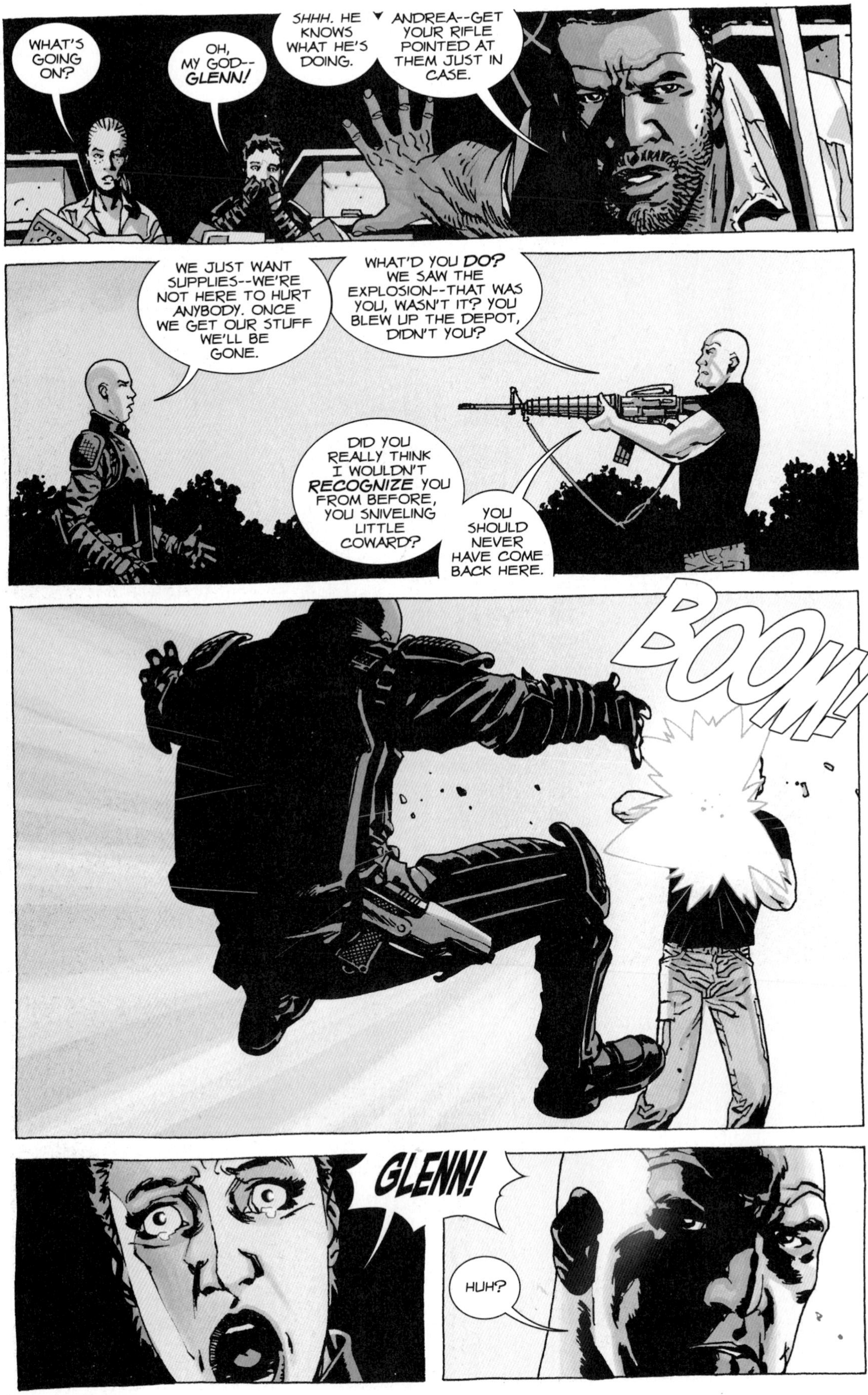
WHAT'S GOING ON?
OH, MY GOD-- GLENN!
SHHH. HE KNOWS WHAT HE'S DOING.
ANDREA--GET YOUR RIFLE POINTED AT THEM JUST IN CASE.
WE JUST WANT SUPPLIES--WE'RE NOT HERE TO HURT ANYBODY. ONCE WE GET OUR STUFF WE'LL BE GONE.
WHAT'D YOU DO? WE SAW THE EXPLOSION--THAT WAS YOU, WASN'T IT? YOU BLEW UP THE DEPOT, DIDN'T YOU?
DID YOU REALLY THINK I WOULDN'T RECOGNIZE YOU FROM BEFORE, YOU SNIVELING LITTLE COWARD?
YOU SHOULD NEVER HAVE COME BACK HERE.
BOOM!
GLENN!
HUH?

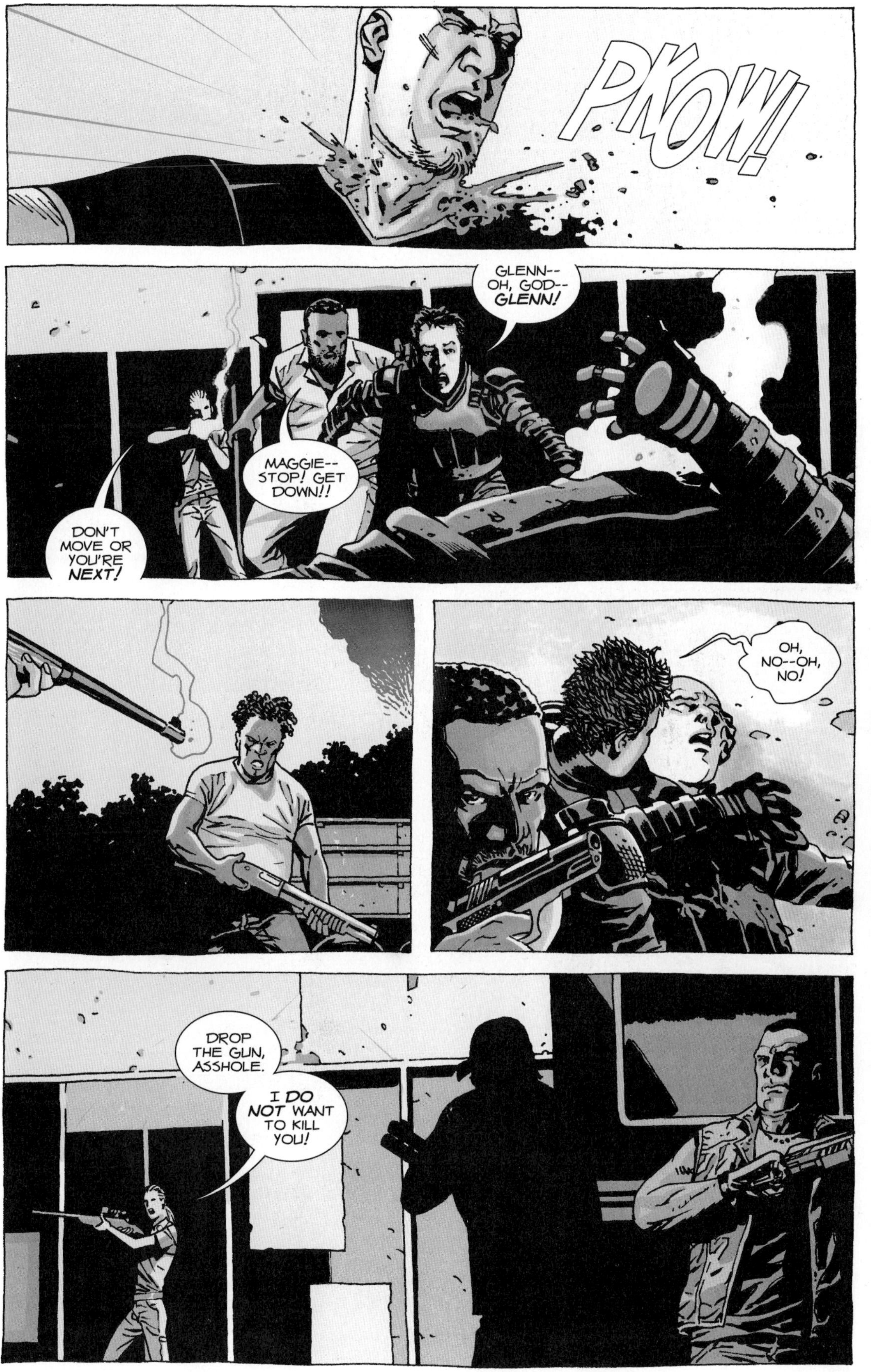
PKOW!
GLENN-- OH, GOD-- GLENN!
MAGGIE-- STOP! GET DOWN!!
DON'T MOVE OR YOU'RE NEXT!
OH, NO--OH, NO!
DROP THE GUN, ASSHOLE.
I DO NOT WANT TO KILL YOU!

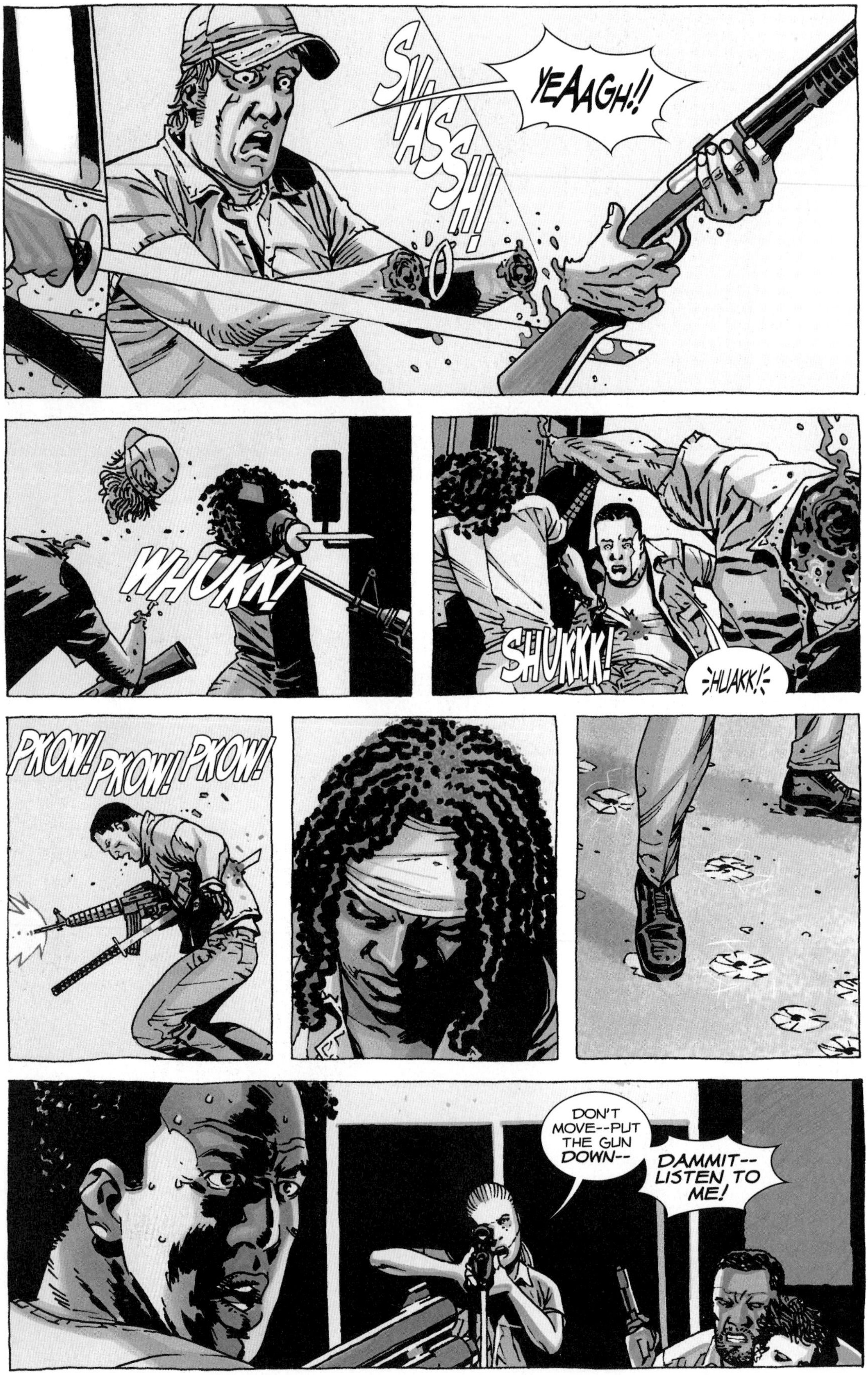
SNASSH!!
YEAAGH!!
WHUKK!
SHUKKK!
HUAKK!
PKOW! PKOW! PKOW!
DON'T MOVE--PUT THE GUN DOWN--
DAMMIT-- LISTEN TO ME!

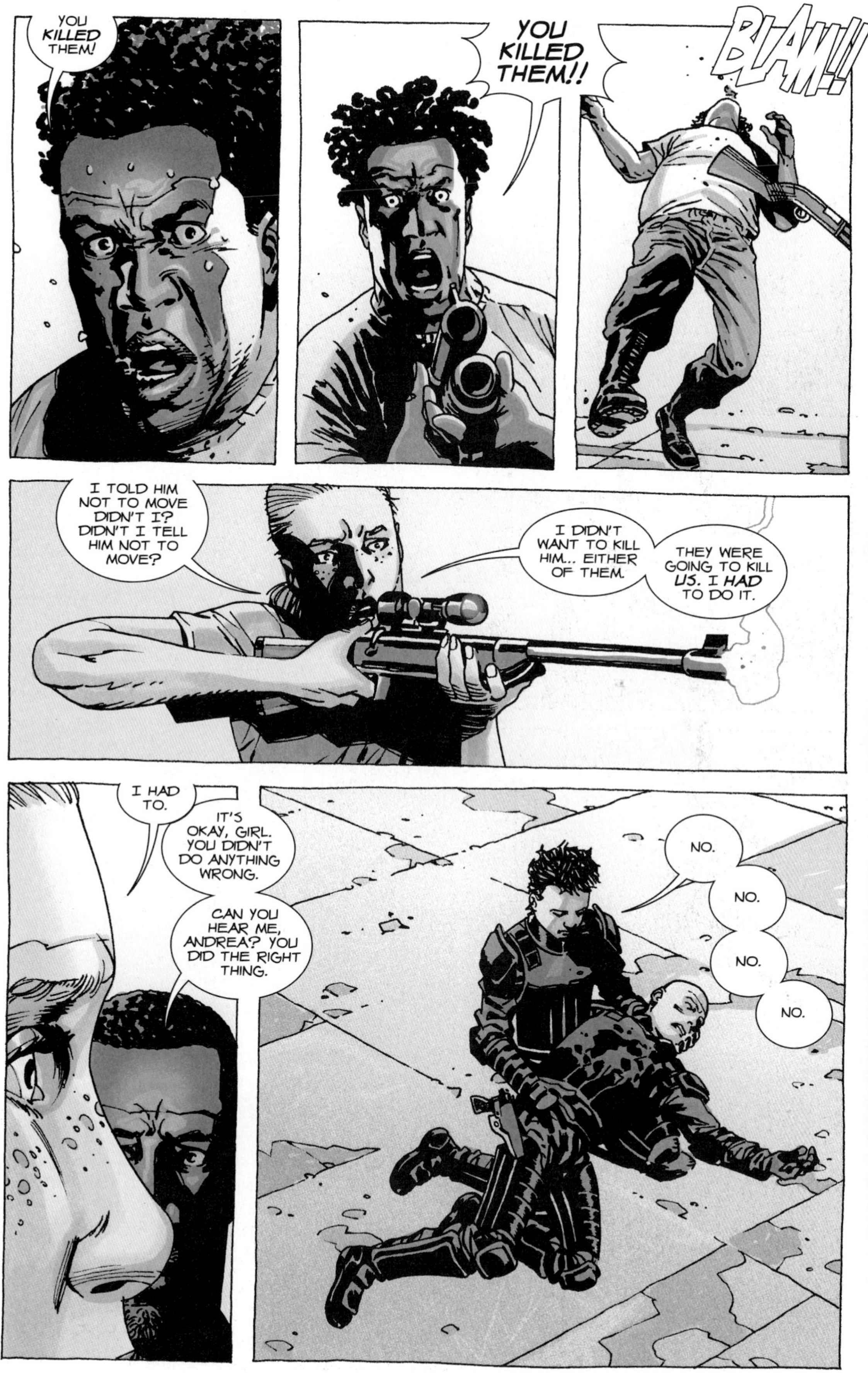
YOU KILLED THEM!
YOU KILLED THEM!!
BLAM!!
I TOLD HIM NOT TO MOVE DIDN'T I? DIDN'T I TELL HIM NOT TO MOVE?
I DIDN'T WANT TO KILL HIM... EITHER OF THEM.
THEY WERE GOING TO KILL US. I HAD TO DO IT.
I HAD TO.
IT'S OKAY, GIRL. YOU DIDN'T DO ANYTHING WRONG.
CAN YOU HEAR ME, ANDREA? YOU DID THE RIGHT THING.
NO.
NO.
NO.
NO.

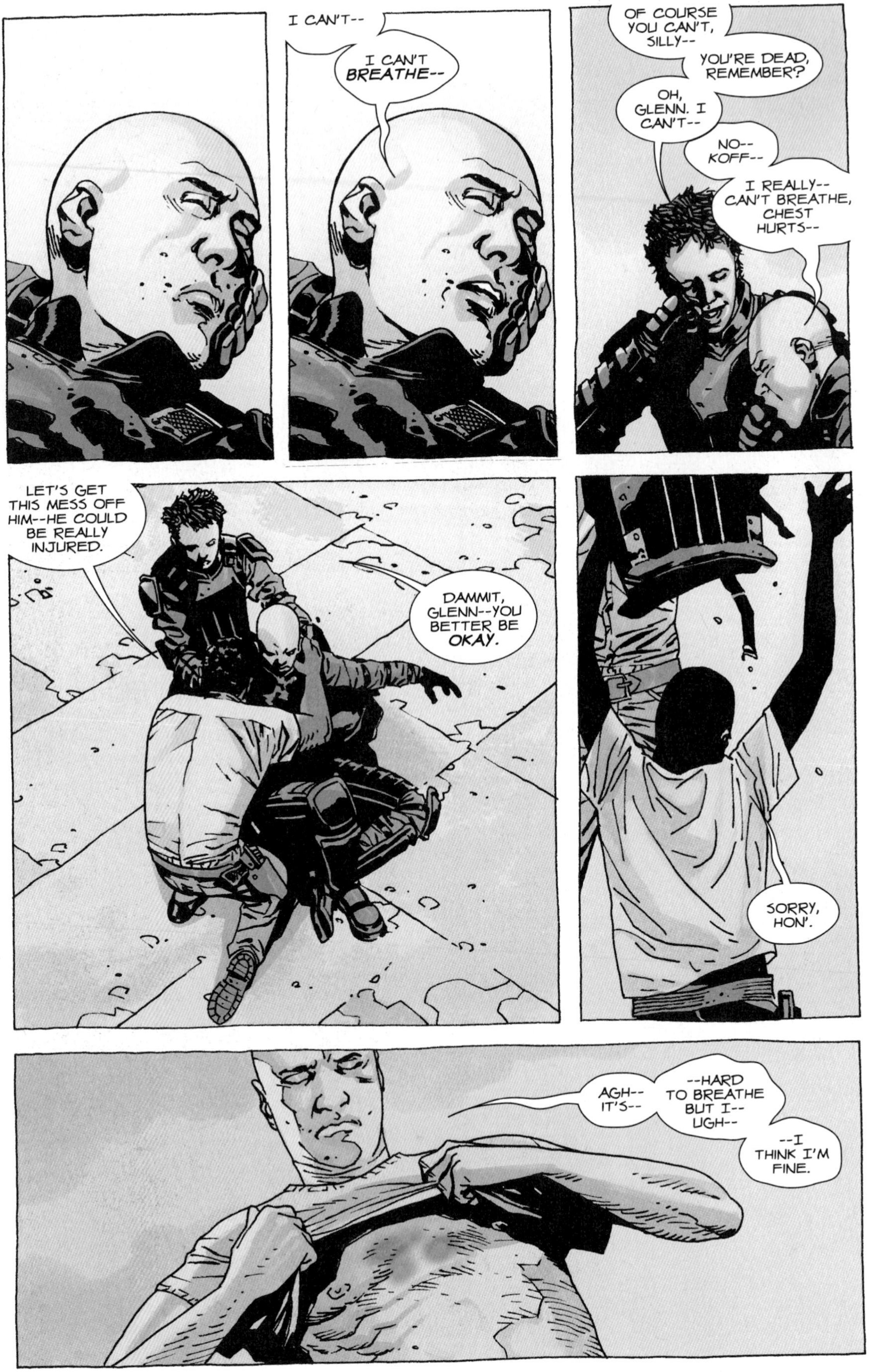
I CAN'T--
I CAN'T BREATHE--
OF COURSE YOU CAN'T, SILLY--
YOU'RE DEAD, REMEMBER?
OH, GLENN. I CAN'T--
NO-- KOFF--
I REALLY-- CAN'T BREATHE, CHEST HURTS--
LET'S GET THIS MESS OFF HIM--HE COULD BE REALLY INJURED.
DAMMIT, GLENN--YOU BETTER BE OKAY.
SORRY, HON'.
AGH-- IT'S--
--HARD TO BREATHE BUT I-- UGH--
--I THINK I'M FINE.

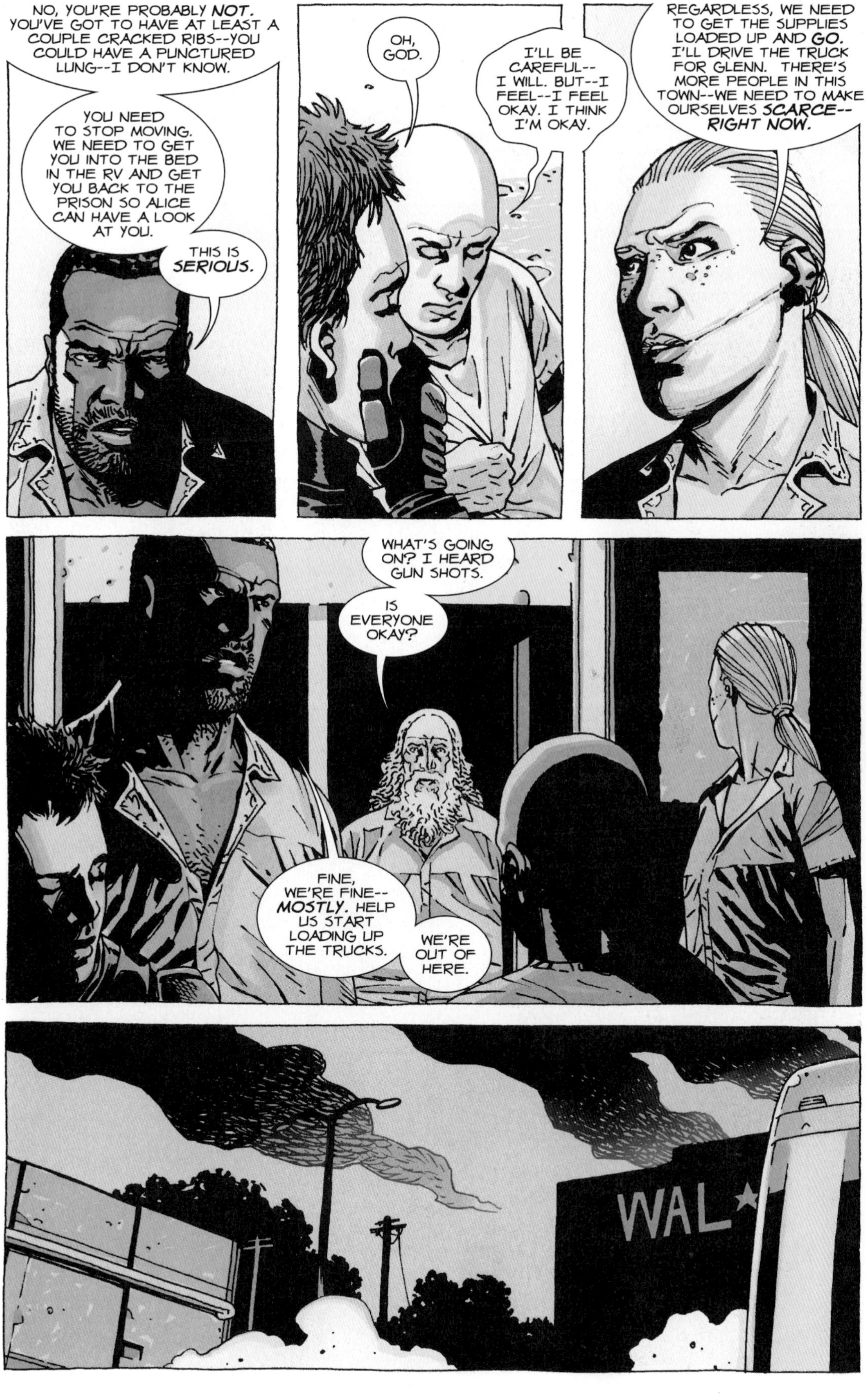
NO, YOU'RE PROBABLY NOT. YOU'VE GOT TO HAVE AT LEAST A COUPLE CRACKED RIBS--YOU COULD HAVE A PUNCTURED LUNG--I DON'T KNOW.
YOU NEED TO STOP MOVING. WE NEED TO GET YOU INTO THE BED IN THE RV AND GET YOU BACK TO THE PRISON SO ALICE CAN HAVE A LOOK AT YOU.
THIS IS SERIOUS.
OH, GOD.
I'LL BE CAREFUL-- I WILL. BUT--I FEEL--I FEEL OKAY. I THINK I'M OKAY.
REGARDLESS, WE NEED TO GET THE SUPPLIES LOADED UP AND GO. I'LL DRIVE THE TRUCK FOR GLENN. THERE'S MORE PEOPLE IN THIS TOWN--WE NEED TO MAKE OURSELVES SCARCE-- RIGHT NOW.
WHAT'S GOING ON? I HEARD GUN SHOTS.
IS EVERYONE OKAY?
FINE, WE'RE FINE-- MOSTLY. HELP US START LOADING UP THE TRUCKS.
WE'RE OUT OF HERE.
WAL★

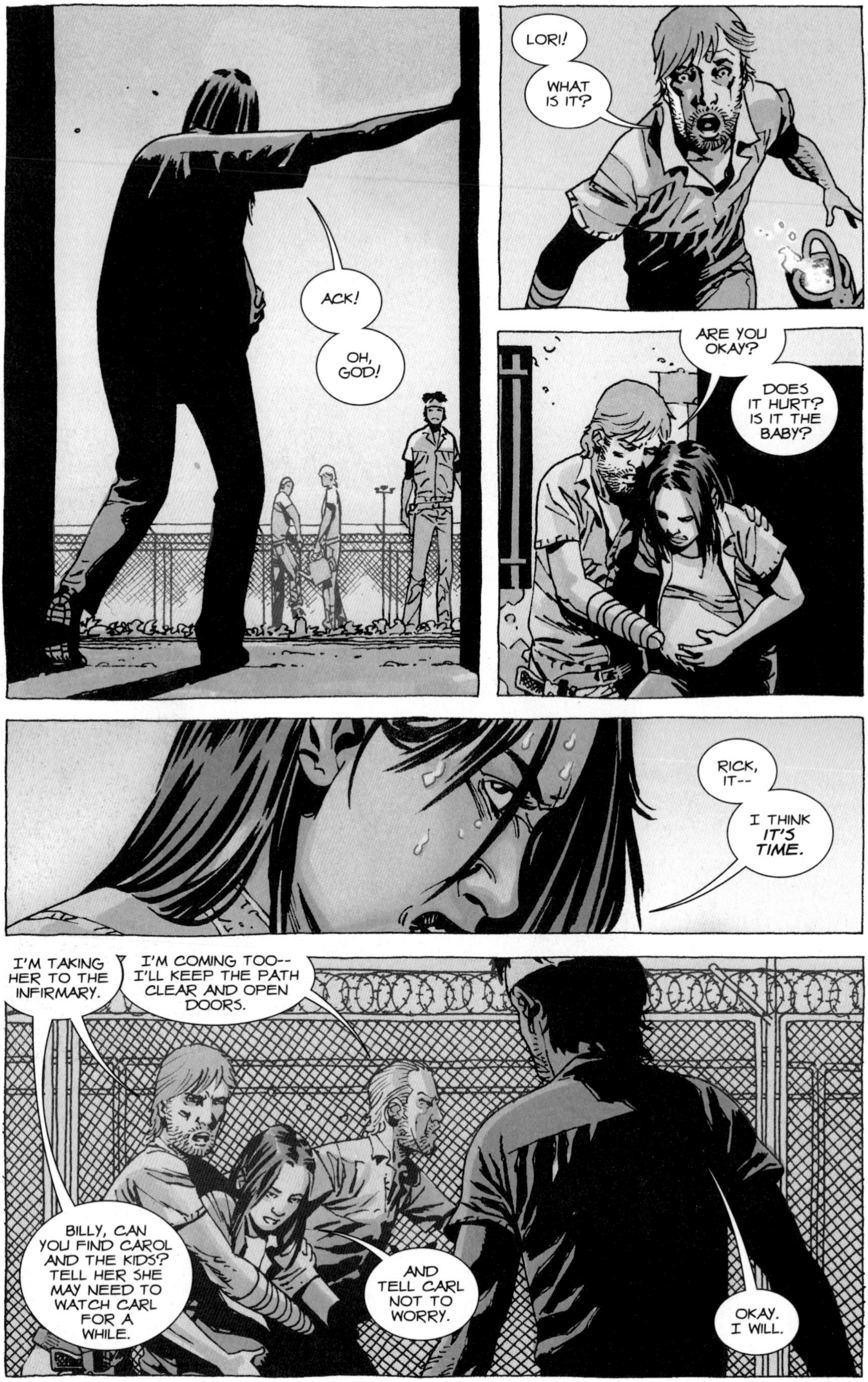
ACK!
OH, GOD!
LORI!
WHAT IS IT?
ARE YOU OKAY?
DOES IT HURT? IS IT THE BABY?
RICK, IT--
I THINK IT'S TIME.
I'M TAKING HER TO THE INFIRMARY.
I'M COMING TOO-- I'LL KEEP THE PATH CLEAR AND OPEN DOORS.
BILLY, CAN YOU FIND CAROL AND THE KIDS? TELL HER SHE MAY NEED TO WATCH CARL FOR A WHILE.
AND TELL CARL NOT TO WORRY.
OKAY. I WILL.

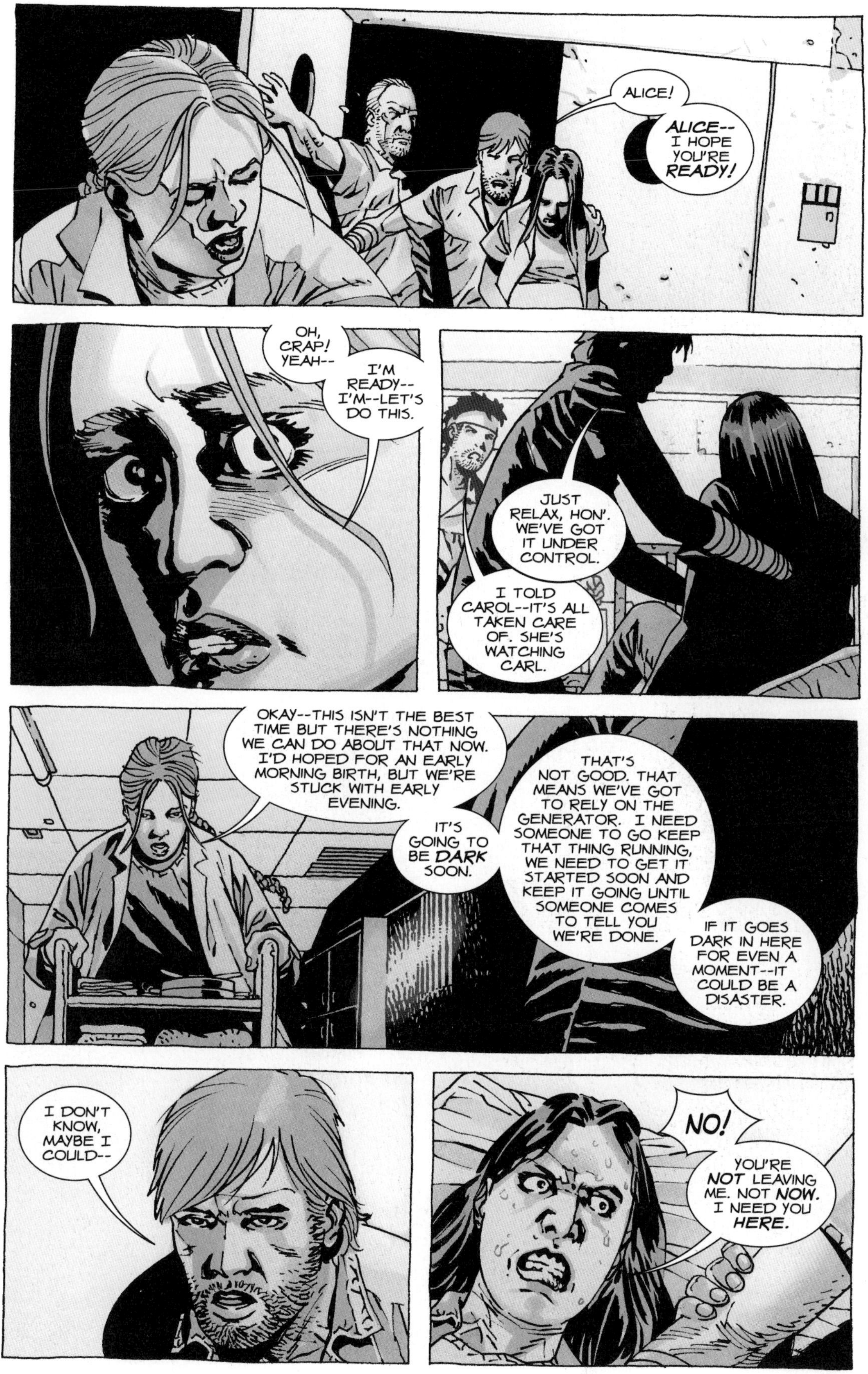
ALICE!
ALICE-- I HOPE YOU'RE READY!
OH, CRAP! YEAH--
I'M READY-- I'M--LET'S DO THIS.
JUST RELAX, HON'. WE'VE GOT IT UNDER CONTROL.
I TOLD CAROL--IT'S ALL TAKEN CARE OF. SHE'S WATCHING CARL.
OKAY--THIS ISN'T THE BEST TIME BUT THERE'S NOTHING WE CAN DO ABOUT THAT NOW. I'D HOPED FOR AN EARLY MORNING BIRTH, BUT WE'RE STUCK WITH EARLY EVENING.
IT'S GOING TO BE DARK SOON.
THAT'S NOT GOOD. THAT MEANS WE'VE GOT TO RELY ON THE GENERATOR. I NEED SOMEONE TO GO KEEP THAT THING RUNNING, WE NEED TO GET IT STARTED SOON AND KEEP IT GOING UNTIL SOMEONE COMES TO TELL YOU WE'RE DONE.
IF IT GOES DARK IN HERE FOR EVEN A MOMENT--IT COULD BE A DISASTER.
I DON'T KNOW, MAYBE I COULD--
NO!
YOU'RE NOT LEAVING ME. NOT NOW. I NEED YOU HERE.

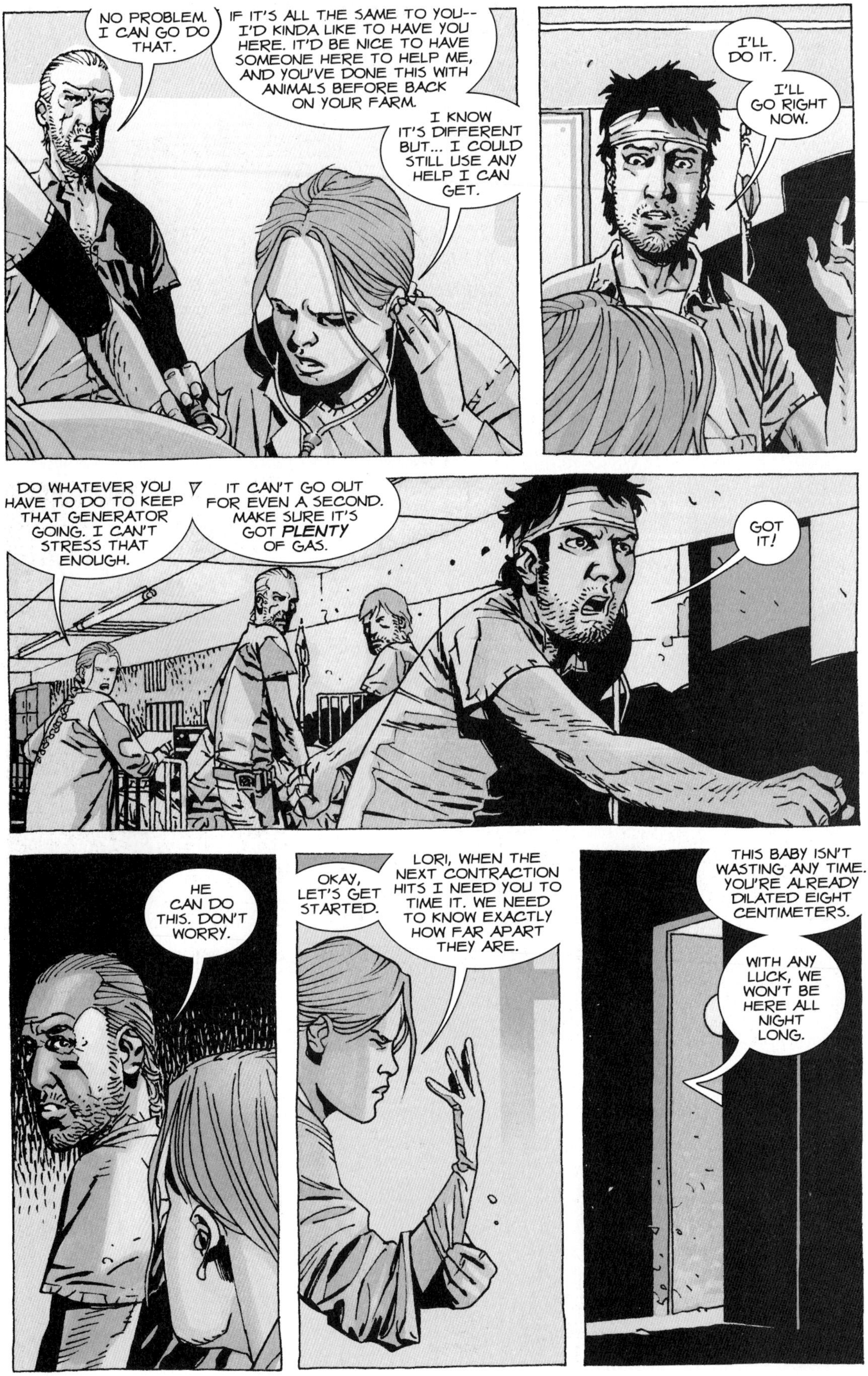
NO PROBLEM. I CAN GO DO THAT.
IF IT'S ALL THE SAME TO YOU-- I'D KINDA LIKE TO HAVE YOU HERE. IT'D BE NICE TO HAVE SOMEONE HERE TO HELP ME, AND YOU'VE DONE THIS WITH ANIMALS BEFORE BACK ON YOUR FARM.
I KNOW IT'S DIFFERENT BUT... I COULD STILL USE ANY HELP I CAN GET.
I'LL DO IT.
I'LL GO RIGHT NOW.
DO WHATEVER YOU HAVE TO DO TO KEEP THAT GENERATOR GOING. I CAN'T STRESS THAT ENOUGH.
IT CAN'T GO OUT FOR EVEN A SECOND. MAKE SURE IT'S GOT PLENTY OF GAS.
GOT IT!
HE CAN DO THIS. DON'T WORRY.
OKAY, LET'S GET STARTED.
LORI, WHEN THE NEXT CONTRACTION HITS I NEED YOU TO TIME IT. WE NEED TO KNOW EXACTLY HOW FAR APART THEY ARE.
THIS BABY ISN'T WASTING ANY TIME. YOU'RE ALREADY DILATED EIGHT CENTIMETERS.
WITH ANY LUCK, WE WON'T BE HERE ALL NIGHT LONG.

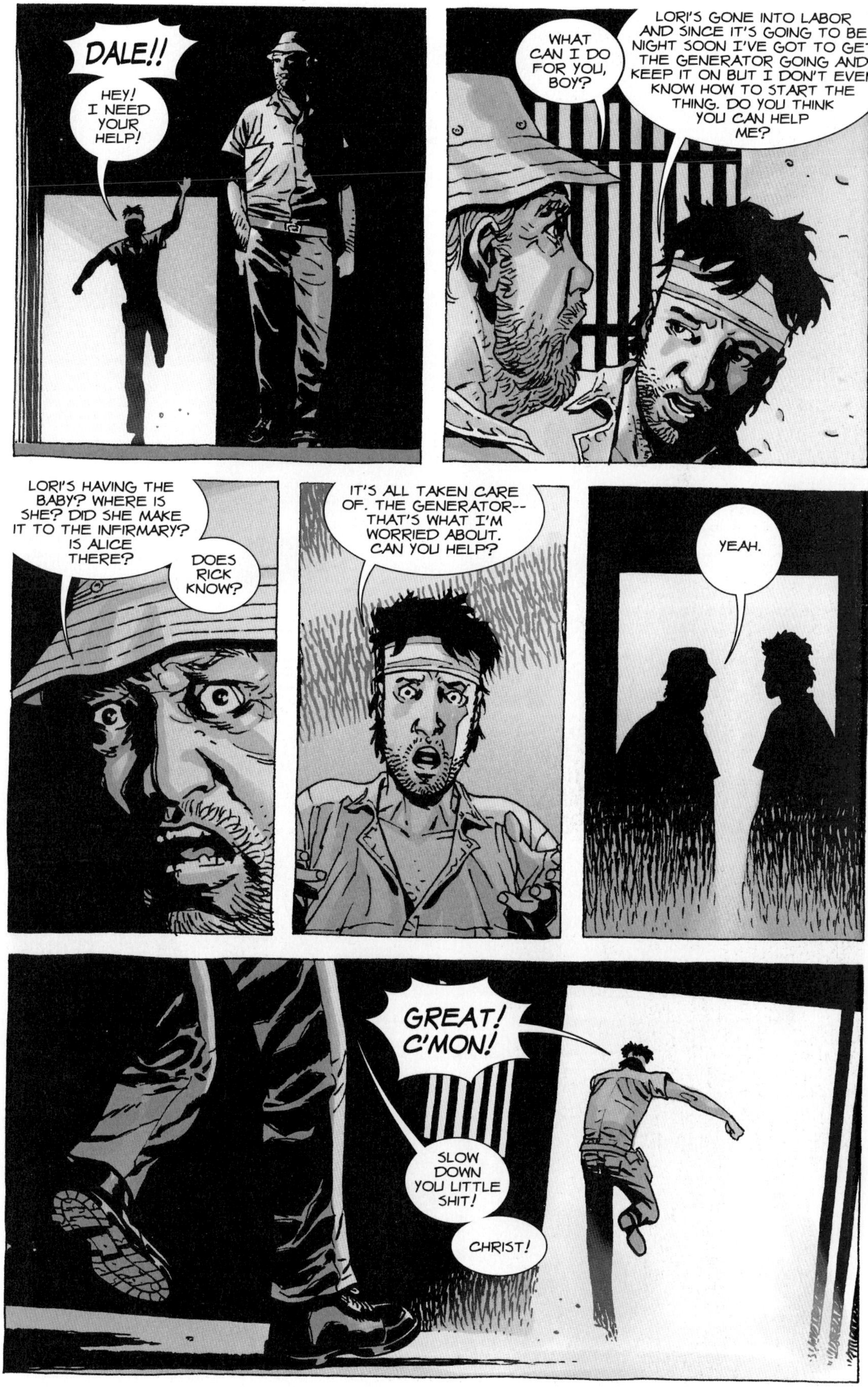
DALE!!
HEY! I NEED YOUR HELP!
WHAT CAN I DO FOR YOU, BOY?
LORI'S GONE INTO LABOR AND SINCE IT'S GOING TO BE NIGHT SOON I'VE GOT TO GET THE GENERATOR GOING AND KEEP IT ON BUT I DON'T EVEN KNOW HOW TO START THE THING. DO YOU THINK YOU CAN HELP ME?
LORI'S HAVING THE BABY? WHERE IS SHE? DID SHE MAKE IT TO THE INFIRMARY? IS ALICE THERE?
DOES RICK KNOW?
IT'S ALL TAKEN CARE OF. THE GENERATOR-- THAT'S WHAT I'M WORRIED ABOUT. CAN YOU HELP?
YEAH.
GREAT! C'MON!
SLOW DOWN YOU LITTLE SHIT!
CHRIST!

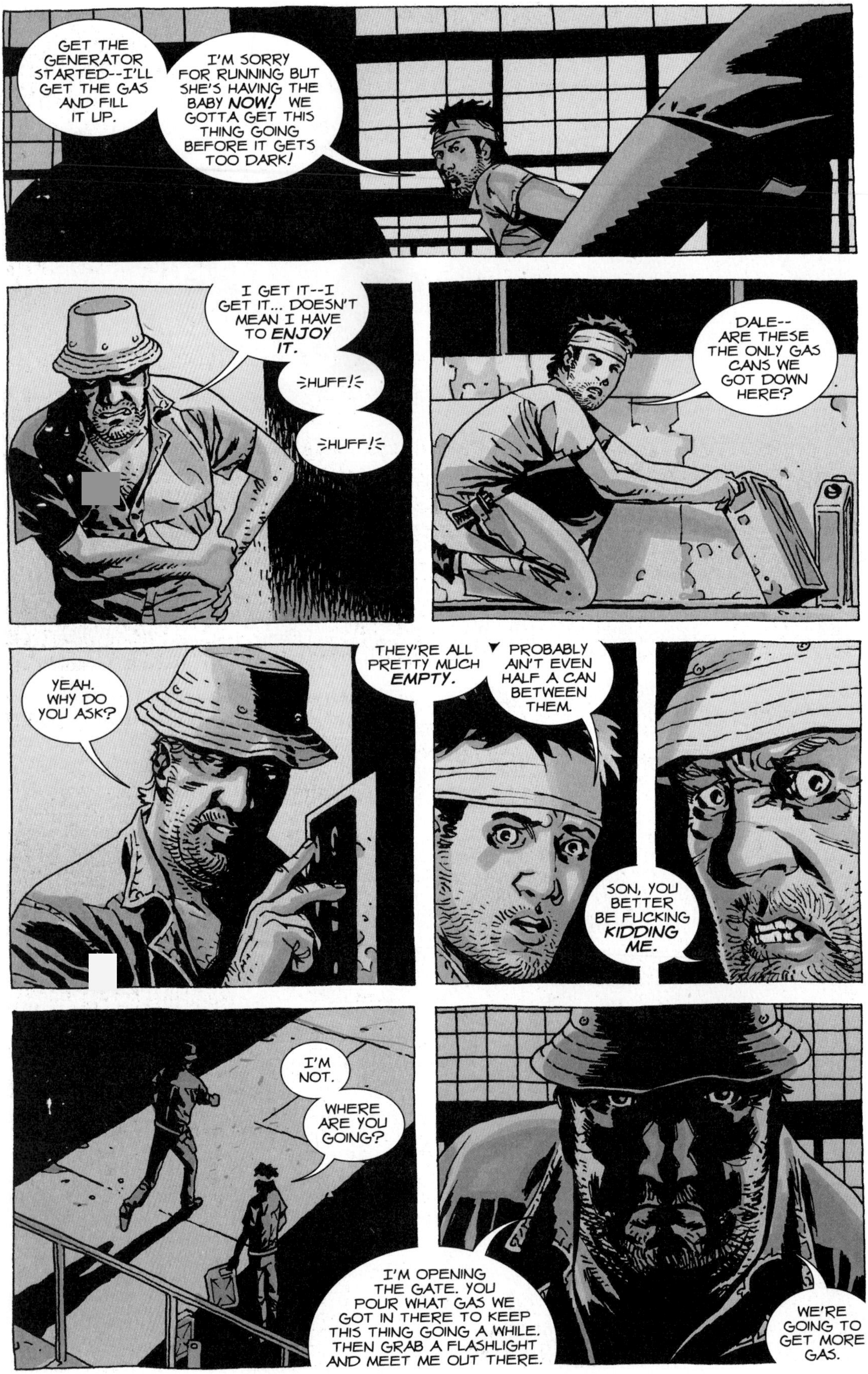
GET THE GENERATOR STARTED--I'LL GET THE GAS AND FILL IT UP.
I'M SORRY FOR RUNNING BUT SHE'S HAVING THE BABY NOW! WE GOTTA GET THIS THING GOING BEFORE IT GETS TOO DARK!
I GET IT--I GET IT... DOESN'T MEAN I HAVE TO ENJOY IT.
HUFF!
HUFF!
DALE-- ARE THESE THE ONLY GAS CANS WE GOT DOWN HERE?
YEAH. WHY DO YOU ASK?
THEY'RE ALL PRETTY MUCH EMPTY.
PROBABLY AIN'T EVEN HALF A CAN BETWEEN THEM.
SON, YOU BETTER BE FUCKING KIDDING ME.
I'M NOT.
WHERE ARE YOU GOING?
I'M OPENING THE GATE. YOU POUR WHAT GAS WE GOT IN THERE TO KEEP THIS THING GOING A WHILE. THEN GRAB A FLASHLIGHT AND MEET ME OUT THERE.
WE'RE GOING TO GET MORE GAS.

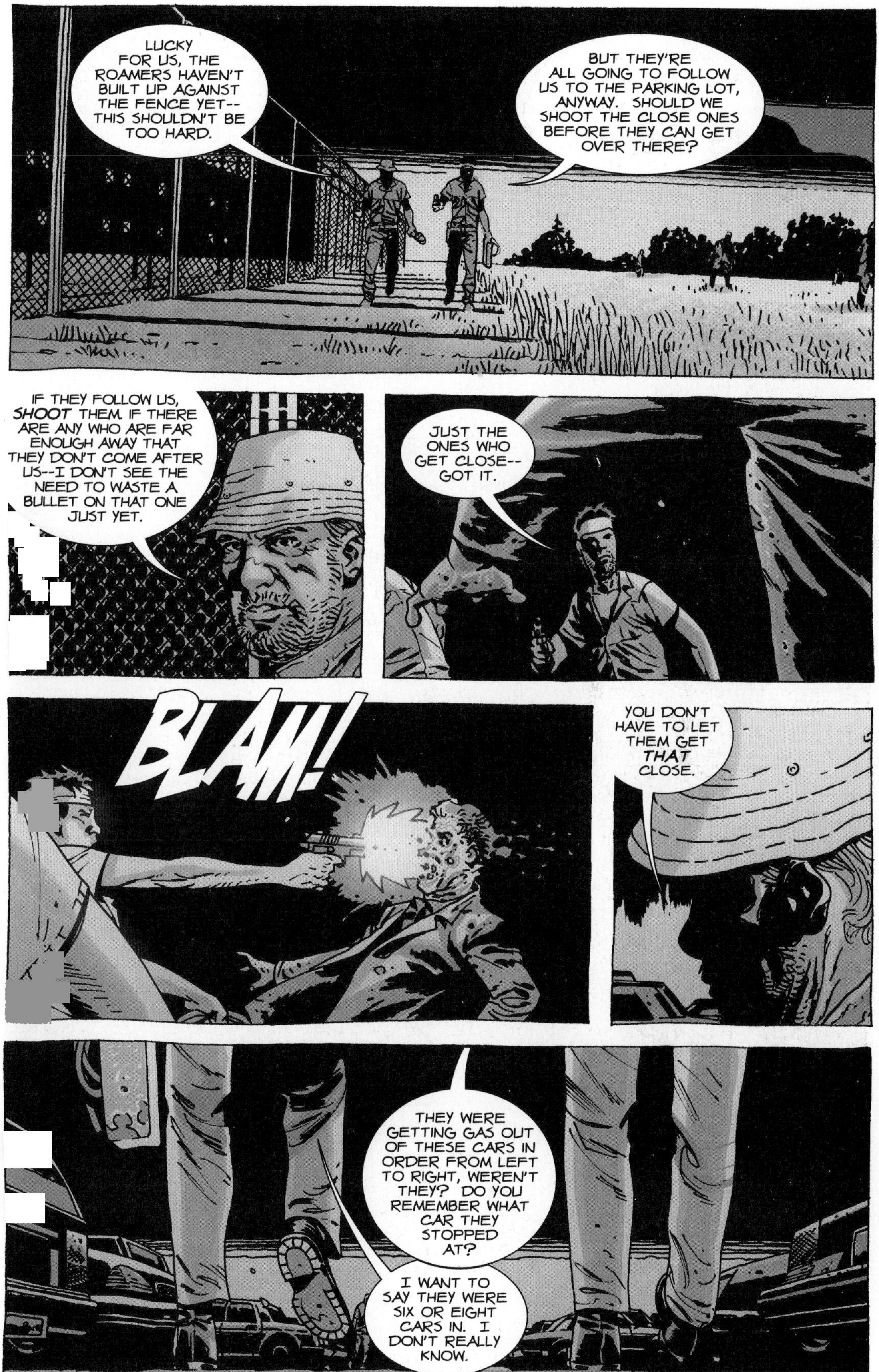
LUCKY FOR US, THE ROAMERS HAVEN'T BUILT UP AGAINST THE FENCE YET-- THIS SHOULDN'T BE TOO HARD.
BUT THEY'RE ALL GOING TO FOLLOW US TO THE PARKING LOT, ANYWAY. SHOULD WE SHOOT THE CLOSE ONES BEFORE THEY CAN GET OVER THERE?
IF THEY FOLLOW US, SHOOT THEM. IF THERE ARE ANY WHO ARE FAR ENOUGH AWAY THAT THEY DON'T COME AFTER US--I DON'T SEE THE NEED TO WASTE A BULLET ON THAT ONE JUST YET.
JUST THE ONES WHO GET CLOSE-- GOT IT.
BLAM!
YOU DON'T HAVE TO LET THEM GET THAT CLOSE.
THEY WERE GETTING GAS OUT OF THESE CARS IN ORDER FROM LEFT TO RIGHT, WEREN'T THEY? DO YOU REMEMBER WHAT CAR THEY STOPPED AT?
I WANT TO SAY THEY WERE SIX OR EIGHT CARS IN. I DON'T REALLY KNOW.

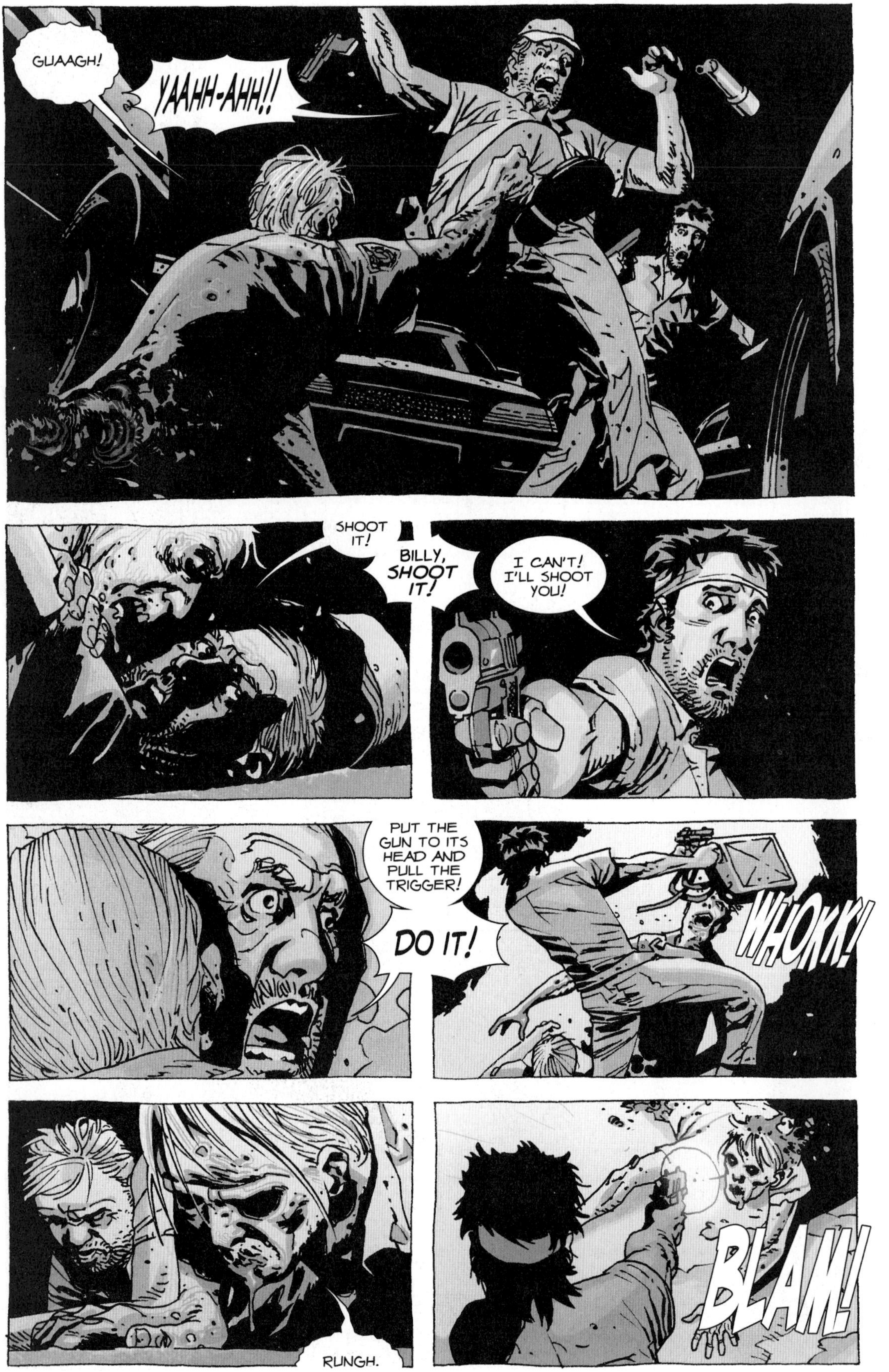
GUAAGH!
YAAHH-AHH!!
SHOOT IT!
BILLY, SHOOT IT!
I CAN'T! I'LL SHOOT YOU!
PUT THE GUN TO ITS HEAD AND PULL THE TRIGGER!
DO IT!
WHOKK!
RUNGH.
BLAM!

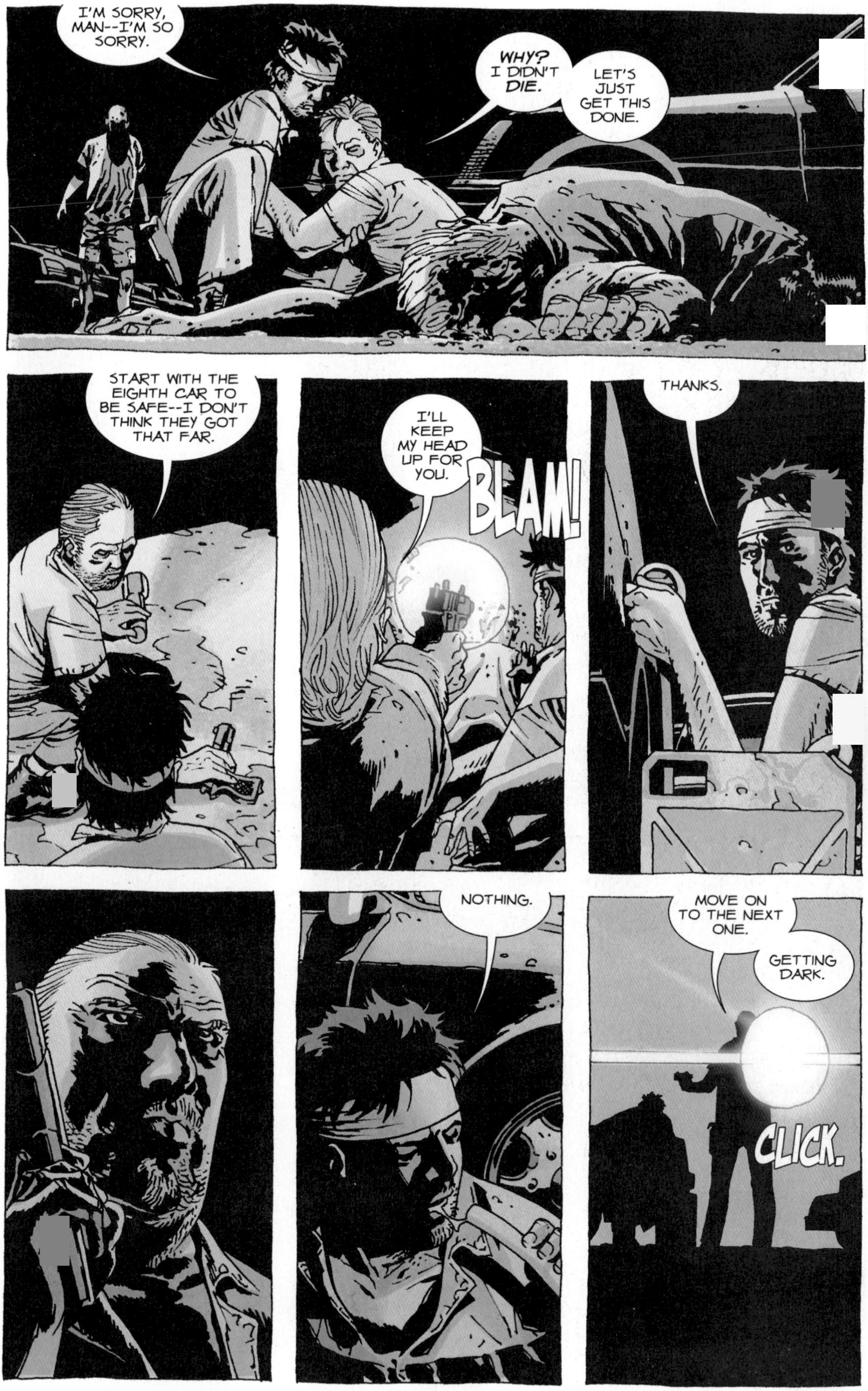
I'M SORRY, MAN--I'M SO SORRY.
WHY? I DIDN'T DIE.
LET'S JUST GET THIS DONE.
START WITH THE EIGHTH CAR TO BE SAFE--I DON'T THINK THEY GOT THAT FAR.
I'LL KEEP MY HEAD UP FOR YOU.
BLAM!
THANKS.
NOTHING.
MOVE ON TO THE NEXT ONE.
GETTING DARK.
CLICK.

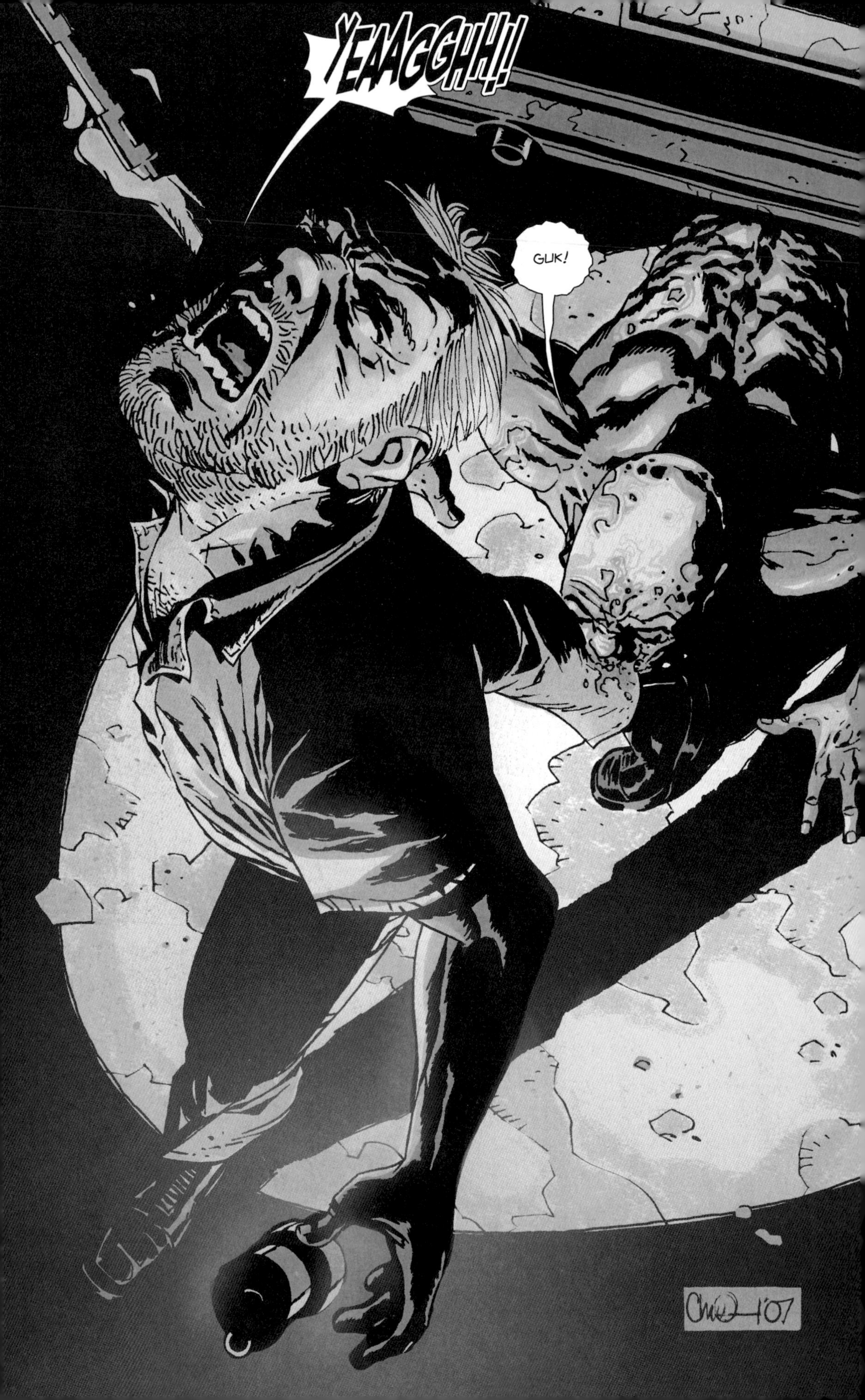
YEAAGGHH!!
GUK!
CM '07

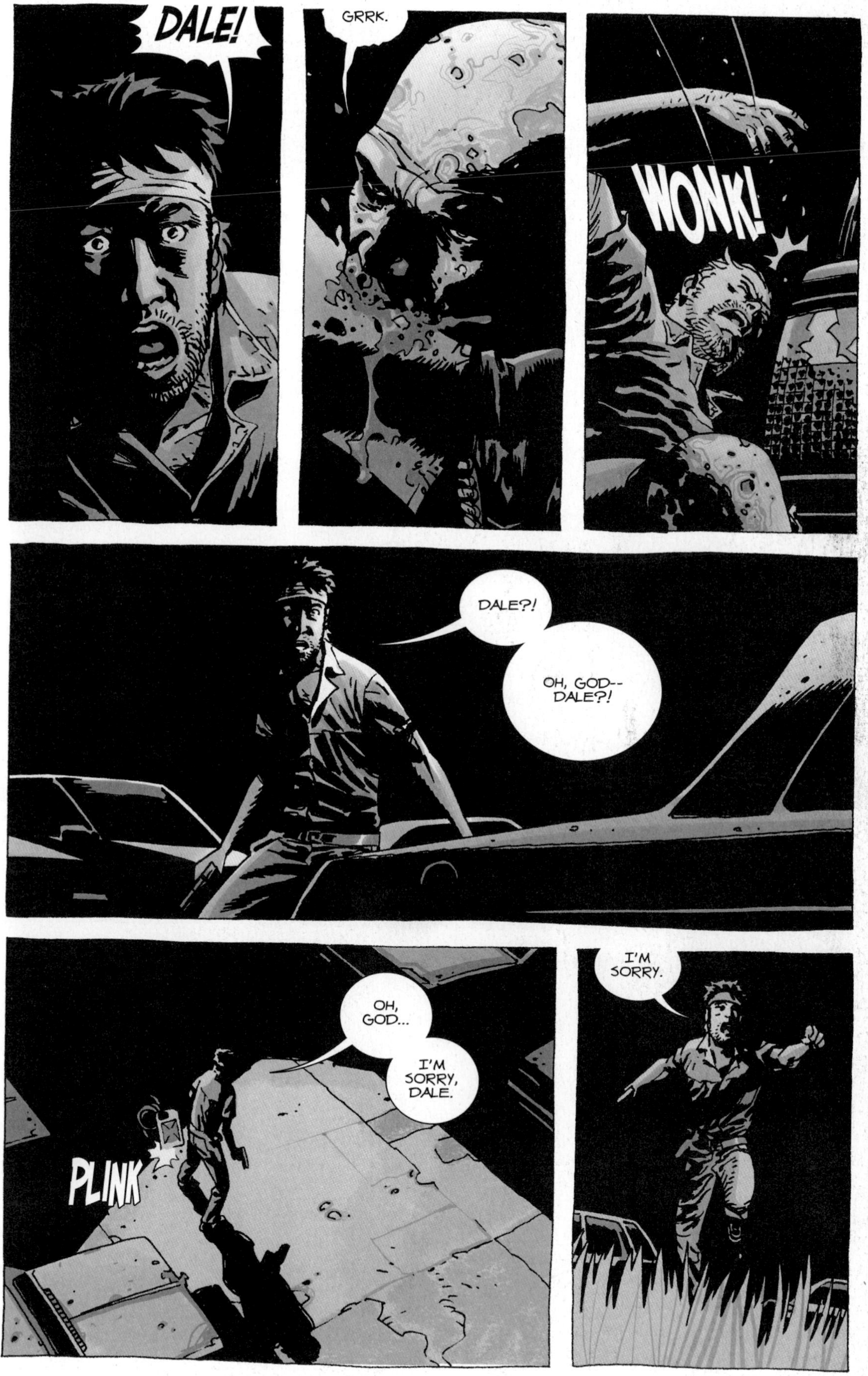
DALE!
GRRK.
WONK!
DALE?!
OH, GOD--
DALE?!
OH,
GOD...
I'M
SORRY,
DALE.
PLINK
I'M
SORRY.

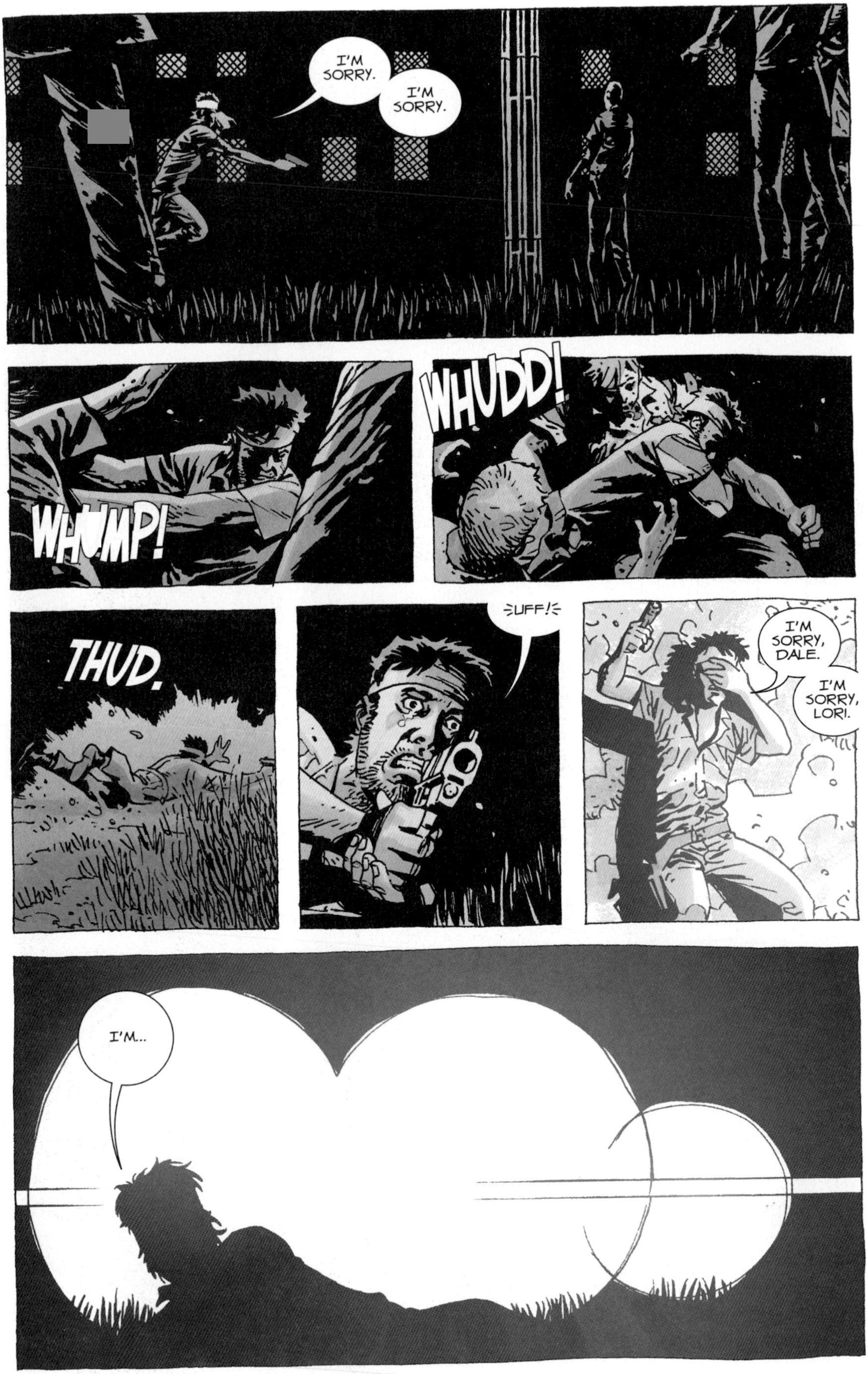
I'M SORRY.
I'M SORRY.
WHUMP!
WHUDD!
THUD.
UFF!
I'M SORRY, DALE.
I'M SORRY, LORI.
I'M...

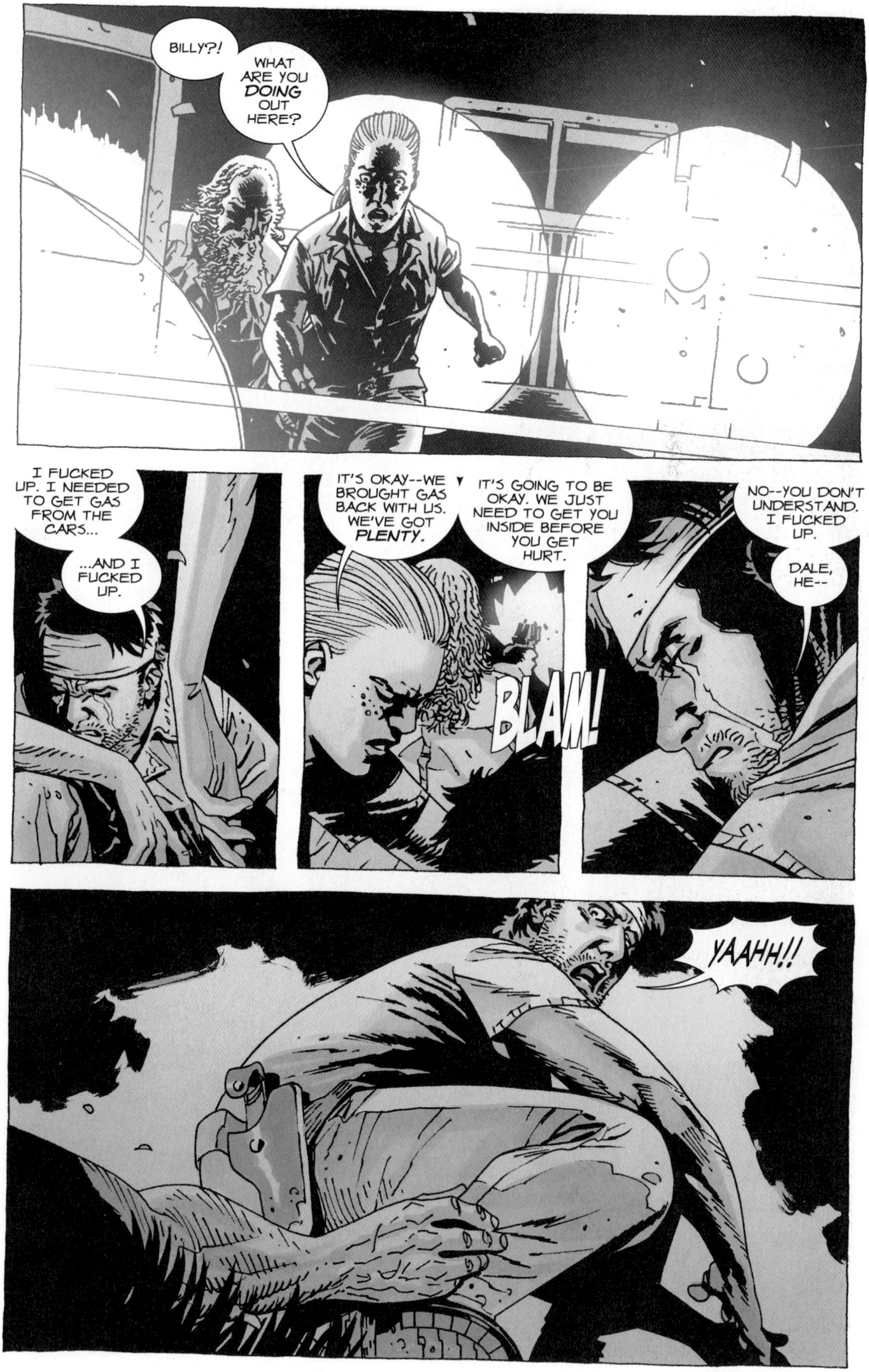
BILLY?!
WHAT ARE YOU DOING OUT HERE?
I FUCKED UP. I NEEDED TO GET GAS FROM THE CARS...
...AND I FUCKED UP.
IT'S OKAY--WE BROUGHT GAS BACK WITH US. WE'VE GOT PLENTY.
IT'S GOING TO BE OKAY. WE JUST NEED TO GET YOU INSIDE BEFORE YOU GET HURT.
BLAM!
NO--YOU DON'T UNDERSTAND. I FUCKED UP.
DALE, HE--
YAAHH!!

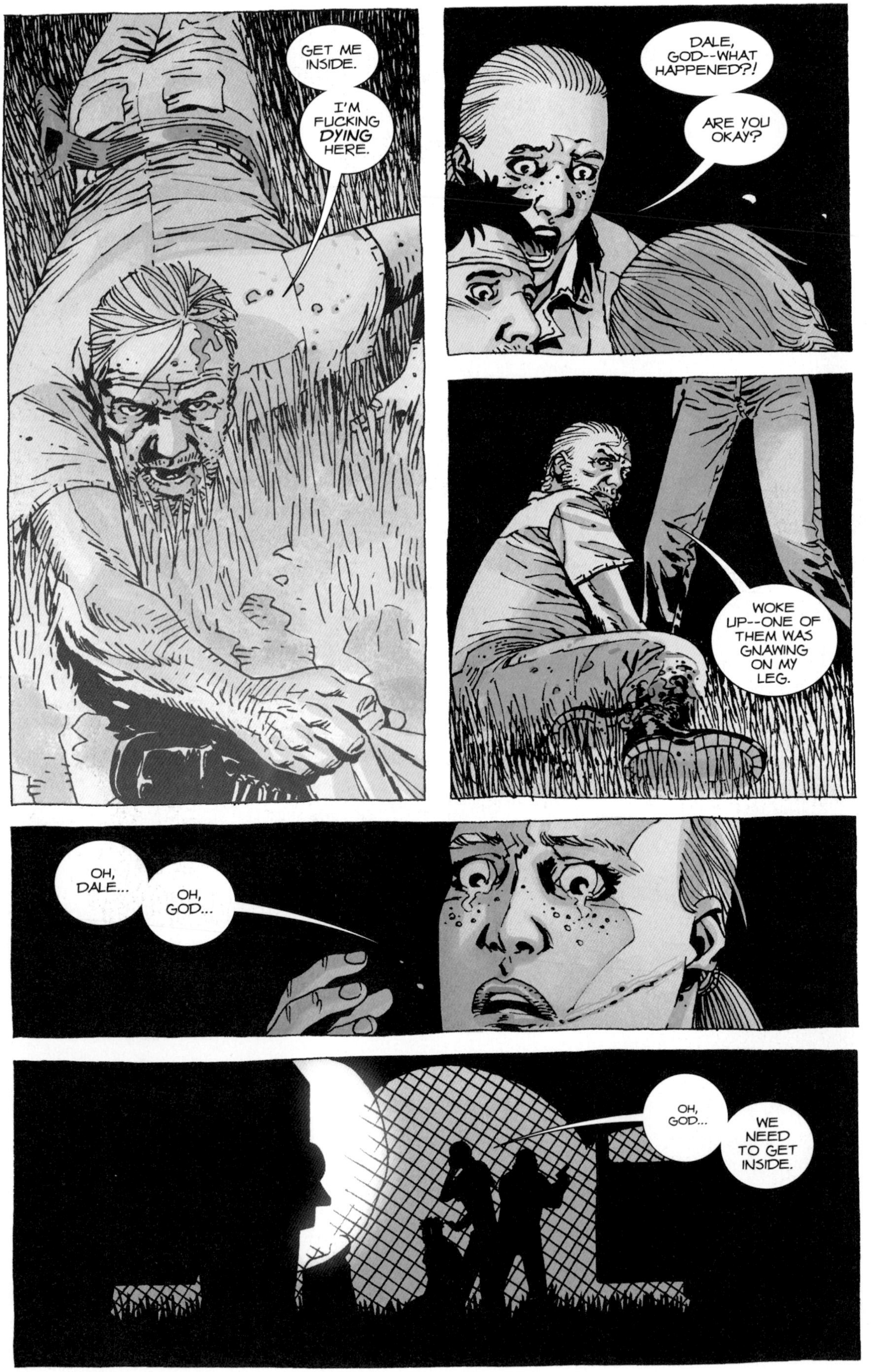
GET ME INSIDE.
I'M FUCKING *DYING* HERE.
DALE, GOD--WHAT HAPPENED?!
ARE YOU OKAY?
WOKE UP--ONE OF THEM WAS GNAWING ON MY LEG.
OH, DALE...
OH, GOD...
OH, GOD...
WE NEED TO GET INSIDE.

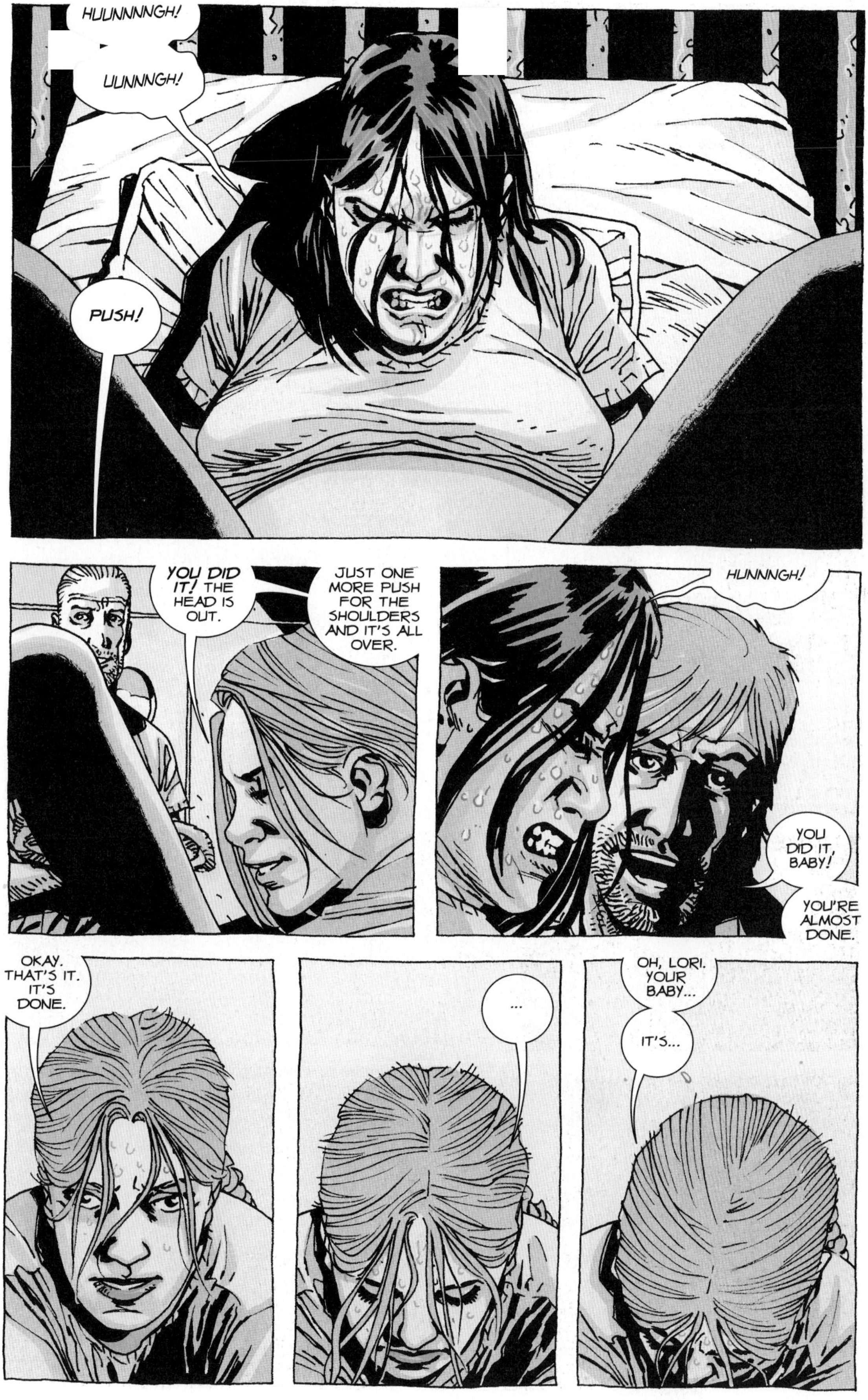
HUUNNNNGH!
UUNNNGH!
PUSH!
YOU DID IT! THE HEAD IS OUT.
JUST ONE MORE PUSH FOR THE SHOULDERS AND IT'S ALL OVER.
HUNNNGH!
YOU DID IT, BABY!
YOU'RE ALMOST DONE.
OKAY. THAT'S IT. IT'S DONE.
...
OH, LORI. YOUR BABY...
IT'S...

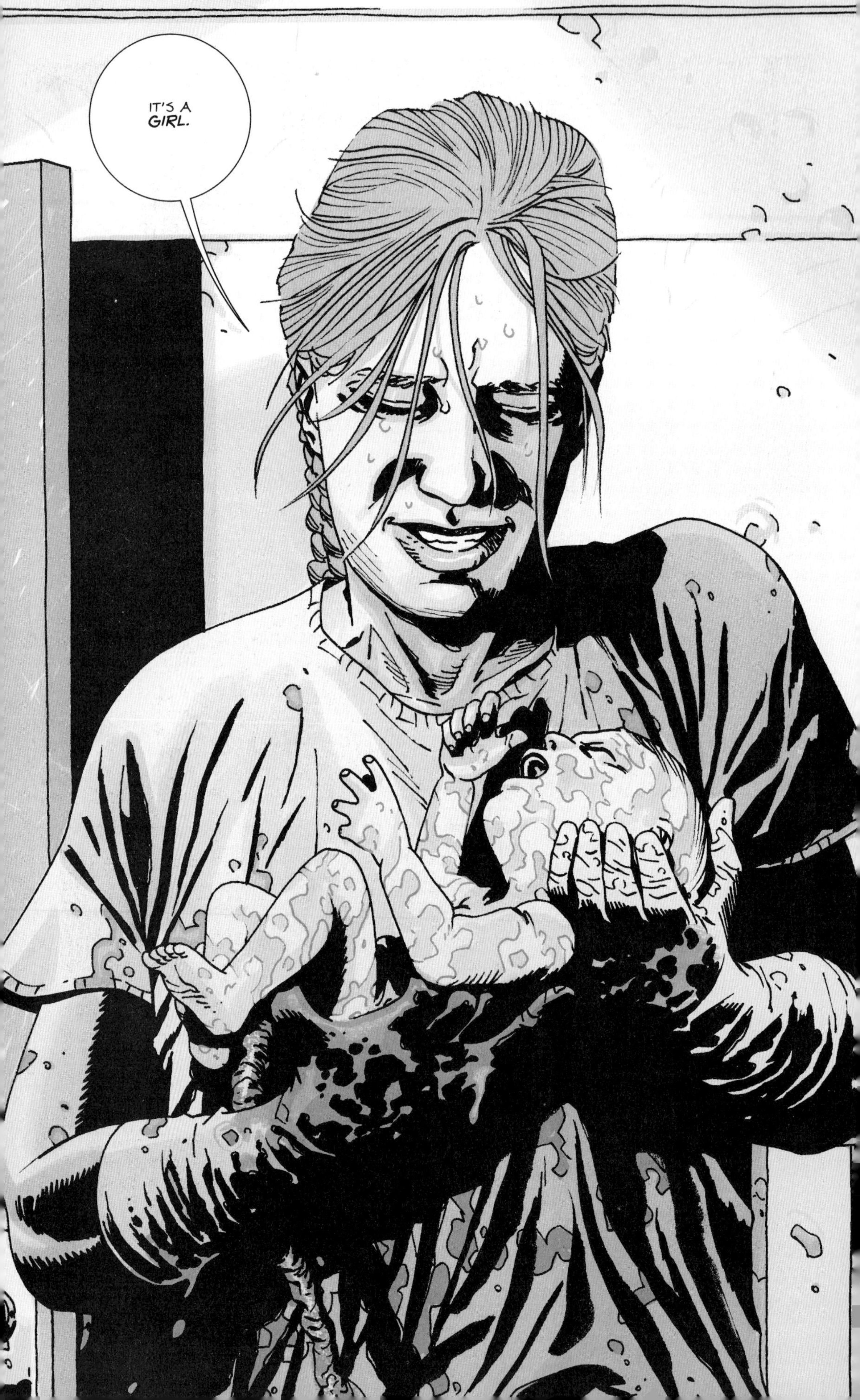
IT'S A GIRL.

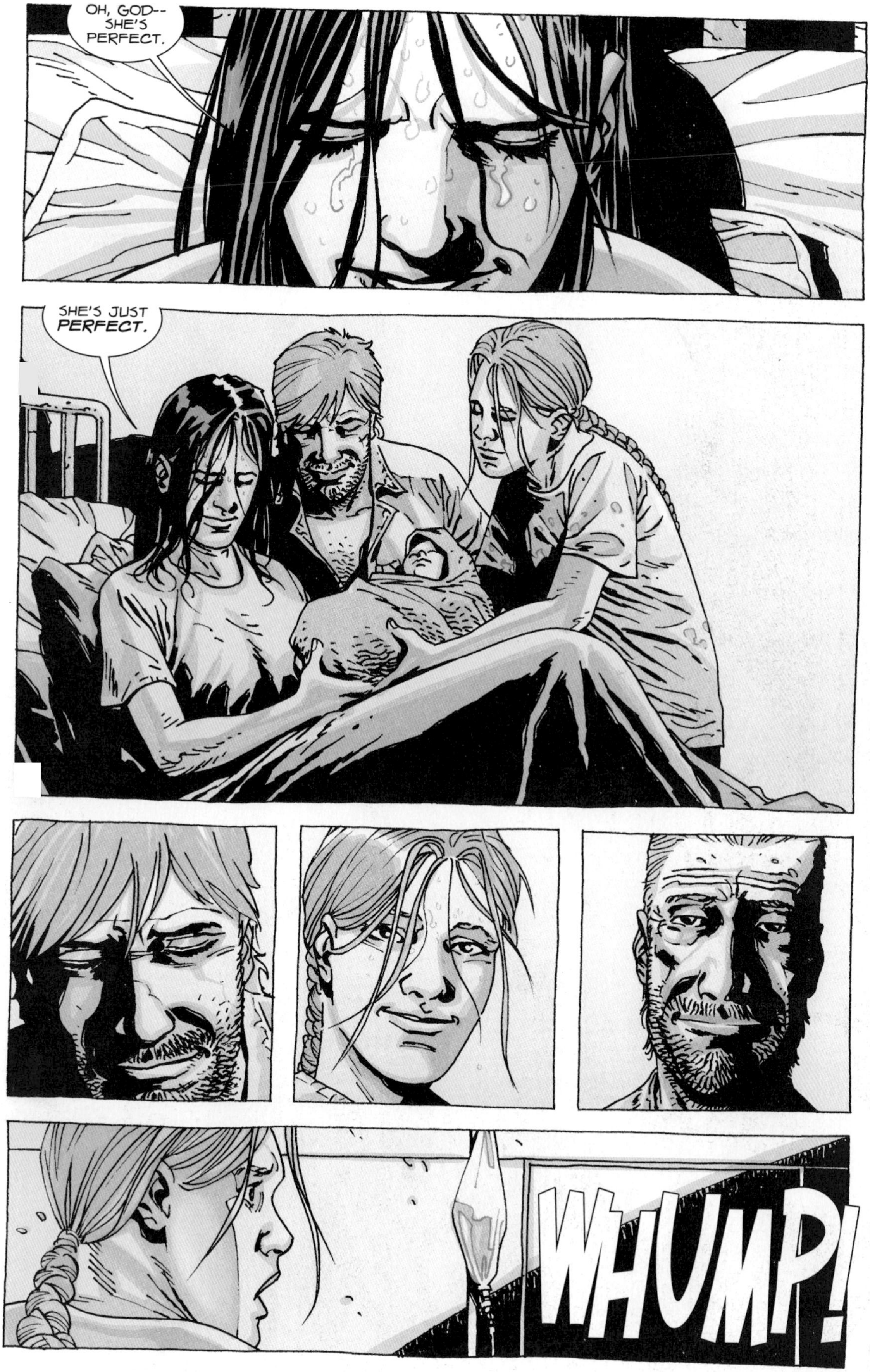
OH, GOD-- SHE'S PERFECT.
SHE'S JUST PERFECT.
WHUMP!

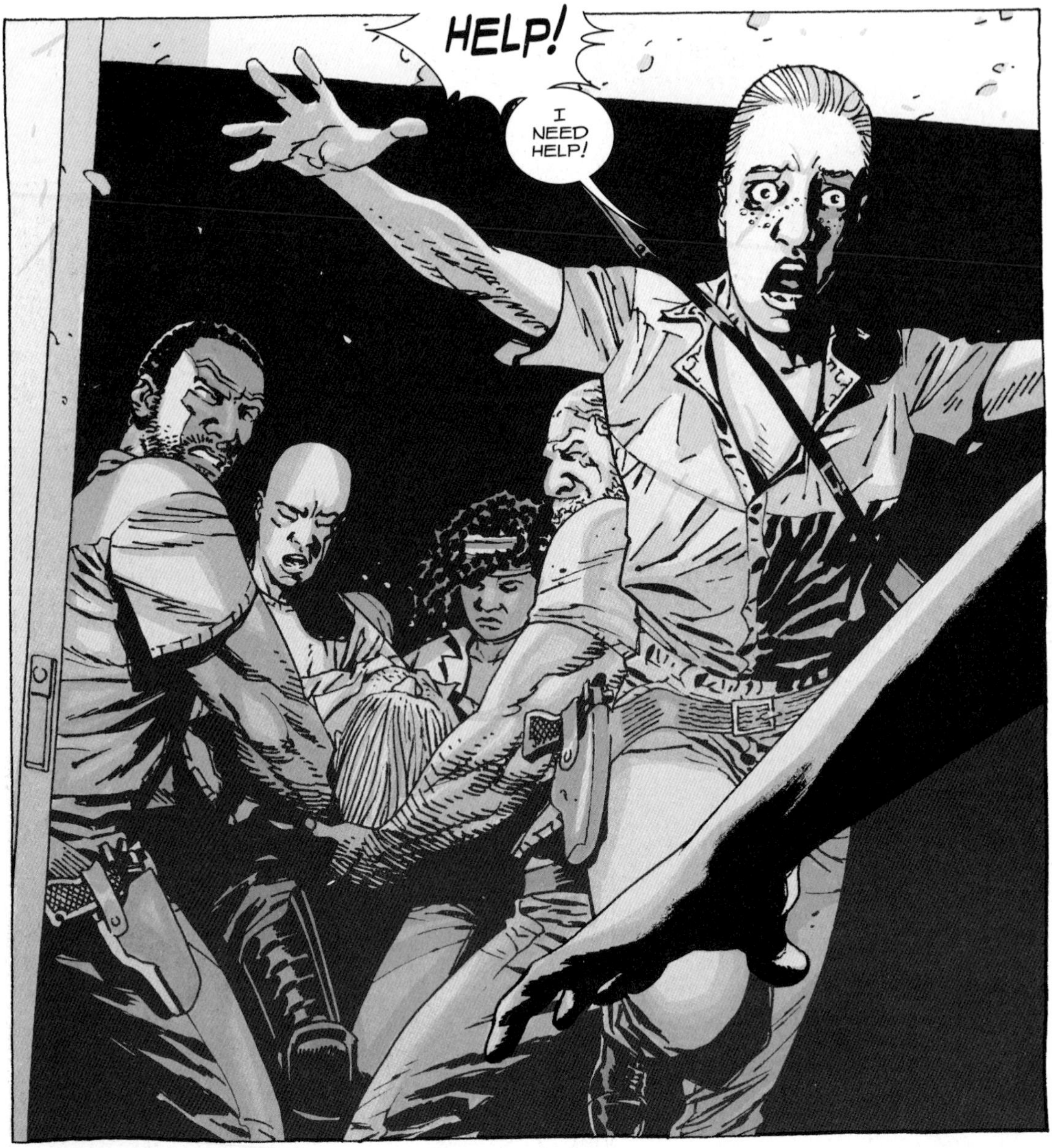
HELP!
I NEED HELP!

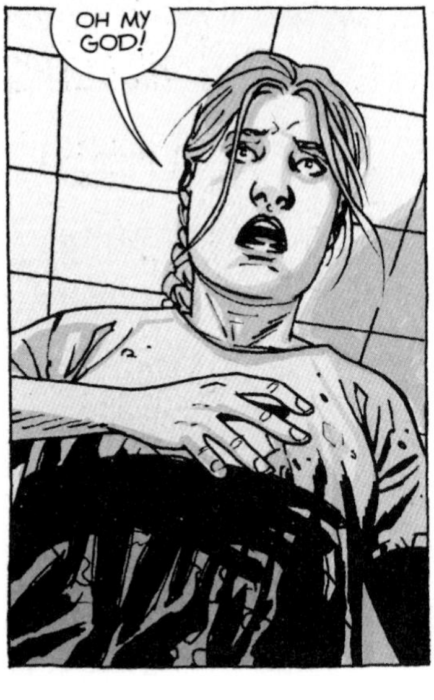
OH MY GOD!

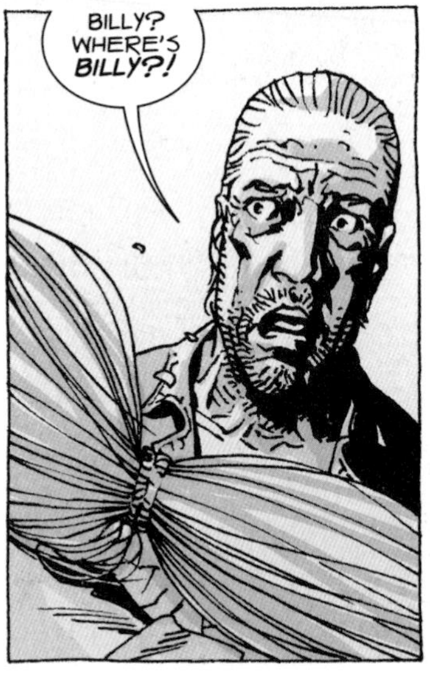
BILLY? WHERE'S BILLY?!

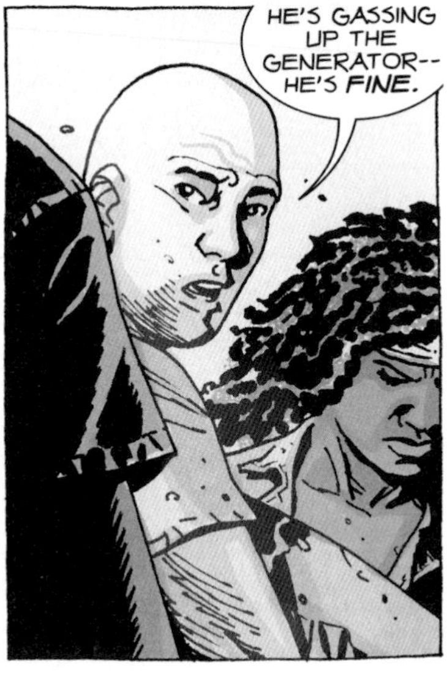
HE'S GASSING UP THE GENERATOR-- HE'S FINE.

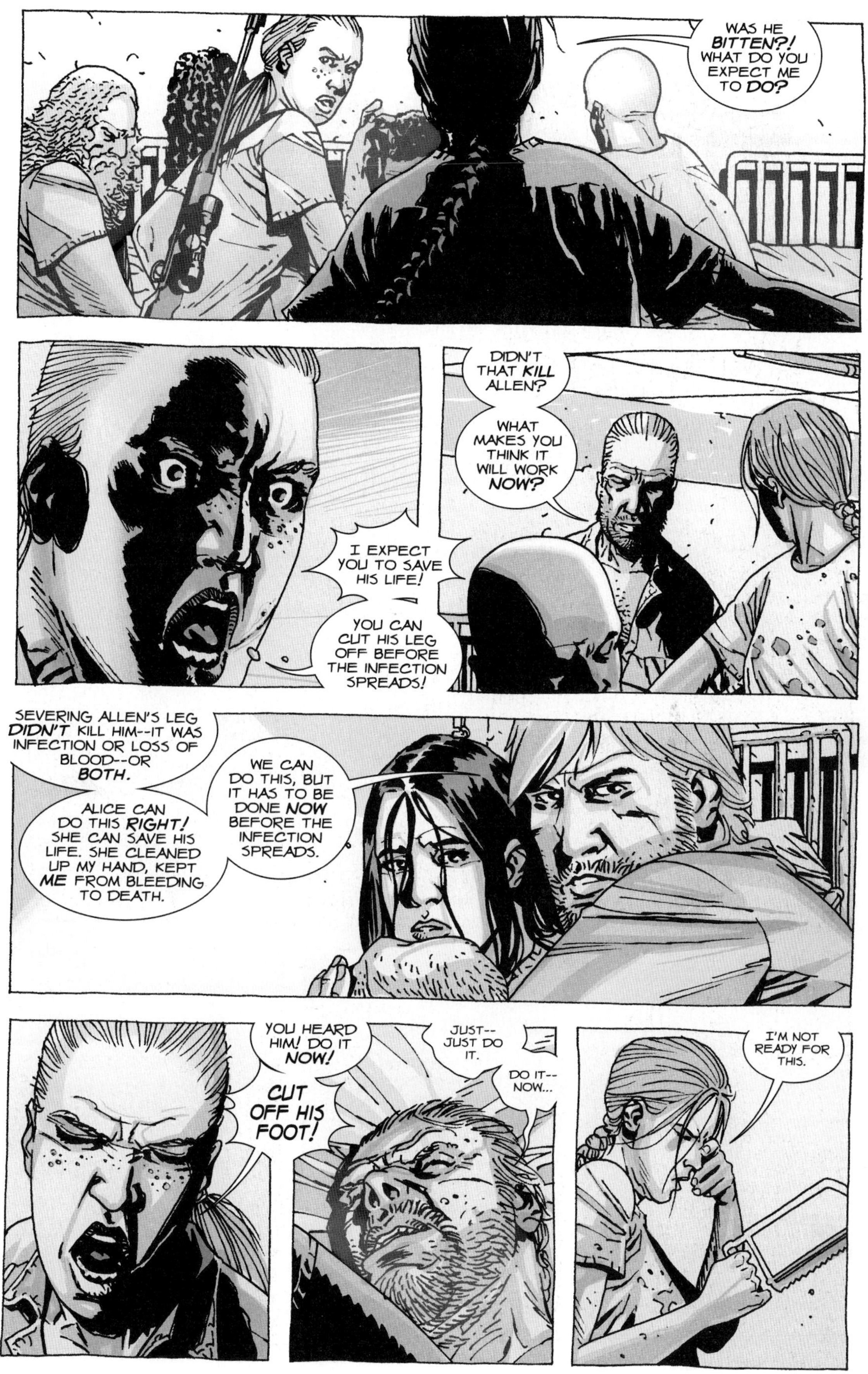
WAS HE BITTEN?! WHAT DO YOU EXPECT ME TO DO?
I EXPECT YOU TO SAVE HIS LIFE!
YOU CAN CUT HIS LEG OFF BEFORE THE INFECTION SPREADS!
DIDN'T THAT KILL ALLEN?
WHAT MAKES YOU THINK IT WILL WORK NOW?
SEVERING ALLEN'S LEG DIDN'T KILL HIM--IT WAS INFECTION OR LOSS OF BLOOD--OR BOTH.
ALICE CAN DO THIS RIGHT! SHE CAN SAVE HIS LIFE. SHE CLEANED UP MY HAND, KEPT ME FROM BLEEDING TO DEATH.
WE CAN DO THIS, BUT IT HAS TO BE DONE NOW BEFORE THE INFECTION SPREADS.
YOU HEARD HIM! DO IT NOW!
CUT OFF HIS FOOT!
JUST-- JUST DO IT.
DO IT-- NOW...
I'M NOT READY FOR THIS.

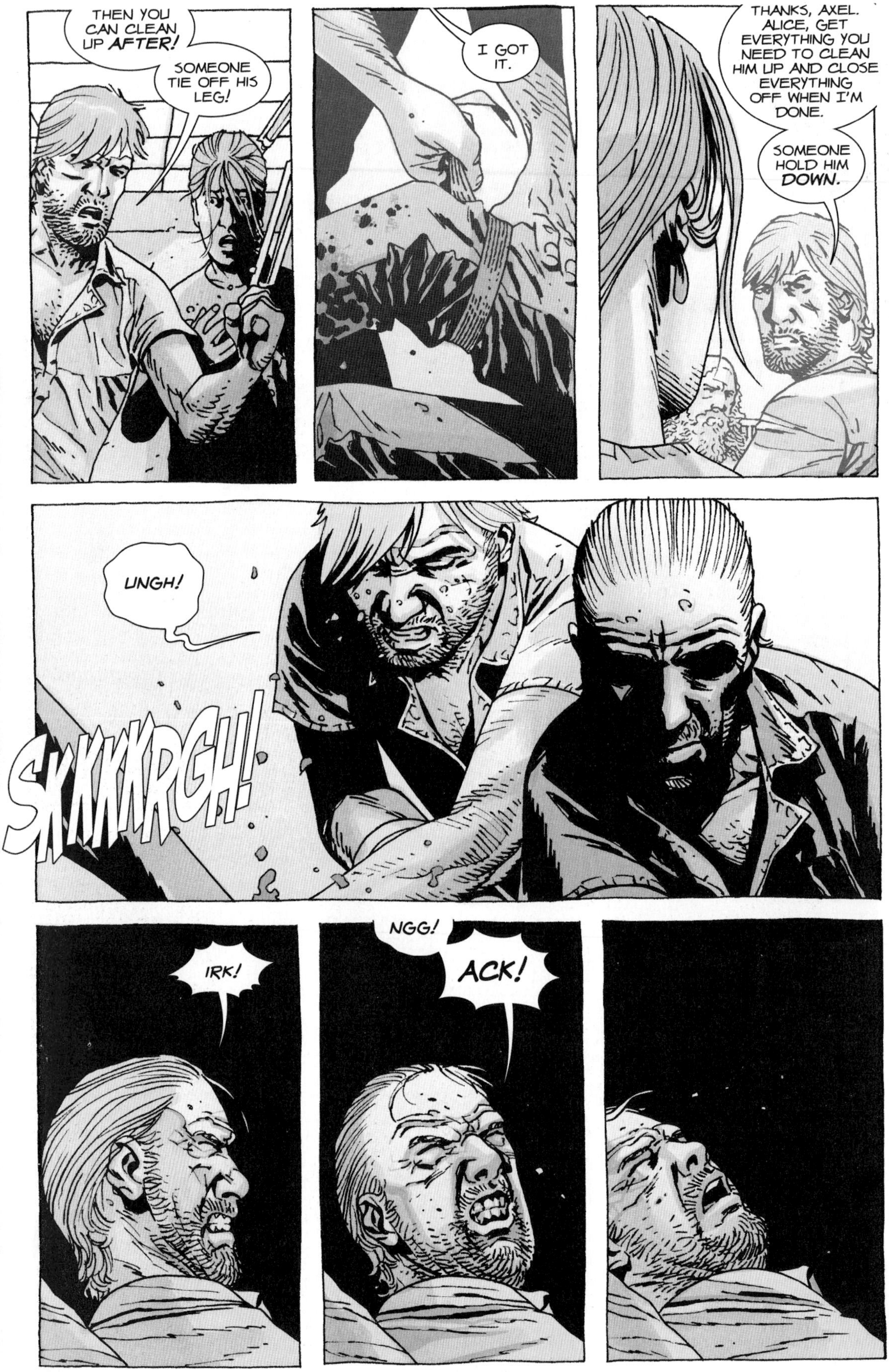
THEN YOU CAN CLEAN UP AFTER!
SOMEONE TIE OFF HIS LEG!
I GOT IT.
THANKS, AXEL. ALICE, GET EVERYTHING YOU NEED TO CLEAN HIM UP AND CLOSE EVERYTHING OFF WHEN I'M DONE.
SOMEONE HOLD HIM DOWN.
UNGH!
SKKKKRGH!
IRK!
NGG!
ACK!

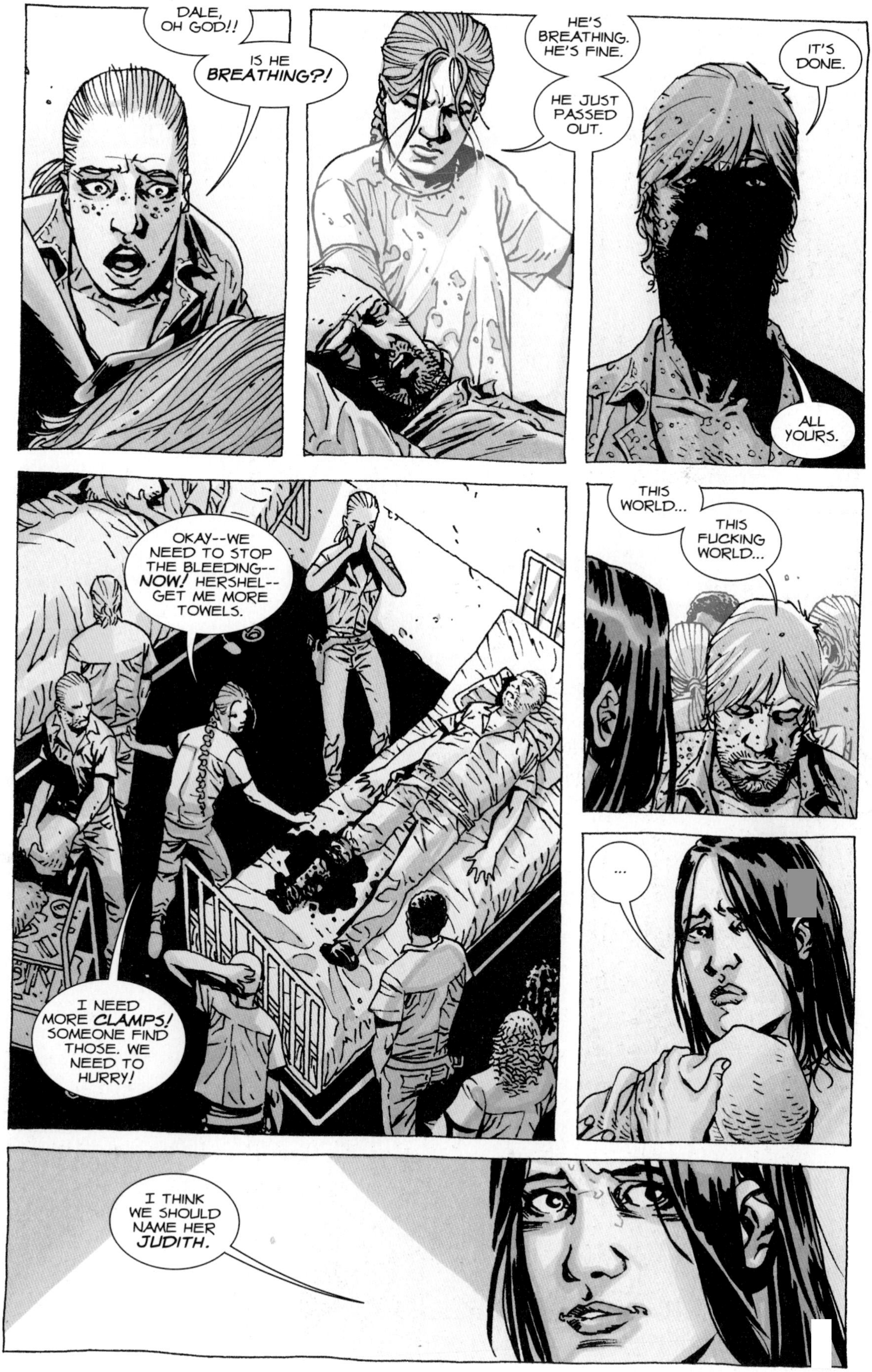
DALE, OH GOD!!
IS HE BREATHING?!
HE'S BREATHING. HE'S FINE.
HE JUST PASSED OUT.
IT'S DONE.
ALL YOURS.
OKAY--WE NEED TO STOP THE BLEEDING-- NOW! HERSHEL-- GET ME MORE TOWELS.
I NEED MORE CLAMPS! SOMEONE FIND THOSE. WE NEED TO HURRY!
THIS WORLD...
THIS FUCKING WORLD...
...
I THINK WE SHOULD NAME HER JUDITH.

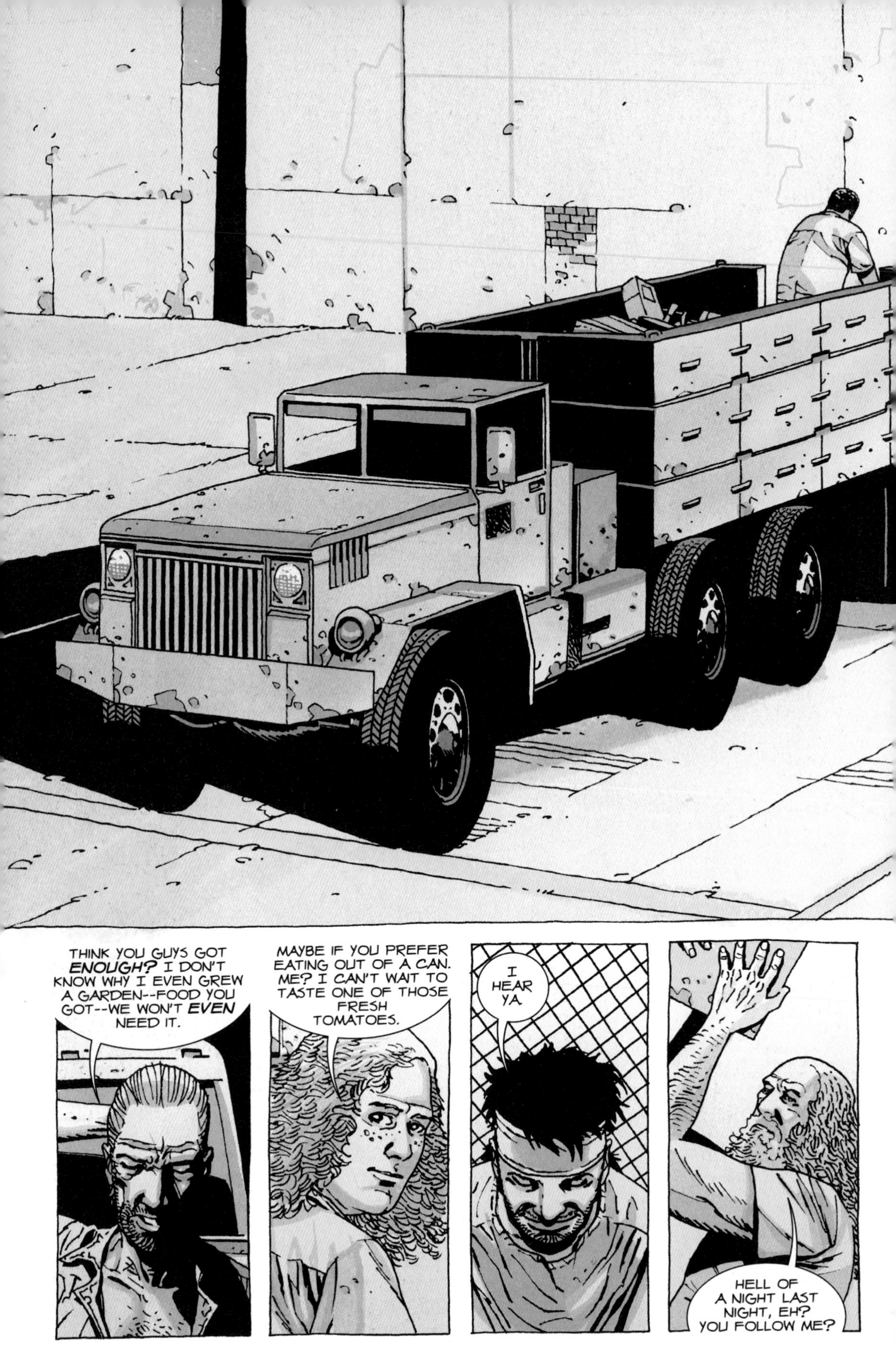
THINK YOU GUYS GOT ENOUGH? I DON'T KNOW WHY I EVEN GREW A GARDEN--FOOD YOU GOT--WE WON'T EVEN NEED IT.
MAYBE IF YOU PREFER EATING OUT OF A CAN. ME? I CAN'T WAIT TO TASTE ONE OF THOSE FRESH TOMATOES.
I HEAR YA.
HELL OF A NIGHT LAST NIGHT, EH? YOU FOLLOW ME?

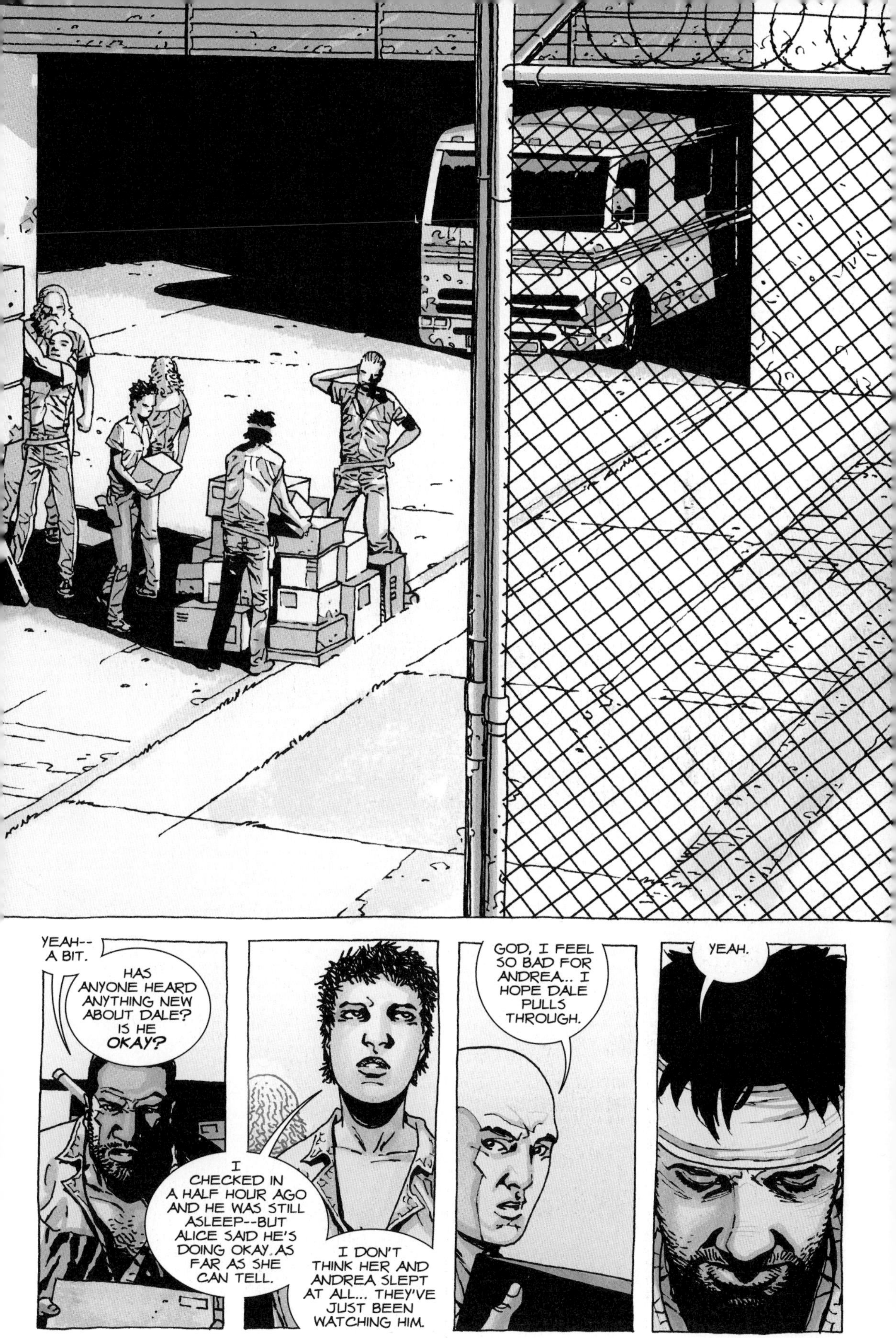
YEAH-- A BIT.
HAS ANYONE HEARD ANYTHING NEW ABOUT DALE? IS HE OKAY?
I CHECKED IN A HALF HOUR AGO AND HE WAS STILL ASLEEP--BUT ALICE SAID HE'S DOING OKAY. AS FAR AS SHE CAN TELL.
I DON'T THINK HER AND ANDREA SLEPT AT ALL... THEY'VE JUST BEEN WATCHING HIM.
GOD, I FEEL SO BAD FOR ANDREA... I HOPE DALE PULLS THROUGH.
YEAH.

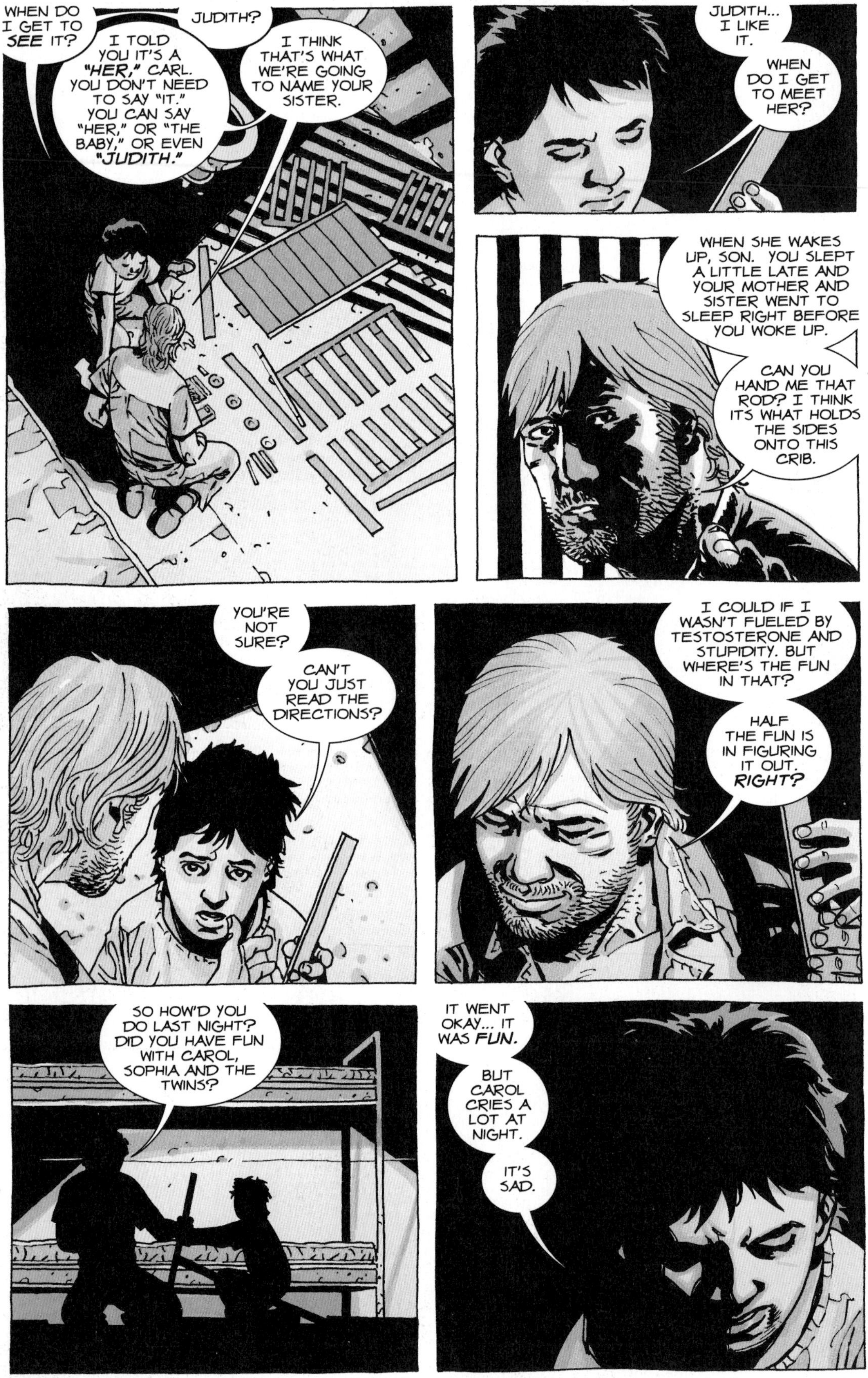
WHEN DO I GET TO SEE IT?
JUDITH?
I TOLD YOU IT'S A "HER," CARL. YOU DON'T NEED TO SAY "IT." YOU CAN SAY "HER," OR "THE BABY," OR EVEN "JUDITH."
I THINK THAT'S WHAT WE'RE GOING TO NAME YOUR SISTER.
JUDITH... I LIKE IT.
WHEN DO I GET TO MEET HER?
WHEN SHE WAKES UP, SON. YOU SLEPT A LITTLE LATE AND YOUR MOTHER AND SISTER WENT TO SLEEP RIGHT BEFORE YOU WOKE UP.
CAN YOU HAND ME THAT ROD? I THINK ITS WHAT HOLDS THE SIDES ONTO THIS CRIB.
YOU'RE NOT SURE?
CAN'T YOU JUST READ THE DIRECTIONS?
I COULD IF I WASN'T FUELED BY TESTOSTERONE AND STUPIDITY. BUT WHERE'S THE FUN IN THAT?
HALF THE FUN IS IN FIGURING IT OUT. RIGHT?
SO HOW'D YOU DO LAST NIGHT? DID YOU HAVE FUN WITH CAROL, SOPHIA AND THE TWINS?
IT WENT OKAY... IT WAS FUN.
BUT CAROL CRIES A LOT AT NIGHT.
IT'S SAD.

EVERYTHING SOUNDS FINE. HE'S OKAY, HE'S JUST *SLEEPING.* I THINK EVERYTHING IS GOING TO BE OKAY. HE DIDN'T LOSE TOO MUCH BLOOD.

THE BABY, THIS, TAPING UP GLENN'S RIBS... WHAT A NIGHT.

YEAH.

UNGH... HEY.

AM I STILL ALIVE?

OH, CRAP-- I'M SORRY, DALE. I DIDN'T MEAN TO WAKE YOU.

IT'S OKAY--YOU'RE JUST DOING YOUR JOB. I THINK I'M RESTED ENOUGH. I FEEL--I FEEL *OKAY.*

I'LL, UH... LEAVE YOU TWO ALONE.

ANDREA?

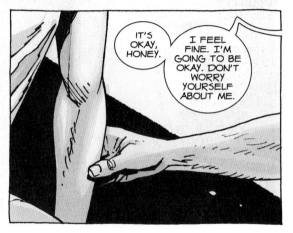

IT'S OKAY, HONEY.

I FEEL FINE. I'M GOING TO BE OKAY. DON'T WORRY YOURSELF ABOUT ME.

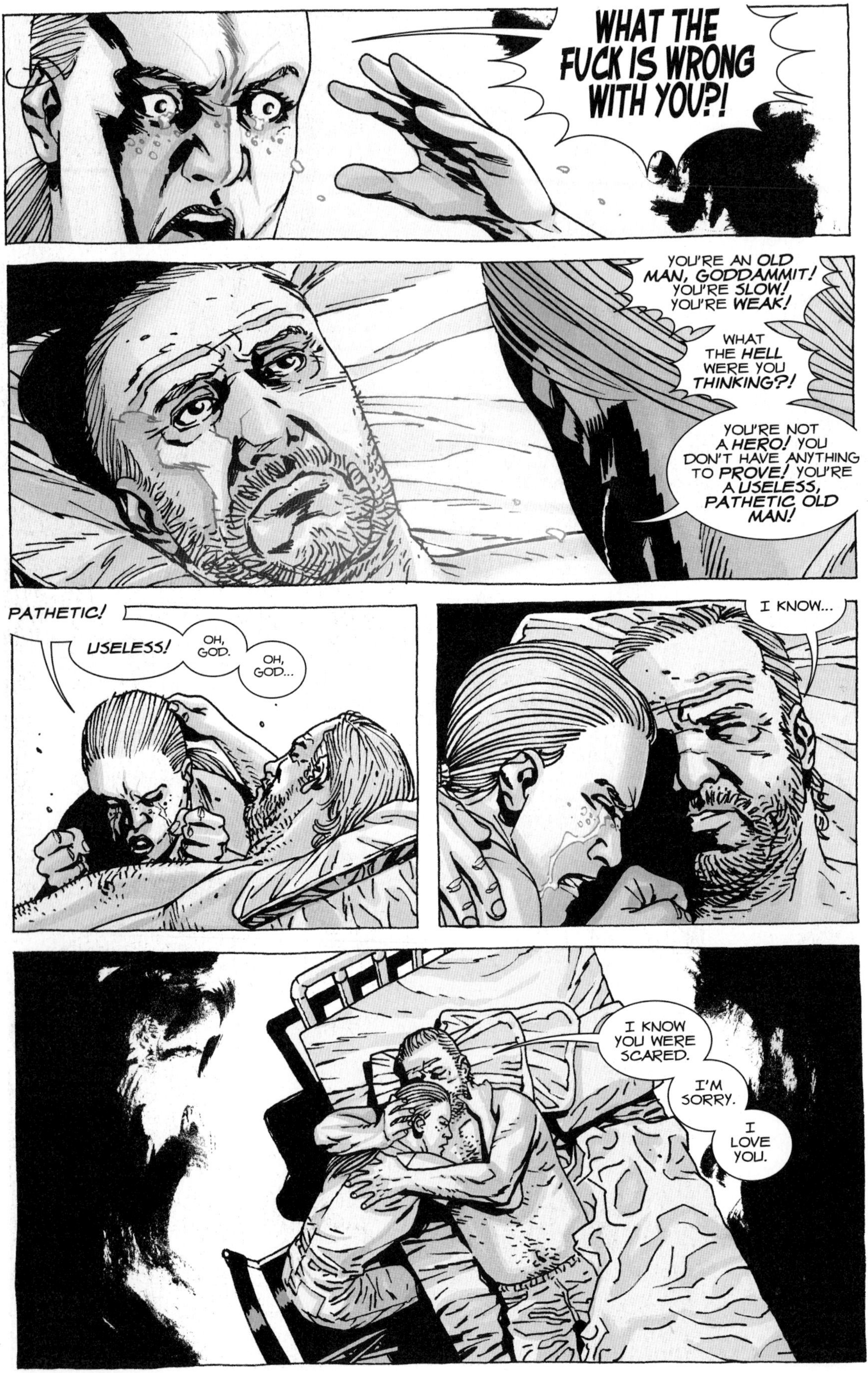
WHAT THE FUCK IS WRONG WITH YOU?!
YOU'RE AN OLD MAN, GODDAMMIT! YOU'RE SLOW! YOU'RE WEAK!
WHAT THE HELL WERE YOU THINKING?!
YOU'RE NOT A HERO! YOU DON'T HAVE ANYTHING TO PROVE! YOU'RE A USELESS, PATHETIC OLD MAN!
PATHETIC!
USELESS!
OH, GOD.
OH, GOD...
I KNOW...
I KNOW YOU WERE SCARED.
I'M SORRY.
I LOVE YOU.

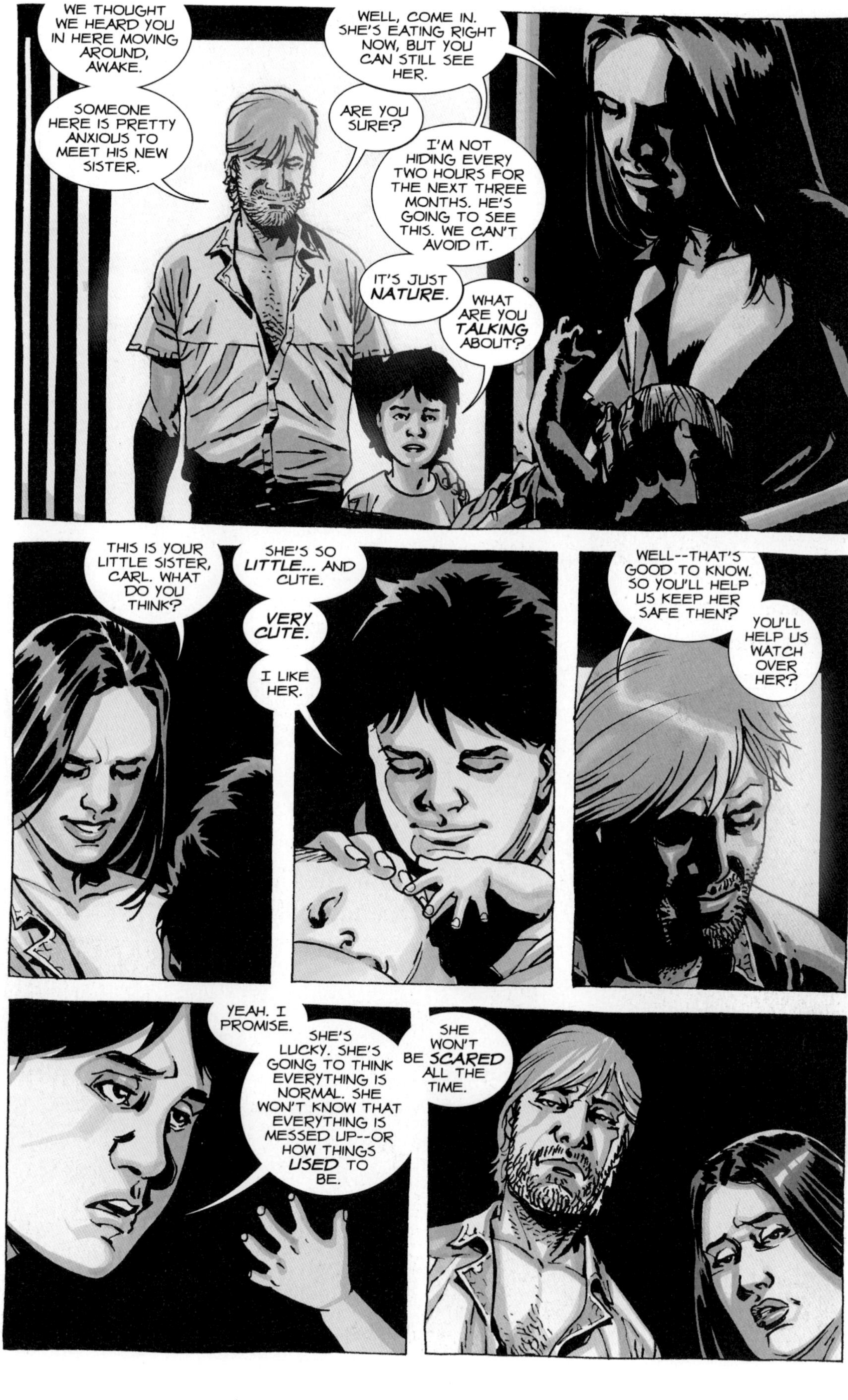
WE THOUGHT WE HEARD YOU IN HERE MOVING AROUND, AWAKE.
SOMEONE HERE IS PRETTY ANXIOUS TO MEET HIS NEW SISTER.
WELL, COME IN. SHE'S EATING RIGHT NOW, BUT YOU CAN STILL SEE HER.
ARE YOU SURE?
I'M NOT HIDING EVERY TWO HOURS FOR THE NEXT THREE MONTHS. HE'S GOING TO SEE THIS. WE CAN'T AVOID IT.
IT'S JUST NATURE.
WHAT ARE YOU TALKING ABOUT?
THIS IS YOUR LITTLE SISTER, CARL. WHAT DO YOU THINK?
SHE'S SO LITTLE... AND CUTE.
VERY CUTE.
I LIKE HER.
WELL--THAT'S GOOD TO KNOW. SO YOU'LL HELP US KEEP HER SAFE THEN?
YOU'LL HELP US WATCH OVER HER?
YEAH. I PROMISE.
SHE'S LUCKY. SHE'S GOING TO THINK EVERYTHING IS NORMAL. SHE WON'T KNOW THAT EVERYTHING IS MESSED UP--OR HOW THINGS USED TO BE.
SHE WON'T BE SCARED ALL THE TIME.

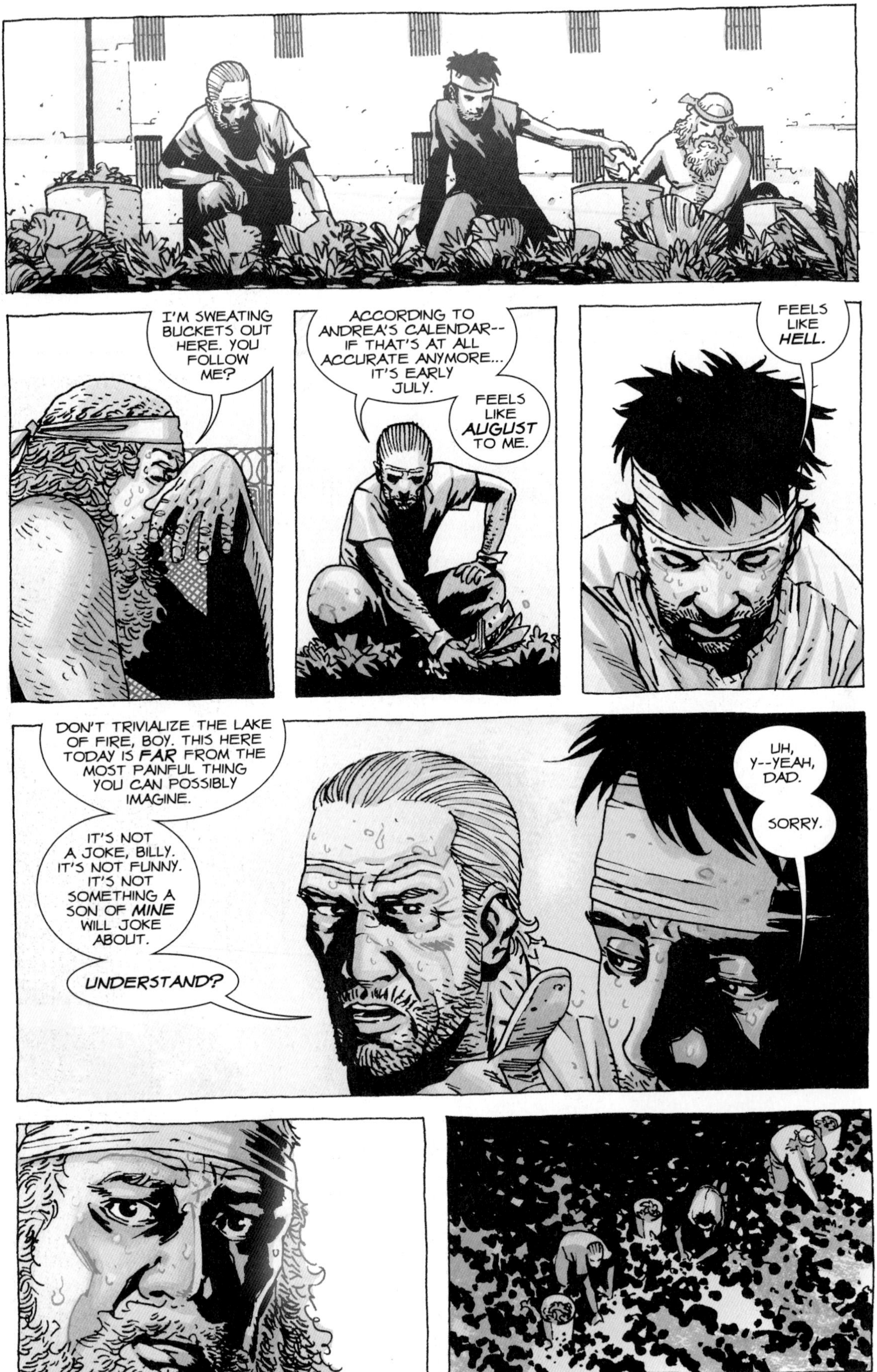
I'M SWEATING BUCKETS OUT HERE. YOU FOLLOW ME?
ACCORDING TO ANDREA'S CALENDAR-- IF THAT'S AT ALL ACCURATE ANYMORE... IT'S EARLY JULY.
FEELS LIKE AUGUST TO ME.
FEELS LIKE HELL.
DON'T TRIVIALIZE THE LAKE OF FIRE, BOY. THIS HERE TODAY IS FAR FROM THE MOST PAINFUL THING YOU CAN POSSIBLY IMAGINE.
IT'S NOT A JOKE, BILLY. IT'S NOT FUNNY. IT'S NOT SOMETHING A SON OF MINE WILL JOKE ABOUT.
UNDERSTAND?
UH, Y--YEAH, DAD.
SORRY.

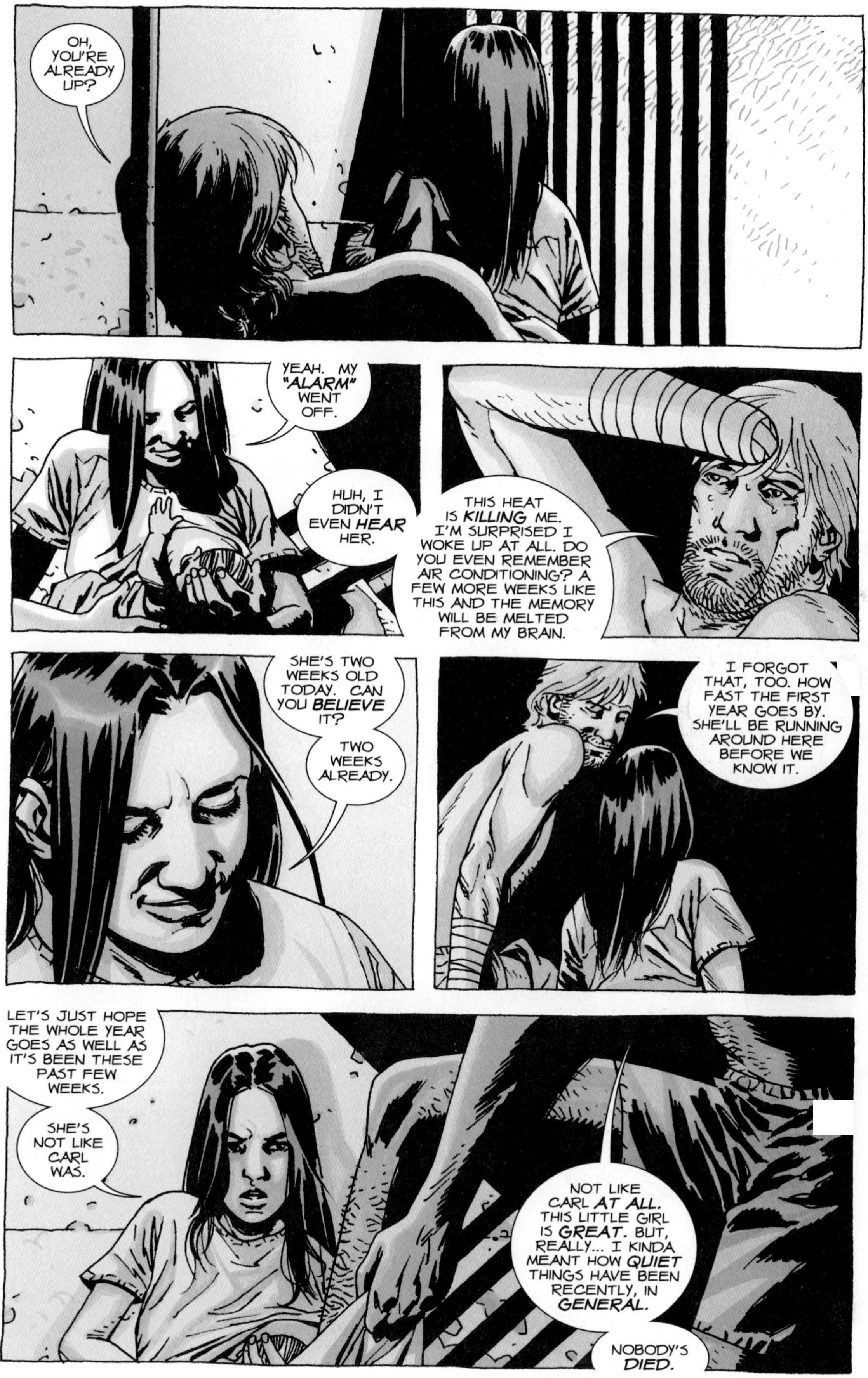
OH, YOU'RE ALREADY UP?
YEAH. MY "ALARM" WENT OFF.
HUH, I DIDN'T EVEN HEAR HER.
THIS HEAT IS KILLING ME. I'M SURPRISED I WOKE UP AT ALL. DO YOU EVEN REMEMBER AIR CONDITIONING? A FEW MORE WEEKS LIKE THIS AND THE MEMORY WILL BE MELTED FROM MY BRAIN.
SHE'S TWO WEEKS OLD TODAY. CAN YOU BELIEVE IT?
TWO WEEKS ALREADY.
I FORGOT THAT, TOO. HOW FAST THE FIRST YEAR GOES BY. SHE'LL BE RUNNING AROUND HERE BEFORE WE KNOW IT.
LET'S JUST HOPE THE WHOLE YEAR GOES AS WELL AS IT'S BEEN THESE PAST FEW WEEKS.
SHE'S NOT LIKE CARL WAS.
NOT LIKE CARL AT ALL. THIS LITTLE GIRL IS GREAT. BUT, REALLY... I KINDA MEANT HOW QUIET THINGS HAVE BEEN RECENTLY, IN GENERAL.
NOBODY'S DIED.

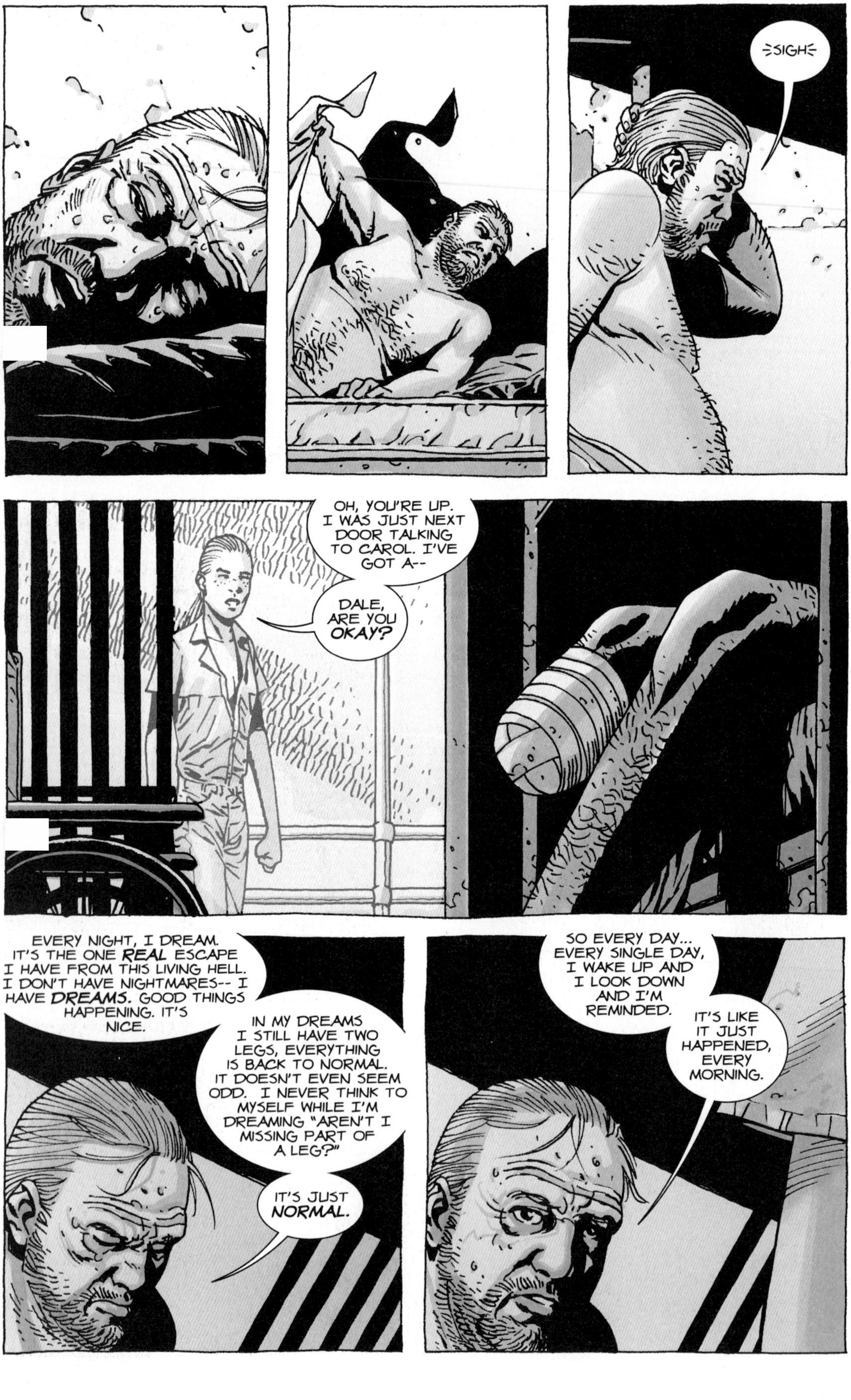
SIGH
OH, YOU'RE UP. I WAS JUST NEXT DOOR TALKING TO CAROL. I'VE GOT A--
DALE, ARE YOU OKAY?
EVERY NIGHT, I DREAM. IT'S THE ONE REAL ESCAPE I HAVE FROM THIS LIVING HELL. I DON'T HAVE NIGHTMARES-- I HAVE DREAMS. GOOD THINGS HAPPENING. IT'S NICE.
IN MY DREAMS I STILL HAVE TWO LEGS, EVERYTHING IS BACK TO NORMAL. IT DOESN'T EVEN SEEM ODD. I NEVER THINK TO MYSELF WHILE I'M DREAMING "AREN'T I MISSING PART OF A LEG?"
IT'S JUST NORMAL.
SO EVERY DAY... EVERY SINGLE DAY, I WAKE UP AND I LOOK DOWN AND I'M REMINDED.
IT'S LIKE IT JUST HAPPENED, EVERY MORNING.

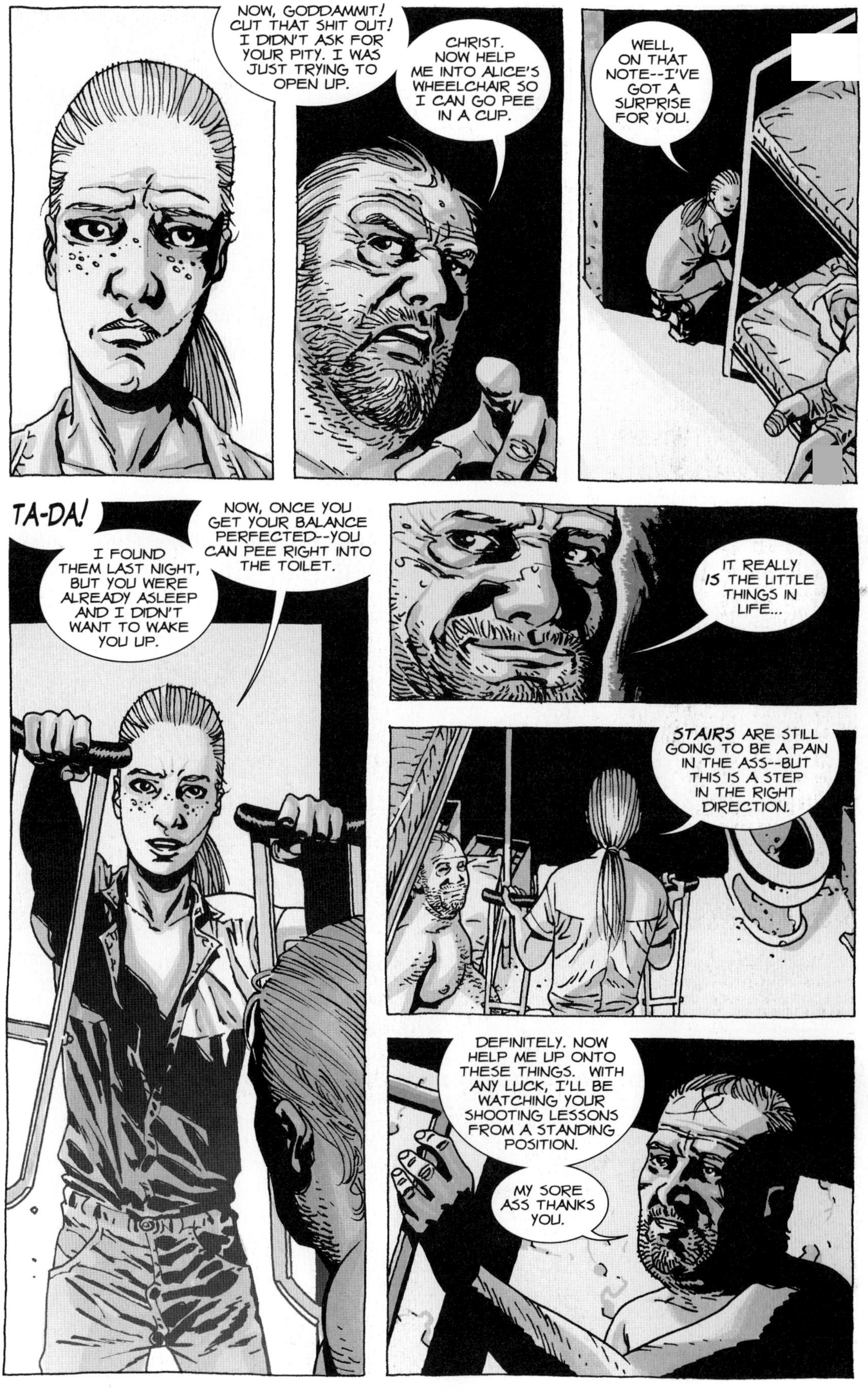
NOW, GODDAMMIT! CUT THAT SHIT OUT! I DIDN'T ASK FOR YOUR PITY. I WAS JUST TRYING TO OPEN UP.
CHRIST. NOW HELP ME INTO ALICE'S WHEELCHAIR SO I CAN GO PEE IN A CUP.
WELL, ON THAT NOTE--I'VE GOT A SURPRISE FOR YOU.
TA-DA!
I FOUND THEM LAST NIGHT, BUT YOU WERE ALREADY ASLEEP AND I DIDN'T WANT TO WAKE YOU UP.
NOW, ONCE YOU GET YOUR BALANCE PERFECTED--YOU CAN PEE RIGHT INTO THE TOILET.
IT REALLY *IS* THE LITTLE THINGS IN LIFE...
STAIRS ARE STILL GOING TO BE A PAIN IN THE ASS--BUT THIS IS A STEP IN THE RIGHT DIRECTION.
DEFINITELY. NOW HELP ME UP ONTO THESE THINGS. WITH ANY LUCK, I'LL BE WATCHING YOUR SHOOTING LESSONS FROM A STANDING POSITION.
MY SORE ASS THANKS YOU.

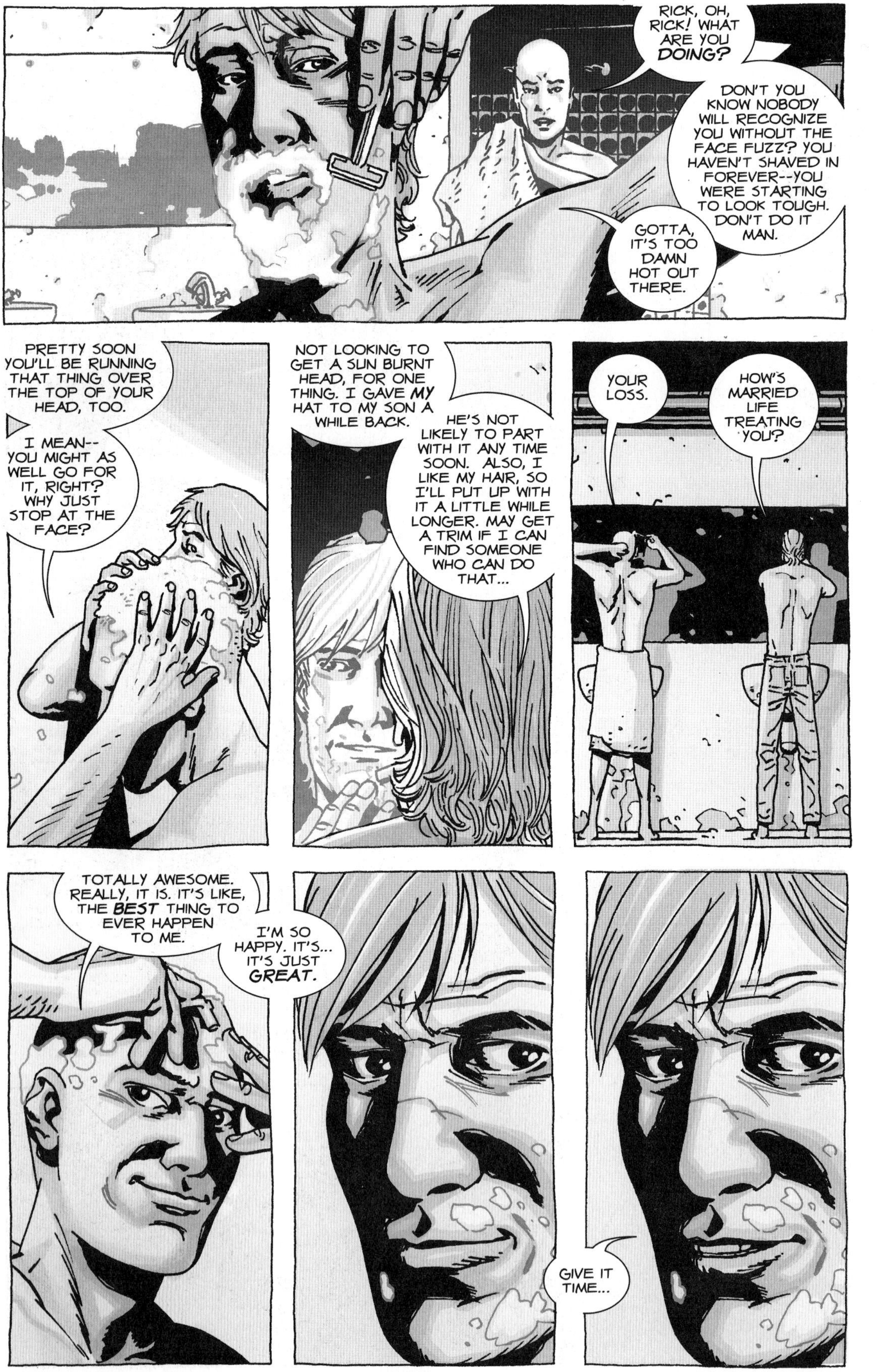
RICK, OH, RICK! WHAT ARE YOU DOING?
DON'T YOU KNOW NOBODY WILL RECOGNIZE YOU WITHOUT THE FACE FUZZ? YOU HAVEN'T SHAVED IN FOREVER--YOU WERE STARTING TO LOOK TOUGH. DON'T DO IT MAN.
GOTTA, IT'S TOO DAMN HOT OUT THERE.
PRETTY SOON YOU'LL BE RUNNING THAT THING OVER THE TOP OF YOUR HEAD, TOO.
I MEAN-- YOU MIGHT AS WELL GO FOR IT, RIGHT? WHY JUST STOP AT THE FACE?
NOT LOOKING TO GET A SUN BURNT HEAD, FOR ONE THING. I GAVE MY HAT TO MY SON A WHILE BACK.
HE'S NOT LIKELY TO PART WITH IT ANY TIME SOON. ALSO, I LIKE MY HAIR, SO I'LL PUT UP WITH IT A LITTLE WHILE LONGER. MAY GET A TRIM IF I CAN FIND SOMEONE WHO CAN DO THAT...
YOUR LOSS.
HOW'S MARRIED LIFE TREATING YOU?
TOTALLY AWESOME. REALLY, IT IS. IT'S LIKE, THE BEST THING TO EVER HAPPEN TO ME.
I'M SO HAPPY. IT'S... IT'S JUST GREAT.
GIVE IT TIME...

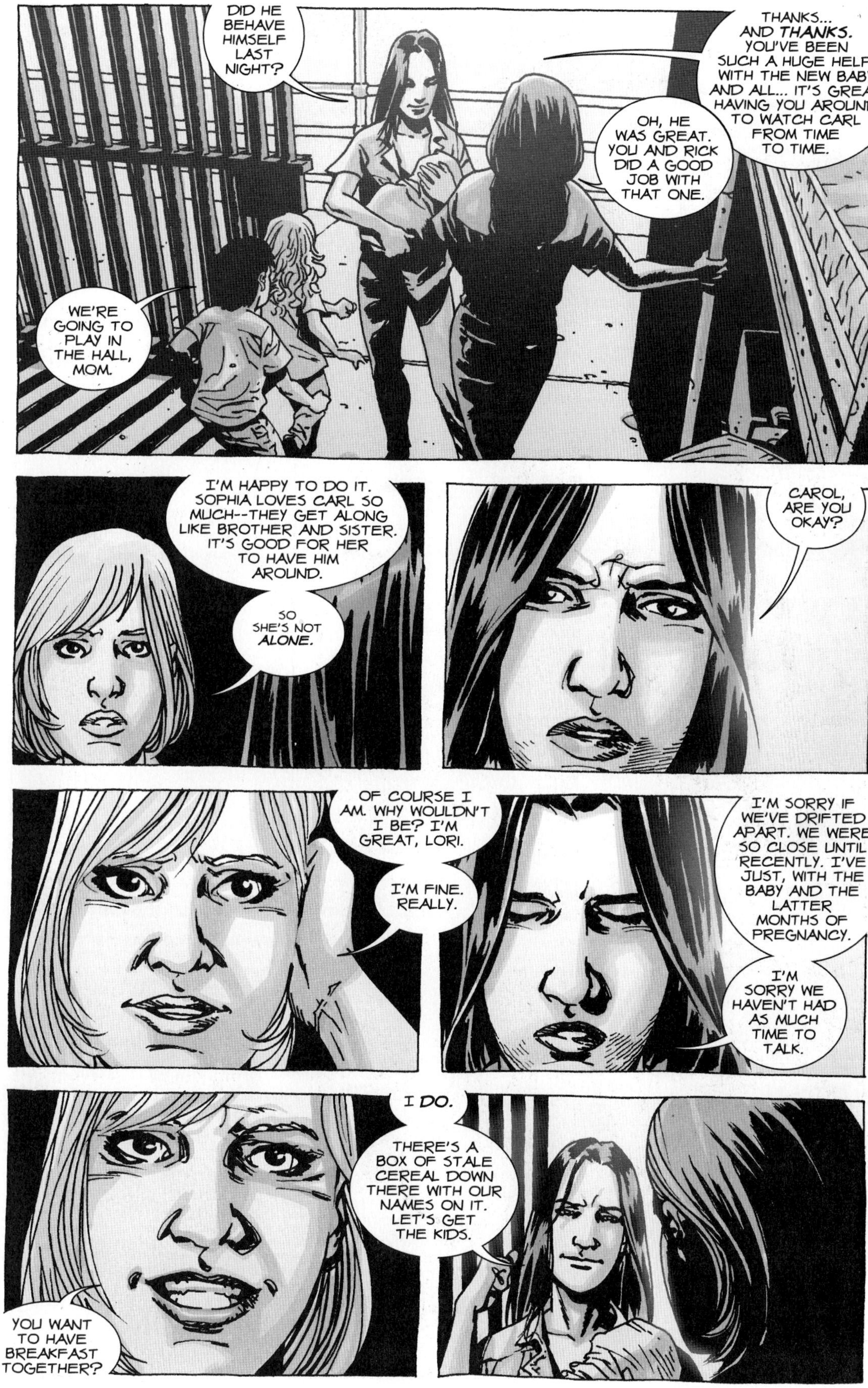
DID HE BEHAVE HIMSELF LAST NIGHT?
OH, HE WAS GREAT. YOU AND RICK DID A GOOD JOB WITH THAT ONE.
THANKS... AND *THANKS.* YOU'VE BEEN SUCH A HUGE HELP, WITH THE NEW BABY AND ALL... IT'S GREAT HAVING YOU AROUND TO WATCH CARL FROM TIME TO TIME.
WE'RE GOING TO PLAY IN THE HALL, MOM.
I'M HAPPY TO DO IT. SOPHIA LOVES CARL SO MUCH--THEY GET ALONG LIKE BROTHER AND SISTER. IT'S GOOD FOR HER TO HAVE HIM AROUND.
SO SHE'S NOT *ALONE.*
CAROL, ARE YOU OKAY?
OF COURSE I AM. WHY WOULDN'T I BE? I'M GREAT, LORI.
I'M FINE. REALLY.
I'M SORRY IF WE'VE DRIFTED APART. WE WERE SO CLOSE UNTIL RECENTLY. I'VE JUST, WITH THE BABY AND THE LATTER MONTHS OF PREGNANCY.
I'M SORRY WE HAVEN'T HAD AS MUCH TIME TO TALK.
YOU WANT TO HAVE BREAKFAST TOGETHER?
I *DO.*
THERE'S A BOX OF STALE CEREAL DOWN THERE WITH OUR NAMES ON IT. LET'S GET THE KIDS.

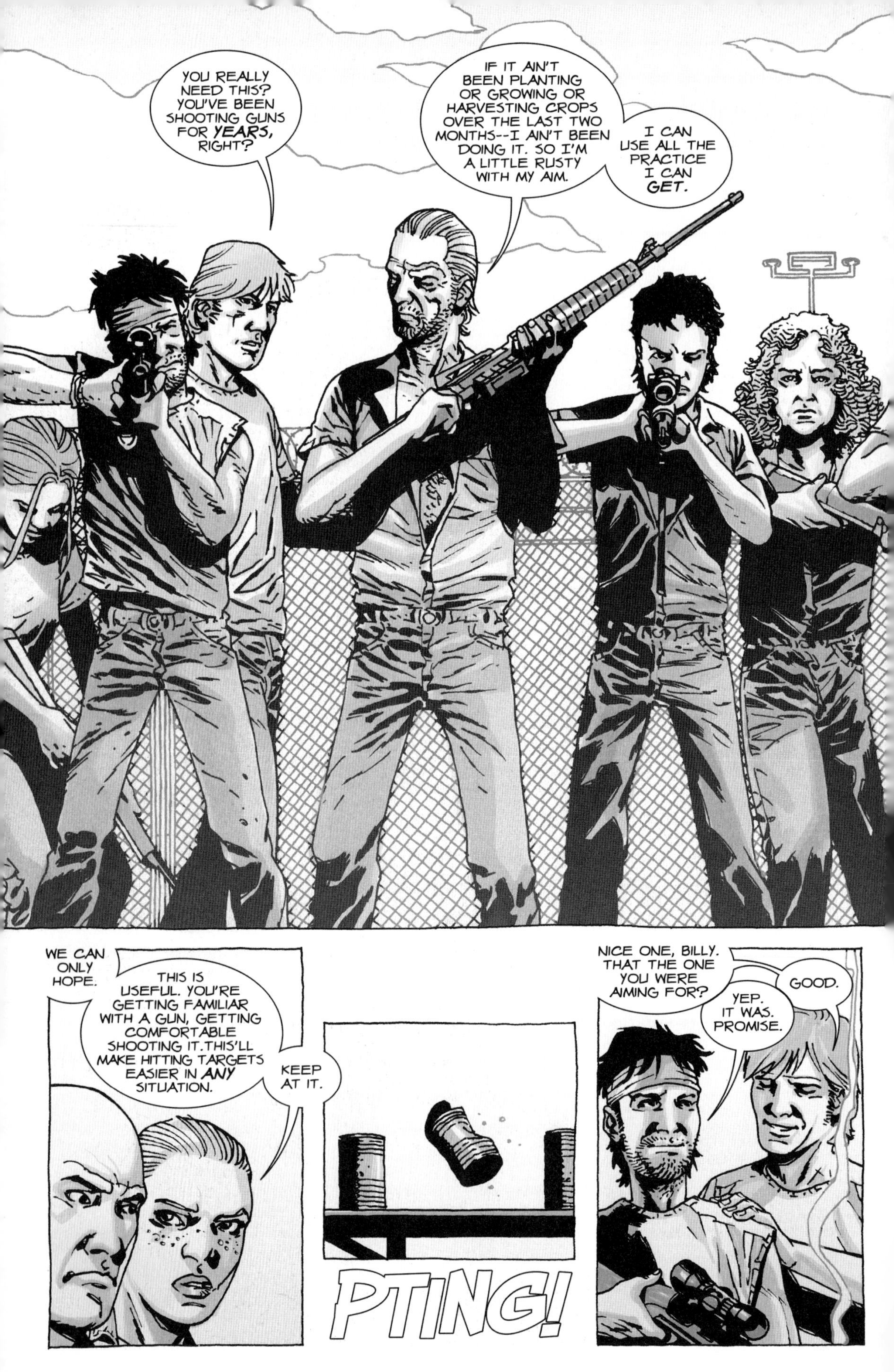
YOU REALLY NEED THIS? YOU'VE BEEN SHOOTING GUNS FOR YEARS, RIGHT?
IF IT AIN'T BEEN PLANTING OR GROWING OR HARVESTING CROPS OVER THE LAST TWO MONTHS--I AIN'T BEEN DOING IT. SO I'M A LITTLE RUSTY WITH MY AIM.
I CAN USE ALL THE PRACTICE I CAN GET.
WE CAN ONLY HOPE.
THIS IS USEFUL. YOU'RE GETTING FAMILIAR WITH A GUN, GETTING COMFORTABLE SHOOTING IT. THIS'LL MAKE HITTING TARGETS EASIER IN ANY SITUATION.
KEEP AT IT.
PTING!
NICE ONE, BILLY. THAT THE ONE YOU WERE AIMING FOR?
GOOD.
YEP. IT WAS. PROMISE.

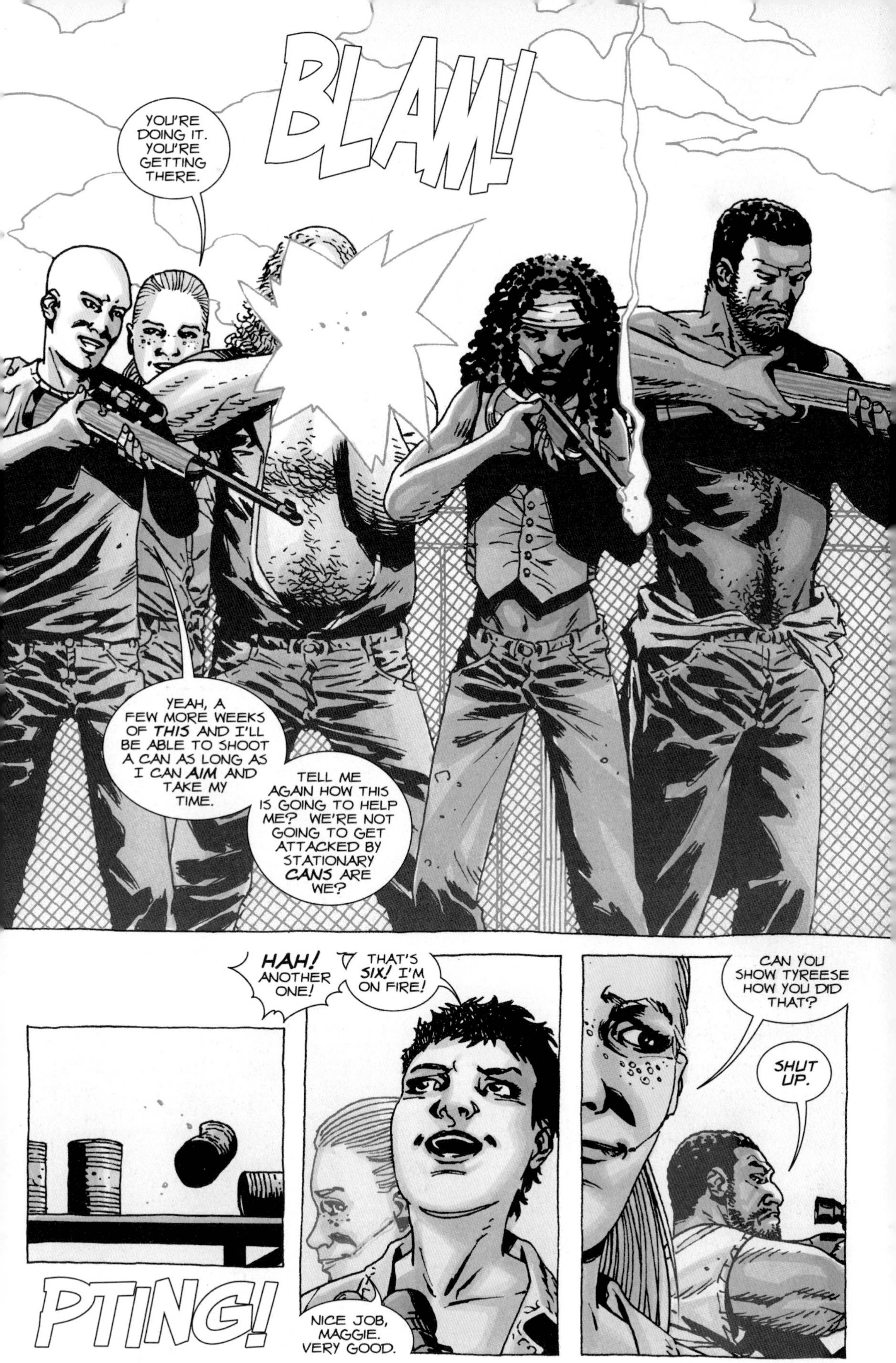
BLAM!
YOU'RE DOING IT. YOU'RE GETTING THERE.
YEAH, A FEW MORE WEEKS OF THIS AND I'LL BE ABLE TO SHOOT A CAN AS LONG AS I CAN AIM AND TAKE MY TIME.
TELL ME AGAIN HOW THIS IS GOING TO HELP ME? WE'RE NOT GOING TO GET ATTACKED BY STATIONARY CANS ARE WE?
PTING!
HAH! ANOTHER ONE!
THAT'S SIX! I'M ON FIRE!
NICE JOB, MAGGIE. VERY GOOD.
CAN YOU SHOW TYREESE HOW YOU DID THAT?
SHUT UP.

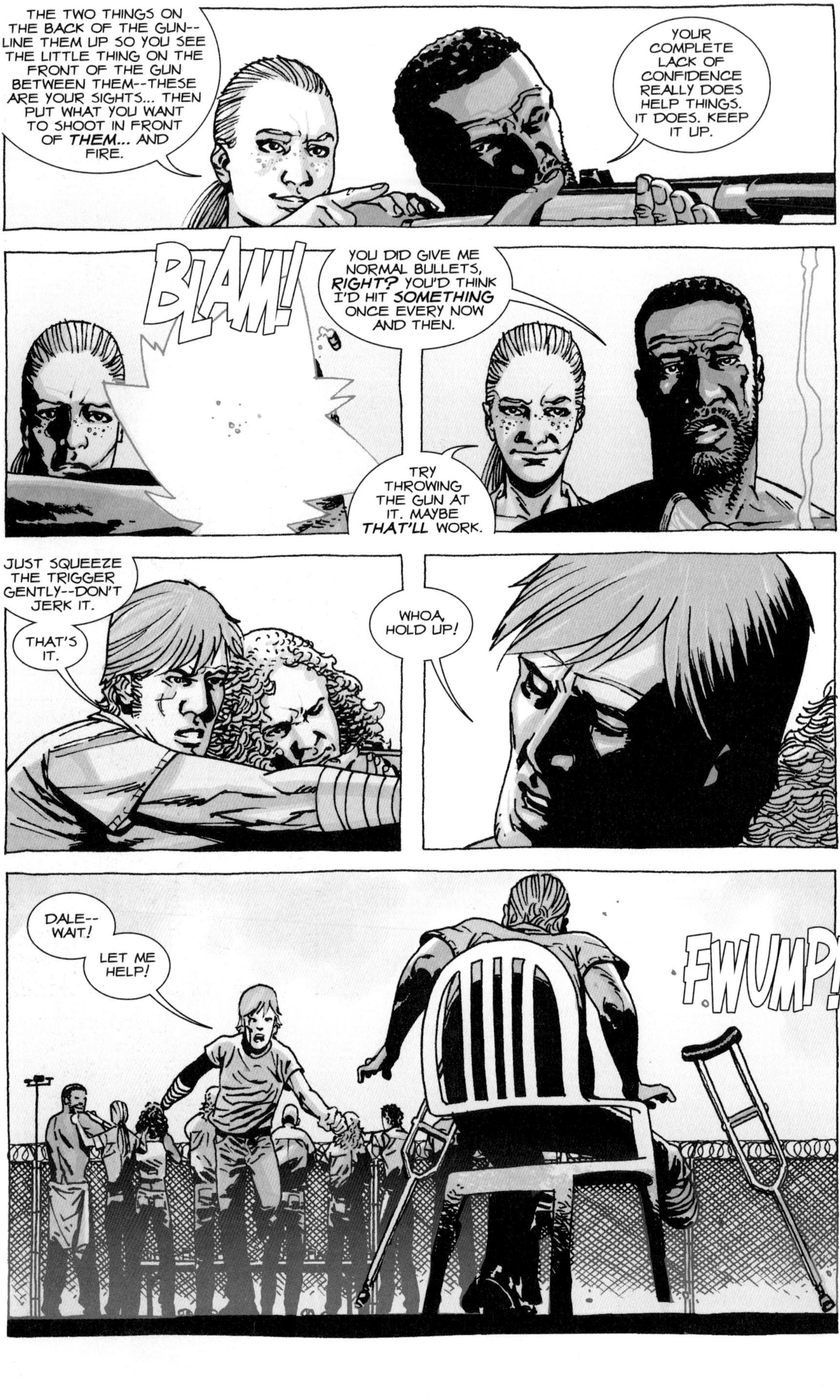
THE TWO THINGS ON THE BACK OF THE GUN--LINE THEM UP SO YOU SEE THE LITTLE THING ON THE FRONT OF THE GUN BETWEEN THEM--THESE ARE YOUR SIGHTS... THEN PUT WHAT YOU WANT TO SHOOT IN FRONT OF *THEM...* AND FIRE.
YOUR COMPLETE LACK OF CONFIDENCE REALLY DOES HELP THINGS. IT DOES. KEEP IT UP.
BLAM!
YOU DID GIVE ME NORMAL BULLETS, *RIGHT?* YOU'D THINK I'D HIT *SOMETHING* ONCE EVERY NOW AND THEN.
TRY THROWING THE GUN AT IT. MAYBE *THAT'LL* WORK.
JUST SQUEEZE THE TRIGGER GENTLY--DON'T JERK IT.
THAT'S IT.
WHOA, HOLD UP!
DALE--WAIT!
LET ME HELP!
FWUMP!

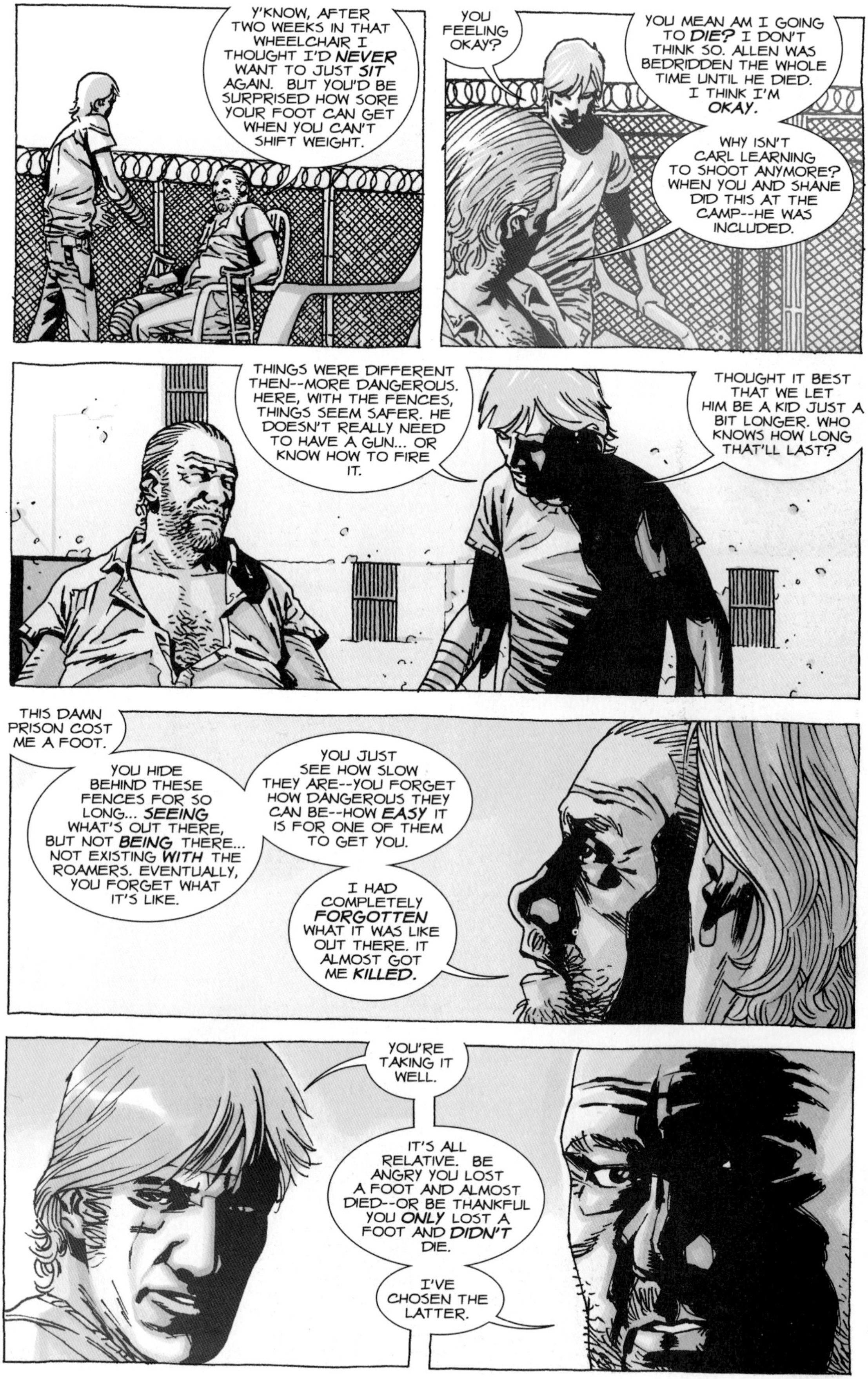
Y'KNOW, AFTER TWO WEEKS IN THAT WHEELCHAIR I THOUGHT I'D NEVER WANT TO JUST SIT AGAIN. BUT YOU'D BE SURPRISED HOW SORE YOUR FOOT CAN GET WHEN YOU CAN'T SHIFT WEIGHT.
YOU FEELING OKAY?
YOU MEAN AM I GOING TO DIE? I DON'T THINK SO. ALLEN WAS BEDRIDDEN THE WHOLE TIME UNTIL HE DIED. I THINK I'M OKAY.
WHY ISN'T CARL LEARNING TO SHOOT ANYMORE? WHEN YOU AND SHANE DID THIS AT THE CAMP--HE WAS INCLUDED.
THINGS WERE DIFFERENT THEN--MORE DANGEROUS. HERE, WITH THE FENCES, THINGS SEEM SAFER. HE DOESN'T REALLY NEED TO HAVE A GUN... OR KNOW HOW TO FIRE IT.
THOUGHT IT BEST THAT WE LET HIM BE A KID JUST A BIT LONGER. WHO KNOWS HOW LONG THAT'LL LAST?
THIS DAMN PRISON COST ME A FOOT.
YOU HIDE BEHIND THESE FENCES FOR SO LONG... SEEING WHAT'S OUT THERE, BUT NOT BEING THERE... NOT EXISTING WITH THE ROAMERS. EVENTUALLY, YOU FORGET WHAT IT'S LIKE.
YOU JUST SEE HOW SLOW THEY ARE--YOU FORGET HOW DANGEROUS THEY CAN BE--HOW EASY IT IS FOR ONE OF THEM TO GET YOU.
I HAD COMPLETELY FORGOTTEN WHAT IT WAS LIKE OUT THERE. IT ALMOST GOT ME KILLED.
YOU'RE TAKING IT WELL.
IT'S ALL RELATIVE. BE ANGRY YOU LOST A FOOT AND ALMOST DIED--OR BE THANKFUL YOU ONLY LOST A FOOT AND DIDN'T DIE.
I'VE CHOSEN THE LATTER.

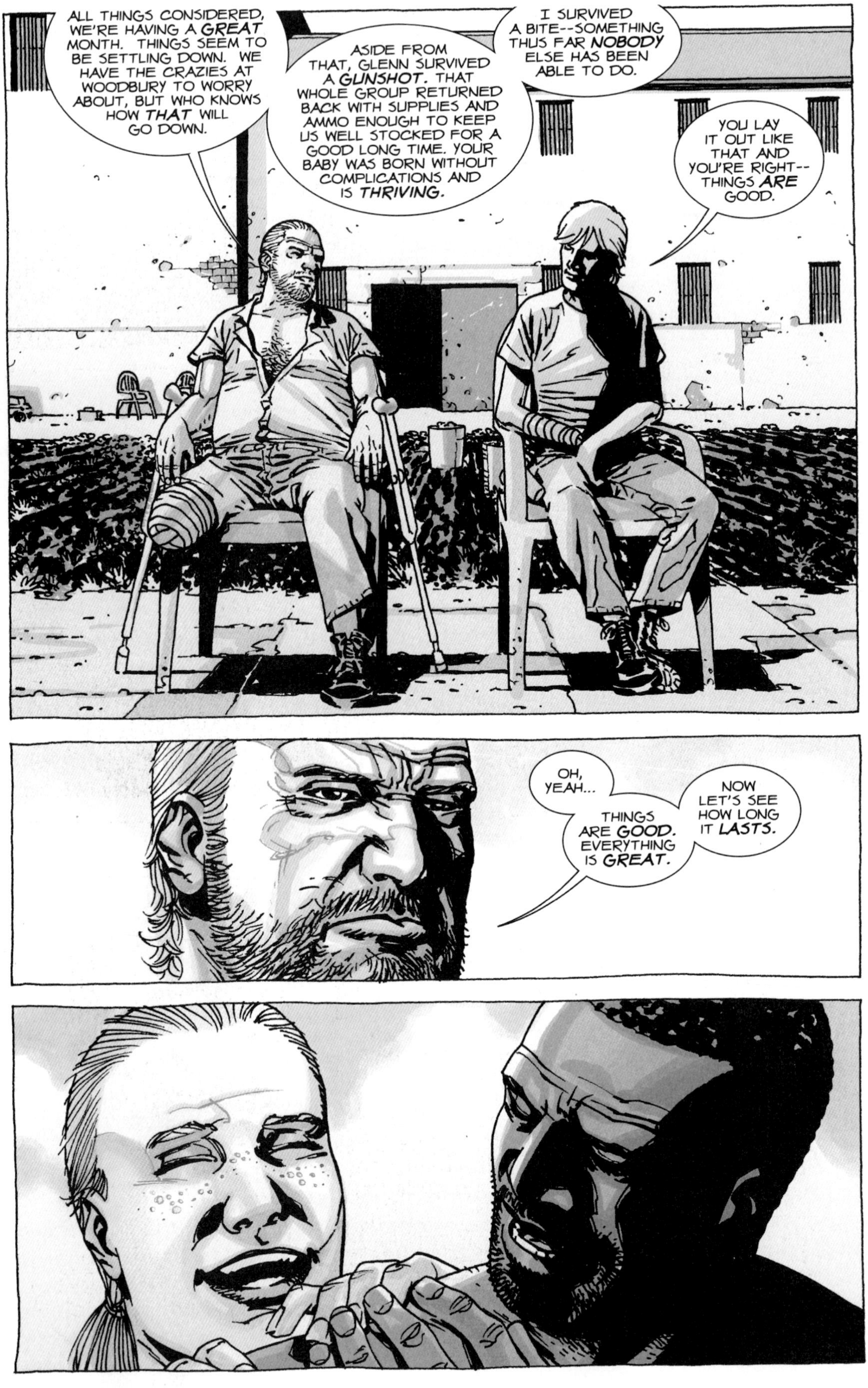
ALL THINGS CONSIDERED, WE'RE HAVING A GREAT MONTH. THINGS SEEM TO BE SETTLING DOWN. WE HAVE THE CRAZIES AT WOODBURY TO WORRY ABOUT, BUT WHO KNOWS HOW THAT WILL GO DOWN.
ASIDE FROM THAT, GLENN SURVIVED A GUNSHOT. THAT WHOLE GROUP RETURNED BACK WITH SUPPLIES AND AMMO ENOUGH TO KEEP US WELL STOCKED FOR A GOOD LONG TIME. YOUR BABY WAS BORN WITHOUT COMPLICATIONS AND IS THRIVING.
I SURVIVED A BITE--SOMETHING THUS FAR NOBODY ELSE HAS BEEN ABLE TO DO.
YOU LAY IT OUT LIKE THAT AND YOU'RE RIGHT-- THINGS ARE GOOD.
OH, YEAH...
THINGS ARE GOOD. EVERYTHING IS GREAT.
NOW LET'S SEE HOW LONG IT LASTS.

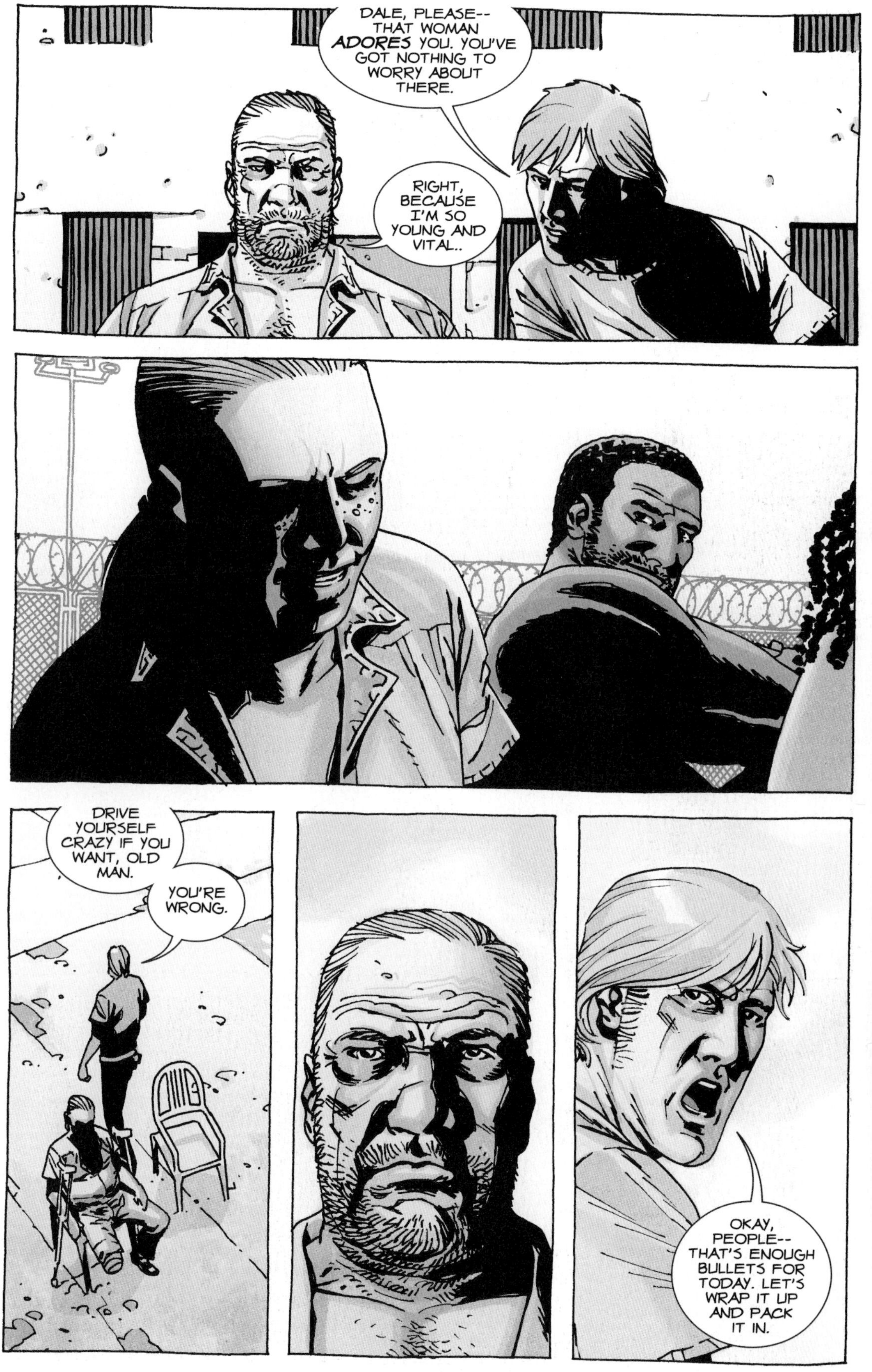
DALE, PLEASE-- THAT WOMAN ADORES YOU. YOU'VE GOT NOTHING TO WORRY ABOUT THERE.
RIGHT, BECAUSE I'M SO YOUNG AND VITAL..
DRIVE YOURSELF CRAZY IF YOU WANT, OLD MAN.
YOU'RE WRONG.
OKAY, PEOPLE-- THAT'S ENOUGH BULLETS FOR TODAY. LET'S WRAP IT UP AND PACK IT IN.

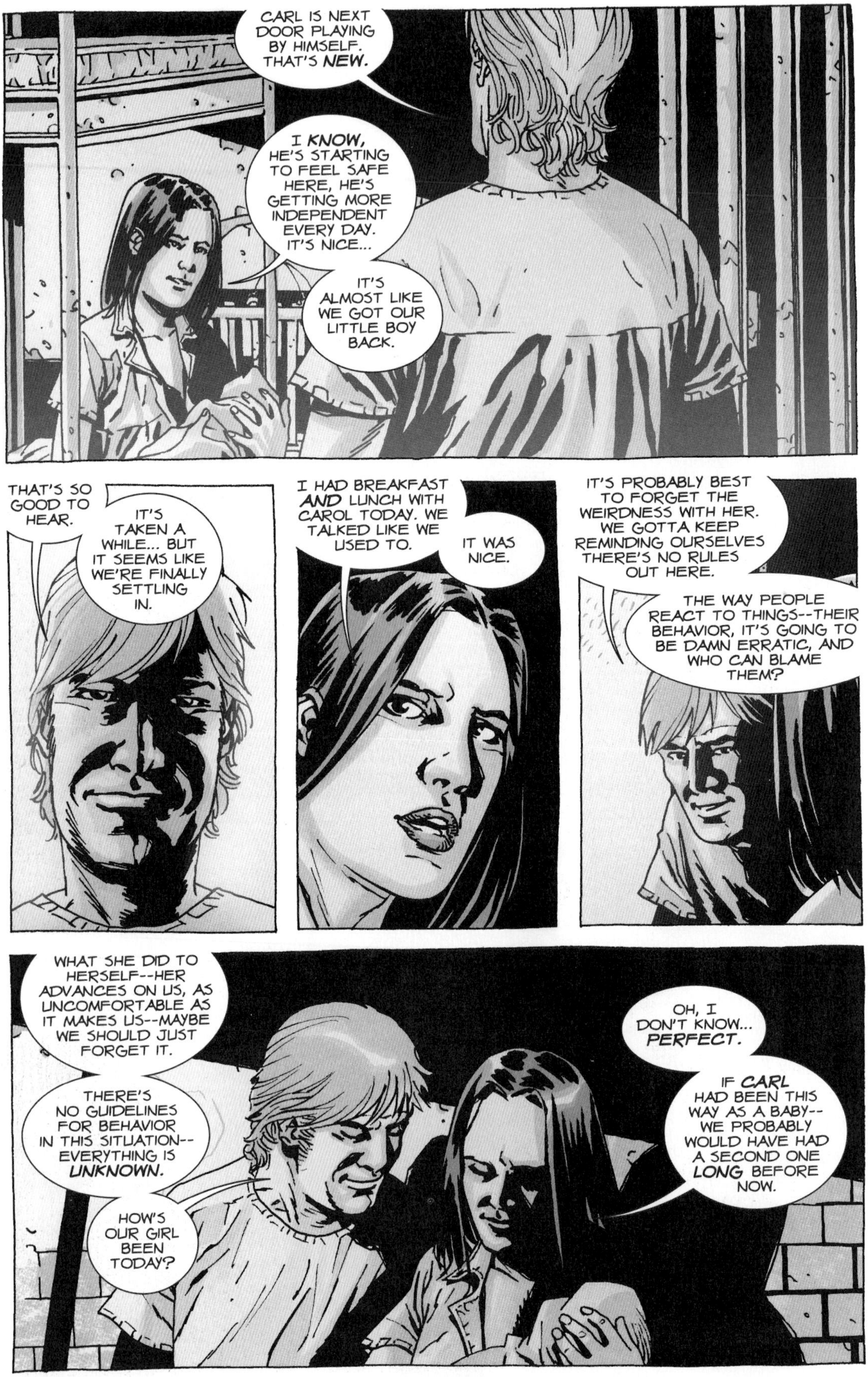
CARL IS NEXT DOOR PLAYING BY HIMSELF. THAT'S NEW.
I KNOW, HE'S STARTING TO FEEL SAFE HERE, HE'S GETTING MORE INDEPENDENT EVERY DAY. IT'S NICE...
IT'S ALMOST LIKE WE GOT OUR LITTLE BOY BACK.
THAT'S SO GOOD TO HEAR.
IT'S TAKEN A WHILE... BUT IT SEEMS LIKE WE'RE FINALLY SETTLING IN.
I HAD BREAKFAST AND LUNCH WITH CAROL TODAY. WE TALKED LIKE WE USED TO.
IT WAS NICE.
IT'S PROBABLY BEST TO FORGET THE WEIRDNESS WITH HER. WE GOTTA KEEP REMINDING OURSELVES THERE'S NO RULES OUT HERE.
THE WAY PEOPLE REACT TO THINGS--THEIR BEHAVIOR, IT'S GOING TO BE DAMN ERRATIC, AND WHO CAN BLAME THEM?
WHAT SHE DID TO HERSELF--HER ADVANCES ON US, AS UNCOMFORTABLE AS IT MAKES US--MAYBE WE SHOULD JUST FORGET IT.
THERE'S NO GUIDELINES FOR BEHAVIOR IN THIS SITUATION--EVERYTHING IS UNKNOWN.
HOW'S OUR GIRL BEEN TODAY?
OH, I DON'T KNOW... PERFECT.
IF CARL HAD BEEN THIS WAY AS A BABY--WE PROBABLY WOULD HAVE HAD A SECOND ONE LONG BEFORE NOW.

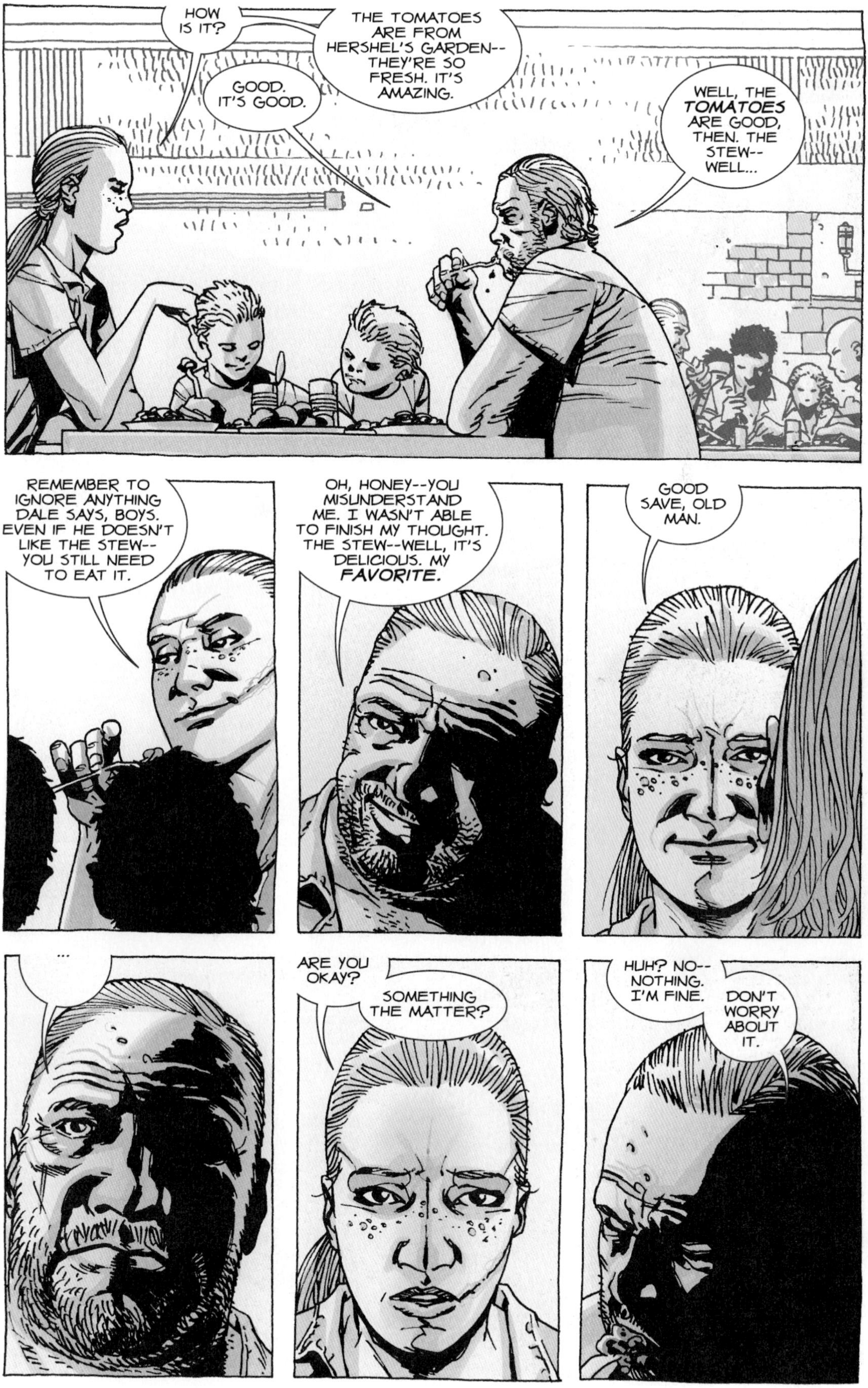
HOW IS IT?
THE TOMATOES ARE FROM HERSHEL'S GARDEN-- THEY'RE SO FRESH. IT'S AMAZING.
GOOD. IT'S GOOD.
WELL, THE *TOMATOES* ARE GOOD, THEN. THE STEW-- WELL...
REMEMBER TO IGNORE ANYTHING DALE SAYS, BOYS. EVEN IF HE DOESN'T LIKE THE STEW-- YOU STILL NEED TO EAT IT.
OH, HONEY--YOU MISUNDERSTAND ME. I WASN'T ABLE TO FINISH MY THOUGHT. THE STEW--WELL, IT'S DELICIOUS. MY *FAVORITE.*
GOOD SAVE, OLD MAN.
...
ARE YOU OKAY?
SOMETHING THE MATTER?
HUH? NO-- NOTHING. I'M FINE.
DON'T WORRY ABOUT IT.

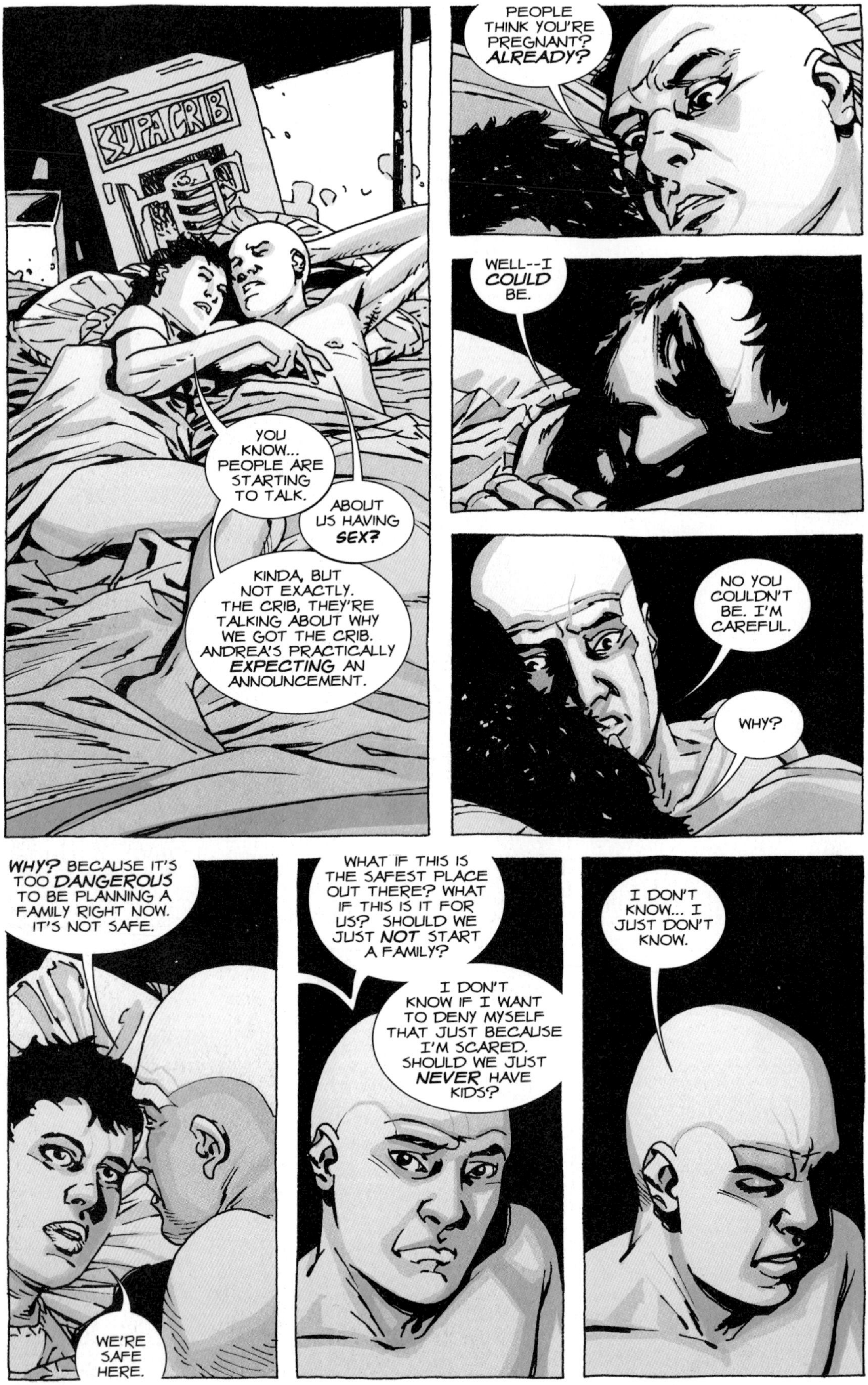
SUPACRIB
YOU KNOW... PEOPLE ARE STARTING TO TALK.
ABOUT US HAVING SEX?
KINDA, BUT NOT EXACTLY. THE CRIB, THEY'RE TALKING ABOUT WHY WE GOT THE CRIB. ANDREA'S PRACTICALLY EXPECTING AN ANNOUNCEMENT.
PEOPLE THINK YOU'RE PREGNANT? ALREADY?
WELL--I COULD BE.
NO YOU COULDN'T BE. I'M CAREFUL.
WHY?
WHY? BECAUSE IT'S TOO DANGEROUS TO BE PLANNING A FAMILY RIGHT NOW. IT'S NOT SAFE.
WE'RE SAFE HERE.
WHAT IF THIS IS THE SAFEST PLACE OUT THERE? WHAT IF THIS IS IT FOR US? SHOULD WE JUST NOT START A FAMILY?
I DON'T KNOW IF I WANT TO DENY MYSELF THAT JUST BECAUSE I'M SCARED. SHOULD WE JUST NEVER HAVE KIDS?
I DON'T KNOW... I JUST DON'T KNOW.

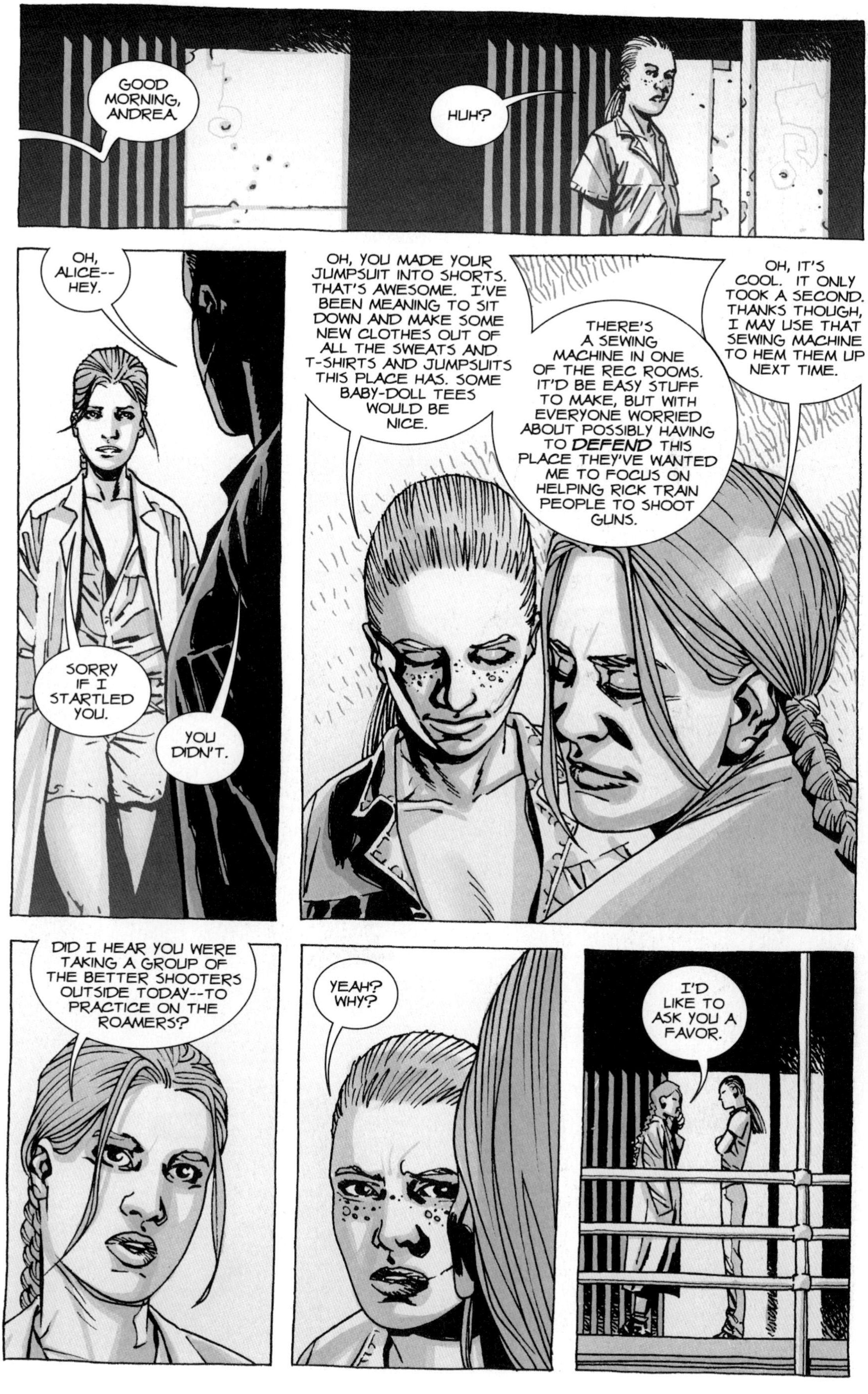
GOOD MORNING, ANDREA.
HUH?
OH, ALICE-- HEY.
SORRY IF I STARTLED YOU.
YOU DIDN'T.
OH, YOU MADE YOUR JUMPSUIT INTO SHORTS. THAT'S AWESOME. I'VE BEEN MEANING TO SIT DOWN AND MAKE SOME NEW CLOTHES OUT OF ALL THE SWEATS AND T-SHIRTS AND JUMPSUITS THIS PLACE HAS. SOME BABY-DOLL TEES WOULD BE NICE.
THERE'S A SEWING MACHINE IN ONE OF THE REC ROOMS. IT'D BE EASY STUFF TO MAKE, BUT WITH EVERYONE WORRIED ABOUT POSSIBLY HAVING TO DEFEND THIS PLACE THEY'VE WANTED ME TO FOCUS ON HELPING RICK TRAIN PEOPLE TO SHOOT GUNS.
OH, IT'S COOL. IT ONLY TOOK A SECOND. THANKS THOUGH, I MAY USE THAT SEWING MACHINE TO HEM THEM UP NEXT TIME.
DID I HEAR YOU WERE TAKING A GROUP OF THE BETTER SHOOTERS OUTSIDE TODAY--TO PRACTICE ON THE ROAMERS?
YEAH? WHY?
I'D LIKE TO ASK YOU A FAVOR.

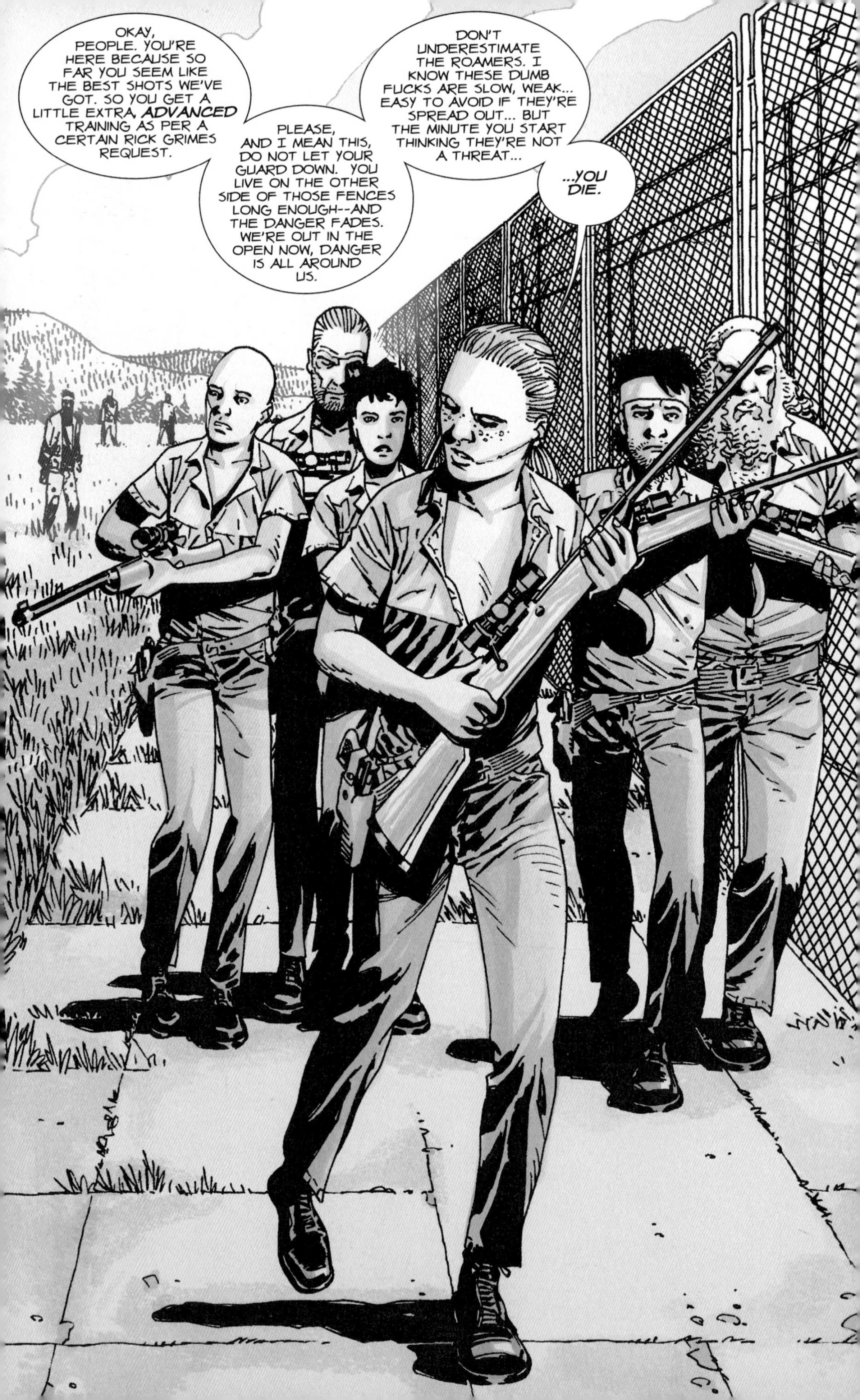
OKAY, PEOPLE. YOU'RE HERE BECAUSE SO FAR YOU SEEM LIKE THE BEST SHOTS WE'VE GOT. SO YOU GET A LITTLE EXTRA, ADVANCED TRAINING AS PER A CERTAIN RICK GRIMES REQUEST.
PLEASE, AND I MEAN THIS, DO NOT LET YOUR GUARD DOWN. YOU LIVE ON THE OTHER SIDE OF THOSE FENCES LONG ENOUGH--AND THE DANGER FADES. WE'RE OUT IN THE OPEN NOW, DANGER IS ALL AROUND US.
DON'T UNDERESTIMATE THE ROAMERS. I KNOW THESE DUMB FUCKS ARE SLOW, WEAK... EASY TO AVOID IF THEY'RE SPREAD OUT... BUT THE MINUTE YOU START THINKING THEY'RE NOT A THREAT...
...YOU DIE.

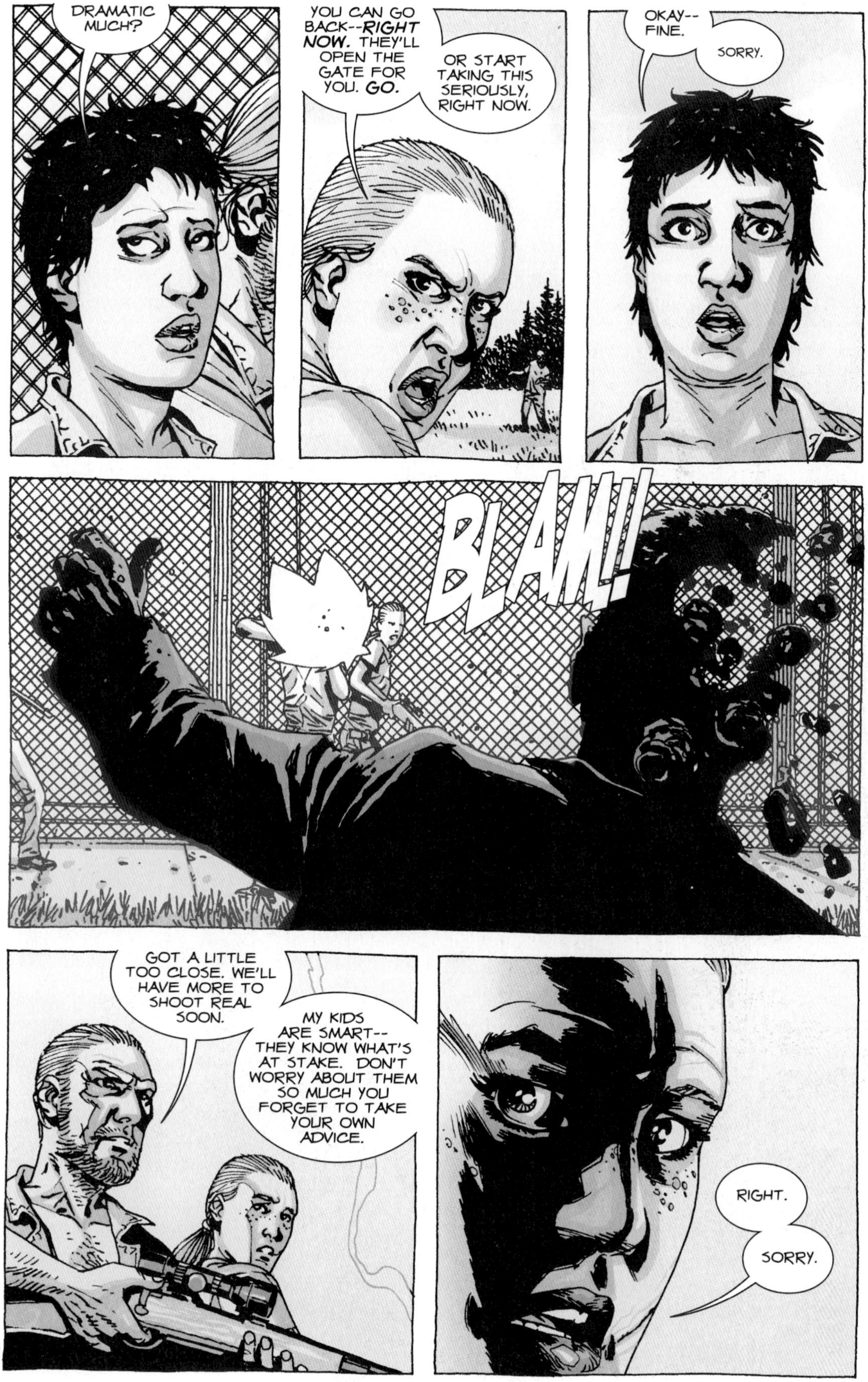
DRAMATIC MUCH?
YOU CAN GO BACK--RIGHT NOW. THEY'LL OPEN THE GATE FOR YOU. GO.
OR START TAKING THIS SERIOUSLY, RIGHT NOW.
OKAY-- FINE.
SORRY.
BLAM!!
GOT A LITTLE TOO CLOSE. WE'LL HAVE MORE TO SHOOT REAL SOON.
MY KIDS ARE SMART-- THEY KNOW WHAT'S AT STAKE. DON'T WORRY ABOUT THEM SO MUCH YOU FORGET TO TAKE YOUR OWN ADVICE.
RIGHT.
SORRY.

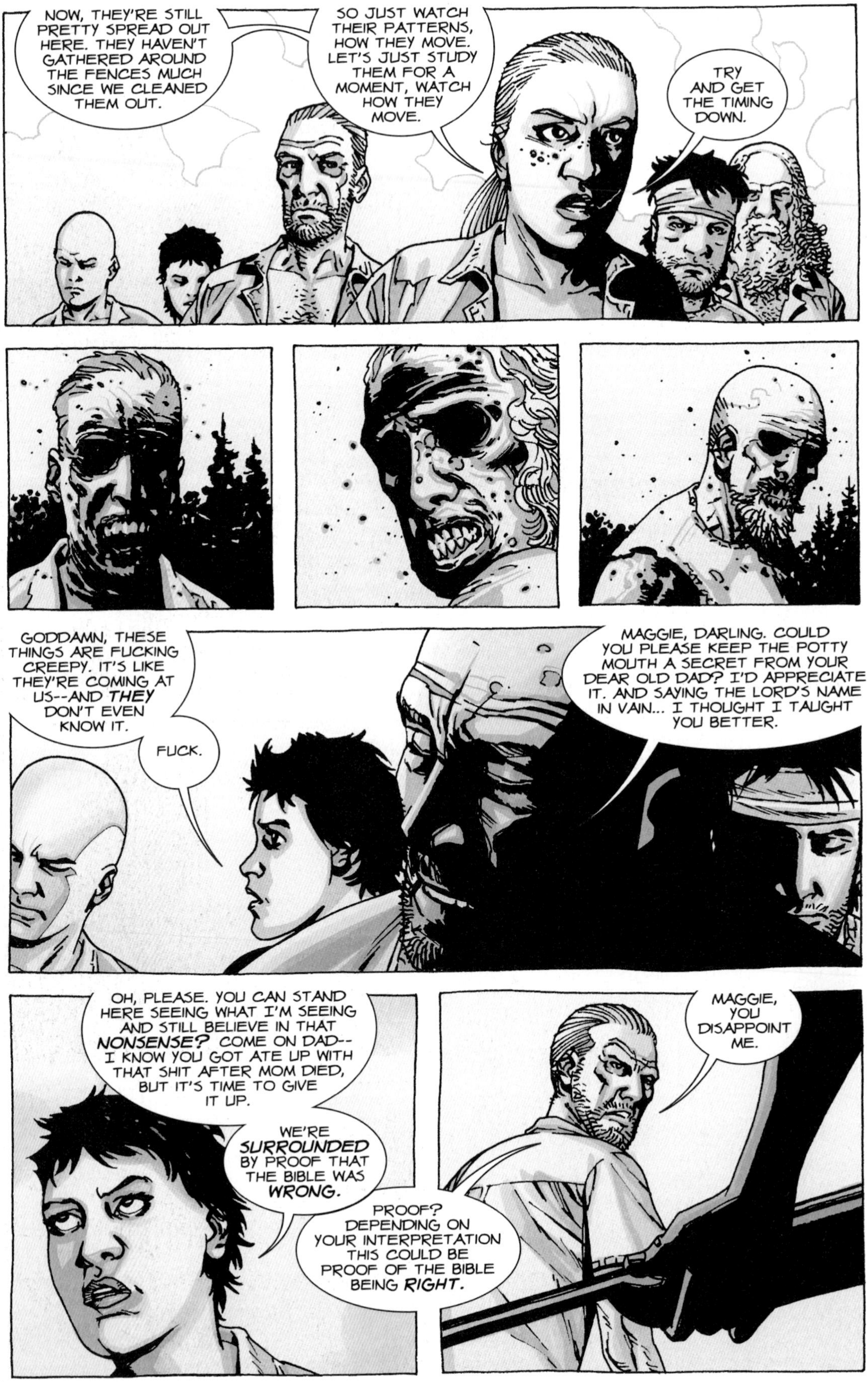
NOW, THEY'RE STILL PRETTY SPREAD OUT HERE. THEY HAVEN'T GATHERED AROUND THE FENCES MUCH SINCE WE CLEANED THEM OUT.
SO JUST WATCH THEIR PATTERNS, HOW THEY MOVE. LET'S JUST STUDY THEM FOR A MOMENT, WATCH HOW THEY MOVE.
TRY AND GET THE TIMING DOWN.
GODDAMN, THESE THINGS ARE FUCKING CREEPY. IT'S LIKE THEY'RE COMING AT US--AND *THEY* DON'T EVEN KNOW IT.
FUCK.
MAGGIE, DARLING. COULD YOU PLEASE KEEP THE POTTY MOUTH A SECRET FROM YOUR DEAR OLD DAD? I'D APPRECIATE IT. AND SAYING THE LORD'S NAME IN VAIN... I THOUGHT I TAUGHT YOU BETTER.
OH, PLEASE. YOU CAN STAND HERE SEEING WHAT I'M SEEING AND STILL BELIEVE IN THAT ***NONSENSE?*** COME ON DAD-- I KNOW YOU GOT ATE UP WITH THAT SHIT AFTER MOM DIED, BUT IT'S TIME TO GIVE IT UP.
WE'RE ***SURROUNDED*** BY PROOF THAT THE BIBLE WAS ***WRONG.***
PROOF? DEPENDING ON YOUR INTERPRETATION THIS COULD BE PROOF OF THE BIBLE BEING ***RIGHT.***
MAGGIE, YOU DISAPPOINT ME.

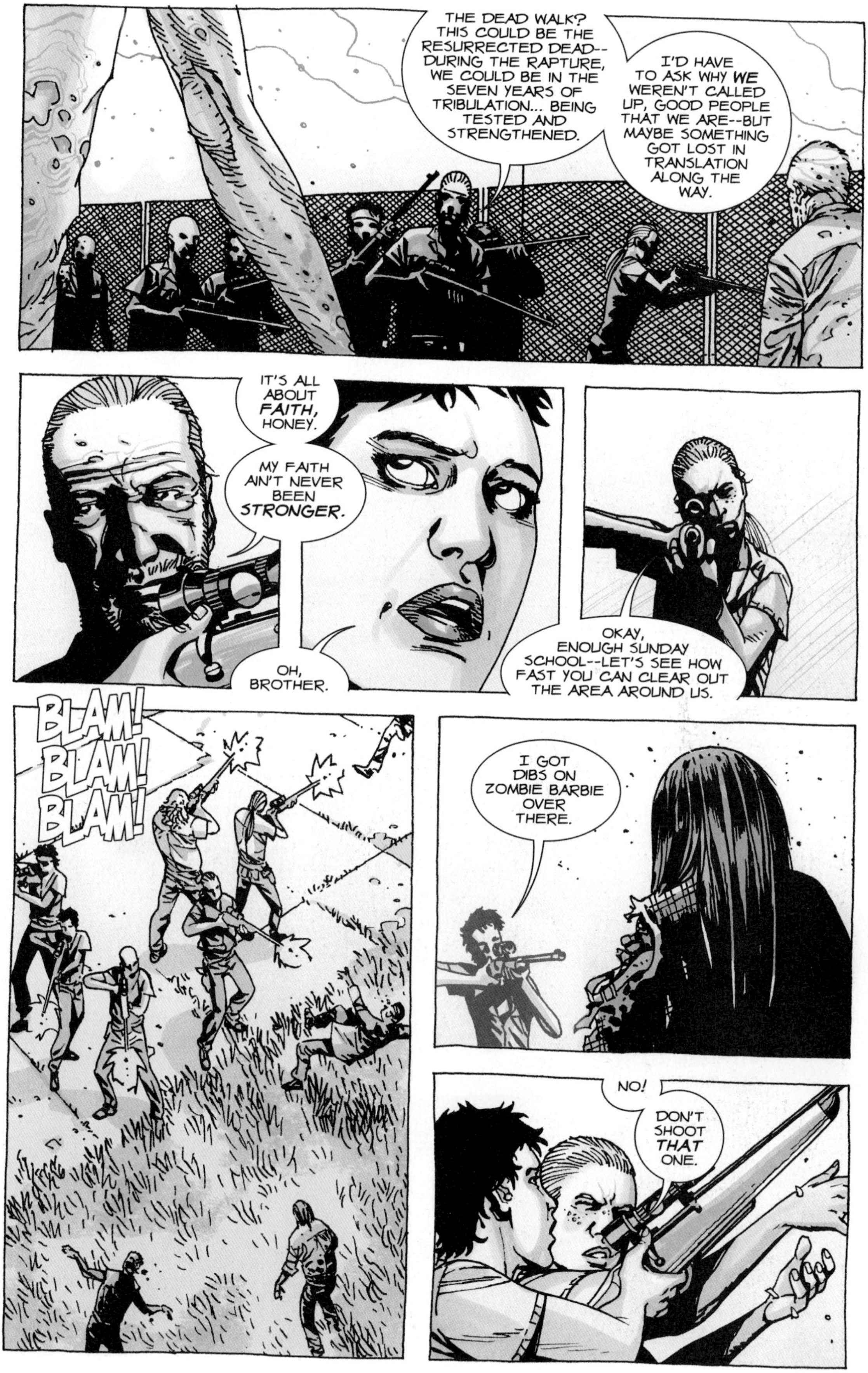
THE DEAD WALK? THIS COULD BE THE RESURRECTED DEAD--DURING THE RAPTURE, WE COULD BE IN THE SEVEN YEARS OF TRIBULATION... BEING TESTED AND STRENGTHENED.
I'D HAVE TO ASK WHY WE WEREN'T CALLED UP, GOOD PEOPLE THAT WE ARE--BUT MAYBE SOMETHING GOT LOST IN TRANSLATION ALONG THE WAY.
IT'S ALL ABOUT FAITH, HONEY.
MY FAITH AIN'T NEVER BEEN STRONGER.
OH, BROTHER.
OKAY, ENOUGH SUNDAY SCHOOL--LET'S SEE HOW FAST YOU CAN CLEAR OUT THE AREA AROUND US.
BLAM! BLAM! BLAM!
I GOT DIBS ON ZOMBIE BARBIE OVER THERE.
NO!
DON'T SHOOT THAT ONE.

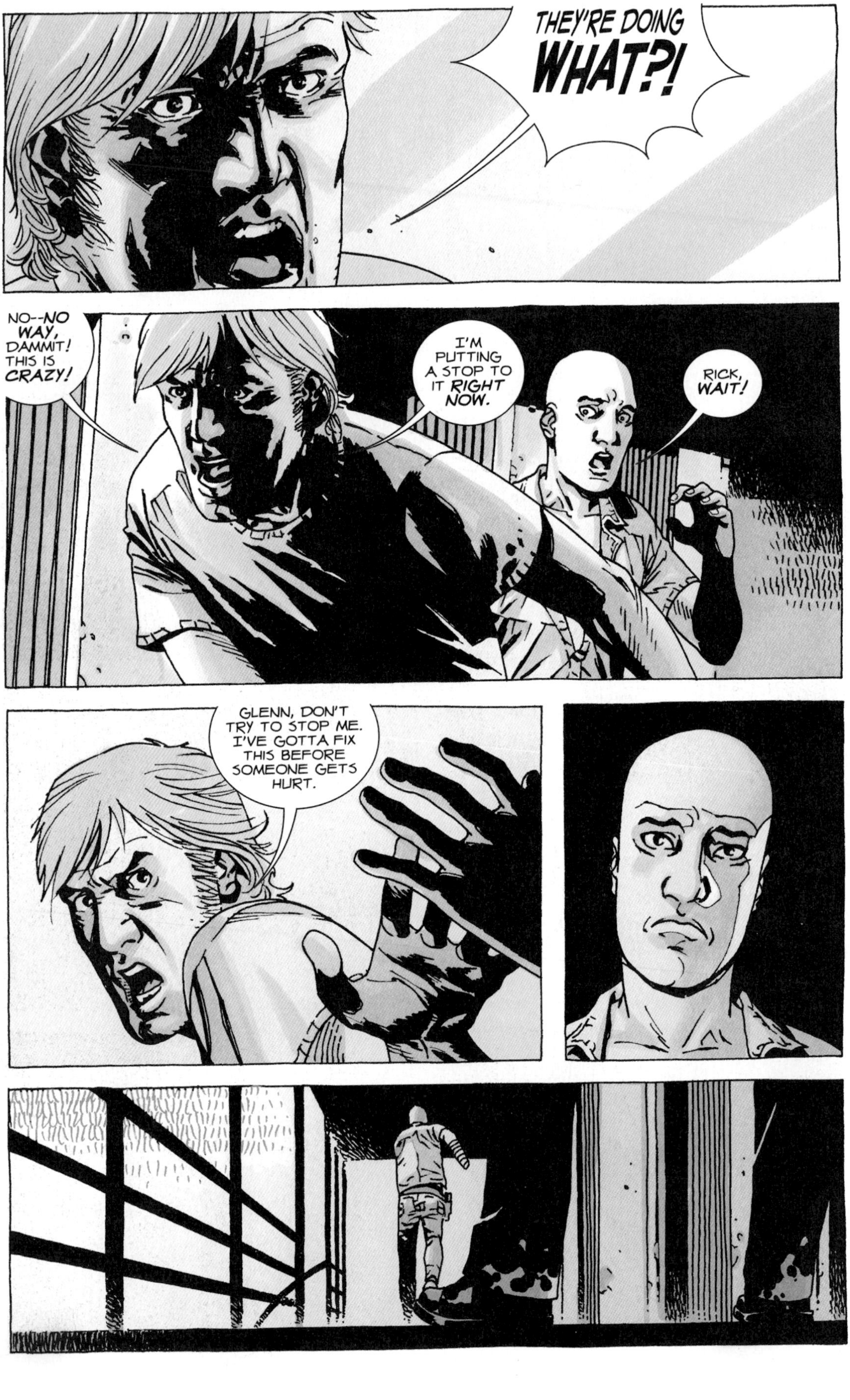
THEY'RE DOING WHAT?!
NO--NO WAY, DAMMIT! THIS IS CRAZY!
I'M PUTTING A STOP TO IT RIGHT NOW.
RICK, WAIT!
GLENN, DON'T TRY TO STOP ME. I'VE GOTTA FIX THIS BEFORE SOMEONE GETS HURT.

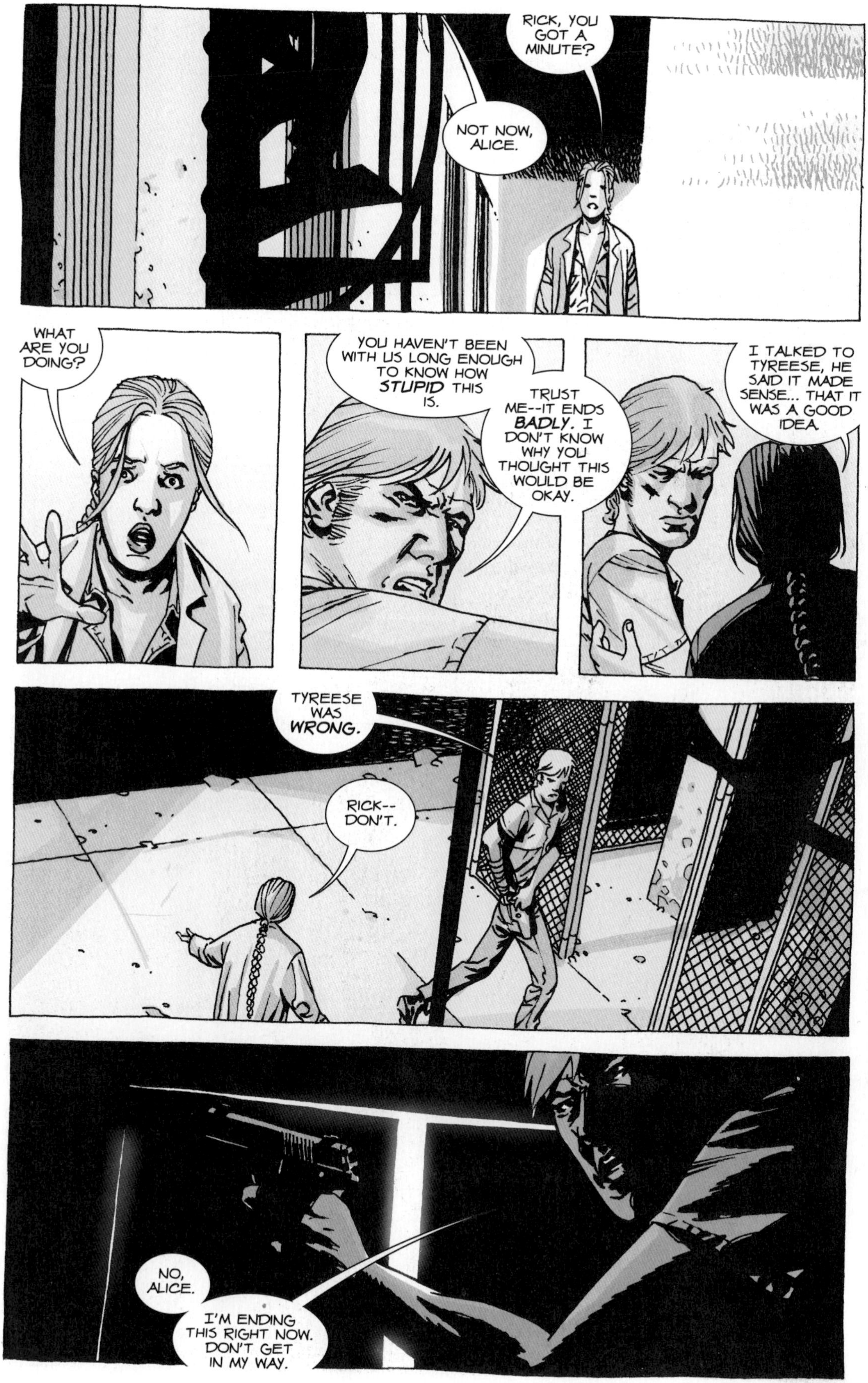
RICK, YOU GOT A MINUTE?
NOT NOW, ALICE.
WHAT ARE YOU DOING?
YOU HAVEN'T BEEN WITH US LONG ENOUGH TO KNOW HOW STUPID THIS IS.
TRUST ME--IT ENDS BADLY. I DON'T KNOW WHY YOU THOUGHT THIS WOULD BE OKAY.
I TALKED TO TYREESE, HE SAID IT MADE SENSE... THAT IT WAS A GOOD IDEA.
TYREESE WAS WRONG.
RICK-- DON'T.
NO, ALICE.
I'M ENDING THIS RIGHT NOW. DON'T GET IN MY WAY.

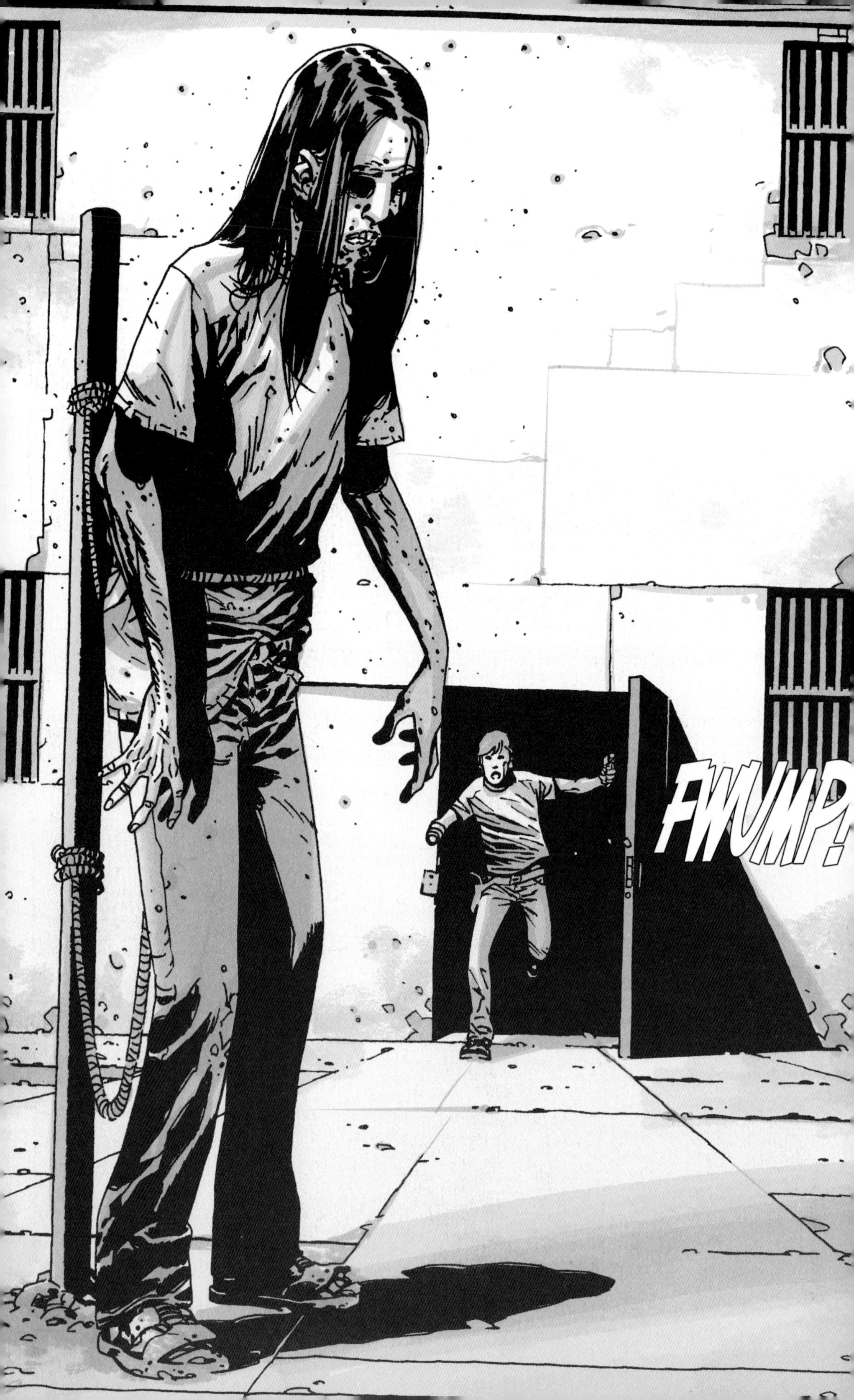
FWUMP!

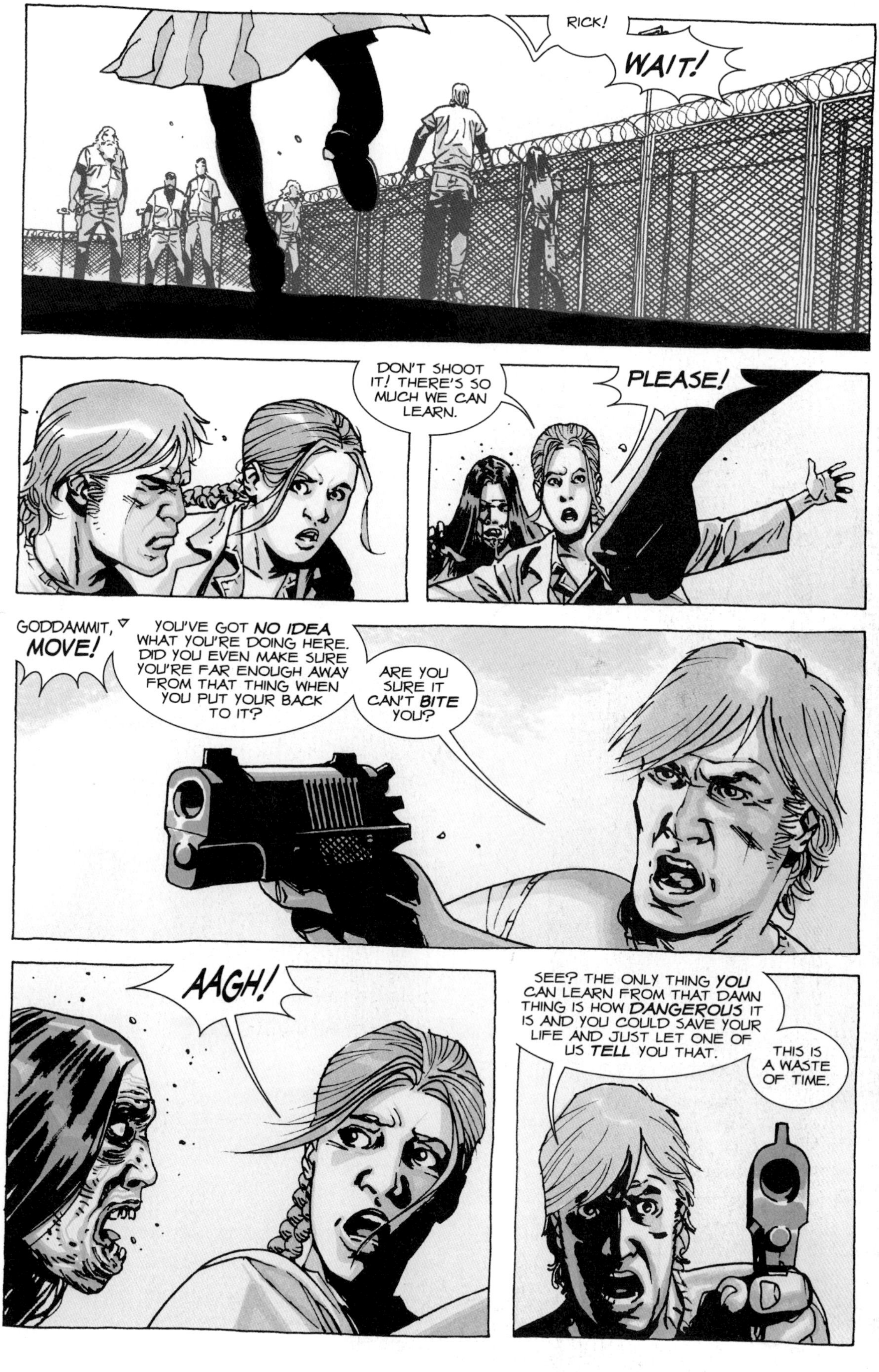
RICK!
WAIT!
DON'T SHOOT IT! THERE'S SO MUCH WE CAN LEARN.
PLEASE!
GODDAMMIT, MOVE!
YOU'VE GOT NO IDEA WHAT YOU'RE DOING HERE. DID YOU EVEN MAKE SURE YOU'RE FAR ENOUGH AWAY FROM THAT THING WHEN YOU PUT YOUR BACK TO IT?
ARE YOU SURE IT CAN'T BITE YOU?
AAGH!
SEE? THE ONLY THING YOU CAN LEARN FROM THAT DAMN THING IS HOW DANGEROUS IT IS AND YOU COULD SAVE YOUR LIFE AND JUST LET ONE OF US TELL YOU THAT.
THIS IS A WASTE OF TIME.

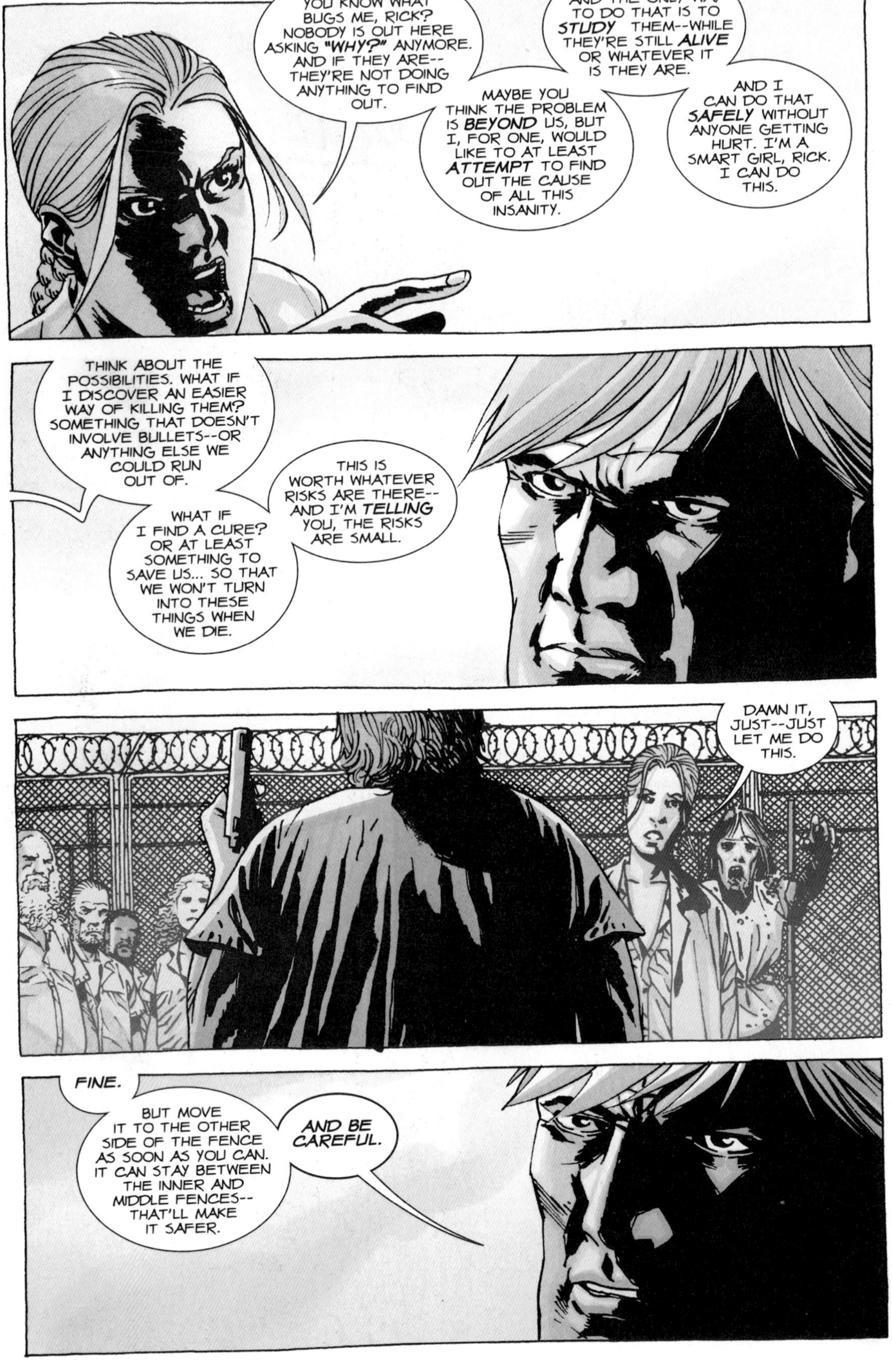
YOU KNOW WHAT BUGS ME, RICK? NOBODY IS OUT HERE ASKING "WHY?" ANYMORE. AND IF THEY ARE-- THEY'RE NOT DOING ANYTHING TO FIND OUT.
MAYBE YOU THINK THE PROBLEM IS BEYOND US, BUT I, FOR ONE, WOULD LIKE TO AT LEAST ATTEMPT TO FIND OUT THE CAUSE OF ALL THIS INSANITY.
AND THE ONLY WAY TO DO THAT IS TO STUDY THEM--WHILE THEY'RE STILL ALIVE OR WHATEVER IT IS THEY ARE.
AND I CAN DO THAT SAFELY WITHOUT ANYONE GETTING HURT. I'M A SMART GIRL, RICK. I CAN DO THIS.
THINK ABOUT THE POSSIBILITIES. WHAT IF I DISCOVER AN EASIER WAY OF KILLING THEM? SOMETHING THAT DOESN'T INVOLVE BULLETS--OR ANYTHING ELSE WE COULD RUN OUT OF.
WHAT IF I FIND A CURE? OR AT LEAST SOMETHING TO SAVE US... SO THAT WE WON'T TURN INTO THESE THINGS WHEN WE DIE.
THIS IS WORTH WHATEVER RISKS ARE THERE-- AND I'M TELLING YOU, THE RISKS ARE SMALL.
DAMN IT, JUST--JUST LET ME DO THIS.
FINE.
BUT MOVE IT TO THE OTHER SIDE OF THE FENCE AS SOON AS YOU CAN. IT CAN STAY BETWEEN THE INNER AND MIDDLE FENCES-- THAT'LL MAKE IT SAFER.
AND BE CAREFUL.

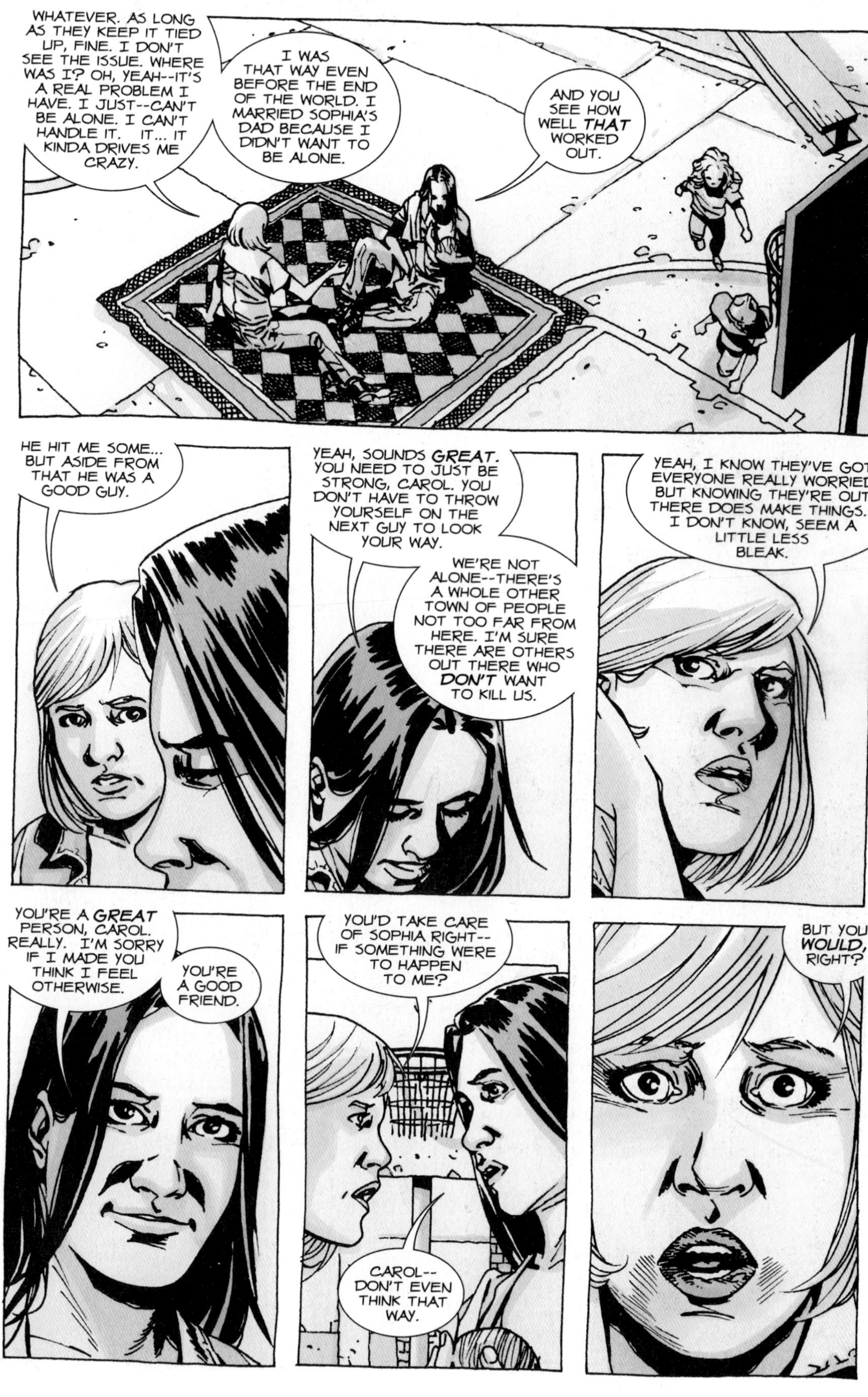
WHATEVER. AS LONG AS THEY KEEP IT TIED UP, FINE. I DON'T SEE THE ISSUE. WHERE WAS I? OH, YEAH--IT'S A REAL PROBLEM I HAVE. I JUST--CAN'T BE ALONE. I CAN'T HANDLE IT. IT... IT KINDA DRIVES ME CRAZY.
I WAS THAT WAY EVEN BEFORE THE END OF THE WORLD. I MARRIED SOPHIA'S DAD BECAUSE I DIDN'T WANT TO BE ALONE.
AND YOU SEE HOW WELL THAT WORKED OUT.
HE HIT ME SOME... BUT ASIDE FROM THAT HE WAS A GOOD GUY.
YEAH, SOUNDS GREAT. YOU NEED TO JUST BE STRONG, CAROL. YOU DON'T HAVE TO THROW YOURSELF ON THE NEXT GUY TO LOOK YOUR WAY.
WE'RE NOT ALONE--THERE'S A WHOLE OTHER TOWN OF PEOPLE NOT TOO FAR FROM HERE. I'M SURE THERE ARE OTHERS OUT THERE WHO DON'T WANT TO KILL US.
YEAH, I KNOW THEY'VE GOT EVERYONE REALLY WORRIED BUT KNOWING THEY'RE OUT THERE DOES MAKE THINGS... I DON'T KNOW, SEEM A LITTLE LESS BLEAK.
YOU'RE A GREAT PERSON, CAROL. REALLY. I'M SORRY IF I MADE YOU THINK I FEEL OTHERWISE.
YOU'RE A GOOD FRIEND.
YOU'D TAKE CARE OF SOPHIA RIGHT--IF SOMETHING WERE TO HAPPEN TO ME?
CAROL--DON'T EVEN THINK THAT WAY.
BUT YOU WOULD, RIGHT?

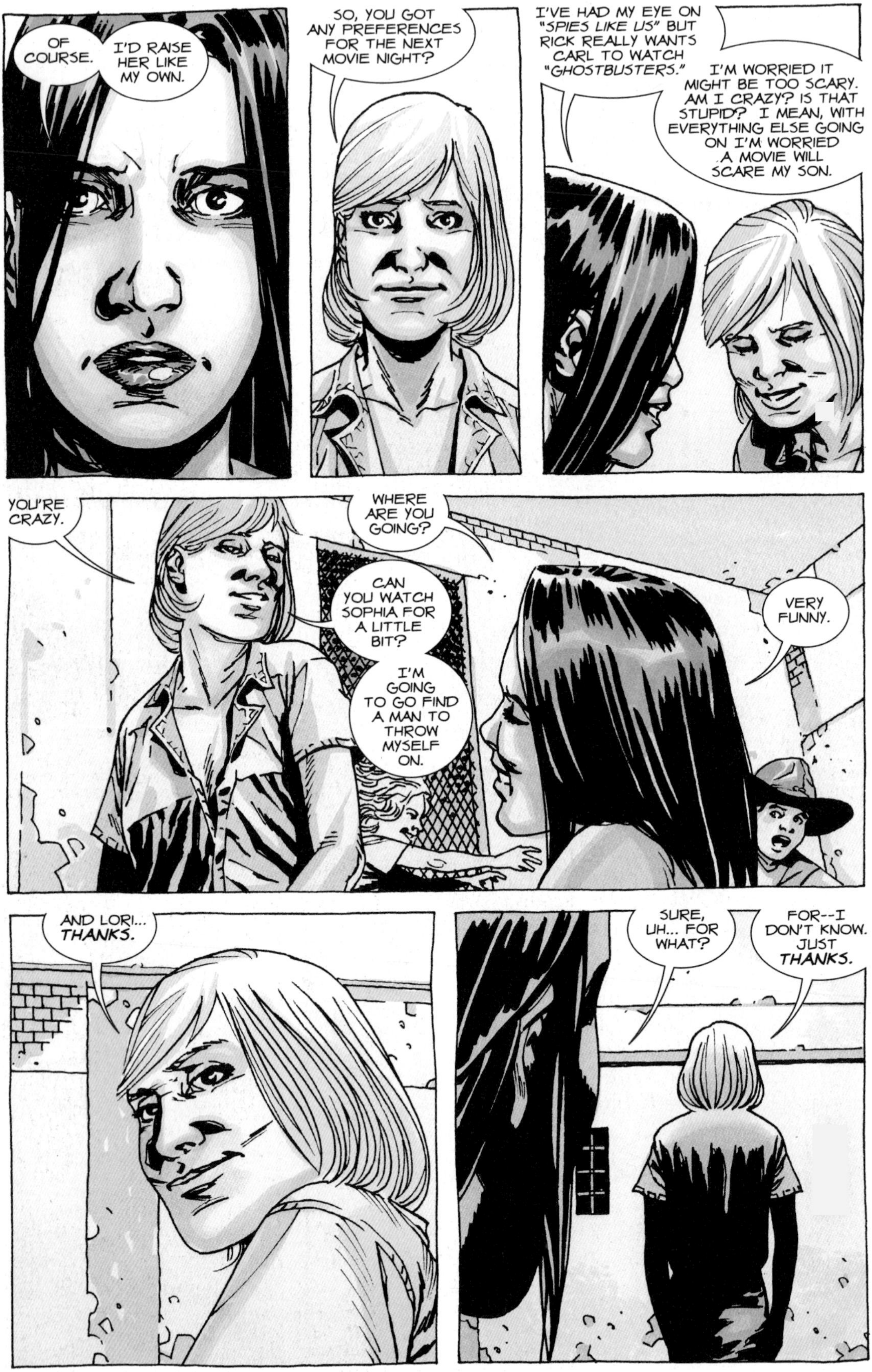
OF COURSE.
I'D RAISE HER LIKE MY OWN.
SO, YOU GOT ANY PREFERENCES FOR THE NEXT MOVIE NIGHT?
I'VE HAD MY EYE ON "SPIES LIKE US" BUT RICK REALLY WANTS CARL TO WATCH "GHOSTBUSTERS."
I'M WORRIED IT MIGHT BE TOO SCARY. AM I CRAZY? IS THAT STUPID? I MEAN, WITH EVERYTHING ELSE GOING ON I'M WORRIED A MOVIE WILL SCARE MY SON.
YOU'RE CRAZY.
WHERE ARE YOU GOING?
CAN YOU WATCH SOPHIA FOR A LITTLE BIT?
I'M GOING TO GO FIND A MAN TO THROW MYSELF ON.
VERY FUNNY.
AND LORI... THANKS.
SURE, UH... FOR WHAT?
FOR--I DON'T KNOW. JUST THANKS.

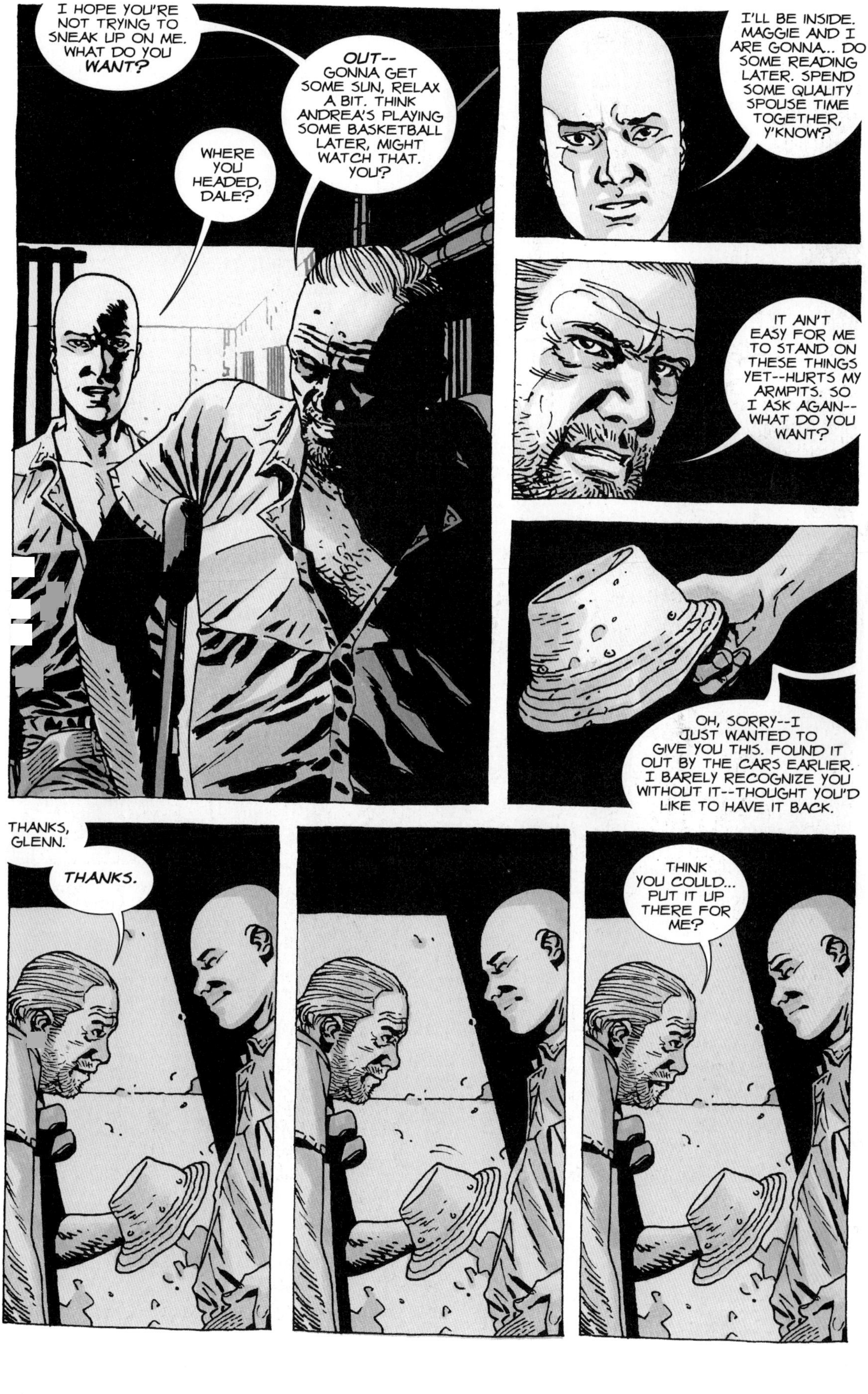
I HOPE YOU'RE NOT TRYING TO SNEAK UP ON ME. WHAT DO YOU *WANT?*
WHERE YOU HEADED, DALE?
OUT-- GONNA GET SOME SUN, RELAX A BIT. THINK ANDREA'S PLAYING SOME BASKETBALL LATER, MIGHT WATCH THAT. YOU?
I'LL BE INSIDE. MAGGIE AND I ARE GONNA.. DO SOME READING LATER. SPEND SOME QUALITY SPOUSE TIME TOGETHER, Y'KNOW?
IT AIN'T EASY FOR ME TO STAND ON THESE THINGS YET--HURTS MY ARMPITS. SO I ASK AGAIN-- WHAT DO YOU WANT?
OH, SORRY--I JUST WANTED TO GIVE YOU THIS. FOUND IT OUT BY THE CARS EARLIER. I BARELY RECOGNIZE YOU WITHOUT IT--THOUGHT YOU'D LIKE TO HAVE IT BACK.
THANKS, GLENN.
THANKS.
THINK YOU COULD... PUT IT UP THERE FOR ME?

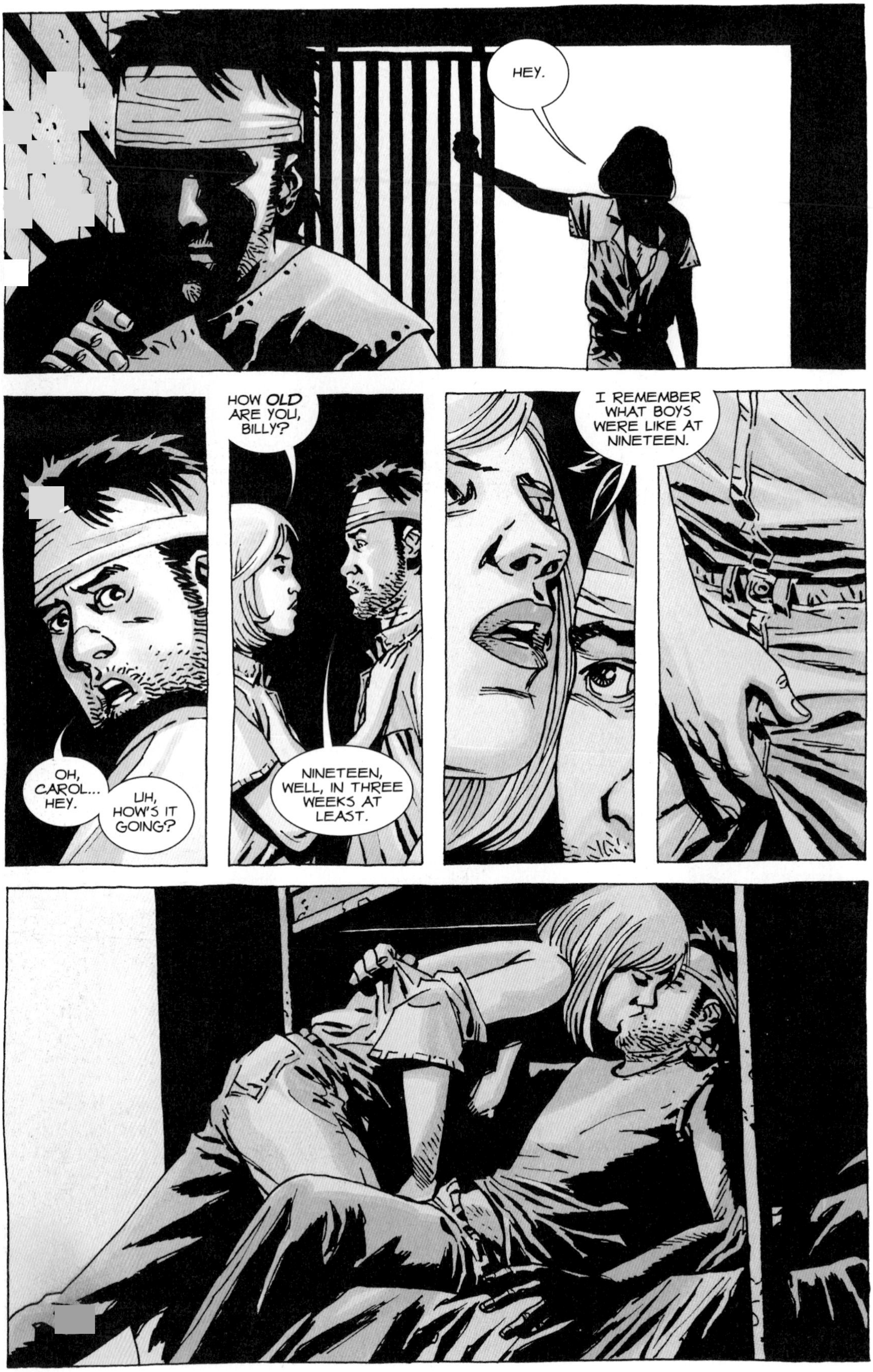
HEY.
OH, CAROL... HEY.
UH, HOW'S IT GOING?
HOW OLD ARE YOU, BILLY?
NINETEEN, WELL, IN THREE WEEKS AT LEAST.
I REMEMBER WHAT BOYS WERE LIKE AT NINETEEN.

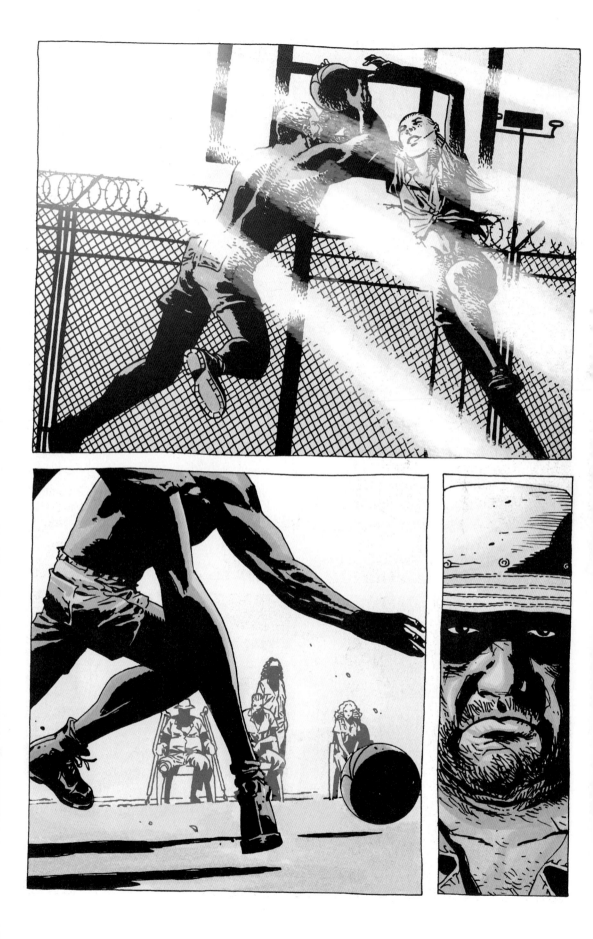

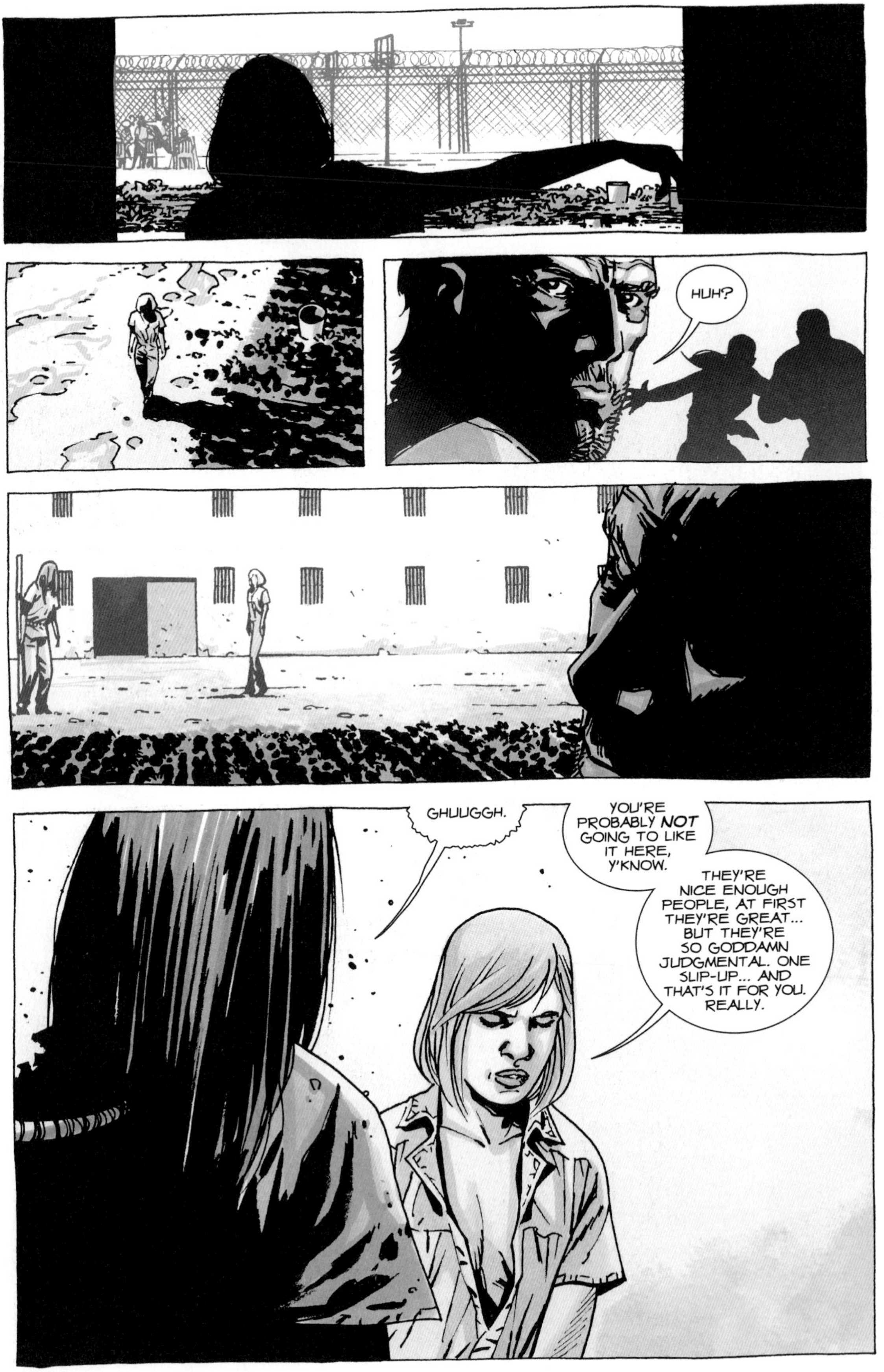
HUH?
GHUUGGH.
YOU'RE PROBABLY NOT GOING TO LIKE IT HERE, Y'KNOW.
THEY'RE NICE ENOUGH PEOPLE, AT FIRST THEY'RE GREAT... BUT THEY'RE SO GODDAMN JUDGMENTAL. ONE SLIP-UP... AND THAT'S IT FOR YOU. REALLY.

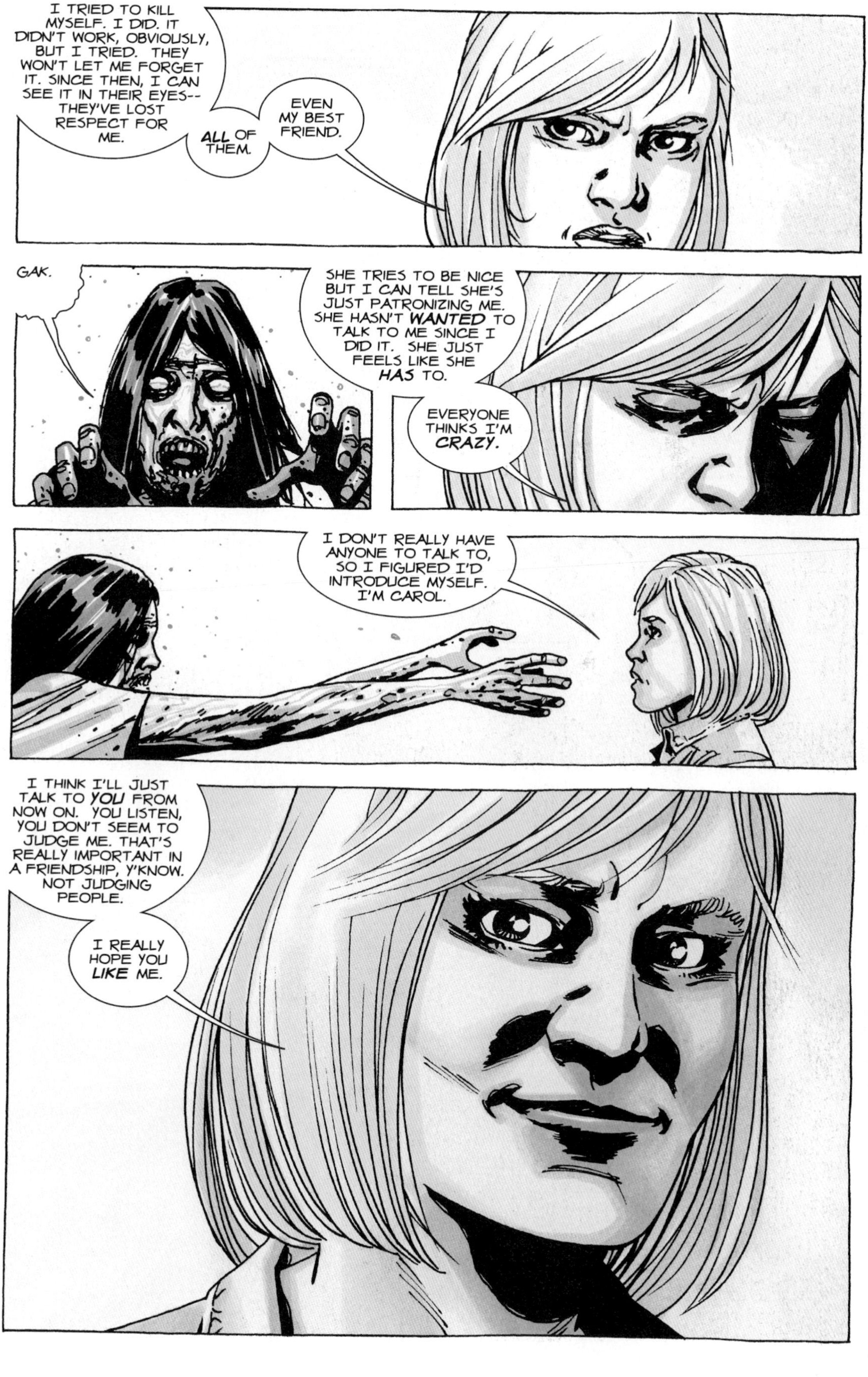
I TRIED TO KILL MYSELF. I DID. IT DIDN'T WORK, OBVIOUSLY, BUT I TRIED. THEY WON'T LET ME FORGET IT. SINCE THEN, I CAN SEE IT IN THEIR EYES-- THEY'VE LOST RESPECT FOR ME.
ALL OF THEM.
EVEN MY BEST FRIEND.
GAK.
SHE TRIES TO BE NICE BUT I CAN TELL SHE'S JUST PATRONIZING ME. SHE HASN'T WANTED TO TALK TO ME SINCE I DID IT. SHE JUST FEELS LIKE SHE HAS TO.
EVERYONE THINKS I'M CRAZY.
I DON'T REALLY HAVE ANYONE TO TALK TO, SO I FIGURED I'D INTRODUCE MYSELF. I'M CAROL.
I THINK I'LL JUST TALK TO YOU FROM NOW ON. YOU LISTEN, YOU DON'T SEEM TO JUDGE ME. THAT'S REALLY IMPORTANT IN A FRIENDSHIP, Y'KNOW. NOT JUDGING PEOPLE.
I REALLY HOPE YOU LIKE ME.

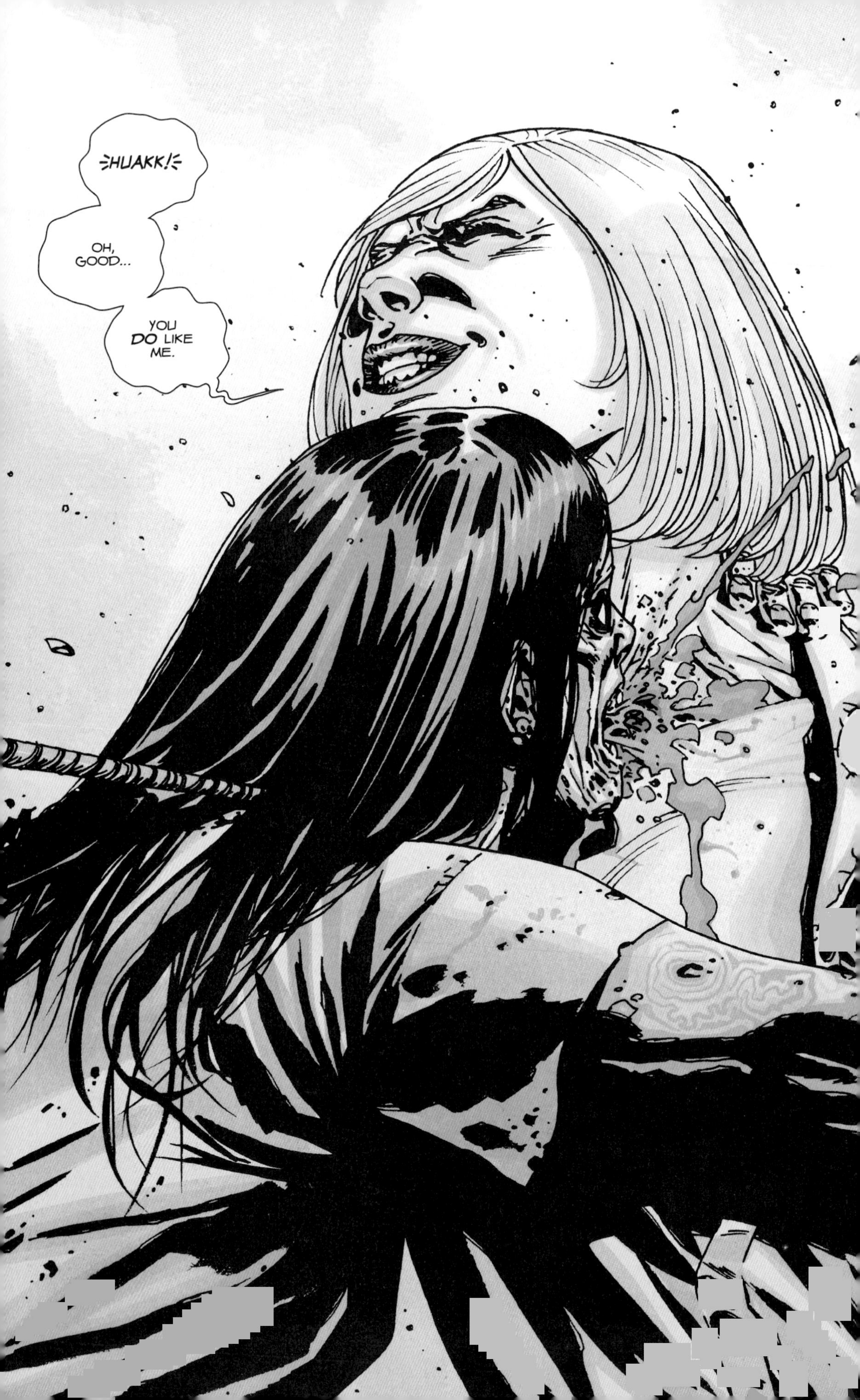

=HUAKK!=
OH, GOOD...
YOU DO LIKE ME.

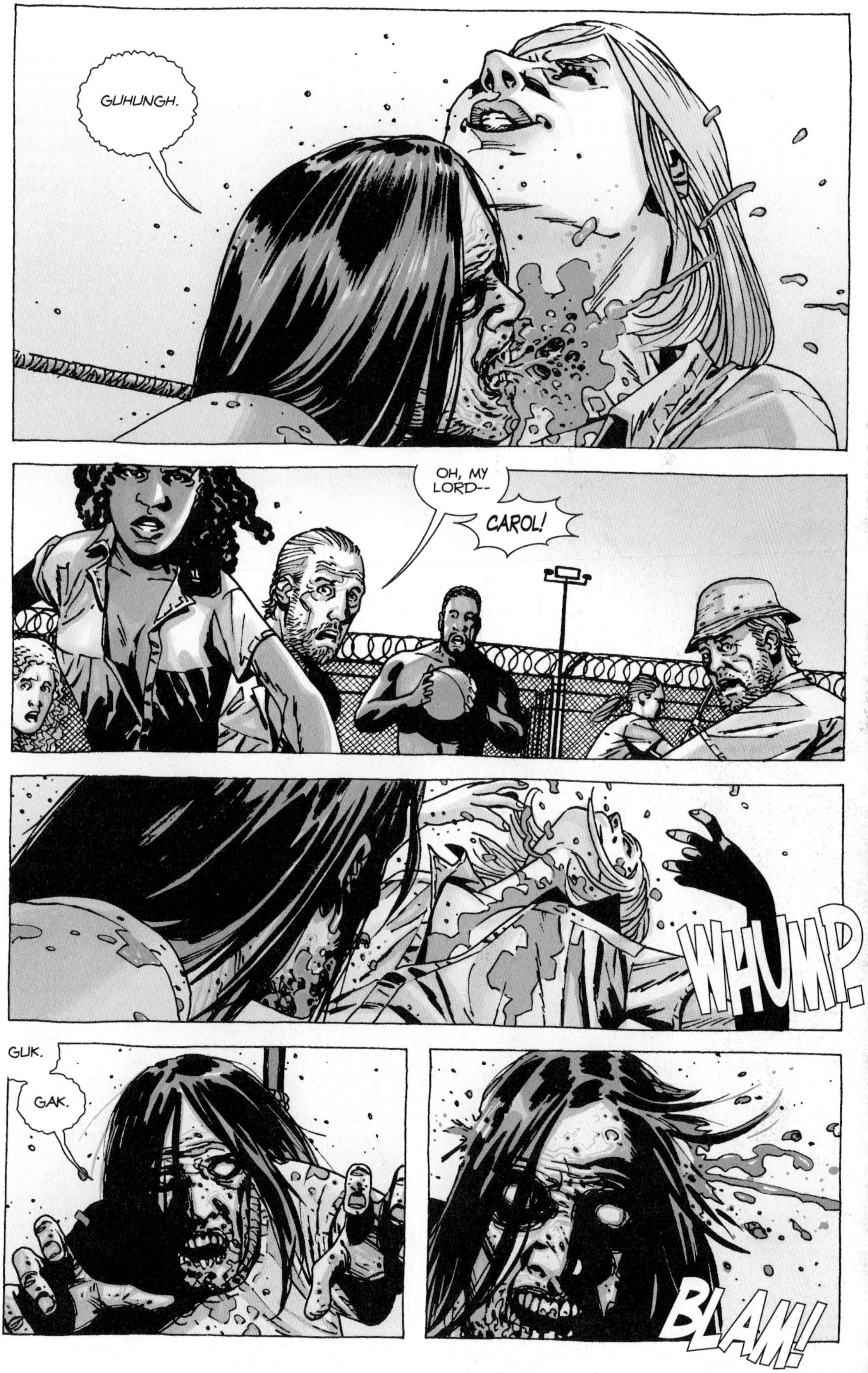
GUHUNGH.
OH, MY LORD--
CAROL!
WHUMP.
GUK.
GAK.
BLAM!

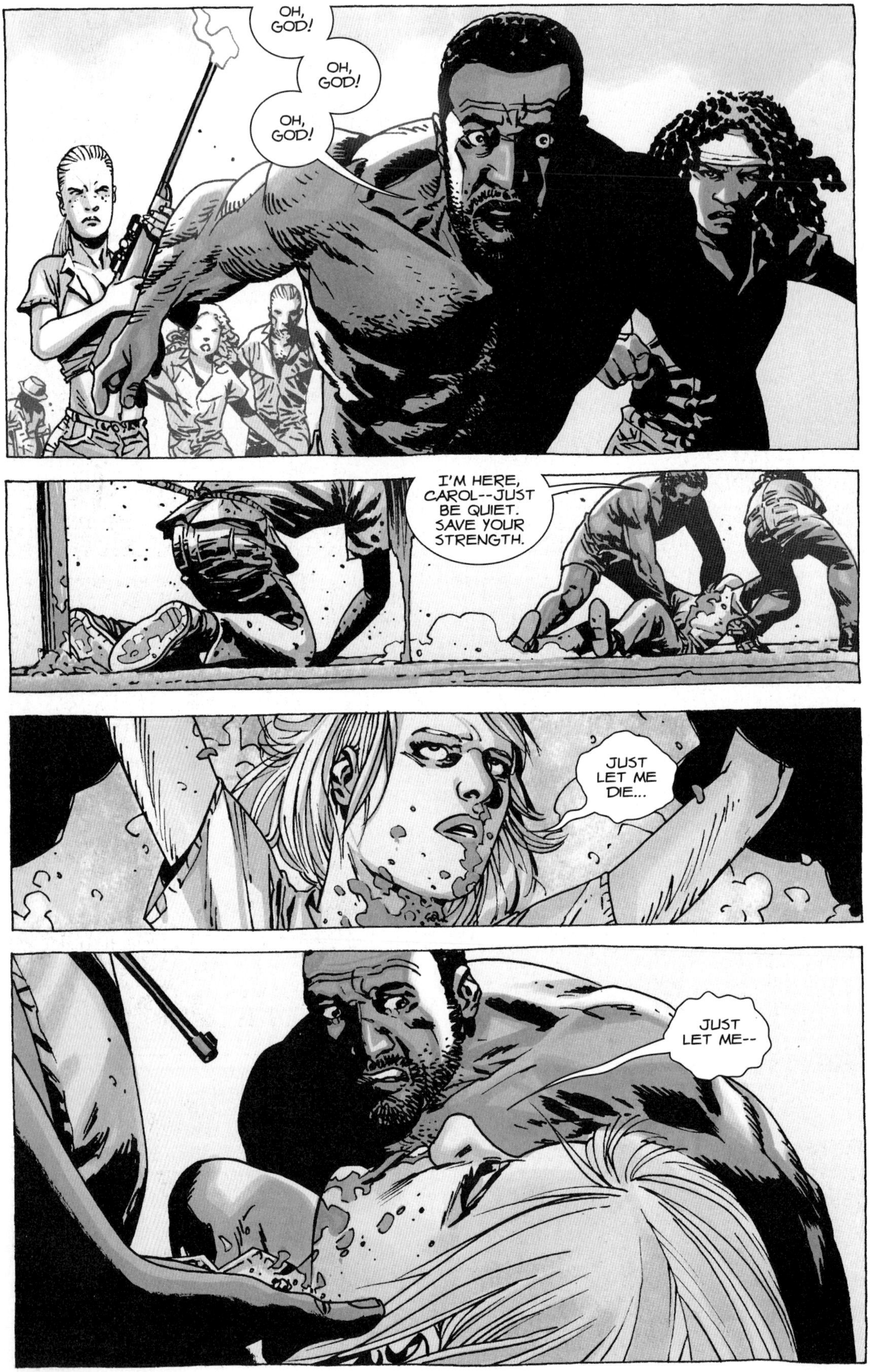
OH, GOD!
OH, GOD!
OH, GOD!
I'M HERE, CAROL--JUST BE QUIET. SAVE YOUR STRENGTH.
JUST LET ME DIE...
JUST LET ME--

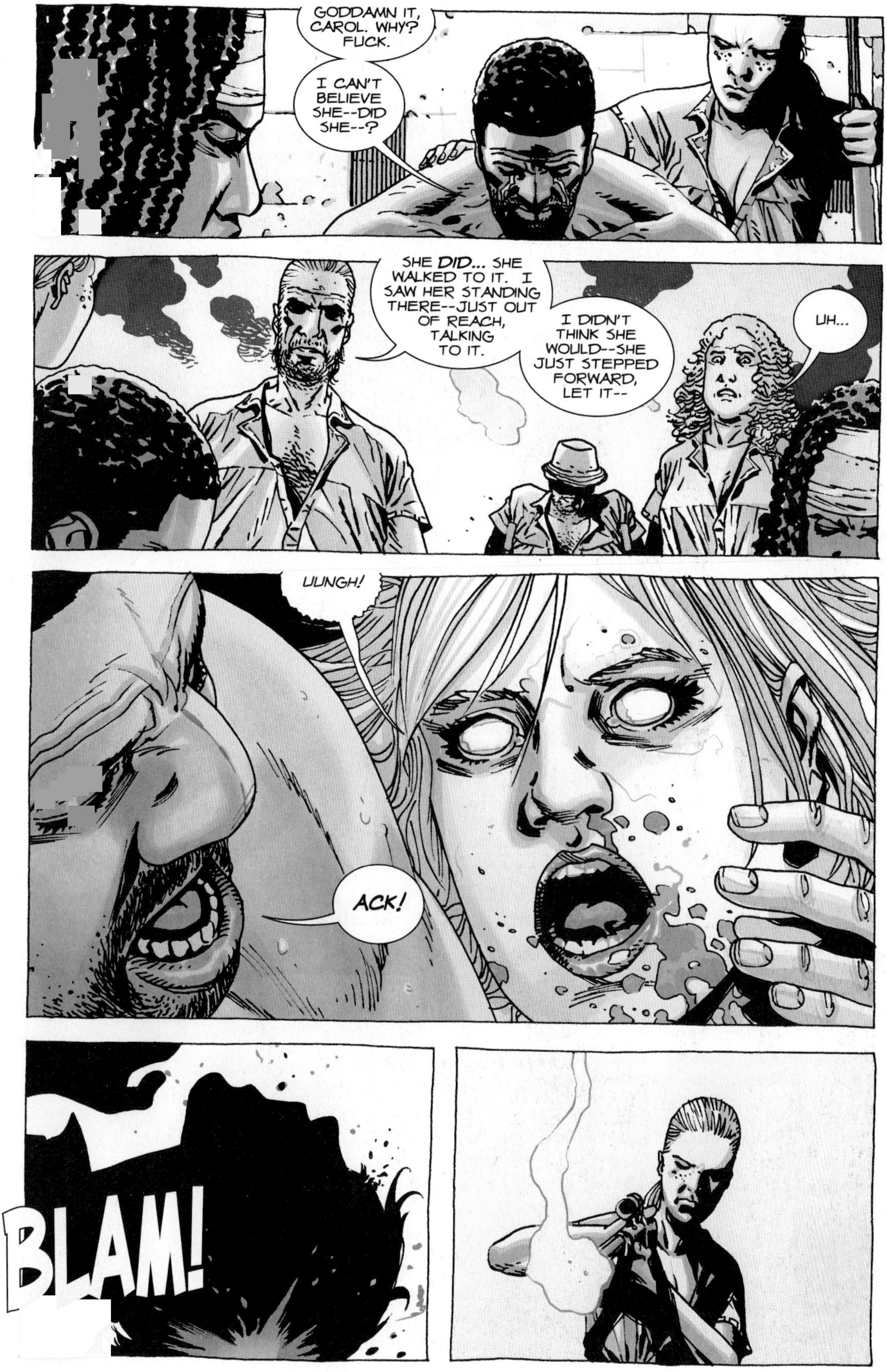
GODDAMN IT, CAROL. WHY? FUCK.
I CAN'T BELIEVE SHE--DID SHE--?
SHE DID... SHE WALKED TO IT. I SAW HER STANDING THERE--JUST OUT OF REACH, TALKING TO IT.
I DIDN'T THINK SHE WOULD--SHE JUST STEPPED FORWARD, LET IT--
UH...
UUNGH!
ACK!
BLAM!

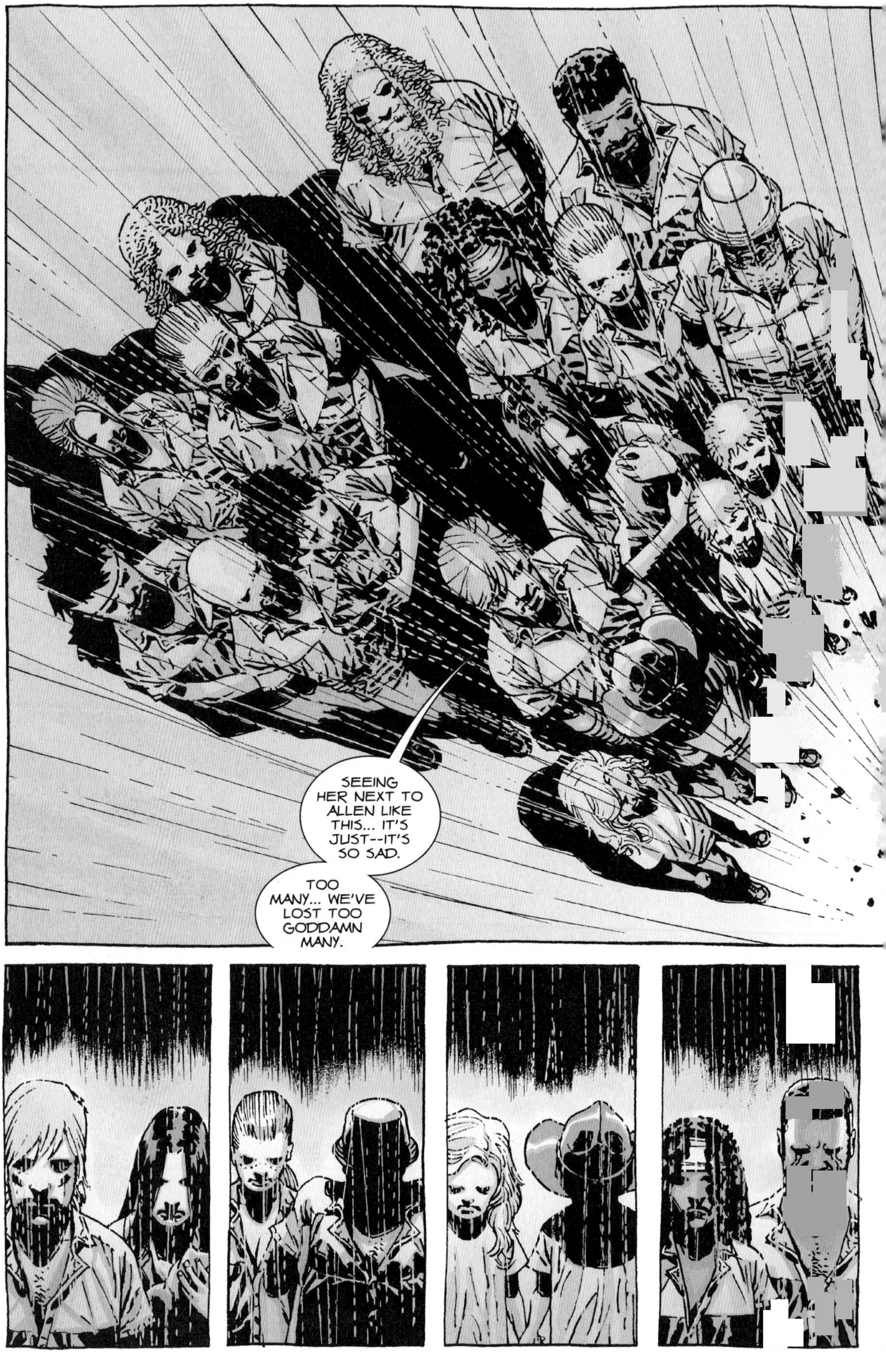
SEEING HER NEXT TO ALLEN LIKE THIS... IT'S JUST--IT'S SO SAD.
TOO MANY... WE'VE LOST TOO GODDAMN MANY.

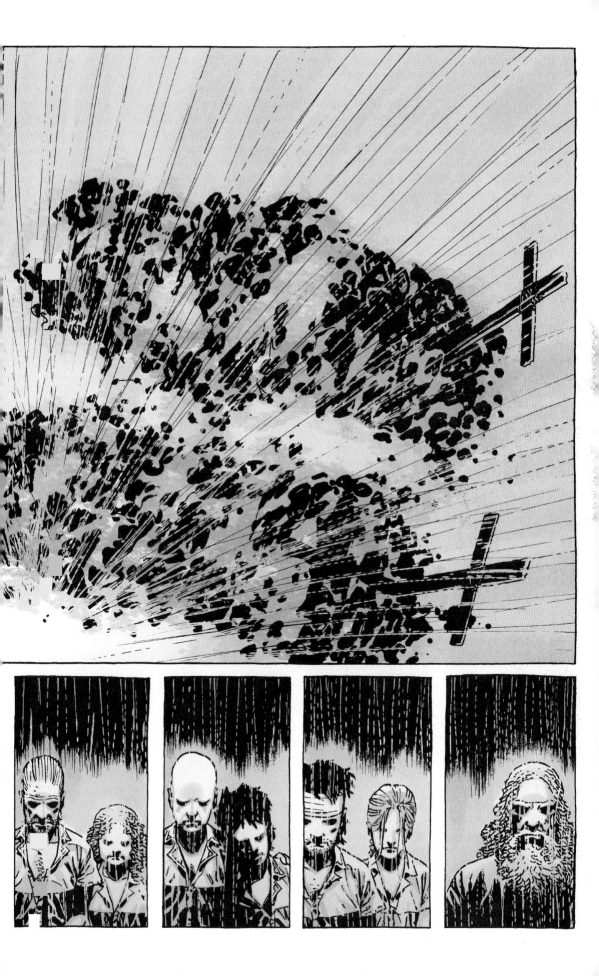

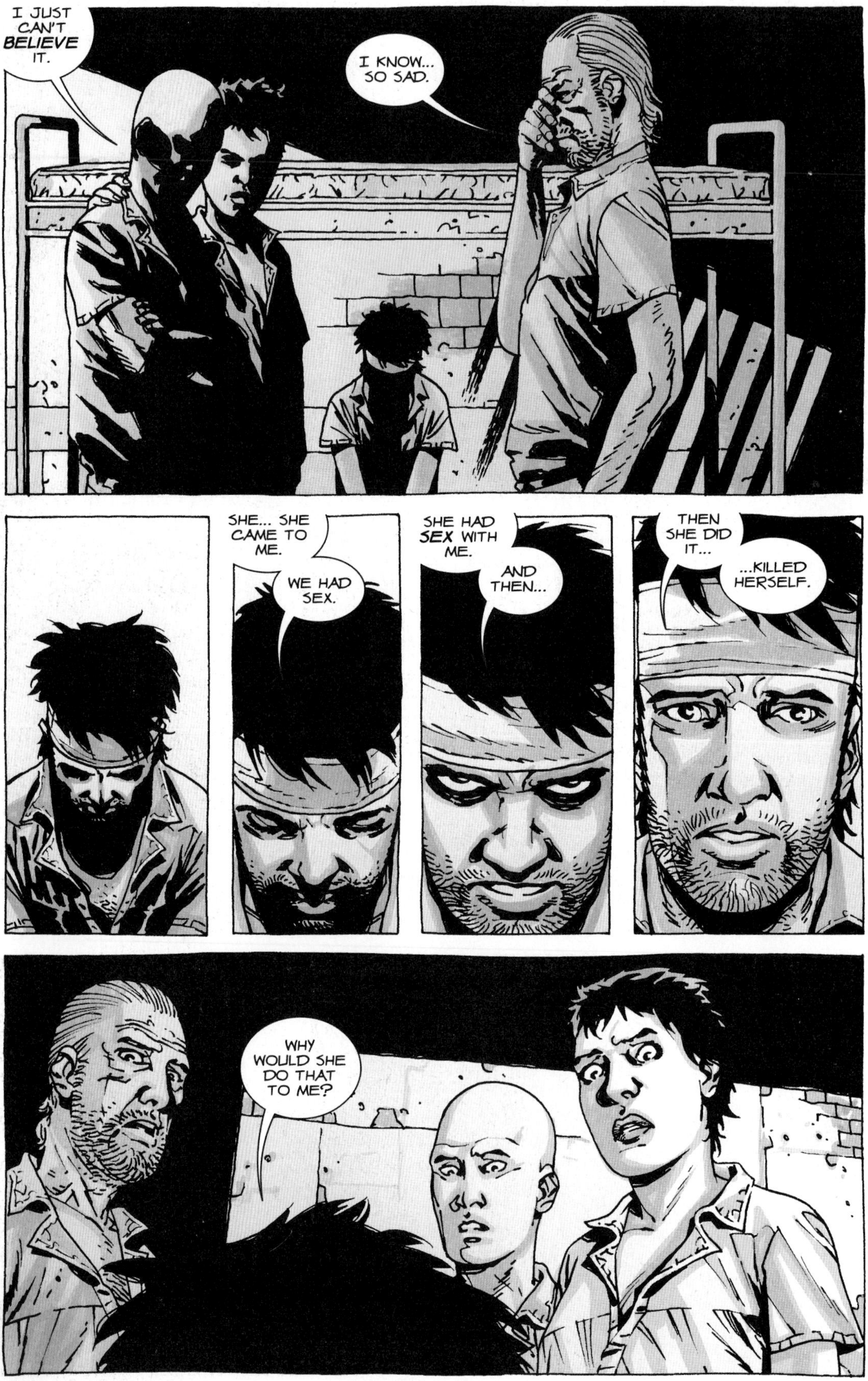
I JUST CAN'T *BELIEVE* IT.
I KNOW... SO SAD.
SHE... SHE CAME TO ME.
WE HAD SEX.
SHE HAD *SEX* WITH ME.
AND THEN...
THEN SHE DID IT...
...KILLED HERSELF.
WHY WOULD SHE DO THAT TO ME?

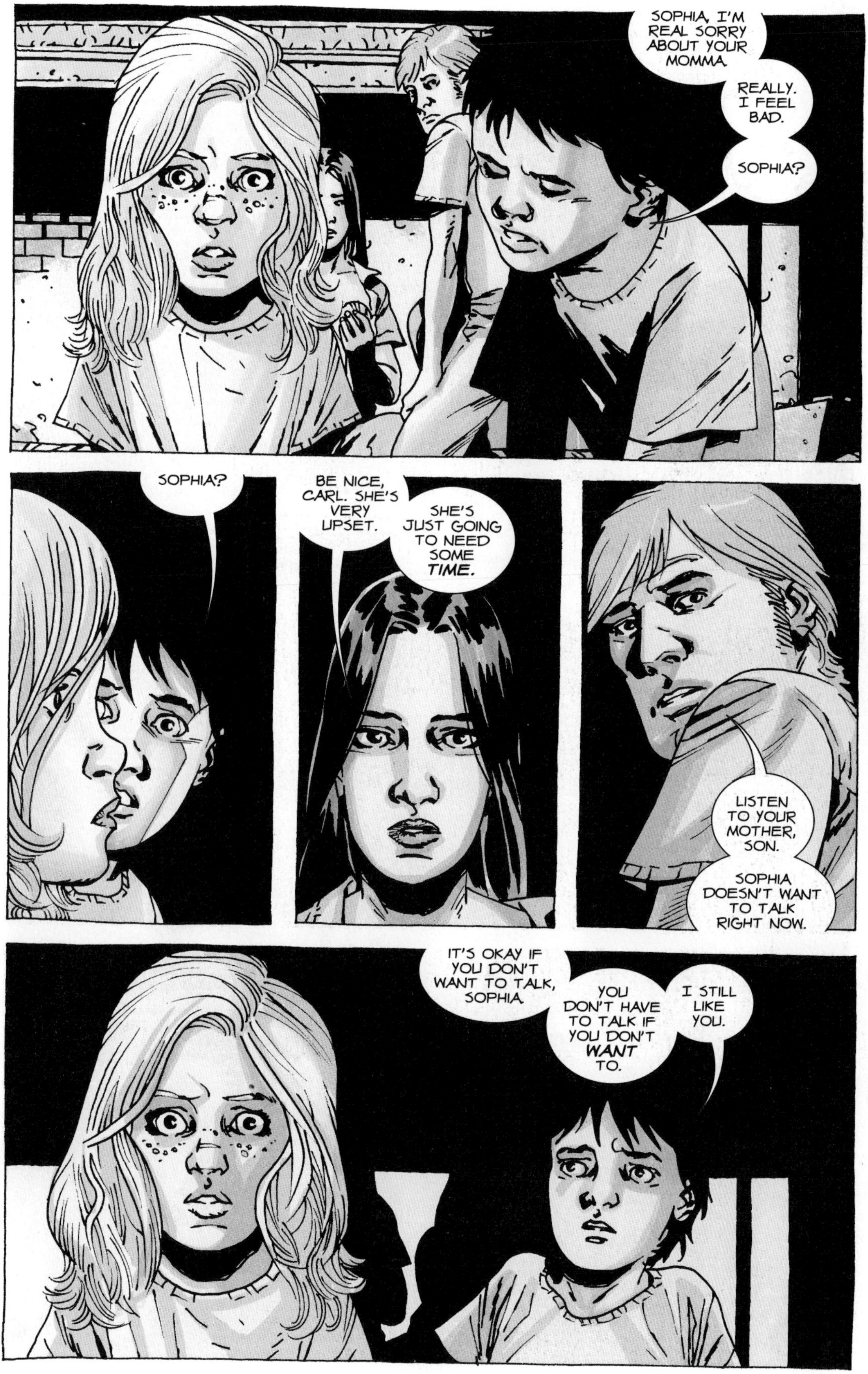
SOPHIA, I'M REAL SORRY ABOUT YOUR MOMMA.
REALLY. I FEEL BAD.
SOPHIA?
SOPHIA?
BE NICE, CARL. SHE'S VERY UPSET.
SHE'S JUST GOING TO NEED SOME TIME.
LISTEN TO YOUR MOTHER, SON.
SOPHIA DOESN'T WANT TO TALK RIGHT NOW.
IT'S OKAY IF YOU DON'T WANT TO TALK, SOPHIA.
YOU DON'T HAVE TO TALK IF YOU DON'T WANT TO.
I STILL LIKE YOU.

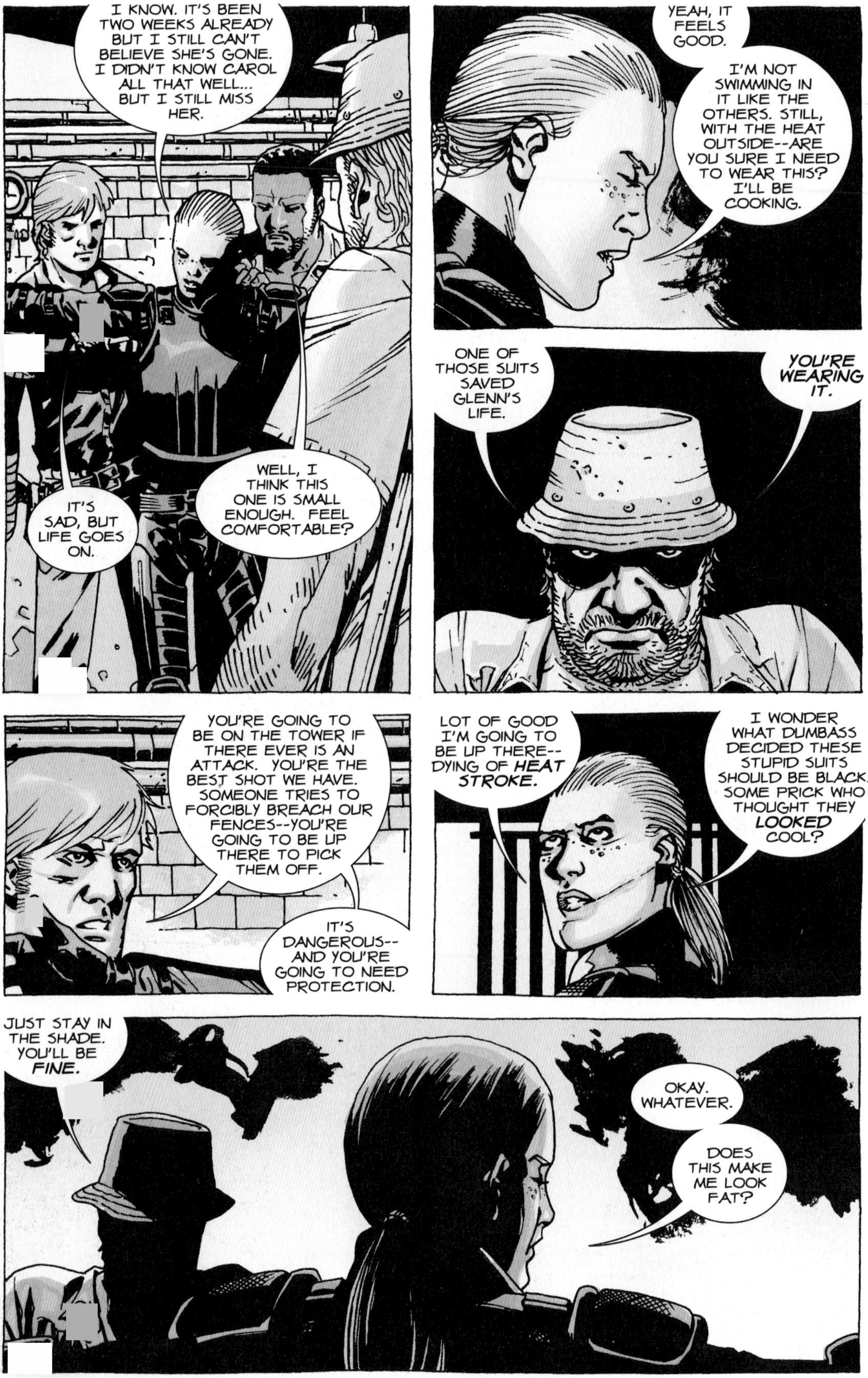
I KNOW. IT'S BEEN TWO WEEKS ALREADY BUT I STILL CAN'T BELIEVE SHE'S GONE. I DIDN'T KNOW CAROL ALL THAT WELL... BUT I STILL MISS HER.
IT'S SAD, BUT LIFE GOES ON.
WELL, I THINK THIS ONE IS SMALL ENOUGH. FEEL COMFORTABLE?
YEAH, IT FEELS GOOD.
I'M NOT SWIMMING IN IT LIKE THE OTHERS. STILL, WITH THE HEAT OUTSIDE--ARE YOU SURE I NEED TO WEAR THIS? I'LL BE COOKING.
ONE OF THOSE SUITS SAVED GLENN'S LIFE.
YOU'RE WEARING IT.
YOU'RE GOING TO BE ON THE TOWER IF THERE EVER IS AN ATTACK. YOU'RE THE BEST SHOT WE HAVE. SOMEONE TRIES TO FORCIBLY BREACH OUR FENCES--YOU'RE GOING TO BE UP THERE TO PICK THEM OFF.
IT'S DANGEROUS--AND YOU'RE GOING TO NEED PROTECTION.
LOT OF GOOD I'M GOING TO BE UP THERE--DYING OF HEAT STROKE.
I WONDER WHAT DUMBASS DECIDED THESE STUPID SUITS SHOULD BE BLACK. SOME PRICK WHO THOUGHT THEY LOOKED COOL?
JUST STAY IN THE SHADE. YOU'LL BE FINE.
OKAY. WHATEVER.
DOES THIS MAKE ME LOOK FAT?

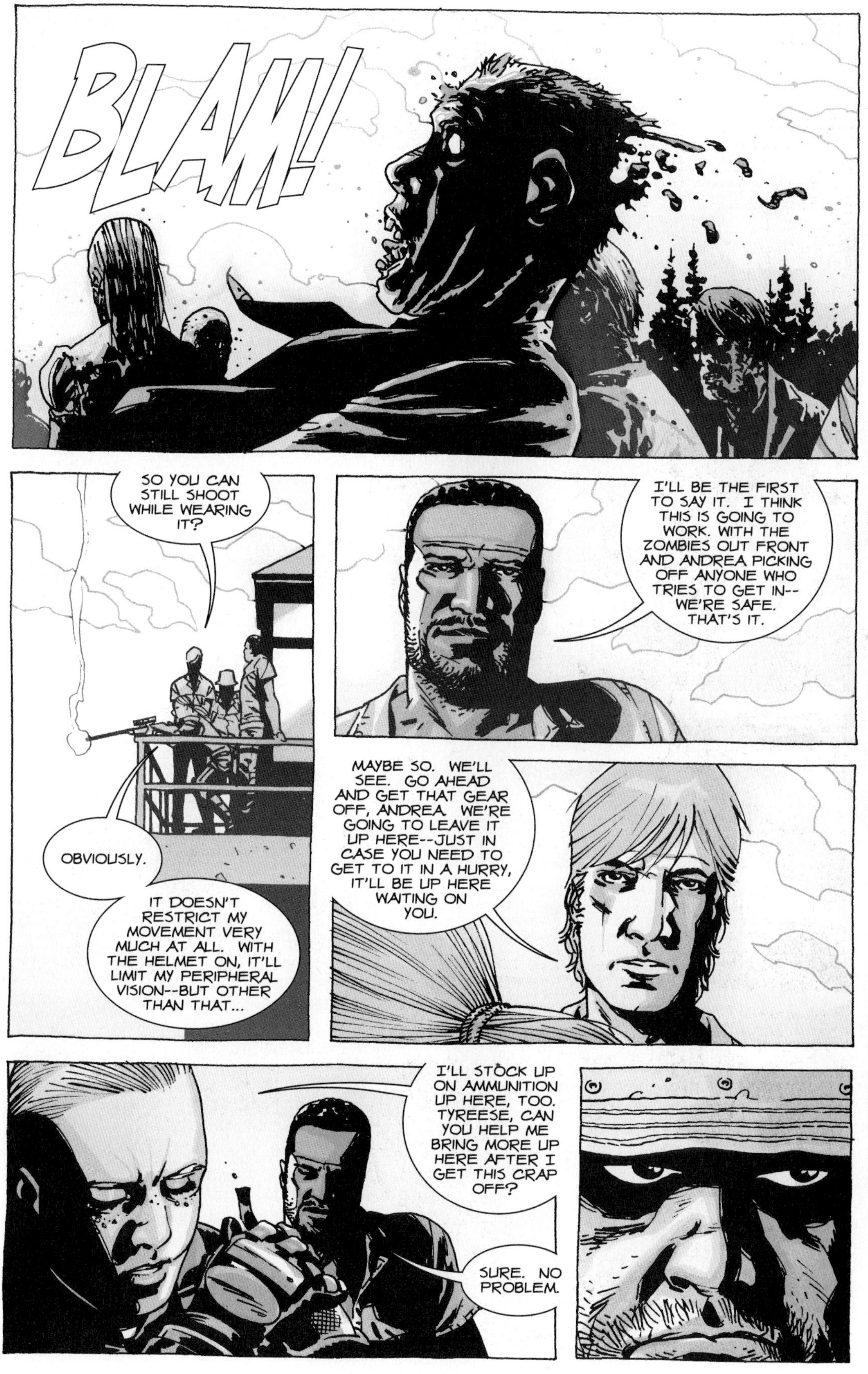
BLAM!
SO YOU CAN STILL SHOOT WHILE WEARING IT?
OBVIOUSLY.
IT DOESN'T RESTRICT MY MOVEMENT VERY MUCH AT ALL. WITH THE HELMET ON, IT'LL LIMIT MY PERIPHERAL VISION--BUT OTHER THAN THAT...
I'LL BE THE FIRST TO SAY IT. I THINK THIS IS GOING TO WORK. WITH THE ZOMBIES OUT FRONT AND ANDREA PICKING OFF ANYONE WHO TRIES TO GET IN-- WE'RE SAFE. THAT'S IT.
MAYBE SO. WE'LL SEE. GO AHEAD AND GET THAT GEAR OFF, ANDREA. WE'RE GOING TO LEAVE IT UP HERE--JUST IN CASE YOU NEED TO GET TO IT IN A HURRY, IT'LL BE UP HERE WAITING ON YOU.
I'LL STOCK UP ON AMMUNITION UP HERE, TOO. TYREESE, CAN YOU HELP ME BRING MORE UP HERE AFTER I GET THIS CRAP OFF?
SURE. NO PROBLEM.

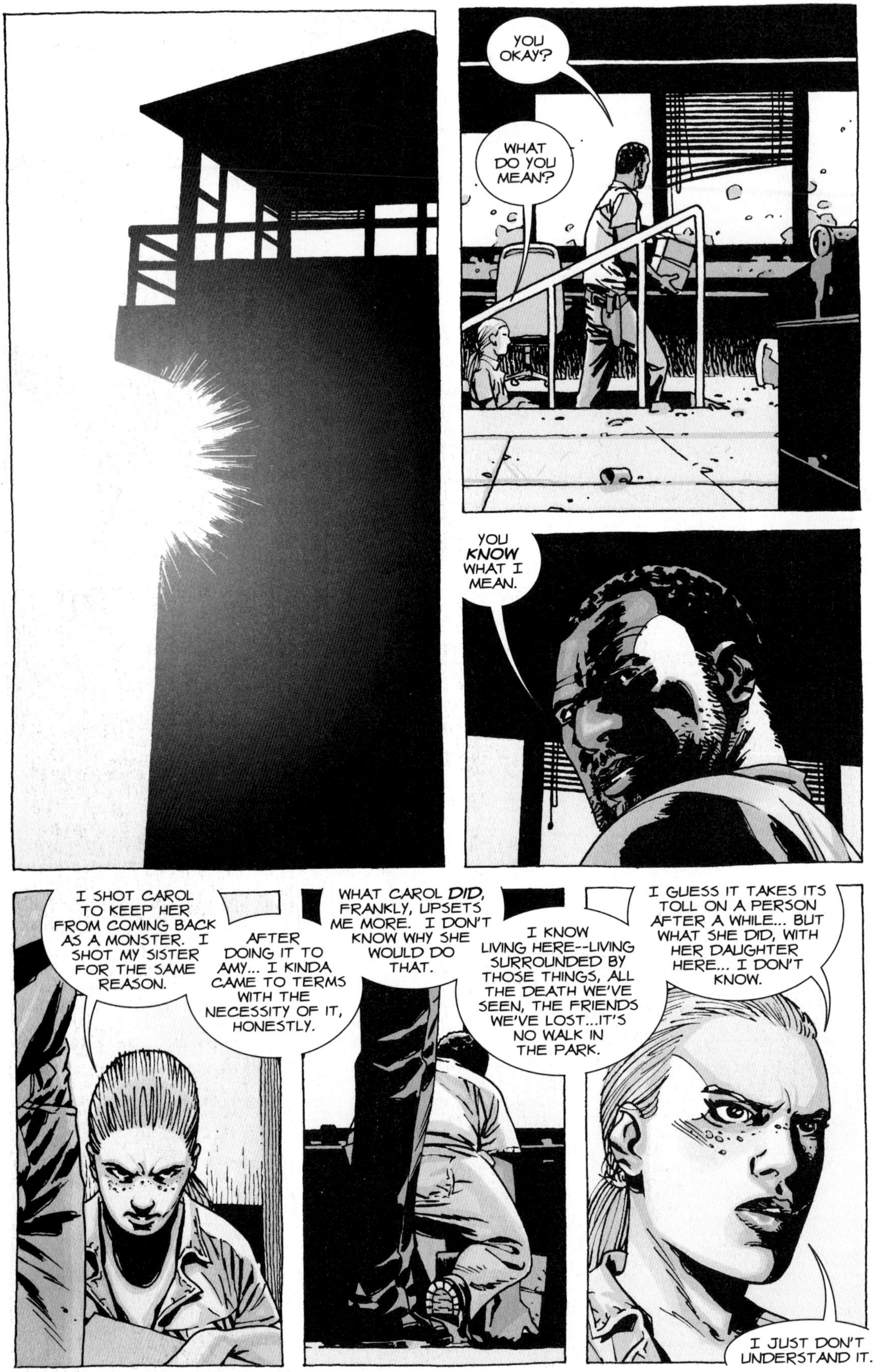
YOU OKAY?
WHAT DO YOU MEAN?
YOU *KNOW* WHAT I MEAN.
I SHOT CAROL TO KEEP HER FROM COMING BACK AS A MONSTER. I SHOT MY SISTER FOR THE SAME REASON.
AFTER DOING IT TO AMY... I KINDA CAME TO TERMS WITH THE NECESSITY OF IT, HONESTLY.
WHAT CAROL *DID*, FRANKLY, UPSETS ME MORE. I DON'T KNOW WHY SHE WOULD DO THAT.
I KNOW LIVING HERE--LIVING SURROUNDED BY THOSE THINGS, ALL THE DEATH WE'VE SEEN, THE FRIENDS WE'VE LOST...IT'S NO WALK IN THE PARK.
I GUESS IT TAKES ITS TOLL ON A PERSON AFTER A WHILE... BUT WHAT SHE DID, WITH HER DAUGHTER HERE... I DON'T KNOW.
I JUST DON'T UNDERSTAND IT.

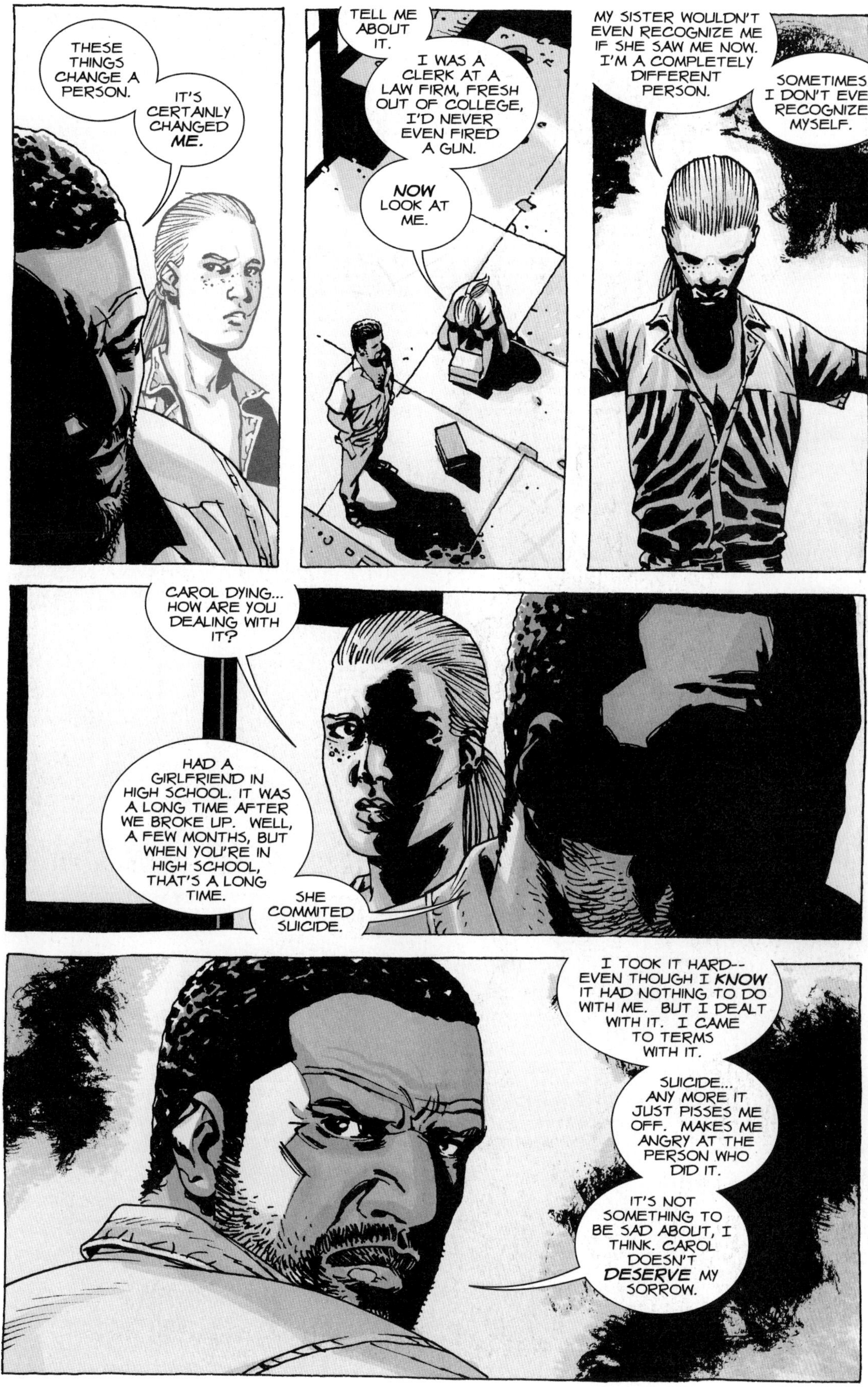
THESE THINGS CHANGE A PERSON.
IT'S CERTAINLY CHANGED *ME.*
TELL ME ABOUT IT.
I WAS A CLERK AT A LAW FIRM, FRESH OUT OF COLLEGE, I'D NEVER EVEN FIRED A GUN.
NOW LOOK AT ME.
MY SISTER WOULDN'T EVEN RECOGNIZE ME IF SHE SAW ME NOW. I'M A COMPLETELY DIFFERENT PERSON.
SOMETIMES I DON'T EVEN RECOGNIZE MYSELF.
CAROL DYING... HOW ARE YOU DEALING WITH IT?
HAD A GIRLFRIEND IN HIGH SCHOOL. IT WAS A LONG TIME AFTER WE BROKE UP. WELL, A FEW MONTHS, BUT WHEN YOU'RE IN HIGH SCHOOL, THAT'S A LONG TIME.
SHE COMMITED SUICIDE.
I TOOK IT HARD-- EVEN THOUGH I *KNOW* IT HAD NOTHING TO DO WITH ME. BUT I DEALT WITH IT. I CAME TO TERMS WITH IT.
SUICIDE... ANY MORE IT JUST PISSES ME OFF. MAKES ME ANGRY AT THE PERSON WHO DID IT.
IT'S NOT SOMETHING TO BE SAD ABOUT, I THINK. CAROL DOESN'T *DESERVE* MY SORROW.

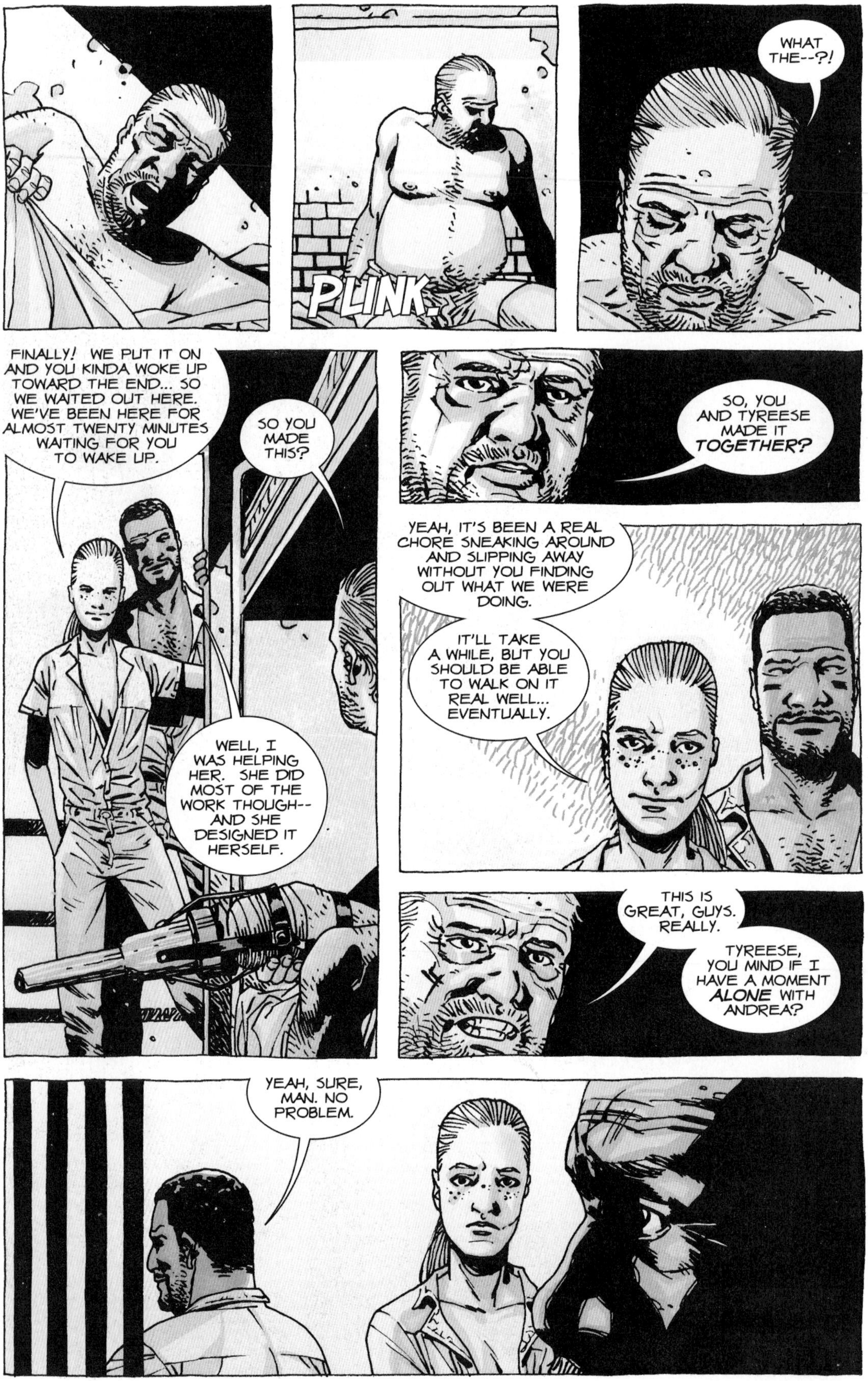
PLINK.
WHAT THE--?!
FINALLY! WE PUT IT ON AND YOU KINDA WOKE UP TOWARD THE END... SO WE WAITED OUT HERE. WE'VE BEEN HERE FOR ALMOST TWENTY MINUTES WAITING FOR YOU TO WAKE UP.
SO YOU MADE THIS?
WELL, I WAS HELPING HER. SHE DID MOST OF THE WORK THOUGH-- AND SHE DESIGNED IT HERSELF.
SO, YOU AND TYREESE MADE IT TOGETHER?
YEAH, IT'S BEEN A REAL CHORE SNEAKING AROUND AND SLIPPING AWAY WITHOUT YOU FINDING OUT WHAT WE WERE DOING.
IT'LL TAKE A WHILE, BUT YOU SHOULD BE ABLE TO WALK ON IT REAL WELL... EVENTUALLY.
THIS IS GREAT, GUYS. REALLY.
TYREESE, YOU MIND IF I HAVE A MOMENT ALONE WITH ANDREA?
YEAH, SURE, MAN. NO PROBLEM.

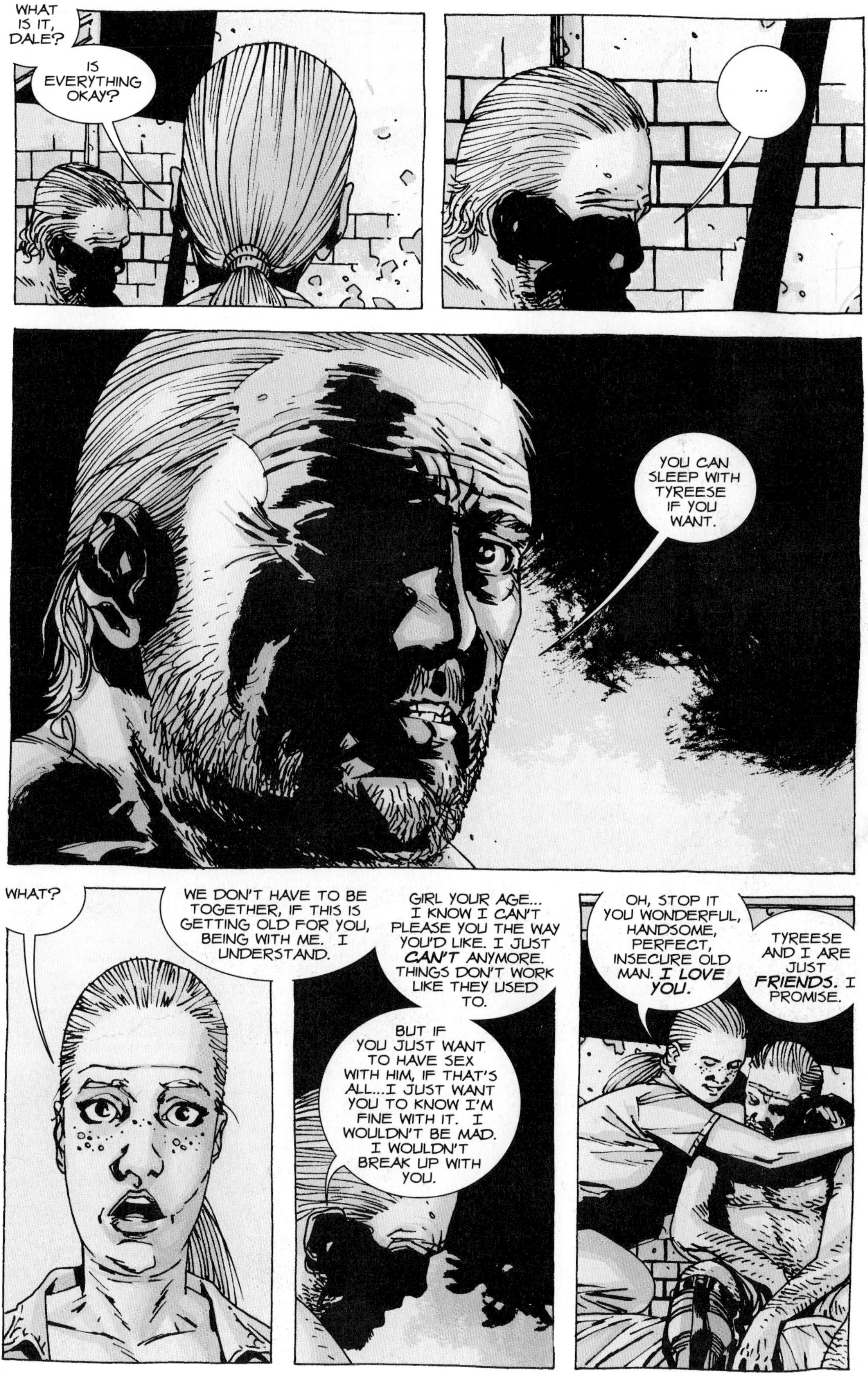
WHAT IS IT, DALE?
IS EVERYTHING OKAY?
...
YOU CAN SLEEP WITH TYREESE IF YOU WANT.
WHAT?
WE DON'T HAVE TO BE TOGETHER, IF THIS IS GETTING OLD FOR YOU, BEING WITH ME. I UNDERSTAND.
GIRL YOUR AGE... I KNOW I CAN'T PLEASE YOU THE WAY YOU'D LIKE. I JUST *CAN'T* ANYMORE. THINGS DON'T WORK LIKE THEY USED TO.
BUT IF YOU JUST WANT TO HAVE SEX WITH HIM, IF THAT'S ALL...I JUST WANT YOU TO KNOW I'M FINE WITH IT. I WOULDN'T BE MAD. I WOULDN'T BREAK UP WITH YOU.
OH, STOP IT YOU WONDERFUL, HANDSOME, PERFECT, INSECURE OLD MAN. **I LOVE YOU.**
TYREESE AND I ARE JUST **FRIENDS.** I PROMISE.

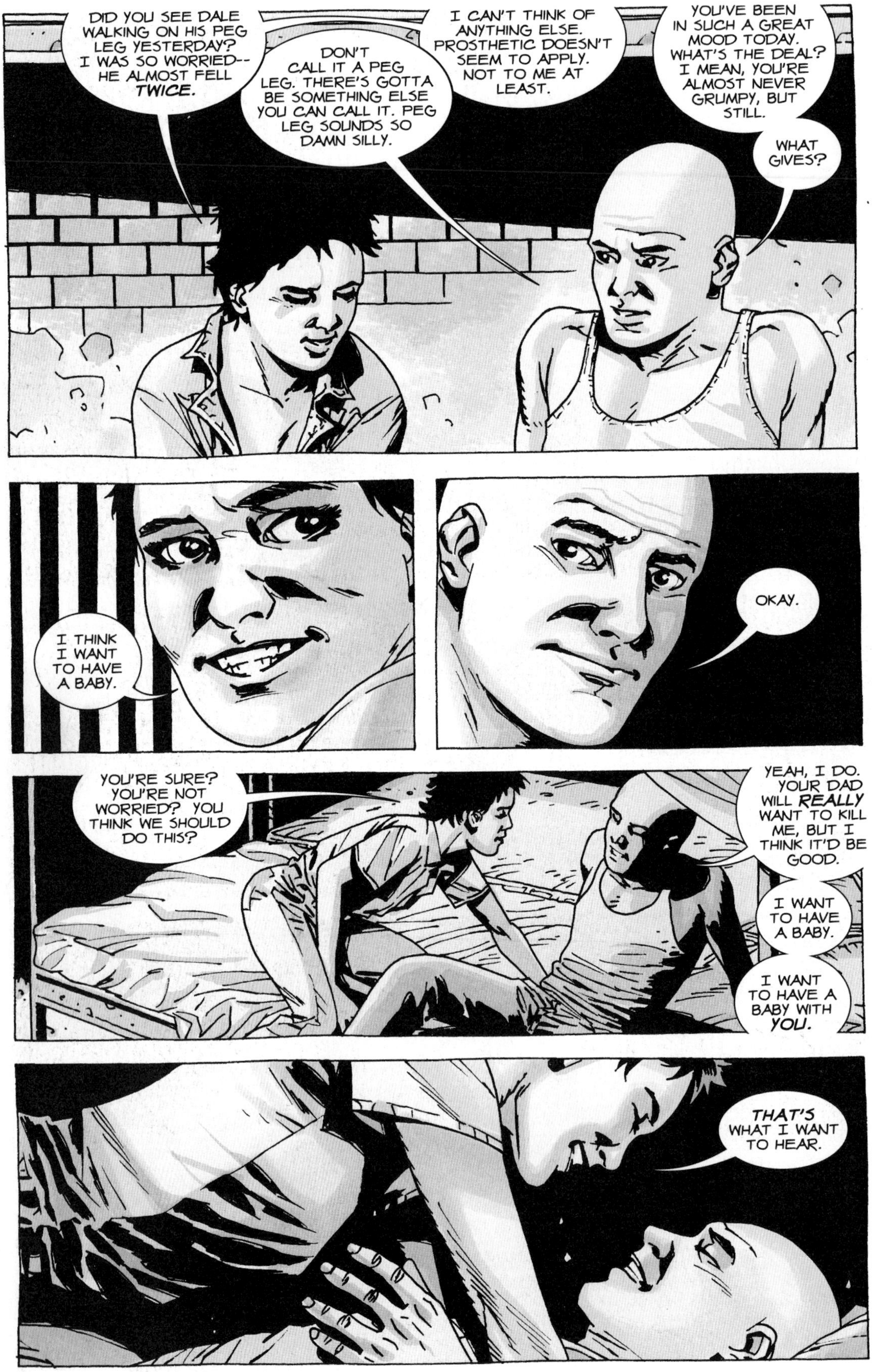
DID YOU SEE DALE WALKING ON HIS PEG LEG YESTERDAY? I WAS SO WORRIED-- HE ALMOST FELL TWICE.
DON'T CALL IT A PEG LEG. THERE'S GOTTA BE SOMETHING ELSE YOU CAN CALL IT. PEG LEG SOUNDS SO DAMN SILLY.
I CAN'T THINK OF ANYTHING ELSE. PROSTHETIC DOESN'T SEEM TO APPLY. NOT TO ME AT LEAST.
YOU'VE BEEN IN SUCH A GREAT MOOD TODAY. WHAT'S THE DEAL? I MEAN, YOU'RE ALMOST NEVER GRUMPY, BUT STILL.
WHAT GIVES?
I THINK I WANT TO HAVE A BABY.
OKAY.
YOU'RE SURE? YOU'RE NOT WORRIED? YOU THINK WE SHOULD DO THIS?
YEAH, I DO. YOUR DAD WILL REALLY WANT TO KILL ME, BUT I THINK IT'D BE GOOD.
I WANT TO HAVE A BABY.
I WANT TO HAVE A BABY WITH YOU.
THAT'S WHAT I WANT TO HEAR.

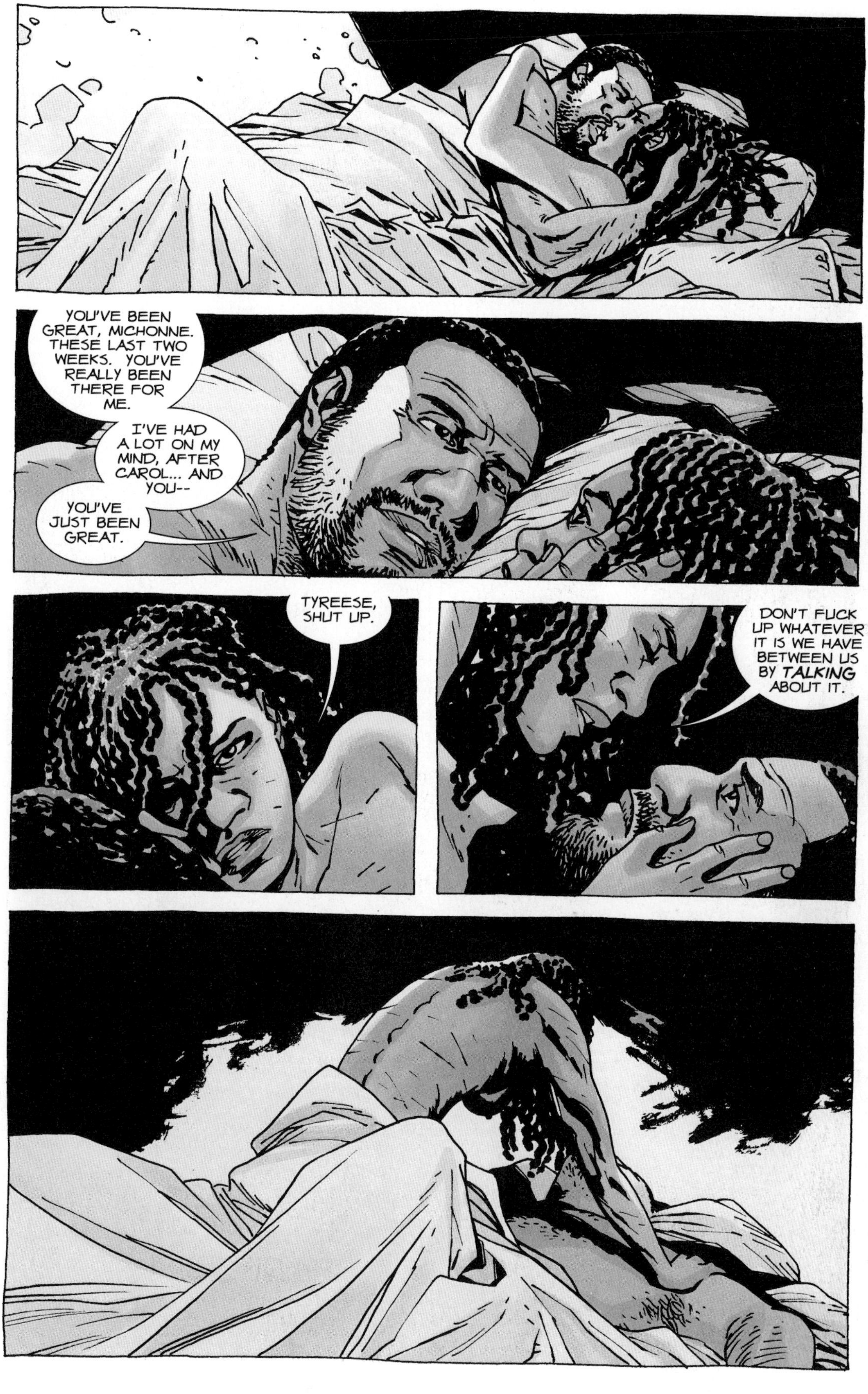
YOU'VE BEEN GREAT, MICHONNE. THESE LAST TWO WEEKS. YOU'VE REALLY BEEN THERE FOR ME.
I'VE HAD A LOT ON MY MIND, AFTER CAROL... AND YOU--
YOU'VE JUST BEEN GREAT.
TYREESE, SHUT UP.
DON'T FUCK UP WHATEVER IT IS WE HAVE BETWEEN US BY TALKING ABOUT IT.

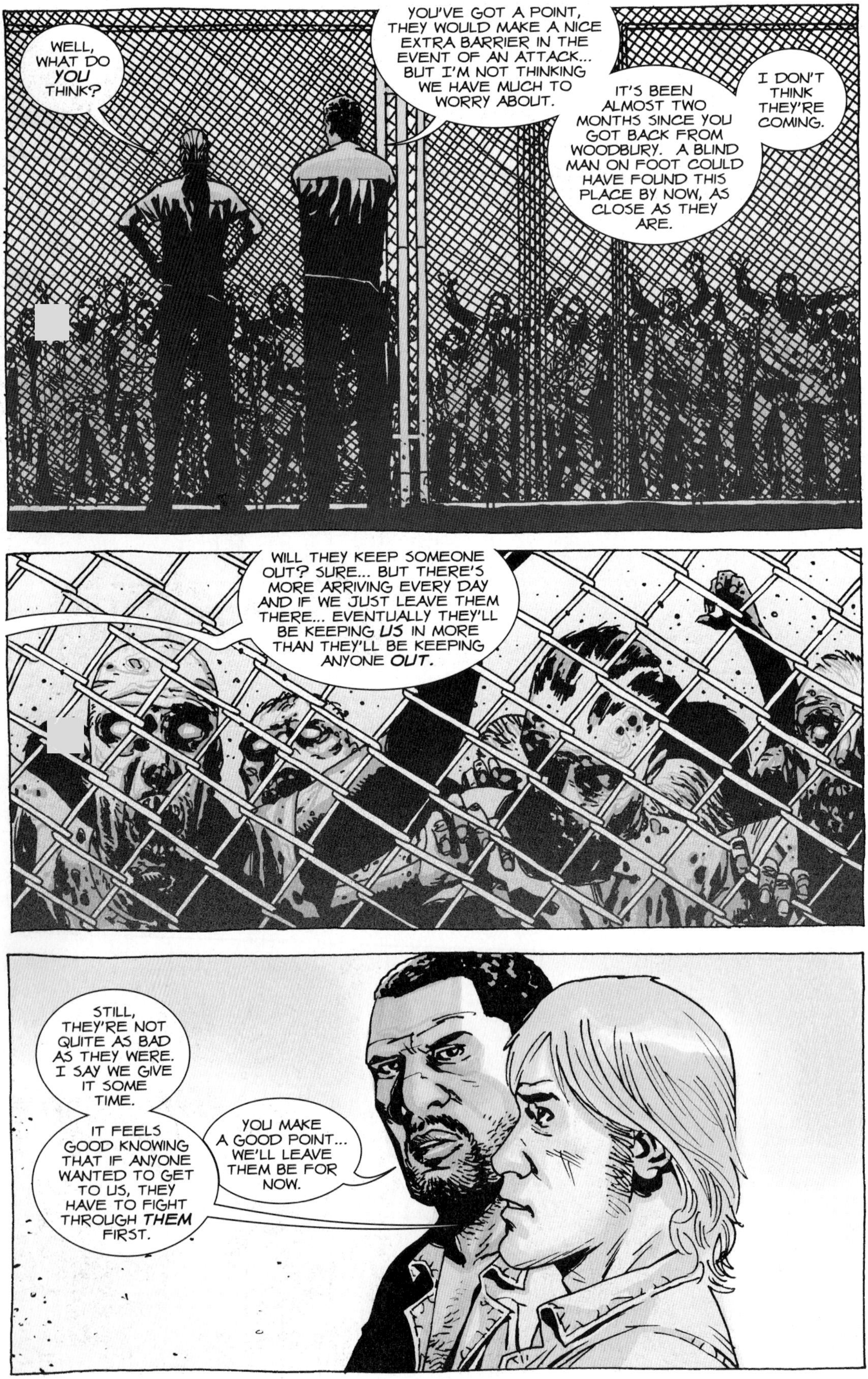
WELL, WHAT DO *YOU* THINK?
YOU'VE GOT A POINT, THEY WOULD MAKE A NICE EXTRA BARRIER IN THE EVENT OF AN ATTACK... BUT I'M NOT THINKING WE HAVE MUCH TO WORRY ABOUT.
IT'S BEEN ALMOST TWO MONTHS SINCE YOU GOT BACK FROM WOODBURY. A BLIND MAN ON FOOT COULD HAVE FOUND THIS PLACE BY NOW, AS CLOSE AS THEY ARE.
I DON'T THINK THEY'RE COMING.
WILL THEY KEEP SOMEONE OUT? SURE... BUT THERE'S MORE ARRIVING EVERY DAY AND IF WE JUST LEAVE THEM THERE... EVENTUALLY THEY'LL BE KEEPING *US* IN MORE THAN THEY'LL BE KEEPING ANYONE *OUT*.
STILL, THEY'RE NOT QUITE AS BAD AS THEY WERE. I SAY WE GIVE IT SOME TIME.
IT FEELS GOOD KNOWING THAT IF ANYONE WANTED TO GET TO US, THEY HAVE TO FIGHT THROUGH *THEM* FIRST.
YOU MAKE A GOOD POINT... WE'LL LEAVE THEM BE FOR NOW.

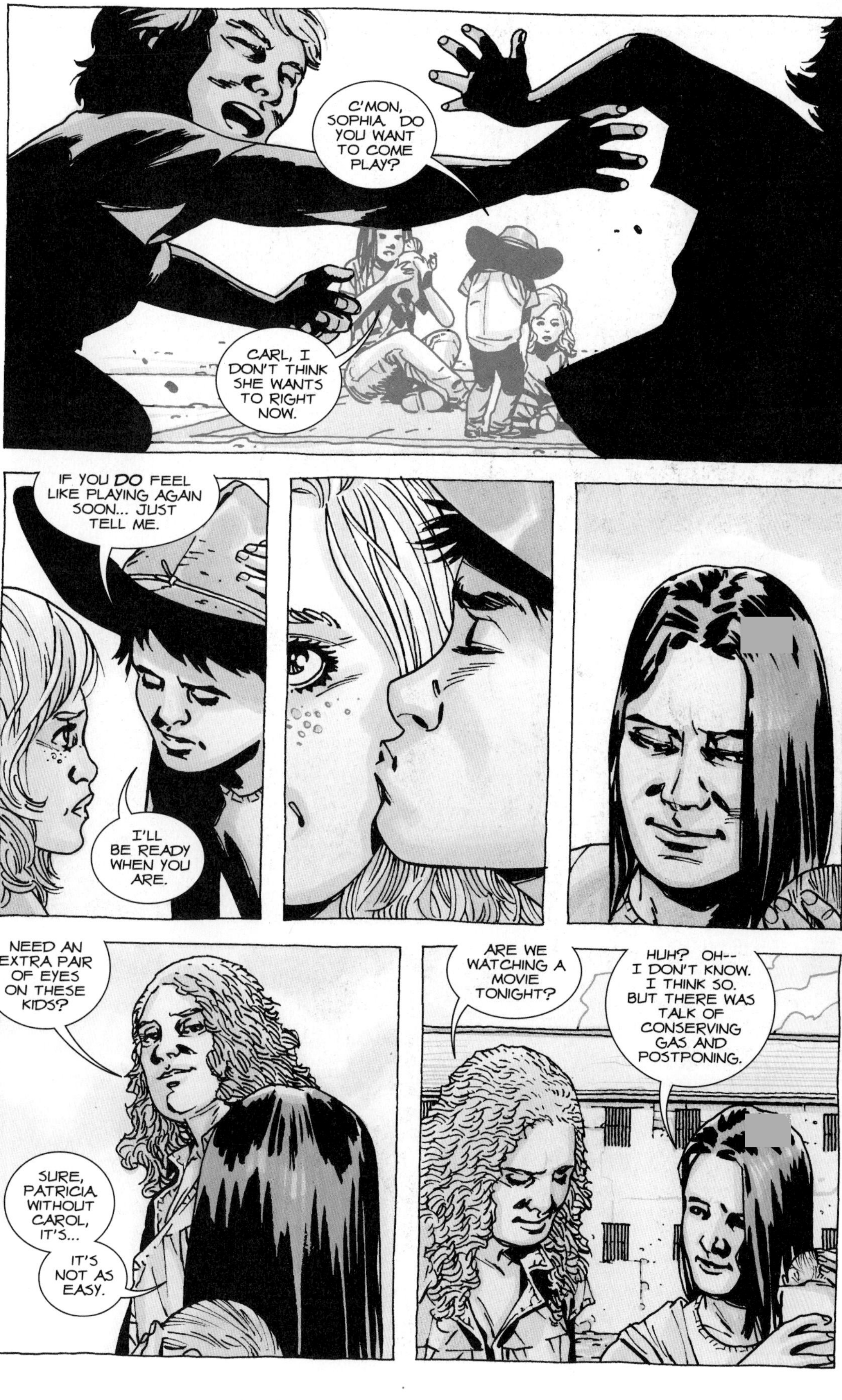
C'MON, SOPHIA. DO YOU WANT TO COME PLAY?
CARL, I DON'T THINK SHE WANTS TO RIGHT NOW.
IF YOU DO FEEL LIKE PLAYING AGAIN SOON... JUST TELL ME.
I'LL BE READY WHEN YOU ARE.
NEED AN EXTRA PAIR OF EYES ON THESE KIDS?
SURE, PATRICIA. WITHOUT CAROL, IT'S...
IT'S NOT AS EASY.
ARE WE WATCHING A MOVIE TONIGHT?
HUH? OH-- I DON'T KNOW. I THINK SO. BUT THERE WAS TALK OF CONSERVING GAS AND POSTPONING.

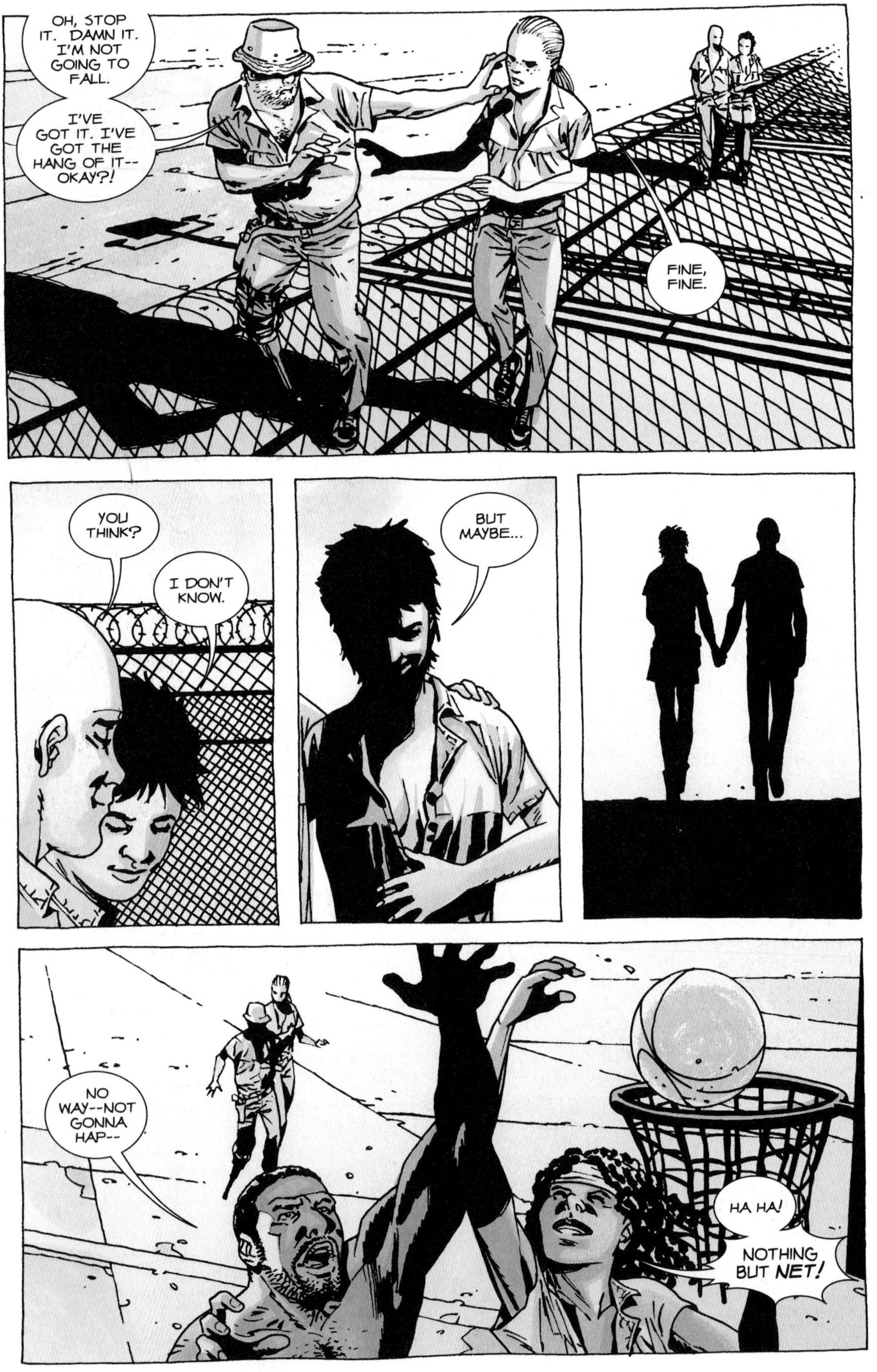

OH, STOP IT. DAMN IT. I'M NOT GOING TO FALL.
I'VE GOT IT. I'VE GOT THE HANG OF IT-- OKAY?!
FINE, FINE.
YOU THINK?
I DON'T KNOW.
BUT MAYBE...
NO WAY--NOT GONNA HAP--
HA HA!
NOTHING BUT **NET!**

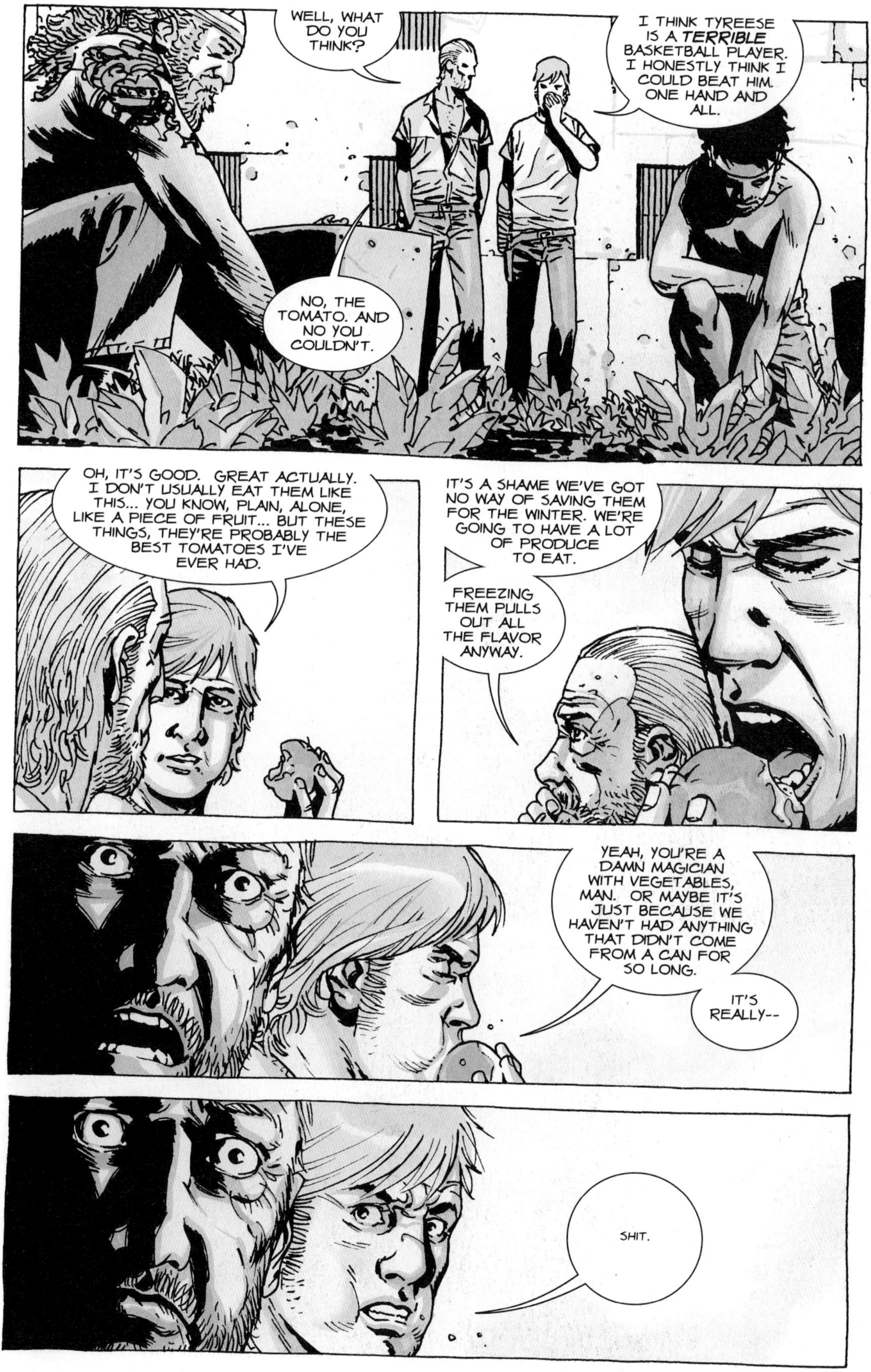
WELL, WHAT DO YOU THINK?
I THINK TYREESE IS A TERRIBLE BASKETBALL PLAYER. I HONESTLY THINK I COULD BEAT HIM. ONE HAND AND ALL.
NO, THE TOMATO. AND NO YOU COULDN'T.
OH, IT'S GOOD. GREAT ACTUALLY. I DON'T USUALLY EAT THEM LIKE THIS... YOU KNOW, PLAIN, ALONE, LIKE A PIECE OF FRUIT... BUT THESE THINGS, THEY'RE PROBABLY THE BEST TOMATOES I'VE EVER HAD.
IT'S A SHAME WE'VE GOT NO WAY OF SAVING THEM FOR THE WINTER. WE'RE GOING TO HAVE A LOT OF PRODUCE TO EAT.
FREEZING THEM PULLS OUT ALL THE FLAVOR ANYWAY.
YEAH, YOU'RE A DAMN MAGICIAN WITH VEGETABLES, MAN. OR MAYBE IT'S JUST BECAUSE WE HAVEN'T HAD ANYTHING THAT DIDN'T COME FROM A CAN FOR SO LONG.
IT'S REALLY--
SHIT.

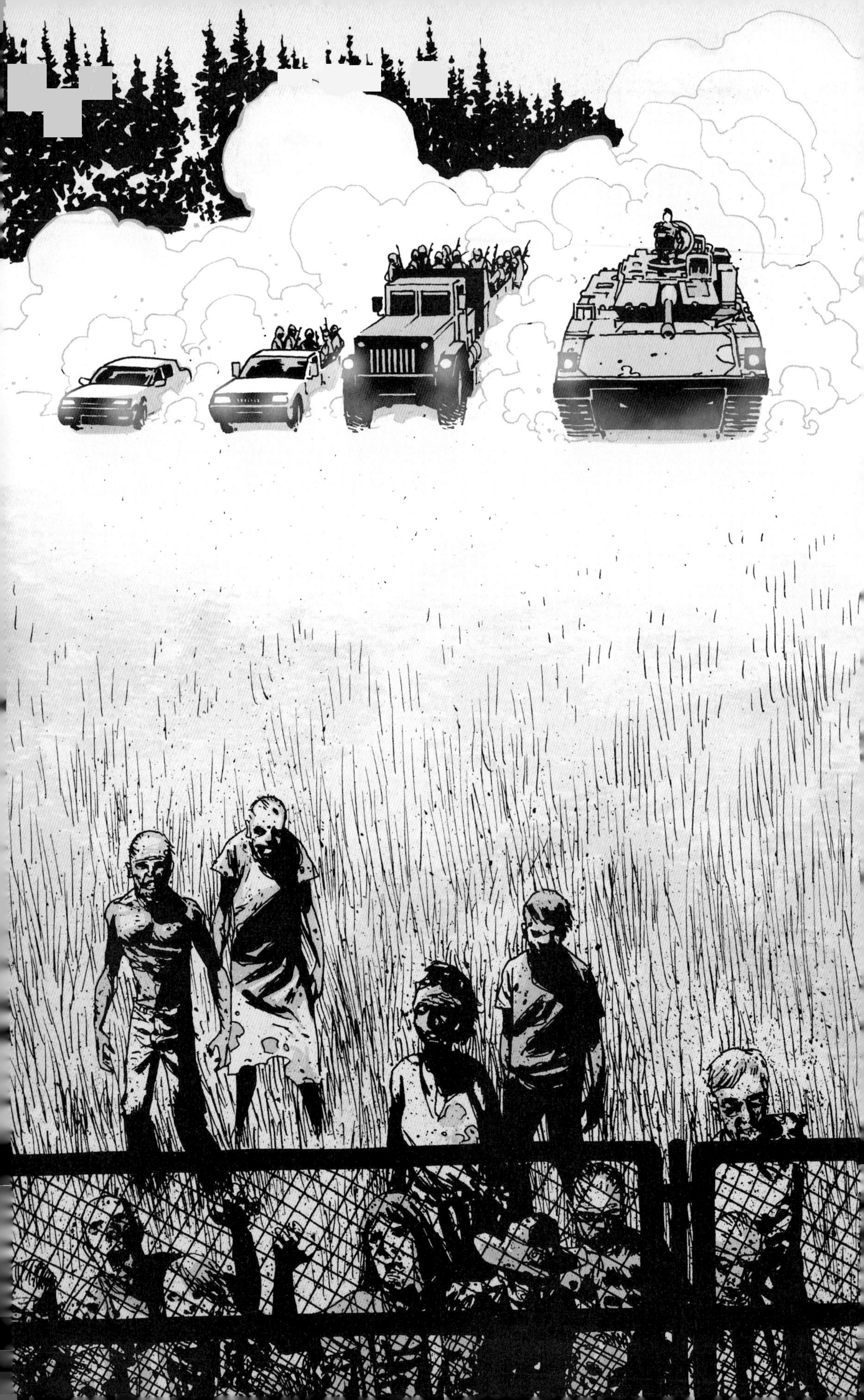

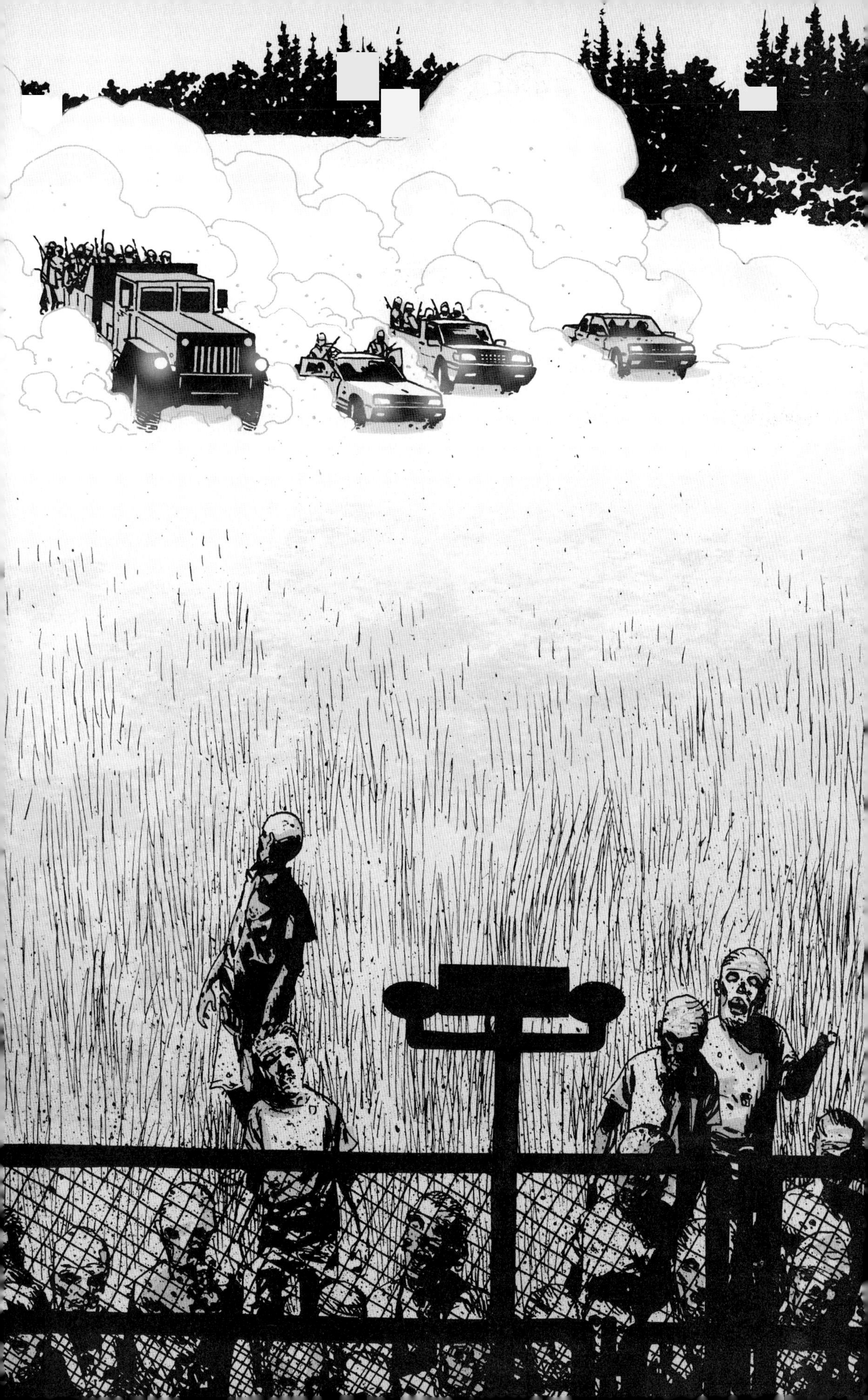

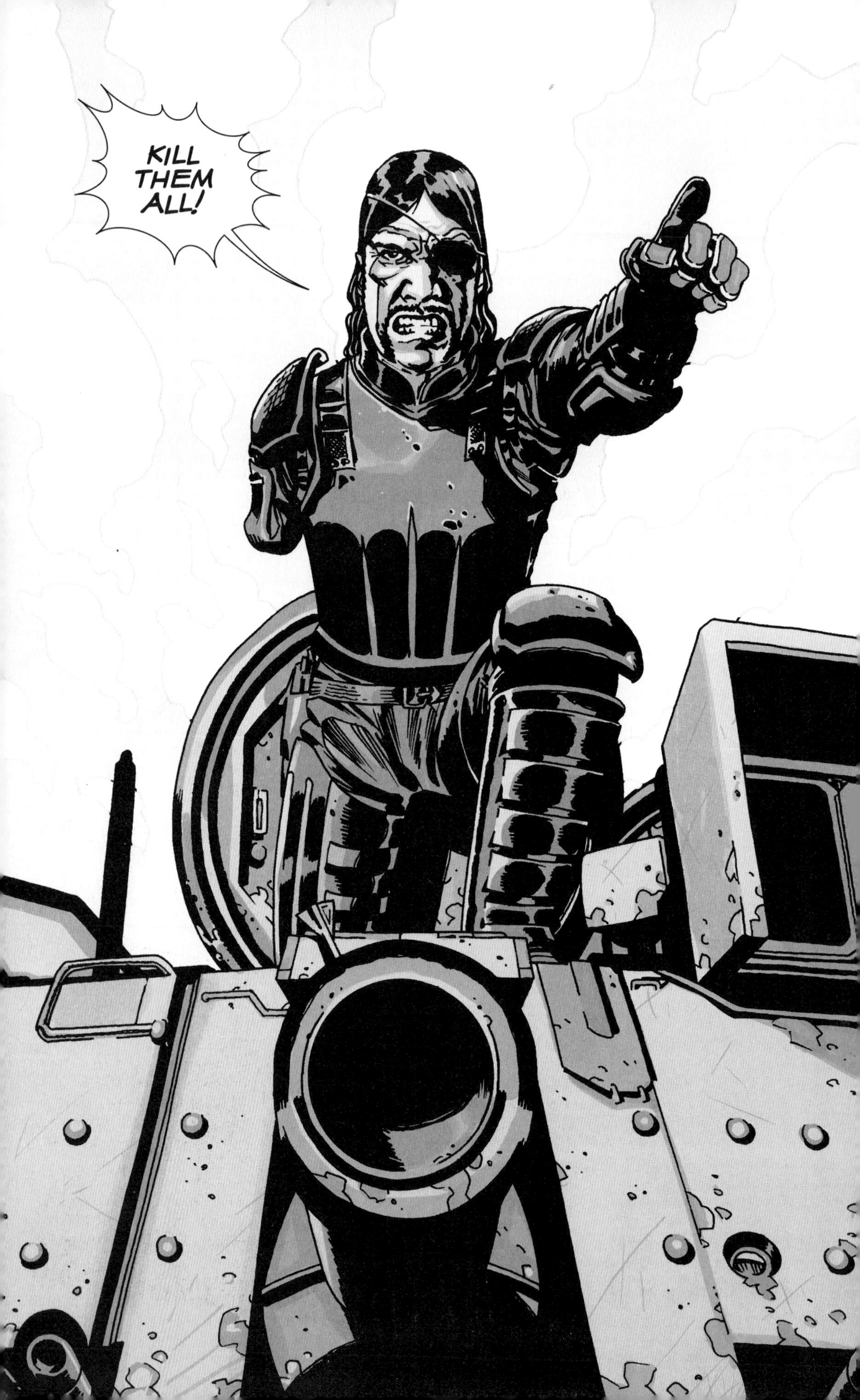
KILL THEM ALL!

TO BE CONTINUED...

MORE GREAT BOOKS FROM ROBERT KIRKMAN & IMAGE COMICS!

WALKING DEAD
HAUNT
BRIT
VOLUME ONE: OLD SOLDIER
THE COMPLETE INVINCIBLE
LIBRARY: VOLUME TWO
BRIT
VOLUME THREE: FUBAR
CAPES
PUNCHING THE CLOCK
THE BOY FROM EARTH

THE ASTOUNDING WOLF-MAN

VO[redacted] TP
ISBN: 978-1-58240-862-0
$14.99

VO[redacted]
ISBN[redacted]978-1-60706-007-9
$14.99

VOL. 3 TP
ISBN: 978-1-60706-111-3
$16.99

BATTLE POPE

VOL. 1: GENESIS TP
ISBN: 978-1-58240-572-8
$14.99

VO[redacted]: MAYHEM TP
ISBN: 978-1-58240-529-2
$12.99

VOL. 3: PILLOW TALK TP
ISBN: 978-1-58240-677-0
$12.99

VO[redacted]: WRATH OF GOD TP
ISBN: 978-1-58240-751-7
$9.99

BRIT

VOL. 1: OLD SOLDIER TP
ISBN: 978-1-58240-678-7
$14.99

VOL. 2: AWOL
ISBN: 978-1-58240-864-4
$14.99

VOL. [redacted]UBAR
ISBN[redacted]978-1-60706-061-1
$16.99

CAPES

VO[redacted]: PUNCHING THE CLOCK TP
ISBN: 978-1-58240-756-2
$17.99

HAUNT

VO[redacted] TP
ISBN: 978-1-60706-154-0
$9.99

INVINCIBLE

VOL. 1: FAMILY MATTERS TP
ISBN: 978-1-58240-711-1
$12.99

VOL. 2: EIGHT IS ENOUGH TP
ISBN: 978-1-58240-347-2
$12.99

VOL. 3: PERFECT STRANGERS TP
ISBN: 978-1-58240-793-7
$12.99

VOL. 4: HEAD OF THE CLASS TP
ISBN: 978-1-58240-440-2
$14.95

VOL. 5: THE FACTS OF LIFE TP
ISBN: 978-1-58240-554-4
$14.99

VOL. 6: A DIFFERENT WORLD TP
ISBN: 978-1-58240-579-7
$14.99

VOL. 7: THREE'S COMPANY TP
ISBN: 978-1-58240-656-5
$14.99

VOL. 8: MY FAVORITE MARTIAN TP
ISBN: 978-1-58240-683-1
$14.99

VOL. 9: OUT OF THIS WORLD TP
ISBN: 978-1-58240-827-9
$14.99

VOL. 10: WHO'S THE BOSS TP
ISBN: 978-1-60706-013-0
$16.99

VOL. 11: HAPPY DAYS TP
ISBN: 978-1-60706-062-8
$16.99

VOL. 12: STILL STANDING TP
ISBN: 978-1-60706-166-3
$16.99

ULTIMATE COLLECTION, VOL. 1 HC
ISBN 978-1-58240-500-1
$34.95

ULTIMATE COLLECTION, VOL. 2 HC
ISBN: 978-1-58240-594-0
$34.99

ULTIMATE COLLECTION, VOL. 3 HC
ISBN: 978-1-58240-763-0
$34.99

ULTIMATE COLLECTION, VOL. 4 HC
ISBN: 978-1-58240-989-4
$34.99

ULTIMATE COLLECTION, VOL. 5 HC
ISBN: 978-1-60706-116-8
$34.99

THE OFFICIAL HANDBOOK OF THE INVINCIBLE UNIVERSE TP
ISBN: 978-1-58240-831-6
$12.99

INVINCIBLE PRESENTS, VOL. 1: ATOM EVE & REX SPLODE TP
ISBN: 978-1-60706-255-4
$14.99

THE COMPLETE INVINCIBLE LIBRARY, VOL. 1 HC
ISBN: 978-1-58240-718-0
$125.00

THE COMPLETE INVINCIBLE LIBRARY, VOL. 2 HC
ISBN: 978-1-60706-112-0
$125.00

THE WALKING DEAD

VOL. 1: DAYS GONE BYE TP
ISBN: 978-1-58240-672-5
$9.99

VOL. 2: MILES BEHIND US TP
ISBN: 978-1-58240-775-3
$14.99

VOL. 3: SAFETY BEHIND BARS TP
ISBN: 978-1-58240-805-7
$14.99

VOL. 4: THE HEART'S DESIRE TP
ISBN: 978-1-58240-530-8
$14.99

VOL. 5: THE BEST DEFENSE TP
ISBN: 978-1-58240-612-1
$14.99

VOL. 6: THIS SORROWFUL LIFE TP
ISBN: 978-1-58240-684-8
$14.99

VOL. 7: THE CALM BEFORE TP
ISBN: 978-1-58240-828-6
$14.99

VOL. 8: MADE TO SUFFER TP
ISBN: 978-1-58240-883-5
$14.99

VOL. 9: HERE WE REMAIN TP
ISBN: 978-1-60706-022-2
$14.99

VOL. 10: WHAT WE BECOME TP
ISBN: 978-1-60706-075-8
$14.99

VOL. 11: FEAR THE HUNTERS TP
ISBN: 978-1-60706-181-6
$14.99

VOL. 12: LIFE AMONG THEM TP
ISBN: 978-1-60706-254-7
$14.99

BOOK ONE HC
ISBN: 978-1-58240-619-0
$29.99

BOOK TWO HC
ISBN: 978-1-58240-698-5
$29.99

BOOK THREE HC
ISBN: 978-1-58240-825-5
$29.99

BOOK FOUR HC
ISBN: 978-1-60706-000-0
$29.99

BOOK FIVE HC
ISBN: 978-1-60706-171-7
$29.99

THE WALKING DEAD DELUXE HARDCOVER, VOL. 2
ISBN: 978-1-60706-029-7
$100.00

REAPER

GRAPHIC NOVEL
ISBN: 978-1-58240-354-2
$6.95

TECH JACKET

VOL. 1: THE BOY FROM EARTH TP
ISBN: 978-1-58240-771-5
$14.99

TALES OF THE REALM

HARDCOVER
ISBN: 978-1-58240-426-0
$34.95

TRADE PAPERBACK
ISBN: 978-1-58240-394-6
$14.95

INVINCIBLE
HAPPY DAYS
THE WALKING DEAD
BOOK ONE
INVINCIBLE
VOLUME ONE
ATOM EVE & REX SPLODE
INVINCIBLE
ULTIMATE COLLECTION
5
THE ASTOUNDING
WOLF-MAN
VOLUME ONE
REAPER
Battle
POPE

TO FIND YOUR NEAREST COMIC BOOK STORE, CALL:
1-888-COMIC-BOOK